I0767971

OATH
OF THE
WOLF

Copyright © 2025 by Elisabeth Wheatley

All Rights Reserved

Published by Book Goblin Books

Human Authored™, Reg #: 6480939, https://authorsguild.org/human

No Generative AI Training Use

For avoidance of doubt, Author reserves the rights, and grants no rights to, reproduce and/or otherwise use the Work in any manner for purposes of training artificial intelligence or machine learning technologies to generate text, text to speech, voice, or audio including without limitation, technologies that are capable of generating works in the same style or genre as the Work, unless individual or entity obtains Author's specific and express permission to do so. Nor does any individual or entity have the right to sublicense others to reproduce and/or otherwise use the Work in any manner for the purposes of training artificial intelligence or machine learning technologies to generate text, text to speech, voice, or audio without Author's specific and express permission.

For inquiries, email support@elisabethwheatley.com

Art Credits

Cover art and design by JV ARTS

Chapter headers and scene breaks by Lindsay Nid

Snapper and Guin art by Morlin Lorenz

Content Disclosure

This book contains descriptions of graphic violence, blood, gore, and consensual sex, as well as mention of sexual violence, miscarriage, infant death, child death, abortion, and other content not suitable for all audiences. Reader discretion is advised.

If you would like more specific information, please email us at support@elisabethwheatley.com with any inquiries.

1

Brynn

Kings were like hearth fires—necessary but best kept at arm's length. It was good to draw close to them, but never too close. The flame might offer protection from other elements, but they were still dangerous. It was best to be known by a king, able to direct his focus, but never the object of his focus. That was where the real danger lay.

Brynn had not needed to think about kings much these past months, but now Ovrek, king of Valdar, wanted something. He had not outright said he wanted something, but he had sent gifts. Sumptuous gifts from far-off lands, the kinds of gifts meant to impress. Kings did not grant such gifts freely. Men like him did not give without expecting to get in return, so what did Ovrek expect?

The riddle had harried Brynn for weeks now and she felt she had only half of it. What was she missing?

"Wife?" Cenric called to her in a way that indicated he'd called more than once.

"Yes?" Brynn smiled up at him, realizing she had been staring at the hearth in the middle of the great hall.

The cacophony of celebration roared around them. At least two hundred people packed into the hall, laughing, singing, and dancing wherever a patch of space could be found.

Cenric gestured to the young man standing before them.

"I wanted to thank you for your wedding gift." Evred was a lanky young man, barely over twenty with a frame that hadn't quite filled out yet.

Brynn inclined her head. "Of course. The blessings of your gods and mine to you and Rowan."

"Your gods and mine," Evred answered, bowing to Brynn. "Rowan wanted to make sure I thanked you before the night was over."

Rowan should have thanked Brynn herself, but Brynn didn't blame her for sending Evred instead. A part of Brynn was relieved that she had. Rowan had been Cenric's concubine, living with him for over a year before he'd married Brynn.

Rowan and Cenric's relationship had already ended by the time Brynn and Cenric had married, but it was still...awkward. There were confused feelings on all sides.

Now Rowan was marrying Evred, a thane in the household of a wealthy Ombra landowner. Brynn and Cenric had been invited. As the alderman and lady of the shire, they had decided it would be rude not to attend.

Brynn had gifted Rowan ten ells of woolen cloth reinforced with spells to ensure they would last longer, along with three strands of colored glass beads, a knife made from Kelethi steel, and copper brooch. They had been the finest gifts Brynn could think of giving while being useful and not too extravagant.

"Is this an Ombra tradition?" Brynn asked, gesturing to the crown of daisies on Evred's head.

"This?" Evred pointed to the flowers and smirked. "No. I lost a wager to my sister."

Brynn stopped herself from frowning. "A wager?"

Evred shrugged, good humor unabated. "Sisters."

"Olfirth has Rowan's silver," Cenric said.

Olfirth was a respected, wealthy thane in Ombra and Evred was a warrior in his service. That was also why this wedding was being hosted in Olfirth's hall. Brynn spied the old thane eyeing her husband from across the room.

Olfirth noticed Brynn watching him and raised his cup in salute. Brynn raised hers in response before sipping from her mead. It was sweet and crisp. Truly, Olfirth had provided the best for this wedding.

"What?" Evred's brows rose in obvious surprise.

"I said Olfirth has agreed to hold the chest until you have a place for it," Cenric repeated.

"What chest?" Evred shook his head. "What silver?"

Cenric blinked at him. "Rowan's dowry."

Evred glanced over his shoulder, but Rowan was at the center of a dance circle, twirling with her sisters and mother.

"Five hundred silver pennings," Cenric explained. "That's the amount I promised to Rowan when she left my household."

Evred coughed. "How much?"

Cenric studied the other man. "You didn't know?"

Evred scratched the back of his neck. "Rowan may have mentioned it, but I must have forgotten."

Brynn herself had almost choked when she heard the amount, but Cenric was generous. That was one reason she loved him so much. She could hardly be surprised when he promised his former concubine almost a decade's worth in wages to start her new life.

Cenric still seemed confused. "You decided to marry a woman and didn't even ask about her dowry?"

Evred glanced to Rowan again. "Forgive me, lord. I didn't."

The young man was smitten and the whole shire knew it. Evred had ridden from Olfirth's farm to Rowan's family home every week over the winter. Not even the cold and the snow had been able to keep him away for long. Men and matrons had teased him while girls had sighed in envy.

Evred was a good man. Brynn could admit she was biased, since the thane had saved her from drowning last autumn. All the same, Rowan was getting a husband who was respected and would make something of himself. Not to mention he adored her. Despite the uneasy nature of the truce between Rowan and Brynn, Brynn was happy for her.

Brynn had married the first time out of duty and the second time out of desperation. A miserable marriage wasn't something she'd wish on anyone.

"Well, go to your bride." Cenric gestured toward Rowan. "I can see that's where you want to be."

Evred didn't need to be told twice. He bowed to Cenric as befitted an alderman and bounded away.

Cenric sighed. "The fool is marrying for love."

Brynn tried not to laugh at that. "Unlike you, who married for wealth and power."

"Exactly," Cenric replied, kissing her temple. "The important things." He slid his arm around her waist, pulling her against him.

Brynn and Cenric might have fallen in love, but that had not been the basis of their marriage. They'd both agreed to this match for practical reasons without ever meeting. Brynn was a highborn sorceress with her own hefty dowry and Cenric was a man of suitable rank in the farthest corner of the kingdom.

The remainder of Brynn's own dowry had arrived in wagons shortly after the roads thawed. Though most of it remained Brynn's personal property, there had been a large sum gifted to Cenric. King Aelgar had made good on his promises.

The household boys had dug a trench to store the chests of silver and precious stones. The bridal hoard now lay buried outside the garden of Cenric and Brynn's longhouse.

Which brought Brynn back to thoughts of kings and their

gifts. Kingship was also like a whirlpool—it tended to drag every-one nearby into its current.

Ovrek had sent them a ship bearing gifts of exotic silk, silver drinking cups, and the pelt of a massive bear.

The bear's phalanges and claws were still attached to the fur, each one almost the length of Brynn's hand. Allegedly, Ovrek had killed the bear himself last summer.

It was not unusual for Hróarr, Cenric's Valdari cousin, to visit. Hróarr and his band of mercenaries often stopped in Ombra on their way up and down the Hyldish coast, between their homeland of Valdar and Kelethi where they worked as mercenaries. Besides them, Ombra saw the occasional trader, but most Valdari were more interested in taking things by force in raids.

Why the gifts from Ovrek? They seemed like the sort of favors meant to impress. According to Cenric, these kinds of gifts had not come before.

As a youth, Cenric had cut his teeth in the armies of Ovrek's conquest. Ovrek had later given him the men to retake Cenric's home of Ombra several years ago.

But Ovrek was no longer Cenric's king.

Cenric now gave his allegiance to Aelgar, Brynn's uncle. Aelgar received the annual tribute of pigs, cattle, wool, and grain from Ombra. Aelgar held Cenric's oaths of fealty.

The gifts had troubled Brynn since their arrival last week. She knew next to nothing about what this Ovrek might want. Cenric and his cousin Hróarr were always happy to tell her about their mentor, but she didn't know enough to judge for herself. All Brynn knew for certain was that Ovrek was a king and kings were dangerous.

Brynn's own veins ran with the blood of at least two kings, more if one cared to look further back in her bloodline. Her entire life she had felt the chains of her lineage locked around her neck. Only recently had she broken free, marrying an upstart alderman as far away from the center of the kingdom as possible.

She'd escaped the plans of her mother and others to use her in their bids for power, at least for now. Perhaps it was paranoia, but Brynn felt as if she was being drawn into a new set of schemes.

"Is something wrong?" Cenric's brow furrowed.

"No." Brynn offered him a smile she didn't feel. "I've just been thinking about Ovrek."

"This again?" Cenric smoothed his thumb over her cheek.

"I know you think it was probably just a gesture of goodwill." Brynn swallowed. "But what if he wants something in return?"

"If there is, I'm sure we'll know soon enough." Cenric sighed. "Ovrek never waits for long. But Morgi has sent me no foretelling of misfortune, so we are left to wait."

Cenric's patron, the goddess of nightmares and foretellings, sent him warnings in his dreams of tragedies and misfortunes. Morgi had saved his life, and Brynn's life, with her warnings in the past. But just because Morgi remained silent did not mean there was no danger.

All the same, Cenric was right. There was nothing they could do tonight or until Ovrek revealed his intentions. They could hardly muster their thanes over gifts.

Anxiety gnawed at Brynn. Should she send word to her uncle? But no, she didn't want to make it sound like her husband was accepting bribes from foreign kings.

Brynn did her best to quash her fears. "We should pay our respects to our host."

"As you say." Cenric folded her hand into his. "It will be fine, love."

Brynn passionately hoped so.

Cenric headed toward where their host sat at the head of his table, tugging Brynn along. They took their place at the mostly empty table, near Olfirth's right hand.

"Alderman." Olfirth raised his horn of mead to Cenric, though the older thane didn't rise.

Cenric had the look of an alderman these days. He seemed to

stand taller now than when Brynn had first met him. He moved more like a leader, more confident of his power.

"Olfirth." Cenric gave an answering nod.

"Lady Brynn." It might have been her imagination, but Olfirth's tone seemed to soften when he spoke to her.

Brynn inclined her head in turn.

Olfirth had helped free her after her abduction by her mother last autumn. But before Brynn had arrived in this far northern land as Cenric's new wife, there had been years of hostilities between the two men.

Their alliance was still new, but it seemed that some of the ice that had settled over their cold impasse was broken. Cenric was proud and often impulsive, but he was teachable.

As Brynn settled on the bench beside Cenric, he pulled her against him, his arm tightening around her waist.

"That dowry was quite generous of you," Olfirth grunted to Cenric. "Five hundred pennings."

Cenric cleared his throat. Under the light it was hard to tell, but Brynn thought her husband might have blushed. "I wish Rowan well." He shot a glance to Brynn as he said it.

Brynn offered a small smile in response. She tried not to be jealous, though the feeling rose up every so often. When Brynn had learned that Rowan was marrying Evred and leaving their village, she had poured out an entire pitcher of milk in thanks to Eponine.

Rowan had run Cenric's household for a year or so while she had been his concubine. Though Brynn still didn't know all the details of that relationship—nor did she want to—she gathered that Rowan was a good woman, just not good for Cenric.

"Evred is a fine thane." Olfirth peered past them to where the young man in question had returned to his bride. "A fine warrior."

Cenric bobbed his head once. "That he is."

"You can never have too many men like him this close to Valdar," Olfirth grumbled. "No offense, lord."

Cenric made a dismissive gesture. "No, it's true."

Cenric was half Valdari. His mother had been from the far northern islands, the daughter of a rich farmer. Cenric, as the youngest of three sons, had been sent to foster with his Valdari uncle as a boy.

He'd been raised to be a warrior in his uncle's household, but fate had other plans. His father and brothers had met early ends in the war of succession in Hylden.

That meant that Cenric had become alderman, but after a lifetime away and fighting for the first king of Valdar, many were suspicious of him. They feared he might be here to take Hylden for Valdar or lead an invasion force.

Marrying a sorceress had helped with those rumors. Cenric was now tied to the royal line from the south, and everyone knew the sorceresses had supported Aelgar.

It might be a coincidence, but why was the king of Valdar, Cenric's former lord, sending bribes the summer after Cenric had married into the bloodline of the Hyldish kings?

Cenric didn't see them as bribes. From their conversations, he saw them as gifts from an old friend. Brynn knew better. Kings did not have *friends,* especially among those who owed them favors.

Olfirth and Cenric were still talking, their words interrupting Brynn's anxious thoughts.

"This is a momentous day for many reasons," Cenric was saying. "Much to celebrate."

"I hope so," Olfirth grumbled back. "Lady Brynn." He bowed slightly to her. "I hear you were hard at work around my farm this morning."

"My wife works too hard." Cenric shook his head in mock disappointment. "It's her one flaw."

"I could not heal everyone," Brynn admitted softly. "Some things are beyond my skill."

A kind of somber agreement came over Olfirth. "Such is the way of things."

Brynn had gotten their group to come early today so that

she could spent a few hours before the wedding healing Olfirth's people. They'd arrived to some twenty or so people from across his lands. There were doubtless more who could have benefitted from a sorceress's power, but those were the ones who had been willing to be seen.

Even among those who had been brave enough to make the journey to Olfirth's hall, not everyone was a candidate for her power. Brynn could heal injuries and help sicknesses, but she could not cure everything.

One woman had come to them saying she was barren. The woman was close to Brynn's age and had looked at her with such desperation, such vulnerability.

Brynn had tried, but there was nothing wrong with the woman's body as far as she could tell. Some things were beyond a sorceress's power. Brynn's power came from life force, from the raw energy of living things, but true mastery over life and death eluded her.

There had also been a young boy who'd lost his hand in an accident with a plough. He had to be in his mid-teens. Brynn had to also sadly tell him that regrowing limbs was beyond her.

In both cases, the barren woman and the maimed boy had nodded numbly, as if they were used to disappointment. As if there was a cauterized scar where hope had once been.

Brynn took another sip of her mead. The drink was thick and golden and seemed to coat her tongue, hinting at the honey used to make it. The mead was strong, blunting the edge of her inner fears and regrets.

Cenric turned to Olfirth as if a thought had occurred to him. "I like your palisade."

"Poles buried a few feet under the ground," Olfirth replied. "We used oak. Harder to work with, but durable and harder to burn."

"Do you have any workmen who could show us how you did it?"

Olfirth seemed to consider that. Brynn wasn't sure whether he was debating the wisdom of helping his rival or perhaps thinking who would be the best to do as Cenric asked. After a moment, Olfirth said, "Most the work was directed by my man Henswin. I can send him and his boys to you after midsummer. Perhaps lend them for a few weeks."

Cenric nodded his agreement. "I'd send men to you to cover their work."

Olfirth seemed pleased by that and offered his hand. Cenric shook it. This was a casual agreement and would probably be reworked in the coming weeks, but it was a start.

Brynn squeezed Cenric's other hand under the table. She had talked to him about this. He needed to accept help and give help to Olfirth—that was how friendships were made. He was taking her advice seriously.

Cenric squeezed back, and it was all she needed.

Behind them, cheers rose. The music stopped.

"Ah." Olfirth set down his drink. "It must be time to escort the couple to their marriage bed."

Brynn glanced over her shoulder, but she couldn't see Rowan and Evred through the press of cheering bodies around them. "Will you attend them?" Brynn asked, looking back to Olfirth.

The old man grumbled something under his breath. "Damned boy has asked me to stand in for his father."

"Oh?"

Olfirth made a dismissive gesture. "His parents died of a fever when he was young. My house girls caught him trying to steal eggs to feed his sister." Olfirth gestured to a figure across the room. "The girl with the flute."

Brynn searched in that direction. The girl with the flute had stepped down and had joined the wedding party, grinning from ear to ear. She was likely in her teens, wearing a daisy crown matching the one Evred wore.

"I took that boy in when he was starving, gave him his battle gear, once he earned it. How does he repay me?" Olfirth made a snorting sound. "Forcing me to walk hundreds of paces in the dark, just to escort him and his new bride from the wedding I hosted to the house I let him build on my land, from my trees."

Brynn took another sip of her mead to hide a smile. Olfirth was not half as cruel or heartless as he wanted the world to believe.

Evred had his own house, which meant Rowan would likely have servants. Evred was not wealthy, but he was respectable. Rowan had done well for herself.

"Olfirth!" As if summoned, Evred appeared, breaking from the crowd, surrounded by his friends and cheering guests. "Lord! My bride and I would have you escort us."

Grumbling under his breath, Olfirth pushed up from the table. "Demanding whelp."

Evred hooked his arm through Olfirth's, pulling the older man to his feet. Brynn had never seen one of Olfirth's men be so forward with him, but it was Evred's wedding. Perhaps he was allowed liberties tonight.

Olfirth went along with the wedding party, a raucous, rowdy bunch. The music began again and the revelers started up a bawdy song, slurring most the words so Brynn couldn't make them out.

Brynn spotted Rowan's mother and her sisters. One of Cenric's thanes walked beside Rowan's father, supporting him with an arm as he was missing part of one leg.

Almost everyone went with them. It was a riotous, gleeful procession.

Esa, Brynn's handmaiden, went arm-in-arm with Kalen, a youth who served Cenric. The boy stumbled a little and Brynn had to wonder if he had been drinking more than he should or if he was just dizzy from dancing. Esa's face was bright and flushed, glowing in the collective joy of the wedding party.

Brynn caught just one glimpse of Rowan. The bride peered up at Evred from under her pale head covering, giggling as he whispered in her ear.

Be happy, Brynn prayed silently in their direction. *Eponine, please let them be happy.*

Whines from her feet drew Brynn's attention.

"Guin?" Glancing under the table, Brynn spotted the young dog.

Guin was only about eight months old, but she had more than tripled in size from when Cenric had first gifted her to Brynn last autumn. Snapper, Cenric's dog, loomed behind her, wagging his tail and looking up at Brynn expectantly.

Brynn scooted back a little to give the puppy room. Guin scampered up her skirts and settled down in Brynn's lap, happy to see over the top of the table.

Guin squirmed, but she let Brynn pet her and ruffle her ears. She knew better than to jump on the table. She was mostly well-behaved, at least when Brynn was watching.

Under the table, Snapper made a whining, forlorn sound. He pawed at Cenric's leg. Cenric reached down and scratched behind his ears.

The two dyrehunds had been exploring the great hall and playing with Olfirth's household dogs, but it seemed they had gotten bored with that.

"Sorry, son." Cenric ruffled Snapper's coat. "You're too big to be a lapdog."

Snapper whined again, as if in protest, but seemed to content himself with the head scratches.

"I love weddings!" Edric cried, stumbling onto the bench beside Cenric, leaning partly on his wife, Gaitha.

"Is that why we didn't have one?" Gaitha quipped, not far behind.

Edric was a thane sworn to Cenric, but the two had been friends for years. Edric was effectively Cenric's right hand man. "We had a southern wedding," Edric snorted back to his wife. "With a priest. Cenric was there." He jabbed a thumb in the direction of his lord.

"I didn't think that was a wedding," Cenric said. "And I don't think you're supposed to stab the priest."

Edric scoffed. "Sack of shit had it coming."

Gaitha made to sit on the bench beside her husband, but he hauled her onto his lap instead. Gaitha was almost a full head taller than Edric, so he was mostly blocked from view, but the thane squeezed his arms around her, seeming quite pleased with the situation.

When Gaitha sat in Edric's lap, Snapper whined again, pawing at Cenric's legs. Brynn could imagine why. If Gaitha could sit in Edric's lap, and Guin could sit in Brynn's lap, why couldn't Snapper sit in Cenric's lap?

"No," Cenric muttered, blocking the dog's efforts. "Not right now." His brow creased and he was probably arguing with Snapper in their minds. All the dyrehunds could speak to Cenric with their minds, though Cenric didn't always like what he heard.

For all her antagonization, Gaitha stroked the top of her husband's head, leaning down to kiss his temple. "Fool," she muttered.

"Good wedding," Edric sighed, looking around the table.

The hall had mostly emptied save for the two couples and a few servants.

"You're not attending the bridal walk?" Gaitha asked Brynn and Cenric.

Cenric took several long moments to respond. "That would be...strange. All things considered."

"I suppose so," Gaitha conceded. "We were going to, but this one is too drunk to walk." She jabbed her forefinger to her husband.

"Drunk? That would be bad manners," Edric shot back.

Gaitha snorted at that. "And we all know you have impeccable manners."

"Olfirth serves good mead." Cenric glanced to Brynn's half-empty cup.

That he did. The golden drink had almost allowed Brynn to

relax—almost.

But surrounded by all this light and laughter and happiness, Brynn was reminded of how much she had to lose. She was happy for the first time since her childhood. In her experience, happiness never lasted for long.

"Is everything alright, Brynn?" Gaitha frowned down from her perch on Edric's thighs.

"I'm just tired," Brynn answered, offering a slight smile. She stroked Guin's fur. The little dog seemed to sense Brynn's unease and smeared her tongue once over Brynn's face.

Cenric rubbed Brynn's back. "It will be fine. I swear it, Brynn." Cenric was certain that Ovrek just wanted to make sure they stayed on friendly terms. He believed the best of his old mentor.

Brynn desperately hoped he was right, but a sinking sense of foreboding told her that he was wrong.

2

Cenric

Cenric's life was perfect.

He was alderman of Ombra like his father and grandfather before him. He had thanes and warriors who were loyal to him and had proven their loyalty in blood. His flocks and herds were flourishing, his fields were planted, and his longstanding rivalry with Olfirth was at last resolved.

Cenric had a beautiful, powerful wife who made him feel he could do anything. Since Brynn, all Ombra had begun to flourish. His estate ran smoother, and his people were healthier. Conflicts that had once seemed unavoidable had been mediated away.

Riding back to his longhouse with Brynn at his side, Cenric felt he could have fought any enemy, scaled any mountain. Their marriage had been unexpected, a falling of the sticks in the right places, but proof that destiny could be kind.

Their group rode into sight of the longhouse in late afternoon, as the sun was sinking toward the mountains.

As their horses crested the hill overlooking their home, all appeared as it should. The bleating of lambs echoed from the fields. Smoke curled lazily from the chimneys of houses and people milled here and there about their business.

"Cenric," Brynn gasped, the alarm in her voice breaking the peace of the moment.

"What's wrong?"

"Ships." Brynn pointed.

Guin perched on the front of Brynn's saddle, head cocked in the same direction. She sniffed at the air, her entire body rigid. She must be picking up Brynn's tension.

Cenric squinted and sure enough, there were two ships pulled ashore along the riverbank. Two ships that had not been there before and couldn't belong to any of his people.

"Valdari?" That was always Brynn's first assumption. She still saw his mother's people as enemies, not that he blamed her.

Cenric shook his head. "I can't tell from this distance."

Brynn glanced at Cenric. "I was promised a remote and isolated land, husband."

"It's not a raid." Edric stood in the stirrups of his own horse, craning his neck to see. "The alarms haven't been raised." The small thane sounded almost disappointed.

Raiding season was about to be in full swing, but raiders would have come under cover of night. They didn't usually drag their boat ashore in full view of the sun.

"Let's see what this is about." Cenric kicked his horse forward and onward to the longhouse, the main residence of his estate.

Brynn steered her horse closer to his, just enough that he noticed. She was protective, this wife of his. He did not feel he needed it, but he didn't entirely mind it, either.

They drew up in the stable yard, the space between the front of the house and the entrance to the stables. Chickens scurried out of their path and dogs barked.

Friends! Snapper rushed to greet Ash, Thorn, and the other dogs.

Cenric home! The other dyrehunds chorused. *Cenric! Brynn!*

Stable boys rushed to meet them and take their horses.

Gannon, one of the younger boys, was the first to reach Cenric. "Valdari, lord!"

"Who leads them? Did they give a name?" He didn't see the red sails of his cousin's ship.

"Berdun, lord. He said he's here to see you." Gannon was breathless, as if he had been fighting to keep everything contained until now.

Brynn dismounted and set Guin down. The little dyrehund leapt to greet the other dogs. Brynn watched Cenric, waving for silence when several of the household girls clustered around her.

"Berdun?" Edric cast a look to Cenric. "Haven't seen that old whoreson in years."

Gaitha dismounted her own horse, leveling a hard look at her husband. "Friend of yours?"

"We know him," Edric answered noncommittally. "He's one of Ovrek's men."

At the name of the Valdari king, Brynn stepped to Cenric's side. She squeezed his arm. "Cenric?"

He hated the worry in her voice. Cenric covered her hand with his. "If they were going to attack, they would have done it already. I'll talk to Berdun and tell you why he's here."

Brynn's fingers tightened and he thought she might argue, but she said, "Be safe."

Cenric kissed her forehead. "I'll tell you everything he says when I return."

Brynn released his arm, though he knew anxiety still radiated through her. Brynn was a strange creature. He had seen her keep her cool in battle and remain calm in the face of armed thanes. She wore composure like a hauberk and serenity like a helm. But her armor always cracked when she looked at him.

"I'll be as safe with them as I was with Olfirth," Cenric promised. He headed down toward the river. "Edric, with me."

Brynn didn't follow or protest further, but she remained in the stable yard, watching.

Thorn, the oldest dyrehund in Ombra, nosed at Brynn's hand, drawing her attention down. He wagged his tail, his one remaining eye fixed on her. Like Olfirth, Thorn was another grizzled warrior with a soft spot for Brynn.

Cenric tried to quash the nagging sense of unease in the back of his mind, yet it lingered.

Shortly after gifts had come for no reason, one of Ovrek's most trusted men came to visit. Cenric wouldn't have been concerned if not for Brynn's worrying these past days. She had predicted Ovrek wanted something, and she was rarely wrong.

Edric turned serious as they walked down the hill toward the village. "It looks like Lady Brynn was right."

Cenric shot him a glare.

"Don't look at me like that. Gaitha overhears things."

"You and your wife gossip too much."

"It's not gossiping if it's your wife," Edric countered.

The longships drew closer. The newcomers rose at their approach. It appeared to be a small crew of less than twenty men across two ships. They were obviously Valdari from their thick woolen clothes and the rings in their beards.

Cenric! Snapper trotted after him, running in lazy circles. *Friends?* He cocked his head at the strange ships, tail wagging.

Ash and a few of the younger dogs followed, though the strangers seemed to be less novel for them. They must have already had time to investigate.

"Where is Berdun?" Cenric called, speaking Valdari

A man with a wide leather girdle around his waist stepped forward to meet them. He was thicker than the last time Cenric had seen him, but mostly the same.

Berdun took a moment, but then his eyes widened. "Cenric? I

didn't recognize you without your beard."

Berdun probably meant nothing by it, but Cenric felt a twinge of *something* at the words. He wasn't clean-shaven, few men this far north were, but he kept it trimmed after the style of Hylden. He used to have braids and rings, but it had made his Hyldish subjects uneasy.

"Alderman, yes?" Berdun bowed to Cenric, acknowledging his superior station.

Cenric reached out and clasped the other man's forearm to show he was unarmed. "It's good to see you, Berdun."

"I still can't believe you're an alderman." Berdun surveyed Cenric and the surrounding village as if this was a marvel worthy of legend.

"My brothers were courteous enough to die," Cenric said drily.

Berdun chuckled at that, then glanced to the thane at Cenric's side. "Edric? Not as skinny as you once were."

"I have a lord who feeds me well." Edric smiled tightly as he spoke the words in Valdari.

Ovrek had promised freedom to any thralls who turned against his enemies. Edric had taken him up on the offer.

Edric had been more skeleton than boy when Cenric had first met him. The Valdari who'd kept Edric as a thrall had thought to make him obey by starving him and when that hadn't worked, had tried beatings.

Edric had laughed hysterically the day he'd stumbled into Ovrek's camp, covered in blood and bruises. They'd all thought him mad, especially when he'd brandished the head of his former master. Edric had killed his master by using the gate of a sheep pen to trap him against the wall, then sawed through the man's neck bit by bit with his own eating knife.

To hear Edric tell the story, his master had screamed and fought, but none of the other thralls had helped him—or Edric, for that matter. When Ovrek's army had taken his late master's farm and Ovrek had offered him the chance to free the other thralls, Edric had declined. He said they hadn't helped him when he'd been starved and beaten, so why should Edric help them? Those men and women had remained thralls.

"It's good to see you, Berdun," Cenric said. "But why are you here? I'm surprised Ovrek can spare you these days."

Berdun exhaled. "Ovrek would invite you to visit him in Istra, to be his guest for the Althing."

The Althing was the largest gathering of people in Valdar. It was a time for disputes to be settled, justice prescribed, and laws decided. Since most of the islands' inhabitants were gathered in one place for a week or more, it was also peak trading season. Whether it was walrus ivory from the farthest northern reaches, woven cloth, newly captured thralls, smoked reindeer, or precious stones from across the sea and beyond, one could trade for it at the Althing. Raids increased in the weeks immediately before the Althing as men tried to acquire goods to trade.

Cenric's great-grandfather had once been chosen as the Lawspeaker, a fact of pride in his mother's family. His great-grandfather had memorized all eighty-six laws of Valdar in those days and had recited them annually for the gathered crowds.

Since Ovrek had taken over Valdar and declared his word as the only law, it had become more of an annual festival.

The Althing had always been held in a great cleared field around Istra and its harbor, so Istra was where the first king of Valdar had established his capital. It was the largest city in Valdar and had nearly one thousand residents when Cenric had seen it last.

"The Althing?" Edric balked at that.

Under different circumstances, Cenric might not have thought anything of this. He might even have been flattered, but Brynn's warnings rippled across his mind.

Berdun must have misinterpreted Cenric's silence. "For old times' sake."

Old times? He had fought alongside Edric, his cousin Hróarr, and many others to bring Valdar under Ovrek's control. Proud and stiff-necked Valdari had been forced to bow before the new king. Cenric's heart thrummed as he considered the possibilities of why Ovrek would want to see him.

"If I go to Istra," Cenric said, "and stay through the Althing, that will be six weeks of absence. During the high raiding season."

"There will be no raids," Berdun promised, with a little too much certainty.

Cenric wasn't sure he believed that. Raiding might sometimes be taxed by jarls and powerful men on the islands, but it wasn't uncommon for individual communities to take it up discreetly, too. A few farmers with spears and a boat might come to steal extra sheep, grain, or iron from undefended settlements along the coast.

Ovrek might be powerful, but Cenric didn't believe for a second he had the power to stop raids altogether. Not unless he had gained omniscience in the past few years.

"Your cousin will be there," Berdun added. "He extends his invitation as well."

Edric folded his arms across his chest but remained silent.

"Ovrek hopes you are on good terms," Berdun pressed. "And he hopes that his gifts prove he is still your friend."

Just as Brynn had predicted, there had been an ulterior motive. Cenric glanced up the hill to the longhouse. Brynn wouldn't like this, but could he really refuse?

Even if Ovrek was a foreign king to him these days, he lived nearer to his lands than Aelgar did. It would be unwise to insult such a powerful man who lived so close.

Cenric's first impulse was to accept. Since his goddess Morgi had not sent him any warnings since the arrival of Ovrek's gifts, he supposed that was likely right.

"I will accept, but I will have to return before midsummer." That was next month, and the sheep would be ready to shed their fleeces. The Althing could last for weeks. "I will also need time to prepare for the journey."

"Excellent." Berdun's answering smile was broad, genuine. He had not wanted to return to Valdar with news of failure. "We leave in a day's time?"

Edric cast Cenric a hard look.

"Three." Cenric would need that time to prepare his people after he told his wife.

Berdun glanced over his shoulder. "What if we settled on two?"

Cenric wasn't expecting that. Habit urged him to leap to obey, to do as his former lord commanded, but a voice in his head that sounded like Brynn told him to be firm. "Not enough time." Cenric tempered the words with an apologetic smile. "I must ready my people."

"Three days, then." Berdun exhaled, lip curled in disappointment, but he did not press the matter. "It will be good to have you back in Istra. We have missed you."

A large part of Cenric was already looking forward to the visit. "I will send servants to see that you are fed and refreshed."

Berdun inclined his head. "We thank you, lord."

Lord? Cenric had been called that for years now, but it felt strange from Berdun's lips. This man had once cursed him to the heart of the Dread Mother for not holding his shield high enough.

"I need to speak to Brynn." Cenric turned. "Edric."

Edric waited until they were out of earshot before questioning him. "What are you doing?"

"It seems I'm going to see Ovrek." Cenric exhaled.

"Why do you think he wants to see you?" Edric asked.

"I don't know."

"Perhaps it's simply a whim," Edric muttered. "Perhaps he wants to take you hunting for giant bears."

"You'll run the shire in my absence," Cenric decided. "Unless you'd rather come with me to Valdar?"

"I'm not going back there," Edric clipped. "I'll have your ship readied, lord. Ten men?"

"That should be fine."

Edric veered off into the village.

Cenric headed back up to the longhouse. People rushed him, asking questions, bringing their fears and concerns. He waved most of them away with wooden assurances. Yes, the Valdari were friends. Yes, they would be leaving soon.

He reached the longhouse and found Brynn in the garden, surrounded by sprouting plants. She sat on a stone by the wall, watching as Guin played with several of the larger dogs.

Brynn had a shawl wrapped around her shoulders, but strands of hair hung free, worked loose from her veil. The tendrils danced in the wind, brushing her cheeks like a caress. A soft smile shaped her face as the puppy hopped and jumped, wrestling with Thorn and the others.

Brynn was beautiful. He could stare at her forever, that slight smile on her face, finally looking at peace. Maybe even happy.

Brynn must have sensed him coming in that sorceress' way of hers. She straightened, her whole body shifting toward him. "Husband?"

He liked it when she called him that, when she claimed him. "Wife." Cenric came nearer and Brynn's brows drew together. He sat beside her, and she shifted, making room for him.

"What's wrong?" Her voice was quiet, small.

"Nothing is wrong."

"Are you lying?"

Cenric hesitated. "Yes."

Brynn clasped her hands in her lap, not taking her eyes off the roughhousing dogs. "Tell me."

Best to get it out, then. "Ovrek has invited me to the Althing."

"Ovrek?" Brynn shot him a look. "Althing?"

"It's a meeting." Cenric paused, considering for a moment. "Most people of the islands gather once a summer to exchange news, trade, and make laws."

Brynn's brow furrowed. "Like the meeting of the Witan?"

"It is similar, yes." The main difference was that the Witan met to advise a king, and the Althing had been a place for landed men to make decisions together.

"So, he did want something," Brynn sighed. It was not a question.

"Yes." Cenric braced himself, not sure how she would take it.

Brynn fell silent again.

He had expected her to argue, expected resistance. Somehow, this was worse. "Brynn?"

"You're going?"

"I told his messenger I would." He braced himself a second time, but she remained silent. "Ovrek is my friend."

"We've just returned home."

"I know."

"Aelgar will not like this," Brynn cautioned.

"Probably not, but it isn't as if he can stop me from meeting with my neighbors."

Brynn took a slow, deep breath. "People already see you as Valdari. I'm trying to make them see you as Hyldish, too, but this will not help."

"You think I don't know that?" Cenric was forever caught between two peoples, two countries, two kings. They jostled him back and forth, like dogs fighting over a bone. "I will try to return quickly." Cenric followed her gaze to the dyrehunds. "The fields are planted, and I have a promise that there will be no raids while I am gone."

"The shire should be fine." Brynn sniffed.

Cenric touched her arm. "Look at me."

Brynn shifted, facing him though her eyes stayed down.

"Either I accept Ovrek's invitation and explain to Aelgar, or I decline the invitation and insult the fiercest warrior I know."

Brynn seemed to consider that, her lips pursed together. Finally, she met his gaze. "When do we leave?"

"We?"

"If you're going to Valdar, I'm going with you." Brynn spoke the words softly, but matter-of-factly. "When do we leave?"

"Valdar is hardly the place for—"

"For what?" Brynn's tone remained soft as she tilted her head to the side, a challenge gleaming in her eyes.

Cenric had been about to say she was a lady but thought better of it. He knew she had fought in the bogs and the killing fields of Hylden, but it didn't fit with his image of her.

"Is it that I am a sorceress?" Brynn cocked her head. "Or perhaps that I am Aelgar's niece?"

Cenric grimaced. "Your uncle will not like you going any more than me."

"No," Brynn agreed. "He will hate it, I suspect. And he's right to." She adjusted her hands in her lap. "He will wonder if you are conspiring against him."

"Do you think I'm conspiring against him?"

"Are you?" Brynn's tone still held no judgment, no hint as to how she might feel about her uncle being betrayed.

"I don't know why Ovrek wants to see me. It could just be to discuss trade routes."

"It could be." Brynn did not sound any more convinced than him.

Cenric studied his wife closely. He was in love with her and often told her as much. They were happy together. But they'd known each other for less than a year. This thing between them was precious, but new—a sapling made of gold. He didn't know how much weight it could bear just yet. "What will you do if Ovrek does not want to discuss trade routes?"

Brynn gripped his hands, tangling her fingers through his. "I'm coming with you." The words were soft, yet spoken like a pledge.

Cenric held onto her, raising their enmeshed hands so he could kiss her knuckles. "We're leaving in three days."

Brynn's shoulders relaxed. She didn't complain about the short notice. "I will prepare the household. And I will be ready." She leaned over and brushed her lips to his. "Thank you."

Any remaining doubts he had were pushed out by the gratitude shining in her eyes.

Brynn rose and headed back into the longhouse. Guin noticed her departure and bounded after her, woofing. Brynn paused in the doorway to lean down and pet her head, rubbing behind the puppy's ears.

Cenric couldn't help smiling as he watched her go. Brynn had known grief, betrayal, abandonment, and pain of every kind, but she had kept her gentleness. She remained soft in defiance of a hard world.

But if it came down to it, if Brynn had to choose between him and Aelgar, would she still choose him? All his life, Cenric had been torn between two countries. It had cost him many things over the years, mostly respect and friendship. He didn't want it to cost him Brynn, too.

Ovrek might be *inviting* him to Istra, but once he was in Istra, within the king's center of power, who knew what other invitations he might have to accept?

Perhaps Brynn would be able to help him with that. She was adept as a politician, and if she wouldn't be able to help him, perhaps she would at least be able to forgive him.

3

Brynn

Brynn was a little surprised Cenric had agreed so easily. She'd anticipated an argument, but she wasn't about to complain.

Aelgar was not going to like this. He might not learn straight-away, but the visit would not go unnoticed.

Brynn would have to present this story carefully. She wasn't sure how yet. That would depend greatly on the outcome of their expedition. The Althing was a time of trade, so perhaps that could be her explanation. She spoke to Cenric to learn what would be most desirable to the people of Valdar and packed jars of honey, casks of blackcurrant wine, and a jar of rare peppercorns that was one of three Brynn had accepted from a merchant in exchange for healing his nephew's broken leg. She also included a basket of old horseshoes. They were useless in their current state, but the iron could be reworked into anything.

They set out at first light, sailing with the emissary's ships flanking Cenric's ship, *Wolf Star*. Daven, Kalen, and several other thanes of the household accompanied them. Brynn had sailed many times before, but never out of sight of land. It was unsettling to have nothing but slate-grey sea in all directions.

The wind whipped off the water, slicing through their layers of clothing like claws of ice. *Ka* shimmered beneath the ship. The sea was alive or at least filled with life. It made Brynn question just what creatures lived beneath the swells and white caps of the waves.

They sailed all day and reached the coast of Valdar near the evening. Their group camped on an abandoned shore, taking shelter in lean-tos pitched on the deck and against the side of the ship.

Cenric spoke easily with Berdun and the other Valdari. It seemed he was friends with many of them.

After the long winter cooped up together and the hard work of spring spent alongside their people, Brynn no longer felt like an outsider in Cenric's life. All the same, it was a stark reminder that he'd had another life—one that had nothing to do with her.

Brynn and Esa sheltered in the back of the ship beneath the canopy. Guin snuggled between them, making contented puppy noises in her sleep.

The deck was hard beneath them, but Brynn woke only once to find Guin snuggling closer. The puppy was growing quickly, her baby softness giving way to the lanky awkwardness of adolescence. She still managed to snuggle between Brynn's neck and shoulder, burrowing down between the blankets. Snapper crawled in with the women sometime in the middle of the night. He wedged himself between Brynn and the side of the ship, snoring happily.

Brynn missed Cenric's warmth and his breathing beside her. It had been months since she'd slept without him and even with Esa and Guin curled beside her, the lack of him felt wrong.

Come morning, she found Cenric first thing. He'd slept in one of the tents and spared a kiss for her, but a glare for Snapper. The dog wagged his tail and didn't seem to care.

They once again set out. The coast of Valdar was not so unlike the coast of Ombra. From what Brynn glimpsed from the deck of the ship, it was a wild northern country, rugged and almost primordial. This was a land that had carried on since the dawn of time, indifferent to the troubles and concerns of mortals.

Their trio of ships continued to sail up the coast, drifting ever closer to the ports of Istra. Brynn wasn't sure what to expect once they reached it, but she kept her head up, searching for any sign that they might be nearing the home of King Ovrek.

Berdun's ship led the way, its grey-washed sails blending with the late afternoon mists. The men laughed and joked, chatter lost beneath the creak of the oars and the dip and swish of the waves.

Their craft began to pass other ships, just a few at first. Ships of the same style as the others. They all had the similar shallow keel and lightweight build, though no two were exactly the same.

Some sails were blue, orange, grey, or red. Some were faded, some bright and freshly dyed. Brynn even spotted one that was striped in white and grey bands.

Berdun's ship disappeared, drifting around a line of trees. *Wolf Star* soon followed as the men rowed.

As they cleared the bend, Brynn got her first sight of Istra. The capital of Valdar sprawled across the bay in a collection of low, loosely ordered buildings that reminded Brynn of mushrooms. Wooden buildings sprung up here and there in different stages of construction, the signs of a young settlement experiencing fast growth.

Brynn would guess it was populated by a thousand or so, which was more than respectable, even by Hyldish terms. There appeared to be docks, forges, trading markets, and ships. Countless ships.

They settled on the water like so many birds, their prows showing carvings of deer, rabbits, and other friendly woodland creatures. Brynn tried to count them and gave up. Perhaps two hundred? With ten to thirty people in each?

Was this normal? Brynn looked to Cenric. He too stared out across the boats, but he didn't seem surprised. Brynn hadn't seen this many ships in one place outside of Ungamot.

"That's a lot of ships, lady," Esa gasped, keeping her voice down. "I didn't think Valdar had many people."

"It doesn't," Brynn agreed. "But they have all come for the Althing."

A sense of danger prickled along Brynn's skin. These were Valdari, the people who had raided her homeland for as long as anyone could remember. Valdari mercenaries had murdered her son after being hired—and failing—to kill her first husband.

Brynn didn't trust them, but half of Cenric had come from this place. Even if she would never belong here, she would brave it to stay with him. Something was wrong about this whole situation and that was why she had to come.

Maybe that made her a fool, but love made her desperate enough to risk everything. Positions could be recovered. Wealth could be restored. Dead loved ones, once lost, were just *gone*.

Cenric and his men rowed after the ship leading them, following it farther into the harbor. They made their way under the shadow of a massive wooden hall not yet darkened with age, perhaps built in the last two years. From the scaffolding near the edges, it appeared some construction was still underway.

The ship came alongside the docks and Cenric's thanes tossed ropes from the deck to men on the shore. They reeled the ship in, bringing it alongside the dock.

Cenric's men began climbing out, carrying their belongings in bundles over their backs.

Guin's ears swiveled around, and she tried to run toward them but Brynn scooped her up. Guin growled but settled in Brynn's arms though her ears remained pricked, curious.

Cenric stepped up onto the docks, speaking with a man that must be some sort of steward or official. He and Cenric clasped forearms. Was this another old friend? Brynn stroked Guin's head, needing something to do with her hands.

Guin was almost too large to carry, but Brynn wasn't ready to stop just yet. There was something grounding about holding the puppy in her arms.

The men chattered in Valdari, Cenric speaking the language easily as he did Hyldish. Brynn knew very little of the language. She might need to hire a local girl to translate for her while she was here.

"Cenric!" roared a familiar voice. The towering figure of Hróarr crashed into her husband.

Snapper barked and hopped in delight, recognizing him.

Cenric and Hróarr greeted one another with claps on the back and excited Valdari words that ran together.

Vana followed him not far behind. As always, she was a vision with her graceful bearing and raven hair mostly covered by a bright yellow veil. Though she was Hróarr's concubine and had been for some years, Vana had been Cenric's first love as a youth. It seemed his life had been abundantly blessed with dark-haired beauties before Brynn. Vana, Cenric, and even Hróarr seemed unbothered by that past infatuation, but it made Brynn's chest twist with discomfort no matter how she tried to stifle the feeling.

Cenric turned around, seeming to remember her. "Brynn." He headed back to the ship, reaching up for her hand.

Brynn passed Guin down first.

Cenric passed the puppy to Vana and Brynn tried to quash her spike of jealousy at that. Why should she care if the stunning woman held her dog?

Cenric turned back to Brynn and caught her around her waist, twirling her around in a circle.

"Cenric!" Brynn yelped, laughing despite herself.

Cenric set her down on the ground, planting a hard kiss on her cheek before reaching up to help Esa down. He set Esa on her feet without twirling her around.

Vana made kissing sounds at the puppy. Guin wiggled, tail

wagging as she licked Vana's cheek. "Such a good little baby," Vana crooned. "What adventures you're having in this far away land."

Brynn held out her arms and Vana handed Guin back to her without complaint. "It's good to see you." Brynn forced a smile.

"And you." Vana's returning smile seemed far more genuine.

"I thought you returned to Kelethi in the spring." Brynn hoped those words didn't sound disappointed.

"We wintered in Istra and the king wanted us to stay for his son's wedding," Vana explained. "The wedding did not happen, but I think this is the longest we've ever stayed in one place." There was something wistful in Vana's tone, something Brynn couldn't quite parse.

"Would you rather be back in Kelethi?" Brynn asked.

Hróarr spent most his time as a mercenary. As his concubine, Vana went with him. The Kelethi always had a use for violent men and the large Valdari and his company of warriors were no exceptions. They spent their summers shedding Kelethi blood in exchange for Kelethi silver and their winters safely back in Valdar before returning to Kelethi every spring.

It was an exciting life that had made Hróarr and all his men wealthy almost overnight, but it was not the sort of life that could be lived for long. The twice-yearly sea crossings and constant movement were a lifestyle that favored the young.

Vana hesitated in answering. "To live on a longship is to make all the world your home, but when all the world is your home, somehow none of it is." She shook her head. "I have enjoyed tending the same hearth these past months, that is all."

Brynn had assumed Vana to be enjoying a life of endless possibilities, but perhaps endless possibilities, like endless journeys, grew tiresome.

"Shall I start unloading, lady?" Esa directed the question at Brynn.

"Wait," Brynn said. "Cenric will tell us where to go."

Kalen called out to several of the Valdari boys, and they scrambled up into the ship to help with the trunks. As they spoke, Kalen gave another string of directions, slipping into the language easily as far as Brynn could tell.

Brynn felt a little relief at that—it was good to have another person who could translate for her if needed.

"It's not the cities of the south," Vana admitted with a sigh. "But Ovrek has done well for himself."

Brynn made no comment. Ovrek appeared to be doing *quite* well for himself, better than she would have thought. Aelgar's cities were larger, the walls more impressive, but that was building on generations of Hyldish kings. Ovrek was the first of his kind, growing a kingdom from the roots up.

That he had accomplished all this in the space of a decade was so impressive it was terrifying.

Guin flailed left and right, mesmerized by the riot of new sights, smells, and sounds, oblivious to the danger that they might be facing.

Cenric returned to stand beside Brynn, offering her a smile. "Welcome to Istra, my love."

Brynn tried not to let her nervousness show, but perhaps some was acceptable. No one would expect her to be completely at ease in a strange land, would they?

"Ovrek wasn't planning for me to bring a wife, so there are some additional preparations being made for us." Cenric sounded at ease, at least. "I'll have the men take the ship down the beach near Hróarr's and set up our tents."

"I see." Brynn surveyed the town around her.

Kalen and the Valdari boys readied the trunks as the ship pushed off rowed by Cenric's thanes, following a waving man who jogged down the beach ahead of them. Presumably, that was one of Hróarr's men who would show them where they could drag the vessel ashore.

Esa hovered at Brynn's back, a satchel slung over her shoulder. She looked small and vulnerable, her auburn curls bouncing round her face like even they were frightened.

Hróarr spoke with the steward in a booming, jovial tone. Brynn might not understand the words, but she recognized the manner. She wondered distantly if perhaps Hróarr was this friendly with everyone. Perhaps this was just how he was.

Cenric glanced to Guin. "We have a meeting. You might want Esa to keep her."

Brynn handed the little dyrehund to Esa and she immediately began whining. Guin whirled on Cenric, ears pinned back as she let off another growl.

Guin never growled at Brynn and not even Esa, but she growled and snarled at Cenric quite often.

Cenric remained silent for another moment. Brynn was getting used to her husband doing that with the dyrehunds, but it was still odd at times.

"What does she say?" Brynn watched as the little dyrehund went back to squirming.

He grimaced slightly. "She still won't speak to me." Cenric could hear the thoughts of all his dyrehunds, and while Guin should be of an age to communicate with him, she hadn't.

Brynn looked to the puppy, tempted to take her back.

"She'll be fine, Brynn." Cenric took her arm and hooked it through his.

"Where are we going?" Brynn inhaled, composing herself.

"We're heading to see Ovrek."

Surprise and consternation almost made her stumble. "So soon?"

"He wanted to see me as soon as I arrived." Cenric said the words calmly, but in a tight way that told her he was bracing himself.

Like most things thus far, Brynn wasn't sure how to take this information. Was this normal?

Kings in Hylden did not send for their aldermen at the drop of a pin, but this was not Hylden. This might be normal, for all she knew.

"But I'm not ready to meet a king." Brynn plucked at the edges of her unadorned mantle, the words tripping out awkwardly. "I'm dressed for traveling."

"So am I," Cenric offered a slight smile. "You don't have to fret, Brynn."

She didn't like any of this, but she refused to miss this meeting just because of her clothes.

Ovrek's steward led them past the docks and dozens of smoking forges into what appeared to be the proper portions of the city. They walked through streets planned out far better than she'd seen in Glasney and even in some parts of Ungamot.

She'd thought Valdar a loose confederation of clan chiefs, jarls, and village headmen. Perhaps what she and her people had heard of them had been understated.

They passed a forge with open walls where men worked at smelting alongside boys covered in soot. They hammered at clumps of glowing ore, shaping the iron into long lengths of spearheads. At least a dozen more were cooling on racks.

Brynn tried not to show a reaction. A gaggle of children rushed past them, play-fighting with sticks that had been fashioned into the likeness of spears. The flaps of their woolen caps flew around their faces, framing ruddy cheeks and snotty noses. They shouted at each other in Valdari, running this way and that.

No one acknowledged them when they raced by, but no one scolded them when they got underfoot, either. The little ones play-fought, sparring with a sloppiness not unlike Guin's play-fighting with Snapper.

Brynn's chest tightened heavily, that distant sadness calling to her the way it did at random times. Her son would never run carefree through streets like this. He'd barely been walking when he had been killed.

"Brynn?" Cenric must have noticed her watching.

Brynn cleared her throat, looking ahead. "Forgive me. They

seem to be having a time of it."

"They're making the most of youth," Cenric chuckled. "We've all had our time with children's games."

Brynn and her sister hadn't. If they had, she didn't remember it. Whenever she had children with Cenric, she hoped they would get to play like this. She hoped they would grow up in a world that was safe enough.

Brynn's chest squeezed a little at the thought. She'd expected to be carrying Cenric's child by now. She was trying to be patient but was bracing herself to be disappointed again this month. Why was it taking so long?

Their group continued their walk up from the docks, accompanied by Hróarr, Vana, Kalen, Esa, and their Valdari attendants. Guin barked once at the playing children, but Esa shushed her.

Words flew past Brynn, conversations between the Valdari. They washed over her like a constant hum, reminding her she was in a foreign place.

Despite the approaching festival, people were hard at work everywhere. Men worked at the forges and along the beach, repairing boats.

This place was abuzz with industry, far more than she had thought to expect. Why did it feel like there was something more to all this work? Like they were preparing for something.

Their small group walked up toward the main hall, looming over the harbor like a crouching beast. Its roof rose to a high peak, thrusting up like a giant's spear. It was by far the largest building in sight, sprawling in a collection of additions with varied stages of weathering, indicating that Ovrek had added to it in phases.

The main entrance of the hall sprawled before them, gaping like an empty maw. A ramp of packed earth shaped into steps with pine beams led up to it. Their group began to ascend the steps.

They drew closer to what must be Ovrek's hall and Brynn could make out collections of shields strung over the main entrance. They were all worn, showing damage, and one had even been split in half. They depicted patterns and shapes, and some had been painted with the likeness of bears, whales, and other animals.

"Shields of the jarls Ovrek defeated," Cenric explained. He pointed to one with a blue stripe down the center. "The shield of Jarl Umar. I collected that one for him." Pride colored her husband's tone at the words.

"Was it a great battle?" Brynn asked.

"It lasted past sundown."

Brynn took that as a *yes*. She adjusted her grip on his arm. She didn't like to think how many times her husband had death's teeth but a hair's breadth from his throat.

"That is Ovrek's battle standard. It means he is home." Cenric pointed to a triangular piece of white cloth emblazoned with the black shape of a twisting serpent.

"A snake?" Brynn stared up curiously. "Are there snakes in Valdar?" Hylden had snakes in the southern part of the kingdom, but Ombra had only the occasional lizard.

"It's to honor Havnar, the First of Fathers," Cenric explained. "These islands were ravaged by a great serpent, a she-troll, and a monstruous wolf. Havnar defeated all three so that his kin could settle these islands. The serpent was the greatest of them all."

Brynn noted that, committing it to memory. She knew Havnar was the ancestor all Valdari worshipped to some extent. They honored the other gods—Llyr of the sea and Gwydrun of the forge, for instance—but Havnar always seemed first among them. "What is a she-troll?"

"I've never had to explain it before," Cenric admitted, brow furrowing. "She was a monster. Half skeleton, half woman."

That made no sense to Brynn, but perhaps it had been a metaphor.

Their group passed under the line of broken shields, into the warmth and smoke of the great hall. Men with braided beards ringed them from all sides, some sitting with cups of mead, others standing to speak in small groups.

Brynn searched for a throne or perhaps a gilded chair, but instead there was a high table. A few people sat drinking, but no one occupied the high seat. Brynn searched the room, aware of several stares directed at her and Cenric.

Esa hovered at their backs, Guin still cradled in her arms. The puppy had stopped struggling and gone silent, probably taking in the newness of the place.

Just as Cenric had stood out in Ungamot, he stood out here. His short-cropped beard and hair marked him as Hyldish, even as his arm rings and wolf's head brooch hinted at Valdari roots.

A man with a white beard arranged in twin braids greeted Hróarr with a massive embrace. He clapped Hróarr on both shoulders, Valdari flowing quickly, almost effusively.

The fork-bearded man briefly greeted Vana. He said something that sounded like a compliment to Hróarr, and the svelte woman bowed. The fork-bearded man clapped Hróarr's shoulder one last time before his attention slid to Cenric. "Cenric!" He stepped toward her husband, greeting him in the same way.

Cenric bowed, slipping easily into Valdari then spoke her name, gesturing to her.

The fork-bearded man rounded his attention on Brynn. He had a way of placing the entirety of his focus on whoever he was speaking to at the time. Hróarr, Vana, and Cenric had all held his total attention and now it was fastened on her.

Brynn dropped into a bow.

"Lady Brynn, welcome to Istra."

Brynn flinched, not expecting to be addressed. "Thank you."

The stranger threw his head back, laughing. He seemed to do that a lot. "Did your husband tell you I was a savage?"

Her mouth went dry and Brynn fought the urge to lick her lips. "Forgive me, lord. I didn't catch your name."

"So formal." The fork-bearded man kept grinning. "I am Ovrek. King of Valdar."

This man was the king of Valdar? Brynn recovered herself and dropped into a deeper bow. "An honor, lord."

"None of that." Ovrek caught her free hand. "Welcome to my home, Lady Brynn. Cenric has asked me to behave, so I will."

Cenric's brow furrowed at that. "Not quite what I said, lord."

Ovrek released Brynn. "You've gotten serious, young wolf. Don't tell me you've become a prudish Hyldishman."

Cenric's answering smile was tight around the corners. "Hopefully not too serious."

"Bah." Ovrek made a waving gesture. "These Hyldish want so badly to be like the great courts of the south. The Kelethi, the Erymayans. Well, I've fought for the Kelethi emperors, and they're overrated. Their wine is good, though. Not to mention their women." Ovrek winked at Brynn at that last part.

Brynn had heard stories of the great cities far across the ocean in the warmer southern seas. There was the seat of a great empire and the fabled golden city of Aureli. She'd heard stories, but she didn't think they could possibly be real. How could there be a city with a thousand times one thousand people? Where could one even find that many people? Who was even able to count that high?

"You're officially an alderman since I last saw you?" Ovrek already knew this so he must be bringing it up to shift the conversation.

"I'm alderman of Ombra now, yes," Cenric confirmed.

"Your lands give allegiance to Aelgar?"

"We pay tribute to him, yes."

Ovrek reacted as if that was the best news he had heard all evening, clapping his hands together. "Excellent! Very good. I am so glad you have brought your wife. So glad." If Ovrek was lying, he was very good at it. "We shall have a feast tonight to welcome the jarls from across Valdar. We hope to see you there."

Cenric smiled. "Of course."

Ovrek wouldn't be upfront. There would be feasting and drinking and only after everyone was glutted and drunk would they discuss the real reason they were here.

Valdari might claim they didn't like courtly games, but their king seemed to play his own version of them.

"Tolvir!" Ovrek shouted across the room. He waved over a young man with a shorter beard, not yet thick enough to braid.

Right away, Brynn noticed the young man must be rich. His tunic was a bright red and trimmed in embroidery to make any seamstress jealous. Silver rings decorated his fingers and arms with one dangling from his left ear.

Tolvir approached and said something to Ovrek in Valdari.

Ovrek wrapped an arm around Tolvir's shoulders, presenting the young man with unmistakable pride. "My son, Tolvir."

Back in Hylden, men with the blood of kings were known as athelings or king-worthy. There were perhaps hundreds of athelings across Hylden, any of whom might one day make a claim to kingship and be confirmed by the Witan. Tolvir would be a Valdari atheling, assuming the Valdari had athelings.

Since Ovrek was their first king, these people would have to sort out succession when the time came. In Hylden, the strength of an atheling's claim tended to be directly correlated to the number of spears he could muster. Lineage mattered, but it meant nothing unless an atheling could prove himself in other men's blood.

Cenric said something in Valdari and Tolvir answered back. Cenric's tone was courteous but guarded with an edge that belied familiarity. Tolvir sounded cocksure and blase, like he knew exactly who his father was and what that made him.

Tolvir was probably still in his teens. Beards made it harder to tell, but she would guess Tolvir was five to seven years younger than her husband. That would mean that Tolvir would have been too young to fight in his father's war of unification.

Brynn inclined her head.

Cenric introduced her in Valdari and Tolvir said something polite back. Cenric switched reverted to Hyldish, probably for her benefit. "We shall see you tonight, lord. Until then, it has been a long journey. I'd like to show my wife to where we will be staying."

"A long journey?" Ovrek guffawed in what Brynn was coming to recognize as a particular way of his. "I've sailed from here to Kelethi and back again, boy. Don't tell me a skip from Hylden is a long journey."

Cenric smiled quietly. "Not all of us can be as hearty as you, lord."

"I remember when you used to drink me under the table, son." Nonetheless, Ovrek shouted to a servant at the edge of the room. He delivered orders in a string of Valdari and the serving woman bowed, gesturing for them to follow her.

Hróarr and Vana stayed behind, taking up a place at one of the tables. Brynn and Cenric followed the maid back down toward the beach outside Ovrek's hall.

Brynn felt eyes on her and glanced back as they left the main hall. Tolvir watched her, his gaze not wavering even after Brynn caught him.

His notice made pinpricks crawl along the back of her neck. She didn't know the boy well enough to read his expression and that made her uneasy. Turning away, Brynn hoped it was nothing.

4

Cenric

Cenric spent the night drinking with Ovrek, Hróarr, and many other friends he hadn't seen in years. Most of them commented on his trimmed beard and all of them made at least one joke about Hylden, but each one congratulated him on retaking Ombra. And they all complimented Brynn. His wife might not have understood the praises given by the Valdari warriors, but she seemed to guess by their tones and expressions.

Cenric complimented their wives and concubines in turn as was the custom. Brynn stayed close to him the whole night, declining an invitation from Vana when several of the women went off together for a short time.

Snapper wandered in and out of the hall, getting pets and scratches where he could, exploring new smells. He and a few other dogs from Ovrek's household tussled over bones on the floor.

As the night wore on, Ovrek announced it was time for gifts.

It was custom for a jarl to give gifts to his warriors at a feast. Some nights he might only be expected to provide choice cuts of meat to his favored men, but the size and number of gifts was dependent on the jarl's wealth and how much he wished to reward his followers.

It seemed that Ovrek had become a jarl of jarls in many ways. Tonight was a special occasion, and the king handed out gifts of finger rings, jeweled daggers, silver coins, and silver brooches, many of them taken directly from his own person.

Ovrek drifted about the room, speaking with the jarls and chieftains and warriors gathered through the hall. Some of these men had been bitter rivals last time Cenric had been here, but one would never know it now. Ovrek placated his enemies with treasure and rewarded his friends with double.

Sifma, Ovrek's wife, was a quiet woman, as stern as her husband was gregarious. She occupied the seat beside Ovrek in her white furs, draped in silver, precious stones, and stamped fabrics that could only have come from beyond the southern seas. As her husband distributed wealth among the men, Sifma gave out gifts to their wives and female companions.

Queen Sifma spoke no Hyldish, but with Cenric as translator, she gifted Brynn a bright blue headscarf made of silk. The fabric was dyed the deep hue of the ocean under a summer sky and must have cost an exorbitant amount even back in its country of origin.

Brynn bowed to the queen, expressing her thanks through Cenric. Despite the language barrier, he noticed her watching silently, reading interactions between the various jarls, their warriors, and their women.

"Cenric!" called a female voice.

Brynn's hand clenched tighter around his arm.

Cenric turned to see a magnificent woman with silver temple rings, dressed in dark, rich blue. Her hair was mostly covered by the veil of a married woman, but it was the same copper red her father's had been before the white took over.

"Lady Tullia," Cenric bowed. "It's good to see you."

"And you." Mischief glinted in Tullia's eye. "Who is this pretty thing on your arm?"

"This is my wife, Lady Brynn, daughter of Eormenulf." Cenric switched into Hyldish for his wife's benefit. "Brynn, this is Lady Tullia, daughter of Ovrek."

Tullia clasped both of Brynn's hands as if they were old friends. "Your father was Eormenulf? I have heard so many tales of him."

Brynn blanched, surprised to hear Hyldish from the other woman. "Thank you, lady."

"Very good, Cenric," Tullia beamed. "I am so proud of you."

Cenric smiled wistfully. "I did nothing to deserve her, I fear. She is my wife only through the gods' generosity."

Tullia laughed at that, leaning toward Brynn as if to share a secret. "You have him well-trained, I see. That is good! Cenric always did need a firm hand."

Cenric's brow furrowed at that.

"But we made a fine warrior out of you." Tullia looked Cenric over with something like fondness. Tullia was much like Ovrek, so magnanimous and friendly, one could almost forget her legendary temper.

"Lady Tullia," Brynn repeated the name slowly, as if committing it to memory. "Am I saying it right?"

"Yes! It's strange, I know. My father named me after a Kelethi lady he knew." Tullia let off a little laugh. "In case you haven't noticed, my father is obsessed with his time in Kelethi." She sighed, releasing Brynn's hands. "I am so pleased you are here. Both of you! I must host you in my house some night and hear all about how our dear boy managed to wed such a fine lady."

"We would be honored," Cenric said.

"Do you have an interpreter?" Tullia asked Brynn. "A servant, perhaps?"

"I was going to find her one tomorrow," Cenric explained.

"Vana is helping me with that."

"No need." Tullia waved her hand dismissively. "I have several Hyldish girls in my household. I will send one to you. If she serves you well, you can keep her."

Brynn's eyes widened in surprise, but if she was scandalized at being given a Hyldish thrall, she had the good grace to hide it. "Thank you." She bowed, hiding her face. "I appreciate your kindness."

"I must go." Tullia pointed to Cenric. "But I will expect to see you again. I demand it."

"Of course." Cenric inclined his head one last time.

Brynn watched Tullia go, people moving out of her way as she marched across the hall, two maids in tow. "Did you ever—?"

"No," Cenric cut her off before Brynn could finish asking the question.

"But she's beautiful."

"She's also Ovrek's daughter and even then, I wasn't fool enough for that." Cenric kissed Brynn's temple. Tullia had been like an older sister to Ovrek's young warriors—a domineering older sister who it was best not to offend. "Let's find a seat, love."

Brynn followed him as he led her through the crowd. "I'm sorry."

"For what?" Cenric found them a spot at one of the many tables, guiding her to a place on the bench beside him.

"I know I have been anxious these past days. Not myself."

Cenric had noticed. He stroked up and down her arm. "I love you."

Brynn flushed, ducking her head.

"Do I not say it often enough?" He lifted her chin back up to meet his gaze.

"No—yes." Brynn cleared her throat. "It's just that anyone could hear."

"I don't mind." Affection for one's spouse was in no way required, but it was hardly forbidden. "Most of them wouldn't understand unless I said it in Valdari—*I love you.*"

Brynn licked her lips. "That's how you say it in Valdari?"

"Yes."

Brynn shifted. "I've heard you say that quite often when we're..."

Cenric raised his eyebrows. "When we're what, love?"

Brynn's cheeks pinkened and she ducked her head. "We're in public."

"Ah, but now I'm thinking about having you in private."

"Cenric!" Brynn covered her face with her hands.

Cenric fought back a laugh, leaning over to kiss her cheek. "You delightful creature."

Brynn giggled despite everything. "You should teach me Valdari."

Cenric rocked back a little at that. Pleasant surprise flushed through him. "You'd want to learn?"

"I would," Brynn murmured. "We deal with them often and I expect..." She paused. "I expect you'll want our children to speak it."

Warmth spread throughout his chest. Cenric had assumed that Brynn, like most of Hylden, merely tolerated his Valdari half. He thought she did it exceptionally well, but he'd tried to stifle that part of himself with her the way he did with everyone else.

But she wanted to share this side of him? She wanted their children to keep his ties to Valdar?

It was such a simple request and yet, Cenric didn't believe he'd ever been so completely accepted before. His friends and kin in Valdar had never been able to accept he was part Hyldish. The people in Hylden were always wary of him being part Valdari.

Brynn had her own fraught history with Valdari, but she was trying. She was trying as no one ever had.

"I'd like that." Cenric fought the sudden urge to sweep her up and kiss her in front of everyone—that might embarrass her too much. "I should have started teaching you sooner." He leaned in, mouth curling with mischief. "Though I have been busy teaching you other things."

Brynn's face flushed even deeper. "Cenric."

He nuzzled her cheek so he could whisper into her ear. "You've been most eager to learn."

Brynn tried to fight her giggle and failed. "Your cousin is heading this way, and he *will* understand what you're saying."

Sure enough, Hróarr lumbered up to their table, sliding in beside them. Vana displayed her silver torque and had what appeared to be a new fur draped around her shoulders.

"I haven't seen some of these men in years," Hróarr sighed. He was a brute most times but spoke in Hyldish so Brynn could understand. "Talk, talk. So much talk."

Cenric chuckled. "I've seen you do your fair share of talking yourself."

"I have good stories to tell!" Hróarr protested. "Been across the sea and down the coast. Most of them have just been farming and trading in the same place."

"I thought we agreed there was nothing wrong with staying in the same place?" Vana's words sounded innocent, but Hróarr tensed.

It was brief, but Cenric knew his kinsman well enough to see it. When neither of the couple elaborated, he changed the subject.

"I've heard that Tagel died," Cenric said. "I was sorry to hear that."

Hróarr grunted. "Man was too young. Had only daughters, too." He lowered his head to take another gulp from his cup. "His neighboring jarls will be dividing up his lands."

"Women can't inherit in Valdar?" Brynn asked, sounding curious.

Hróarr laughed. "Not these days. Women jarls aren't much good to a warrior king."

Brynn blinked at Hróarr, seeming confused.

Vana elbowed Hróarr and muttered something too quiet for

Cenric to catch.

Hróarr cleared his throat, though he didn't sound exactly sorry. "Ovrek gives you land, you owe Ovrek service in times of war. That's the agreement."

Cenric almost reminded his cousin that Brynn and her sistren had been the ones to put the king of Hylden on the throne. But something in his cousin's words nagged at him. "Ovrek gave you land."

Hróarr didn't meet Cenric's eyes. "He did."

Brynn stiffened at his side, but Cenric focused on his cousin.

Years ago, Ovrek had given Cenric the men to retake Ombra. They had been former thralls and castoffs, but they had been sworn into his service. Brynn might be rubbing off on him, but it occurred to Cenric that Ovrek might feel he'd given Cenric land, too.

"Is Ovrek at war?"

"Not yet." Hróarr took another gulp from his cup.

Cenric heard the unspoken meaning—there would be war soon. His whole body tensed unconsciously, bracing the way he did for blows when he stood behind a shield. He squeezed Brynn tighter, the impulse to protect her leaping to the fore of his mind.

"Cenric!" As if their words had summoned him, Ovrek swaggered up to them. The king moved alone through the swell of people, not attended by servants or attendants here in his own hall. Ovrek took a place on a stool, dragging it so that he closed off the small half-circle the four of them had made. "Hróarr! Two of my finest boys are now men grown." Ovrek spoke in Hyldish for Brynn's benefit. He faced Brynn, the twin braids of his beard wagging as he did. "How are you finding the hospitality of my hall, lady?"

Brynn offered a soft smile. "You are more than generous, lord."

"You do me great honor by coming on such short notice," Ovrek said to Cenric, still speaking in Hyldish. "You are favored of Aelgar, I hear?"

Cenric wasn't sure how to answer. "He is generous enough to tolerate me."

Ovrek laughed. "You and your foretelling and hound-speaking." Ovrek tugged at the braids on his chin. "Can you speak to this one?" He gestured to Snapper under the table.

Friend? Snapper asked, wagging his tail at the king.

"This is Snapper." Cenric scratched Snapper's rump, earning a string of happy thoughts from the dyrehund. "He's one of my dogs, yes."

"What's he saying right now?"

Snapper cocked his head at Cenric, sensing that they were talking about him.

"He's asking if you can be friends." That was what Snapper usually wanted to know.

"Would you like to be friends, son?" Ovrek lowered a hand toward the dog.

Friends! Snapper's tail thrashed wildly as he stepped forward, licking the back of Ovrek's knuckles.

"Good dog." Ovrek rubbed Snapper's ribs and earned an appreciative snort from the dyrehund. "I saw you brought another one." Ovrek patted Snapper one last time. "A pup?"

Cenric indicated his wife. "That is Brynn's dog." The dyrehunds did not understand ownership in the way humans did, but Guin definitely favored Brynn.

"I see. And you hunt with them?"

"We do," Cenric said. "They're good trackers."

"Can you still throw a javelin like you used to?" Ovrek quirked a brow.

"I can still kill what I aim at." Cenric hadn't had as much time to hunt lately, but he was still proficient.

"I should like to see that. A hunt with mind-speaking dogs," Ovrek mused. "I shall have to visit your land."

"That would be an honor." Cenric felt Brynn's eyes on him

and added, "King Aelgar would be pleased to meet you, I am sure."

Ovrek gave no sign that was anything other than what he wanted to hear. He turned his attention to Hróarr. "I'm glad we were able to get him to come."

Hróarr inclined his head. "It has been too long since my cousin was in the fatherland."

That wasn't entirely true. Cenric had been in one of the southern towns last autumn, searching for the man who had killed Brynn's son. But it was probably unwise to boast of abducting Valdari warriors.

"Indeed!" Ovrek pointed a thick finger at Cenric. "You and I must speak tomorrow."

Brynn went rigid at his side, but she hid it on her face well.

"I shall await your summons," Cenric said.

"Bah!" Ovrek laughed at that. "No, son. Just find me when you can. I will be with the shipbuilders all day. Work of kingship and all that."

Cenric inclined his head. "I will."

"Here." Ovrek removed a large silver cuff from his wrist and handed it to Cenric. At a glance, Cenric guessed it was easily worth a good mare back in Hylden. "I am honored by the presence of a brave warrior and alderman of Hylden."

It would have been an insult to refuse, so Cenric accepted the gift with a bow. "You honor me." He turned to Brynn and slid the cuff over her forearm.

She seemed surprised, but didn't protest, adjusting the silver circlet over her sleeve. Brynn might not understand the significance of it, but from the way Ovrek followed the gesture, he seemed to catch Cenric's intent.

I'm keeping Brynn.

Ovrek turned to Hróarr. "And you!" Ovrek took a ring from his finger, studded with a large ruby. "It is always good to have you here."

Hróarr inclined his head, accepting the gift with both hands.

"You honor me." He also handed the ring to Vana and she began to plait it into the end of a braid.

They exchanged stories—all in Hyldish—reminiscing about the years past when Cenric and Hróarr had fought for Ovrek's kingdom. Ovrek spoke to Brynn kindly, at least from what Cenric could see.

"Your father was King Eormenulf, yes?" Ovrek stroked the tendrils of his beard as if in thought. "The Great Wolf."

Cenric had almost forgotten that was the meaning of his dead father-in-law's name. It seemed a rather Valdari name for a Hyldish king.

"Yes, lord," Brynn said.

"He was a fine warrior. He gave me a fierce battle when I faced him. I wished I could have fought him again." It was as high a compliment as Ovrek could give an enemy, or even a friend.

"Thank you, lord." Brynn did not ask just when or where Ovrek had fought against her father's thanes, and that was likely for the best.

"But a king's daughter?" Ovrek's brows rose, looking to Cenric. "Impressive, my son. You must be truly loyal to Aelgar if he wasted his niece on you."

Cenric heard the jest, but Brynn flinched.

"I asked to marry Cenric." Brynn fingered the silver cuff with her free hand. "I wanted..." She trailed off, looking to him.

"He's jesting, love." Cenric slipped his arm around her, looking to Ovrek. "In Hylden, we only take one wife, so I had to make sure the one I chose was exceptional."

Ovrek chuckled. "That is good. I recommend only taking one wife." He nodded across the room to where Sifma was handing out gifts much like her husband was. "Sifma is a wonderful woman. An excellent queen. She helps keep our children in line. And she manages my household well, including the concubines."

Brynn inhaled at that, though Cenric wasn't sure why. It was well-known that many aldermen and wealthy men in Hylden often kept concubines. A few generations ago, multiple wives had been normal.

But all of Hylden had started to rethink that practice after the war of King Offa's sons. Generations ago, King Offa had collected the wives and daughters of his defeated enemies the way Ovrek collected shields. Before his death, King Offa had sired ten sons with six different women. After his death, the in-fighting between the different factions and mothers' supporters had created a glut of violence. There were old battlefields where scavengers still found bones, iron spearheads, and the occasional coin. Stories claimed that the Cerin River had turned rusty with blood.

It was too expensive for a poor man to have multiple women. It was too dangerous for a rich man. Some men got away with it due to losing most their offspring as children and infants, but many did not. Not without losing their family's integrity in the process. It wasn't worth it.

Not to mention that the last time one of Cenric's relatives had tried keeping multiple women, Morgi had sent him nightmares of having his manhood eaten by rats until he'd stopped. For whatever reason, Morgi did not approve of polygamy.

"Tolvir and Tullia are Sifma's children, then?" Brynn asked the question politely, curiously.

"Yes." Ovrek glanced fondly to his wife. "They get their good looks from her, as you can see." He chuckled. "But I might get another son by winter, should the First of Fathers be so good."

Brynn made no response to that, though her brows wrinkled slightly.

Ovrek leveled a pointed look to Cenric. "Find me tomorrow."

Cenric inclined his head as Ovrek took his leave, moving off through the crowd. That left him with Brynn, Hróarr, and Vana once again.

Hróarr cast Cenric a meaningful look.

There would be a reckoning tomorrow, one way or another. Cenric would hear why Ovrek had sent for him. But that was tomorrow.

Tonight, Cenric wanted to drink with his friends and introduce them to his wife. Brynn remained tense at his side, but she continued smiling, bowing, and charming in that quiet, gentle way of hers. These people were strangers, foreigners, and she might have seen them as enemies, but she showed them the same deference she showed everyone.

They stayed at the feast until late into the night. Well after dark, they finally returned to where their people had set up their tents beside Hróarr's camp.

Brynn and Cenric's tent was large, as fitted their station. It even had its own brazier filled with hot coals to stave off the evening chill. Inside, Esa and Kalen had finished setting up their own bedrolls and the larger one intended for Brynn and Cenric. The tent was not home, but it was far more luxurious than Cenric was used to when he traveled.

Guin whined at the sight of Brynn, pulling against her collar and scrabbling at the earth. She had been tied by a loose ribbon to one of the center braces.

Brynn knelt to greet the pup, freeing her. Now that Brynn was here, the puppy shouldn't wander far.

Snapper greeted the puppy, licking her happily and wagging his tail. Guin yipped, her smaller tail thrashing even faster than his.

Cenric unfastened the brooch at his shoulder and removed his mantle. Stepping up behind Brynn, he wrapped his arms around her, pulling her into his chest. She clasped his arms, her back melting against him. He inhaled, smelling her hair and that indescribable scent that was somehow *her*.

"Have you eaten?" Cenric asked, glancing at Kalen and Esa.

"Not yet, lord, but there's a piglet on the spit outside."

Cenric nodded to the two of them. "Go. Both of you."

Esa and Kalen bowed and slipped out. Kalen kept close beside Esa, which should reassure Brynn.

"Do you think we'll be back in the next fortnight?" Brynn's

question came soft, quiet the moment the tent flaps stilled.

Outside came the low chatter of their thanes and Hróarr's people around the campfire. If Cenric listened, he could hear the soft murmur of the waves along the beach.

"Yes." Cenric chose to believe that they would be home soon. If they weren't it would mean something went terribly wrong.

"If we aren't?" Brynn squeezed his arm.

"We will." Cenric didn't plan to spend an entire raiding season away from his lands, promise from Ovrek or no.

Brynn exhaled a long breath. She tilted her head back.

"I'm sorry to be keeping you from home," he said.

Brynn twisted in his arms, facing him. Her fingers stroked his jaw, a featherlight caress. "You are my home."

Cenric couldn't hold back anymore and kissed her. Her mouth was soft, giving. He wrapped an arm around her, pulling her flush against him.

The night's chill clawed at his back, but Brynn's gentle warmth beckoned him. He clenched her backside, pulling her against his hardening groin.

Cenric nuzzled her hair, nipping at the top of her ear.

She wanted to learn Valdari. Even amongst total strangers who didn't speak her language, she had spent the whole evening showing nothing but courtesy to his old friends. He ached to show his appreciation, to show what her effort meant to him. He felt intensely loved at the moment and he wanted her to feel the same.

Cenric swept his tongue over the tip of her nose, making her yelp.

"Cenric!" She wiped at her nose, giggling.

He caught her and licked her cheek. She let off a shriek that devolved into laughter.

"Stop!" Brynn shook with giggles, hiding her face with her arms.

"Well?" Cenric kissed the top of her head. "I won't even have to take your clothes off."

Brynn bit her lower lip. "Alright."

"Is that a *yes?*"

"Yes," Brynn whispered.

Victorious, Cenric scooped her up into his arms.

She giggled, arms wrapping around his neck as he carried her to the pallet they would share. He enjoyed seeing her like this—giddy and flushed with delight.

Cenric laid her down on the pallet and knelt between her legs, lifting her skirts. He started at her ankles, leaving kisses above her knees and a trail up her inner thighs. "My sweet wife," he murmured, inhaling her musky scent.

He nuzzled the hair between her legs, his tongue teasing her open as she spread for him. He found the bud at her apex and stroked her with his tongue, making her sigh as she laid back.

"Oh, that's good," Brynn whispered, still trying to keep quiet. "You make me feel so good."

That was exactly what Cenric wanted to hear. They would see how long she was able to keep her voice down.

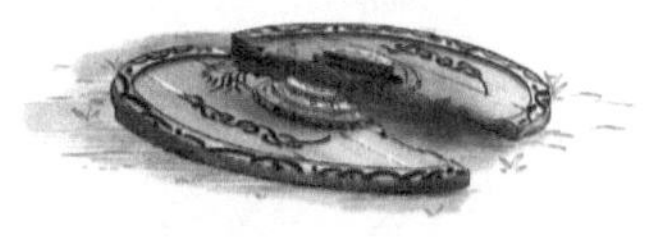

Snapper whined, blood soaking his fur. Cenric? *He whimpered.* Cenric? *Snapper struggled to reach him, growing weaker by the moment. His back legs dragged on the ground, mangled and useless.* Hurt. Snapper hurt.

It's alright, *Cenric sent back, lying.*

Armored bodies lay all around them on the riverbank of Ombra.

Smoke filled the sky as the village burned. Screams rent the air, men shouted, and weapons clashed as the last of the survivors fought a losing battle.

Cenric couldn't move, the sharp pain in his ribs and chest kept him pinned to the ground. An arrow pierced through his neck, just above his collarbone. A dark bird fluttered overhead—a crow come to feast on the dead.

Cenric. *Snapper collapsed at his side, letting off soft cries.*

Good dog, *Cenric told him.* You were so brave.

Good dog. *Snapper tried to press closer to Cenric's side. His breathing grew shallow, barely audible. He sank into the ground, leaning heavily against Cenric's armored side.*

Snapper?

No response. Snapper lay motionless.

Fighting tears, Cenric struggled to turn his head. Everything was a blur of burning houses and rushing bodies. Valdari voices shouted, mixed with Hyldish screams.

A thud beside Cenric drew his attention. A banner had been staked on the riverbank just a few steps away. It fluttered and rippled, the familiar outline of a black serpent writhing over the expanse of dead men.

King Ovrek had taken Ombra.

Cenric jolted awake with weight nudging him to the side. A paw stuck into his ribs. Snapper was trying to shove Cenric out of the way so he could get between him and Brynn.

Cenric grabbed Snapper by the scruff of his neck, wrestling the dyrehund to his other side.

Brynn. Snapper huffed indignantly. *Cenric.* Snapper wanted to sleep next to Cenric and Brynn at the same time and getting in the middle was the only way to achieve that.

No, Cenric sniped back. *Brynn is for me.* All the same, Cenric scratched the rough fur around Snapper's neck, relieved to find the dog alive, well, and unharmed. He reached for his own neck, letting out a breath when there was no hard arrow shaft jutting out of his flesh.

He patted Snapper's ribs as the dog groused, settling down on Cenric's far side.

Snapper?

The dyrehund lifted his head, ears forward.

You're a good dog.

Snapper's tail thumped. *Good dog!*

The soft murmur of the waves along the beach was a stark contrast to the screams from his foretelling. He lay in the quiet as his heart slowed and he let his breathing match Brynn's steady rhythm.

As he drifted back off to sleep, it occurred to him that Brynn had been right about Ovrek once again.

5

Brynn

Brynn fell asleep thinking she couldn't possibly be happier than she already was.

Cenric was a good man. He was often complicated, but good nonetheless.

It filled her with a sense of dread. She'd been happy other times in her life, just before tragedy had struck. What misfortunes might be ahead?

Snapper tried to wedge himself between Brynn and Cenric in the middle of the night. Before Brynn could realize what was happening, Cenric dragged him out of the way.

Brynn relaxed into her husband, melting into the safety of his arms. Guin lay close on Brynn's other side, curled into a little grey ball.

Esa and Kalen slept quietly on their separate pallets. Outside the tent, Istra was mostly silent, save for the waves crashing on the shore. Brynn drifted back off to sleep with Cenric's arms coiled around her.

The next morning, Cenric rose early to meet with Ovrek. He kissed her, his hand lingering on her shoulder. Glancing to Kalen and Esa still on their pallets, he said, "I need to speak to you."

Those words never signaled anything good. "What is it?"

"A foretelling," Cenric exhaled. At her tensing shoulders, he added, "We have time, but…"

Kalen stirred. The boy didn't rise, but he was close to waking.

Cenric gave her a reassuring smile that did nothing to quell the uneasiness deep in her gut. "I will tell you more tonight."

When they could talk away from listening ears, he meant.

The comfort Brynn had taken in her husband last night was snuffed out in a moment. Dread coiled through her, but she tried to push it down.

Things would work out. They had to.

She helped Cenric don his tunic and pin his mantle in place so Kalen could go on sleeping. He reached for his sword belt and Brynn stiffened.

"I don't plan to need it." He buckled it around his waist calmly, casting her a smile that was almost forlorn. "But I'd rather have it today."

Brynn smoothed his mantle over the sword, partially covering it. "Does it have anything to do with your foretelling?"

"Yes and no. There is time, love," he promised her. "I will tell you more tonight." Cenric pressed a kiss to her forehead before striding from their tent.

Brynn watched him walk out of sight from the entry way, Snapper trotting happily at his heels.

If Cenric chose to side with Ovrek instead of Aelgar, Brynn wasn't sure what she would do. Last autumn, she would have sided with her uncle, but now…

No one had loved Brynn before, not like this. No one had cared for her this much since her sister's death.

Brynn would try to persuade Cenric to remain loyal to Aelgar, but if he didn't? Would she leave him? Could she bring herself to do it? Just the thought sent a pang through her chest.

It turned out Daven and several of Cenric's thanes all spoke Valdari as well. Were Brynn and Esa the only ones in their party who didn't?

Laden with pots of honey, casks of wine, peppercorns, and iron, Brynn sent Daven and a few others into the gathering on a large field where the thick of the trading seemed to be taking place. There would be silks, precious metals, rare stones, and even some foreign spices, but all of that could be acquired farther south.

Brynn wanted cloth. While no one would be naked anytime soon, much of their household needed new clothes. Many of the youths who worked in the longhouse wore clothes that had been patched, repaired, and handed down since the days when Cenric's mother had been lady of Ombra. Brynn didn't blame Rowan for the oversight. Rowan had never run a great household before and had done an excellent job all things considered, but it was something that may take time to fix.

Brynn had considered seeking girls across the shire to work for her in weaving and spinning, but that might have to wait for another year. If they could acquire the cloth they needed here in Valdar, that would save Brynn, Esa, and the other women of the household months of work.

If possible, she wanted the men to acquire walrus ivory, too.

That would be rare back in Hylden and there was an almost endless number of things that could be made from the large tusks.

Brynn and Esa took Guin for a walk in the crisp seaside air. They walked along a rocky stretch of beach, watching as Guin leapt at the waves and chased gulls. A few of the town dogs padded up to Guin and she dropped onto her belly in a play stance.

Another of the dogs pounced and Guin wrestled with the larger animals, growling her little puppy sounds.

"Such a fierce girl," Brynn laughed.

"She'll be as big as them soon," Esa said. "She's more than doubled in size since you got her."

It was true. Guin would outgrow being carried soon. Brynn felt a little sad at that thought.

"Will you take her hunting, do you think?"

"Maybe." Brynn watched as the puppy sniffed at the ground, nosing out the remains of a mussel shell. "But we'll see if Guin takes to it when she's bigger."

Guin turned at her name, like she usually did. She dropped back on her haunches, ears forward. Her paws had grown out of proportion to the rest of her, making her awkward on her feet.

She let off a low yip, leaping toward a speck of motion on the rocks. A crab scuttled away from her, and she leapt around it, ears forward as she sniffed it. The other dogs followed her, rushing to see what had drawn her attention.

Brynn inhaled slowly. The world was rich with *ka*. Overflowing with it. She had always thought of these northern islands as stark and barren, but they teemed with life. She could feel the power swelling from the forest to the sea. Even from the rocks, though not as strong.

Behind them, the town was very much alive. Most of it was certainly the jarls and others gathered here for the Althing, but not all.

"Kalen says that the dyrehunds are unmatched trackers." Esa watched the puppy as she scurried back and forth. "He says I should come hunting. If you'll allow it, of course."

"You speak with Kalen often?" Brynn tried not to sound too teasing.

"We've done nothing wrong." Esa answered a little too quickly, the words tripping over each other in their haste to get out. "I like him, is all."

She smiled at the girl, a sad twisting in her chest. At Esa's age, Brynn had been embroiled in a war for her family's survival. She'd barely had time to notice boys, much less act on it. "Kalen is a fine young man." Brynn didn't insult Esa by telling her to be careful.

Esa knew well enough. Besides, Kalen was probably the safest object of Esa's affections there could be.

Brynn sensed someone approaching and turned. The young woman was likely around Esa's age and dressed plainly but appeared clean and well-fed. Brynn's brow furrowed at the sight of her. She had an unusual amount of *ka* in her body, shimmering off her in golden whisps.

The girl was a sorceress. She wasn't summoning *ka* to herself strategically, quite the opposite. It was the wild, accidental way of drawing power that marked younger, unpracticed Istovari.

Brynn almost took a step back but suppressed her shock by the time the girl reached them.

Guin yipped at the girl, her tail stiffening as she moved closer to Brynn. The little dog had become more protective since arriving in Istra. Maybe Cenric had told her to guard Brynn or something of that nature. Guin did not speak to Cenric, but he still tried speaking to her.

The girl greeted them with a low bow, dark hair catching in the wind. "Lady, you are Brynn of Ombra?" Her Hyldish was heavily accented and spoken hesitantly, but Brynn understood it well enough.

"I am." Brynn folded her hands before her, fighting to remain composed.

"I am handmaiden to Lady Tullia. She has sent me to serve you however I may."

Brynn had almost forgotten Tullia's promise to provide a translator. "Yes. My thanks to your mistress." Brynn glanced at Esa.

From Esa's expression, she could see the girl's *ka* as well.

Brynn would need to think of how to address this, if at all. "What is your name?"

"Lena." The girl's eyes remained downcast.

"Where..." Brynn hesitated. "You are from Hylden?" Tullia had already hinted at that.

"My mother was Hyldish." Lena's gaze wavered, as if searching the ground for something. "She taught me her language."

A sinking sense of suspicion mixed with dread pooled in Brynn's gut. Did Tullia know what this thrall girl was? Did Tullia intend this as a message?

Brynn glanced past Lena, noticing several young men heading in their direction. "Child, did you bring an escort?"

"No, lady," Lena answered, head remaining firmly down. "They followed me here."

Brynn straightened. The three young men appeared to be approaching them directly.

"Lady Brynn!" called one of the men in the front, shading his eyes against the rising sun. "Is that you?"

Brynn saw no point in lying. "Yes. Why were you following my interpreter?"

The leader spread his hands toward Brynn in the universal gesture of peace. "I knew my sister was to send you a servant. It seemed the easiest way to find you."

"Your sister?"

"Tullia." The young man drew closer, keeping his hands in sight. "I am Tolvir. We met briefly yesterday."

Up close, Brynn now recognized him. "Yes." She inclined her head.

Brynn hadn't realized Tolvir spoke Hyldish. His mastery of the language seemed shakier than his sister's, but she could understand him.

The two youths at his sides appeared to be about his same age, dressed in embroidered tunics with iron arm rings. Belts of ornately patterned tablet weaving lashed their waists in addition to their leather knife belts. They were wealthy young men, probably his companions.

Lena drew back from them. Esa did not.

Esa knew as well as Brynn that if it came to real danger, all three boys wore no armor, and their woolen tunics would be short work for Brynn.

"If you seek my husband, he is with your father this morning."

Tolvir cleared his throat. "You are a sorceress, yes?"

Brynn thought that common knowledge. "I am."

"You can heal illness, yes?" Tolvir shuffled, glancing at one of his companions.

Brynn chose to be honest. "Some things, yes."

"I would ask a favor from you." Tolvir adjusted his hand on the hilt of the dagger at his hip, leaning back with an air of forced nonchalance.

"A favor?"

"For a lady in the king's household."

Brynn inhaled a slow breath to hide her apprehension. "And who is this lady?"

"Gistrid, concubine to the king."

Brynn's instincts flinched at that. The king's concubine needed healing? It was not terribly suspicious by itself, but Brynn was all too familiar with the intrigue and politics that could be tangled up with the consorts of kings. Her own mother had been concubine to Eormenulf.

"I see." If Brynn refused, she might be denying a woman the only help she could get. Many ailments, injuries, and illnesses could only be addressed with the help of a sorceress. "Where is Lady Gistrid?"

"She is in her longhouse," Tolvir explained. "I could take you there."

Brynn hesitated. There didn't seem to be a reason to refuse, but a nagging feeling told her she was missing something.

"Lady?" Esa saw her hesitation and looked askance. "What's wrong?"

Brynn inhaled. Perhaps she should have accepted Vana's invitation to the queen's weaving house today, then she might have had Vana for advice. But Vana had said no one else there would speak Hyldish, so Brynn had declined for fear of offending someone by accident. "Lead the way." Healing wasn't something Brynn liked to withhold, even if she needed to be careful.

Tolvir smiled, his shoulders relaxing a little. "We are grateful. This way."

Esa collected Guin, who squirmed and whined, so Brynn stooped to take her.

The puppy clambered up so that her front paws were resting on Brynn's shoulder, her haunches cradled by Brynn's arms. She sniffed at the air, head thrown back to enjoy the smells she hadn't caught from the ground.

Brynn followed the trio of young men back up from the beach to the series of dwellings and outbuildings Ovrek had constructed for himself. Servants, messengers, and visitors trailed past them as they walked. Some people did bow to Tolvir, but most either didn't notice him or didn't care.

Lena trailed after Brynn as Tolvir and his friends took them to what appeared to be a respectably sized house. It was not as grand as Olfirth's hall, but it was worthy of a great lady.

Tolvir shouted and a woman with greyed hair under her veil answered the door. He exchanged low words with the woman, several names passing back and forth.

The woman cast a look to Brynn, then back to Tolvir.

"What is she saying?" Brynn asked.

"She's saying it was discussed last night, and my mother Sifma didn't want you to help," Tolvir grated.

Brynn turned to Lena. She wanted to make sure she understood. "Queen Sifma doesn't want me trying to help Ovrek's concubine?"

"Yes," Lena confirmed.

"I don't wish to offend the queen." Whatever the queen's reasons, Brynn didn't want to go against Sifma's wishes. She didn't want to make unnecessary enemies.

"Wait." Tolvir gestured for Brynn to stop. He spoke several hurried phrases to the elderly servant and the woman let off a sharp exhale before shutting the door.

"Are we being turned away?" Brynn asked.

"She's asking Gistrid." Tolvir stepped from one foot to the other, not quite meeting Brynn's eye.

This situation was a little odd, but Brynn didn't see how to remove herself from it without causing trouble.

A few moments later, the woman with the greyed hair returned, looking grim. She beckoned to Brynn, waving her inside.

Brynn moved forward as Tolvir stepped aside. She cast him a questioning look.

"No men inside but my father." Tolvir offered a slight bow. "We will wait here."

That made sense.

Brynn stepped into the house to find a single room lined with furs, the scent of sweet oils permeating the air. Two other thrall girls worked around the fire, one preparing what appeared to be a midday meal and another stood guard at the brazier, watching the flames. Several other handmaidens moved to and fro, and three more attended a lounging figure near the back.

The woman Brynn assumed to be Ovrek's concubine leaned against a pile of furs and pillows. She was young, younger than Brynn, though older than Esa.

Straightaway, Brynn's chest clenched.

Gistrid lay listless with a faint yellow tint to her skin. Away from the sight of men, her hair lay uncovered over her pillows. Her eyes were half shut, and the smell of sickness infused the room.

Her body was alight with *ka,* the signs of a body fighting hard to survive. Was this the woman Ovrek hoped would give him another son?

"Lady Gistrid?" Brynn asked the question gently.

The woman's eyes flicked up at her name.

Brynn bowed, showing respect. Whether she carried the title of queen or not, this woman was consort to a king.

Gistrid said something in slurred Valdari.

Lena answered. Several of the other handmaidens spoke amongst each other.

Even from beside the door, Brynn suspected how this would go. "What ails her?"

"She has been bleeding," Lena explained. "She's been drowsy and weak."

Brynn grimaced. She didn't have the heart to tell them that Gistrid's pregnancy was already over. A pregnant woman's body glowed with *ka* and while Gistrid's body was still full of it, there was too much focused in her abdomen. That was the sign of a body trying to save itself.

"Can you help her?" Lena asked.

From the way the other girls watched with large eyes, they hoped she could. It seemed odd that Tolvir had requested help, not Ovrek. That was one more thing about this situation that made her scalp prickle. Brynn was already going behind Sifma's back by doing this. Was she defying Ovrek in some way as well?

The woman with the greyed hair kept speaking.

"If she is able to bear a son for the king, it would be a great service," the translator added.

Brynn's chest tightened a little more. "How long has she been like this?"

Lena repeated the question and one of the other handmaidens answered. "Three days, lady. Her women have been doing what they can."

Brynn hesitated. Had they been hiding her illness, or perhaps its severity, from Ovrek?

"It came upon her quickly," Lena interpreted. "Sudden pains and...tiredness?"

"Has anyone else fallen ill like her?" Brynn tried to hide her unease.

"No, lady," Lena answered after translating the question for the others.

That did not sound like disease, but Brynn would still try to be careful. "How far along is she?" Ovrek had mentioned winter, but clearly there were things Ovrek did not know.

"Almost three months, lady," Lena replied.

"Her first?"

"Yes," Lena confirmed.

Brynn fought to keep her outward reaction neutral. Gistrid's belly was unusually large for so early in pregnancy, especially for a first.

One of the handmaidens added something, gesturing for Lena to explain.

"Her belly began swelling two days ago," Lena translated.

"I see." This was bad. Brynn held out a hand to the concubine. "May I touch you?"

Lena translated and Gistrid nodded, closing her eyes once again. She appeared only partially aware of what was happening.

Brynn grasped Gistrid's hand to find it cold. She crouched beside the other woman, focusing her power.

Kneeling, Brynn closed her eyes. She could feel the other woman's *ka* more clearly with contact. It confirmed her suspicion that this wasn't disease. The damage was focused low in Gistrid's belly. At first, she thought it was Gistrid's womb, but no.

Brynn bowed, focusing. She wasn't sure, but she thought the swollen, enlarged thing in Gistrid's abdomen was her liver. Fissures ran through it, countless tiny cracks. Combined with the suddenness of this ailment...

There was also damage to Gistrid's heart and her labored breathing warned of difficulty with her lungs. The liver was vital to balancing the blood, so that made sense.

Brynn felt other smaller pools of *ka* scattered over Gistrid's body, mostly on her skin. "I am going to check your arm." Brynn waited a moment, giving Lena time to translate.

When Gistrid didn't respond, Brynn pushed up Gistrid's sleeve, exposing a bruise on the younger woman's wrist. At least twenty others peppered her body from what Brynn could sense.

"What happened here?" Brynn asked, looking to the nearest handmaiden. Gistrid was Ovrek's concubine. Had he...?

It took a long set of heartbeats while Lena translated Brynn's question and the other woman's response.

"They don't know," Lena said. "This just happened."

Brynn carefully pulled Gistrid's sleeve back down, thinking. A damaged liver, swollen abdomen, strained heart and lungs, and bruising that had happened suddenly.

Gistrid had been poisoned.

While the implications of that poured through Brynn's head, she tried to focus. Where to start with healing?

For all her experience treating ailments and injuries, Brynn had little experience with poison. Most people didn't have the chance to seek a sorceress's help at all.

Should she start with the liver and work outwards toward the heart and lungs or start with the heart and lungs and work inward toward the liver? Brynn's mother would have known.

Shoving that thought down, Brynn decided to start with the most damaged organ. Livers were generally resilient, and this one had put up a valiant fight, but it was losing.

Brynn channeled power into Gistrid's abdomen, careful so as not to overwhelm her body with power. Assuming Gistrid had been poisoned days ago, the poison should be mostly out of her body by now, even if its effects remained. But what if it wasn't?

Would healing the organ trap the remaining poison inside? Brynn didn't know that, either, but if she did nothing, Gistrid was going to die.

"Esa."

"Yes, lady?" Esa stepped forward, Guin in her arms.

Brynn gestured to Lena. "Can you watch my dog?"

Lena hesitated but took Guin from Esa.

Guin licked Lena's cheek once, signaling her acceptance of the situation.

Lena flinched as if startled but stroked the puppy all the same.

"What should I do?" Esa crouched beside Brynn, eyes wide with worry. She too must see the advanced state of damage in Gistrid's body.

"We're going to start with her liver. I'll direct the healing, but I may need you to channel more power into me."

It was how they usually did things when the work was too complex for Esa's skill. The young sorceress rested her hand on Brynn's shoulder and power trickled into Brynn. With an extra source of *ka*, Brynn began to work.

Bodies wanted to be whole. They were meant to survive. Even in their battered state, Gistrid's organs soaked up the healing power. Focusing, Brynn was careful to channel her power slowly enough that Gistrid's body could soak it up.

Poison, unlike infections, could not be made stronger with *ka*. Assuming Brynn was right about it being poison and assuming she was right about it already being outside Gistrid's body, there shouldn't be any harm to giving her more power.

Brynn did her best to guide her healing spells, but organs were complex. She preferred to let the body guide the healing whenever possible.

Power poured from Brynn and into Gistrid. The liver remained swollen, but it was not so tangled, and Brynn no longer felt the broken fissures.

Moving onto Gistrid's heart and lungs, Brynn worked to

strengthen those as well.

Gistrid exhaled a sharp breath, her eyes flying open.

Her handmaidens leaned over her, flocking to her side with concern. The eldest, who appeared to be the senior, asked a question.

Gistrid answered, shaking as Brynn continued to work.

The extra fluid in Gistrid's body would need to be expelled on its own when she made water, but Brynn felt the rest of her body sliding into wholeness.

Gistrid sat up, trembling and still yellowed, but alert. She pulled up her sleeve. The bruises remained—bruises were always last to heal—but even they had faded. She turned to Brynn and uttered something low. Brynn didn't need a translator to know it was gratitude.

Gistrid's nearest handmaiden let off a cry of relief and a collective sigh seemed to go through them all.

The senior of the servants smoothed back Gistrid's hair in an almost motherly way. From the age of that servant, Brynn had to wonder if she had been Gistrid's nursemaid or had some other history with the girl.

Gistrid asked Brynn a question.

Lena spoke. "Lady Gistrid asks what ailed her."

Now came the difficult part. Brynn didn't know what to say besides the truth. "You were poisoned, lady."

Lena blinked at Brynn in shock. It wasn't until Gistrid demanded a translation that Lena spoke.

As Lena's explanation poured out, Gistrid's face hardened. She barked something to one of her handmaidens, then a crisp command to Lena.

"She asks if you were able to spare her child, lady."

Brynn shook her head sadly. "The child is already gone. She should continue miscarrying over the next few days."

Lena repeated the words.

Gistrid replied in a firm, insistent tone.

Lena spoke softly. "She asks if there is nothing you can do."

"I'm sorry." Brynn ducked her head. "There isn't. I was lucky to be able to save you."

Gistrid turned away, her face hidden.

Even if Gistrid had no affection at all for Ovrek, bearing a king a son was one of the surest ways for a concubine to ensure her own status and safety. Brynn's mother had made it clear Eormenulf had wanted a son and dismissed her when Brynn had been his second disappointment.

Gistrid seemed genuinely upset by the loss, but Brynn needed to make one thing clear.

"Lady, it is possible someone wanted to hurt you or your child or both. You must be careful."

As the words came to Gistrid through Lena, the consort barked something hard, sounding dismissive.

"Lady Gistrid says all her servants are loyal and none of them would think to harm her."

"Be that as it may—"

Gistrid gave a sharp order in Valdari, leaning on her nearest servant as she stood.

"The lady thanks you for your service and asks that you leave her."

Brynn felt she had done something wrong but didn't know what.

Gistrid made a sharp shooing motion and Brynn didn't need a translator to understand she was being dismissed.

"The lady says she will inform Queen Sifma, but you are no longer needed," Lena said.

Brynn bowed. "Please tell the lady to send for me if there is anything more I can do." She felt defeated, powerless. This girl needed help, protection. Brynn had the strength to offer both, and yet neither. What was she supposed to do?

Lena translated the words as Brynn and Esa bowed to Gistrid one last time.

Leaving Gistrid's house, Brynn felt her chest tightening with dread. Ovrek's concubine had been poisoned, either intentionally or not. People ate bad or contaminated food all the time, yet it seemed too great a coincidence. That woman lived surrounded by servants and luxury, why would she be poisoned, but not her servants, unless it was intentional?

Gistrid had been poisoned all at once if the damage to her body was any indication. There had been no fissures in different stages of healing, they had all been about the same.

That meant someone had given her a lethal dose of *something* that was nonetheless taking days to work. If the goal had been to kill, why not use something that killed quickly? There were plenty of plants that would have made short work of taking a life, even in small doses.

"Well?" Tolvir almost ran into Brynn the moment she emerged from the house.

Brynn startled, sidestepping to avoid him.

"Were you able to help?"

Brynn thought a silent prayer before answering. "I think so. She's still weak, but she should pull through." She didn't add that Gistrid had already miscarried or that her illness had not been natural.

"I am grateful, Lady Brynn." Tolvir offered a lopsided grin, a look that showed his father's likeness. "I hope there is some way I can repay you."

Brynn disliked everything about this situation. She couldn't stop wondering why Tolvir had been the one to ask for help or why Gistrid had been poisoned. "Thank you, lord. I hope you will excuse me."

Tolvir inclined his head. "Of course."

Brynn took Guin back from Lena as she and Esa followed silently. Brynn led them back toward the beach and their camp between Hróarr and Cenric's ships.

"You think she was poisoned on purpose, lady?" Esa asked

quietly.

"Yes." Brynn inhaled a deep breath. "Maybe. I need to talk to Cenric." He should be able to give her advice.

"And if she was?" Esa asked. "What does that mean?"

"I don't know," Brynn answered honestly. She glanced over at Lena, but the girl followed along quietly.

6

Cenric

Cenric found Ovrek in the shipyards, as he had said. The sun was relentless in summer, turning the water into a glaring expanse of light.

Ovrek's men were hard at work building ships. Dozens of them, from the look of it. Ships sat along the beach and inside workshops in all stages of repair and construction. Ovrek was building himself a fleet.

The specter of last night's foretelling hovered in the back of Cenric's mind. Were these portents of his own impending death?

Ships were the pride of the Valdari. In a land lacking the fertile farmland and lush jewel mines of the south, their ships were their greatest achievement. Ovrek and his veterans loved to tell tales of how their longships had outrun the Kelethi navy. After decades as mercenaries, their relationship with the Kelethi emperor had soured. Cenric still wasn't clear on what had happened. There were whispers it had involved the emperor's mistress, but Ovrek himself had never confirmed that.

Cenric approached Ovrek as the king finished speaking to several of the workmen in the process of layering boards into a ship's hull. The Valdari king had no attendants or guards in sight, almost as if he dared his enemies to attack him in broad daylight, surrounded by his own men.

"Cenric!" Ovrek barreled toward him. "How did you sleep, my friend?" He addressed Cenric in Valdari now that Brynn wasn't here.

The king wore no visible weapon, but didn't mention Cenric's sword at his hip, either. In the warring days, he'd ordered his men to carry their arms at all times.

"Well enough, lord." Cenric clasped forearms with the king, coming to stand beside him as he watched the mast of a ship raised and hammered into place.

Friend! Snapper cried, greeting Ovrek with his tongue lolling out one side.

"And you, you mighty beast!" Ovrek rubbed Snapper's sides, earning happy yips from the dyrehund.

Cenric searched down the beach, looking for Brynn. She'd planned to take Guin and Esa for a walk this morning, but he didn't see her from this side of the bay.

"It has been too long." Ovrek took in the work around him. "Two years?"

"Closer to three." Cenric adjusted his cloak.

"How does lordship suit you?"

"It suits me well enough." Being a lord had its own set of inconveniences and burdens, but Cenric enjoyed his life.

"At peace with your father's countrymen?"

"Mostly."

"Mostly?" Ovrek's head tilted at that as if to angle his ears to the word.

Cenric decided there was no harm in honesty. "Leofstan, the

alderman to the south, seems uninterested in friendship."

"Why would you say that?" Ovrek seemed just a little too interested from the way his shoulders shifted.

This past spring, Leofstan's shepherds had begun crossing boundary stones north to graze their sheep on Cenric's lands. They swore ignorance when confronted by the Ombra shepherds. For now, the incidents were annoyances at worst, but they were the kind of small slights that might swell into feuds over time. Shepherds were as proud as thanes and men had been killed over less. Leofstan had ignored Cenric's messengers and done nothing to stop the incidents.

Cenric had to assume the shepherds grazed their flocks on his fields with Leofstan's approval. "Aldermen are no different from jarls," he said wryly. "We always want what the others have."

"Mmm." Ovrek stroked his beard, seeming to think. It wasn't like Ovrek to stall, but that was what the man seemed to be doing.

"Why am I here, Ovrek?" Cenric had never needed pretense with his mentor before. "Unless, of course, Valdar has been so dull without me."

Ovrek did not respond to his humor. "Walk with me and tell me about this new wife of yours."

Cenric went rigid, humor gone, but he fell in beside the king. They walked side by side, Snapper trailing after them. "Brynn is a fine woman," Cenric answered. "What do you want to know?"

"She's kin to several kings?"

"Dead ones, for the most part." Cenric kept his gaze neutral and straight ahead.

"Niece to the current king?"

"She is." Cenric cast Ovrek a sidelong glance. "Is there something in particular you want to know?"

"You must have done a great service to Aelgar for him to wed you to his niece."

Cenric stopped, facing Ovrek. "Aelgar married her to me to get rid of her. He fears she could still try to take the kingship from him, but Hylden would never accept me as king." When Cenric finished, he stared down his former liege lord. He had been learning the art of politics from Brynn, but with Ovrek, he would rather be honest. It seemed like he and Ovrek owed each other that much.

Ovrek threw back his head and laughed. "I have always liked that about you, son." He clapped Cenric on the shoulder. "Straightforward. Very Valdari."

Cenric dared to smile back.

Ovrek cleared his throat, eyes shining with mirth. "You do not care for Aelgar, then?"

Cenric surveyed the beach littered with ships. "I must make peace with my neighbors." He glanced to Ovrek. "Whoever they happen to be."

Ovrek made a sound of understanding. "Aelgar has sorceresses, yes?"

Cenric hesitated. "They supported his rise."

"But?"

Cenric was sure Brynn would be upset if he revealed this part, but Ovrek almost certainly knew already. "There is a faction of sorceresses that would seek to put a sorceress on the throne."

"I heard there was an attempt to make your wife queen."

"Your ears must be long indeed, lord." Cenric suspected Ovrek had spies in Hylden, but he hadn't been sure—until now. Then again, perhaps it had been Hróarr. It stung to think of his cousin being a spy, but then again, why should he have kept it secret? Hróarr and several of his men had been injured in her mother's attempt to abduct Brynn and they had spent weeks recovering and repairing the damage before sailing home last fall. "But if you heard that, then you must also have heard my wife has no desire to be queen."

"Are you sure?" Ovrek clasped his hands behind his back, looking across the beach and to the men at work across it, toiling like so many bees in a hive. "Power is a thrill like nothing I know."

Ovrek winked at Cenric. "And I have known many thrills."

"She..." Cenric wasn't sure how to explain it. *She chose me,* he thought to himself. *She's a sorceress and a king's daughter, but she chose me.*

Cenric had seen Brynn tear a ship to pieces and flatten trees with her spells. He had seen her charm warlords and cajole even the fiercest warriors into friendship. He had no doubt Brynn could be queen if she wished it, but instead she spent her days as lady of Ombra, managing his house and serving his people. She could be anything she chose, yet she chose him.

Cenric thought of the story of Eponine, the moon goddess who had left life in the stars for the love of a shepherd. There were times with Brynn when he felt like that shepherd, a mere man somehow permitted to touch divinity.

"Brynn chose me."

"How long have you been married?" Ovrek pressed.

Cenric didn't like what Ovrek was implying, but it wasn't anything the older man wouldn't already know. "Seven months."

"Seven months," Ovrek repeated the words slowly, deliberately, like he was chewing on them. "You think you know her so well? Sifma still surprises me after decades."

"I can manage my own house," Cenric snapped. "Is there anything else you would like to say about my wife?"

Ovrek tsked. "I meant no offense, son."

Cenric chose not to answer.

"You are quite taken with her." Ovrek made a dismissive gesture in the air. "Come." He beckoned, continuing his walk down the beach.

Cenric shifted to follow the king. He'd moved his right foot back, braced in a battle stance without realizing it.

"Would you fight for Aelgar if he called on you?" Ovrek was finally getting to the point, it seemed.

"Depends," Cenric admitted.

"On what?" Ovrek cast Cenric a sidelong glance.

"Why he wanted me to fight." Cenric tilted his head toward the sky. "And if there might be more compelling reasons not to fight."

Ovrek was quiet for a long moment, as if for effect. "I'm going to take Hylden."

Even without his foretelling last night, the words would not have been surprising. Perhaps Cenric had spent too much time with the likes of Aelgar, but it was refreshing to have the truth out in the open. "You sound confident."

"You doubt I could do it?" Ovrek gestured to the beach. "Five thousand men will sail before midsummer. And whoever joins us once we reach Hylden." Ovrek gave Cenric a significant look.

War.

Cenric thought of his thanes back in Ombra. Many of them, like Edric, had once been thralls in Valdar, but they had fought in Ovrek's war, and he had rewarded them with wealth and freedom. Offensive war was always preferable, when there was treasure, thralls, and land to be taken. Many of Cenric's thanes would be happy for the chance at such wealth.

But Cenric also thought of his fields and flocks. Men fighting would mean fewer to plant, plough, and reap. Fewer to tend the animals.

Most of all, he thought of Brynn. Thought of how she described the war to establish Aelgar. This would break her heart.

But Morgi seemed to be warning Cenric that if he went against Ovrek, he would lose.

"I cut the throat of a young stallion on the first snows and released him," Ovrek said. "When we tracked him down, he had bled out facing the southern sea."

A stallion? Ovrek must be serious if he was willing to sacrifice such a valuable creature for his auguries. Since not everyone had Cenric's foretellings, those who wished to know the future had to resort to other means.

Ovrek's eyes glinted with excitement as he spoke. "I sacrificed bullocks and boars to the Grandfather Yew. The ground soaked up their blood, leaving nothing behind."

That meant the offerings had been accepted. The Grandfather Yew was the most holy place in Valdar, deep in the forest and visited only for sacrifices.

"I struck a new sword against a Hyldish helm, and the helm split in two," Ovrek continued. "A random sword that had never been tested. Can you believe it?"

Cenric remained silent. That was a strong sign indeed.

"The omens are good." Ovrek punched a fist into his opposite hand. "The First of Fathers blesses me in this conquest."

All of these signs combined would mean Ovrek was assured of success. Whether he had interpreted the signs correctly or not, it hardly mattered. Enough wars had been won on confidence.

"You're quiet, son," Ovrek chuckled. "The Cenric I knew would have been slavering for the chance at battle-glory."

"The Cenric you knew did not have lands and their people to consider." Cenric chose not to mention Brynn again. He would prefer Ovrek stop thinking about her. A part of him wished he hadn't brought her here at all, though he couldn't have said why.

"Your lands and people will be fine," Ovrek assured him. "Ombra is in the perfect place to land an army." He gestured to his ships. "You have hundreds of abandoned farms in need of farmers. I have hundreds of farmers in need of farms."

Since the war to establish Aelgar as king of Hylden had emptied many of the shires and farms in the south, the northern lands had slowly lost their people to the warmer, gentler lands. Ombra had the land to support more.

"Troublemakers and criminals, I am sure," Cenric clipped, trying to sound joking, but failing.

Ovrek chuckled at that, still not matching Cenric's tone. "I am not satisfied with a kingdom, young wolf. I will create an empire."

"An empire?" Cenric had rarely ever heard the word. "You mean like the Kelethi?"

Ovrek shrugged. "Why not?"

"They have centuries, hundreds of years of legacy at their backs." Even Cenric knew the Kelethi Empire had already been old when his ancestors first met the dyrehunds.

"Do you know how empires start?" Ovrek faced Cenric, eyes bright. "Men like me. Men with ambition. Men who see not what is, but what could be." He gestured across the beach. "You think the first days of Kelethi were grander than this?"

Cenric studied the ships again, wondering if what Ovrek claimed was true. Was it possible the first Valdari king could also become its first emperor?

"I have one hundred men and their households I would send to you," Ovrek said.

"For what purpose?"

"To serve you," Ovrek answered, as if it was obvious. "You could settle them where you wish. Your lands are in need of people, and I have more people than I know what to do with."

"You would make Ombra a colony?" Cenric only knew the word from Hróarr. It was not one he used often. "A vassal region of your realm?"

Ovrek spread his hands in a gesture of goodwill. "You know me, Cenric. Wealth and glory follow me like a cloud. Have I ever failed to reward those who serve me?"

Cenric supposed that was true. He folded his arms across his chest, thinking. But what was there to think about? Ovrek was offering him friendship and Morgi had already shown him the alternative.

"You don't even have to go to war," Ovrek added. "Not just yet."

What Ovrek was describing was no mass raid or even an invasion. He wanted to set up a stronghold in the north, the mainland closest to Valdar. From there, it would be that much easier for his army to march south into Hylden while being supported by their kin in Ombra.

Cenric did have vast swaths of land, empty farms, and abandoned fields. Ombra could reasonably support thousands more than it currently did. He imagined one day having a massive hall like Ovrek, a city of several thousand around it unlike the few hundred that currently lived at the foot of his longhouse. Perhaps it was possible.

And Ovrek was old while his son was young and unliked. Ombra might easily break from Valdar after Ovrek's death to become its own kingdom. If Cenric took this deal, his children might one day be kings in their own right. What was to say otherwise?

"I will have to hear more about this," Cenric answered, stroking his beard. He realized now that it was a habit he had picked up from Ovrek.

"As soon as you make the decision, I will send the farmers to you," Ovrek said. "Sooner is better, if you want them to help with the fall harvest and ready their own winter stores."

"I must confer with my advisors." Cenric needed to discuss this with Edric and his other men, not to mention the leaders of his various villages across his lands. Not all of them would agree, no matter what, but the appearance of deference went a long way to keep them from fostering resentment.

The king made a noncommittal sound. "And your wife?"

Cenric couldn't speak for Brynn. He honestly wasn't sure what she would say. Brynn was his best and most trusted advisor, but that was not what Ovrek would want to hear. "I am the alderman, not her."

Ovrek chuckled, seeming pleased.

7

Brynn

Someone had intentionally poisoned Ovrek's concubine. As much as Brynn didn't want to believe it, the more she considered it, the more likely it seemed.

Simple bad meat or moldy grain wouldn't have caused that kind of damage to her organs. Nor would it have affected her, but no one else. Intentional poisoning was the only logical explanation.

Worst of all, Brynn had no way of guessing why. There might be any myriad of reasons to poison a woman close to Ovrek. Brynn had no idea how many concubines he might have. It might be a way of getting rid of competition for another desperate woman. It might be something even more complex. There were thousands of people here for the Althing. Any one of them might have a reason to not want Ovrek to have another heir. Then again, it had been Sifma who had not wanted Brynn to attend Gistrid. That did seem suspicious and surely Sifma, as mother of Tolvir, would have her reasons.

This was an emergency, but Brynn had to wait until Cenric returned. She didn't want to send for him and risk drawing the attention of the king—or the culprit.

Not a day here and already she was getting dragged into the intrigues of this place.

Brynn made her way back toward the beach with Esa, Lena, and Guin. Daven and the others might not be back for a time, but at least Brynn would have the chance to clear her thoughts.

People milled in every direction, carrying bundles and barrels and even leading live animals. The Althing was getting underway, and more people were arriving by the hour.

"Lady Brynn!" A woman in rich blue burst through the crowd, flanked by servants and guards. People parted before her like sheep before a shepherd.

Brynn turned and dropped into a bow as soon as she saw who it was. "Lady Tullia."

Guin went rigid, standing close to Brynn's side. Esa fell silent at her back. Lena's head dropped and she seemed to shrink into the background.

"There you are!" Tullia cried, sweeping in to catch Brynn's hands. "You are a difficult woman to track down. Even after I sent you a spy!" At that last part, Tullia cast a knowing look to Lena.

Lena kept her head down, shoulders hunching.

Brynn wondered once again if Tullia knew Lena was Istovari. "Were you seeking me, lady?"

"It so happens I was." Tullia came to stand beside Brynn, tucking Brynn's arm through hers as if they were sisters or close friends. "Where has that husband of yours gotten to?"

"My husband went to meet your father this morning, I am afraid." Brynn wondered how long he would be gone. "I do not know when he will return."

"Late, if I were to guess." Tullia eyed the crowd as if she was looking for someone. "My father has much to show him."

A pit of dread seemed to open up in Brynn's belly, but she forced her face to remain friendly. "I am sure."

Tullia let off a Valdari curse. "So many people here. My father has built the largest fleet ever seen in Valdar."

"You must be very proud." Brynn offered a polite smile. "I can tell my husband you wanted to speak with him."

"It is you I wished to speak with." Tullia seemed to give up trying to find whoever she was looking for in the crowd. "Have you visited the bazaar yet, Lady Brynn?"

Brynn chose her next words carefully. "No, lady. I sent my men there this morning."

"You have been working hard, it seems."

"I dislike being idle." Brynn had the impulse to clasp her hands together, but she tried to remain relaxed, at least on the outside. These Valdari royalty made her nervous.

Guin plopped back on her haunches, staring at Tullia with interest. She peered up at the Valdari woman and then to Brynn as if asking whether she should growl.

"Would you like me to show you?" Tullia asked. "It is not every day that I meet someone of my own station."

"Your station?"

Tullia's eyes sparkled. "The daughter of a king."

Esa shifted, but remained silent as befitted her age and rank. Lena made no sound at all. She didn't even move. She reminded Brynn of fawns that laid still in the brambles, motionless even at the approach of hounds.

What would be the correct response? Brynn could refuse and risk offending Tullia.

Again, Brynn had to wonder if Tullia knew Lena was Istovari or if it was coincidence. Was Brynn being threatened?

She wished again she'd accepted Vana's invitation for today. Vana made Brynn uneasy, especially because she still hadn't gotten up the courage to ask Cenric about his past with the gorgeous Valdari woman. But Brynn had allowed that to influence her decisions when Vana had made good efforts to be friends. Vana also seemed to be close with Queen Sifma. This whole situation could have been avoided if Brynn had controlled her feelings.

"That should be alright," Brynn conceded.

"Excellent!" Tullia clapped her hands together and in that moment Brynn could see the resemblance to Ovrek. "Do you have anything to trade?"

"I sent my men to do the trading for me."

"You sent men to do your trading?" Tullia's brows rose in mock consternation. "You must have faith in them indeed."

Brynn offered a wry smile. "They are sworn to die for me. The least they can do is barter for me."

Tullia laughed at that, a great belly laugh. "Fair enough."

"They also speak the language," Brynn admitted, then added. "Your interpreter had not arrived last night when we made this plan."

"Yes." Tullia glanced over her shoulder to Lena. "That one lacks the backbone for bartering, I think. Far too timid."

If possible, Lena shrank even more into herself.

"Just as well. This way, Lady Brynn." Tullia tugged Brynn through the crowd, her servants and attendants falling in around her.

Guin padded alongside Brynn's skirts, tail and ears up as she investigated their surroundings.

Brynn noticed that two of Tullia's attendants were lanky men made bulky by their weapons. They also appeared to be wearing mail under their cloaks. How odd that Tullia had armed guards when her father did not.

"Do you like them?" Tullia asked, glancing over her shoulder. "I picked them up in Kersus. All the great ladies there have eunuchs as guards. They don't speak Valdari yet, but we are working on that."

Brynn's mother had told her of the Kelethi practice of mutilating boys and young men. Brynn didn't know where Kersus was, but she assumed somewhere in the southeast.

Making eunuchs had been outlawed for decades, but the Kelethi government was still almost entirely run by the household eunuchs of powerful families. So, slaves were castrated elsewhere and brought into the empire after. With their manhood completely severed, not only were eunuchs left with no place in society beyond what their masters offered but they were left unable to urinate without assistance. Brynn's mother had told her in a detached, scholarly tone that they carried quills for the purpose.

It had sounded horrific then and seemed equally horrific now, but Brynn tried to mask her thoughts.

"I've been wanting to buy another eunuch," Tullia mused. "One that has his letters and can write for me. I'd like to have a written history of Valdar and my father's conquests. What do you think?"

"I think you are quite far-thinking, lady." Brynn chose her words carefully. "Very learned as well."

Tullia was magnificent in every way. As tall as a man and dressed in lush fabrics, she moved with utter confidence. She spoke Hyldish effortlessly. Everything about her testified to a quick mind and indomitable personality. Tullia seemed like a woman who had yet to meet an obstacle she could not overcome through sheer force of will.

It was hard to guess her age, but she must be around thirty, assuming Ovrek had been about thirty when he married Sifma, who was probably younger. Tullia was at the age where she had both the gift of experience and the zeal of youth.

"I speak Valdari, Hyldish, Ramthi, and a little Azric." Tullia sounded flippant, as if those foreign tongues had come easily to her and were barely worth mentioning. "Writing does challenge me, but I can make myself understood in most ports. For years, I handled trade with the south for my father."

"You must be very well-traveled."

"More than most, but less than some." Tullia smiled almost wistfully. "My husband and I sailed to Kelethi and back a few times. That was exciting."

"It sounds like it." Brynn didn't have to feign her sincerity. "Will I meet your husband?"

Tullia shook her head. "He's dead."

"I'm sorry."

"Thank you. He was an oaf, but an agreeable oaf. I only wish I'd gotten a son from him before he died." Tullia let off a sigh that sounded regretful, but not particularly grieved.

Then again, Brynn didn't know this woman at all. Who was she to judge whether Tullia was grieving?

"My father will hand me off to another oaf, and I will try to manage this one better. Meanwhile, my dear brother will keep swyving his way through the house thralls all while pining over the girl who rejected him."

Brynn had no idea how to respond to that.

Tullia waved her hand in the air. "My brother thinks using his cock makes him a man." Tullia laughed, shaking her head. She indicated her eunuchs. "I have better men right here and neither one has a cock."

"I think we have all wished to be men at some point," Brynn admitted softly. She had—as soon as she had been able to understand why she had been such a disappointment to her father.

"Why should I wish to be a man?" Tullia demanded. "What is wrong with being a woman?"

"I meant no offense."

Tullia waved her hand as if to say it was nothing. "I used to spar with spears against Cenric and the others around his age. Did he tell you that?"

"No," Brynn admitted. "But Cenric has not told me much of his training."

"I see," Tullia muttered, all traces of her former humor gone. "My father taught me. I helped teach the boys in my father's army.

Before Tolvir was born, he took me everywhere. Called me his little shadow."

"My husband holds you in high regard," Brynn added hurriedly. She didn't want Tullia angry with Cenric. "I'd never heard of Berdun, either."

In truth, they hadn't discussed war overmuch in the past seven months of their marriage. Their life had been filled with the slow season of winter, then the hurried preparations through the lean spring months. It had been easy to forget for a time who they were, and that politics would always find them. For a few months, Brynn enjoyed peace.

"You're quite fond of him," Tullia noted, changing the subject. She seemed to do that frequently, ploughing hard into one topic and then equally hard into another the next moment.

"I am," Brynn conceded.

"You chose to marry him?"

Brynn inclined her head. "I did. I am very happy with him."

Tullia made an interested sound at that. "Is he a good husband?"

"Very good." Brynn allowed herself to smile.

Tullia snorted. "Though I suppose you haven't known anything different."

Brynn almost corrected Tullia, but she didn't want to argue.

They had reached the large field set with tents and wagons. Most of the attendants of the Althing had arrived by ship, but some had come over land.

Valdari voices chattered in all directions as men and women bartered. The peak of the Valdari trading season was happening before their eyes. Woodsmoke filled the air along with the scent of cooking meat. A short, stocky horse was led past, pulling a cart piled with furs and a gaggle of children riding on top.

People bowed to Tullia, clearly recognizing her. She acknowledged only a few, but even if she had wanted to acknowledge all of them, it would have been impossible.

Tullia seemed prepared to drop the subject of Cenric, but Brynn felt the need to defend him, if indeed he was being attacked.

"Cenric is a good man." Brynn hoped that would make her point without directly contradicting the other woman.

"He's young," Tullia replied. "Especially for an alderman."

Brynn demurred. "We are of an age."

Tullia seemed to consider that for a long moment, as if she'd never seen a man's youth as a good thing. "Wouldn't you prefer a more accomplished man?"

Brynn was no longer sure about the point of this conversation. "I am sure Cenric will accomplish much yet."

"I suppose so. I wouldn't have married him myself, but I'm sure you had your reasons." Tullia sounded as if she couldn't imagine what those reasons might have been.

Brynn didn't want to defend her choice of husband, nor did she want to try to convince Tullia of Cenric's virtues, so she remained silent.

"Gistrid was betrothed to my brother last autumn. Did you know that?" Tullia cast Brynn a pointed look. She must know Brynn had been to see Gistrid and who had been with her. "They were inseparable for a time, should have been married by now, but come spring, Gistrid and her kinsmen had grown more ambitious."

"I did not know that." Brynn knew next to nothing about these people, though she did now recall Vana had said something about Tolvir's wedding and that it had been called off.

"Little whore wanted to marry my father instead." Tullia scoffed at that. "But even though she refuses to look at him now, the fool boy is still besotted."

That might explain why Tolvir had been the one to ask for Brynn's help.

"Not that I blame her entirely," Tullia admitted. "My brother is a waste of good air. He wouldn't last a week without my mother to protect him."

Brynn chose not to comment. She could think of several practical reasons why Gistrid might want to marry a current king over a potential future king, especially when Ovrek was the first and the Valdari had still not decided on their manner of succession.

"My father wouldn't let Gistrid have the title of wife." Tullia smiled humorlessly. "Out of respect for my mother, you see." She kept her gaze ahead. "But he offered Gistrid concubinage instead and the little bitch accepted. Hopes to get a son so she'll secure her position after my father's death. As if the man won't outlive us all for spite." Tullia tossed back her head with a bitter laugh. "She just wants to use my father. And both my parents let her. She's like a seagull fighting for scraps of my father's legacy."

That was not so different from what someone had once said about Brynn.

Brynn had been just a few weeks from the birth of her son when she had overhead her first husband, drunk and angry, ranting to one of his thanes about her. A whore, Paega had called her. A little vulture just waiting to claim his lands and wealth, who had only wanted a baby to make sure she held onto them after his death.

"If the gods are just, she'll die screaming in childbirth," Paega had sneered. "It would serve her right." When Paega had thrown open the door and seen Brynn there, they both froze in shock. Paega was the first to speak. "Brynn," he had slurred, "you weren't supposed to hear that." It was the one time he'd ever expressed anything like regret toward her.

Brynn had mostly stopped shedding tears over him by that point, but she had sobbed herself to sleep that night. To this day, she didn't understand why Paega hated her so much.

Tullia shrugged as if none of it mattered. "I didn't realize pennyroyal could be so devastating."

"What?" Brynn wasn't sure she had heard correctly.

Pennyroyal—used to repel fleas, cure some skin ailments, and induce miscarriage. It could also be highly poisonous.

"It's nothing." Had Tullia just confessed to poisoning Gistrid? "I had the chance to buy this one eunuch skilled in apothecary last summer. I should have bought him. My mother could use the help, I think."

"Why are you telling me all this?" Brynn asked softly. "I don't understand."

"Because you have a great deal of power, but no friends in Valdar, and you want what I want."

No friends? That stung, but Brynn supposed it was true. Vana and Hróarr only tolerated her for the sake of Cenric.

"What is it that we want?" Brynn asked.

"To stop a Valdari invasion of Hylden."

Brynn inhaled sharply before she could stop herself.

"Don't act surprised. You're clever enough to know that's what's coming. You think Ovrek built all those ships for trade?"

Brynn was close to the fire now. She needed to be careful lest she was burned. "Why would you want to stop that?" Brynn would expect Tullia would support the expansion of Ovrek's domain.

"Any army led by my father now will be cursed." Tullia watched two boys drag a pig along by a rope.

"What makes you say that?" Brynn tried not to sound too curious, but the certainty in Tullia's voice was hard to miss.

"My father was too long abroad, I fear. The ways of the south have clouded his judgment."

Brynn continued to walk beside the other woman, sensing that Tullia was choosing her words carefully.

"He has forgotten the honor due our ancestors, in particular the First of Fathers."

Brynn remained silent. She didn't know enough about the ways of Valdar to understand what that might mean.

"My husband confronted my father about his profanities." Tullia's tone turned icy, as if she was fighting to keep every hint of emotion from her voice. "Ovrek did not care for it." Tullia pointed to Lena. "He plans to invade your country. He plans to burn your farms and make your sorceresses thralls."

So, Tullia *did* know.

"He is doomed, but that does not mean he cannot do great harm to you and your people before the wrath of Havnar takes its course. It is in all our best interest to stop him."

"I am not sure what I can do," Brynn answered honestly.

"Neither am I," Tullia admitted. "Not yet."

A girl with wispy curls toddled along beside her father. She was still young enough to show her bare calves. Her dark brown tunic had been carefully and subtly repaired many times, but Brynn could see the signs.

The child stared with wide eyes at the sight of Tullia, tugging on her father's sleeve. "Da!" the child cried. "Da!" She pointed furiously at Tullia, eyes wide in awe. She spoke a string of excited Valdari.

The child's father tried to shush her, tugging her along. He ducked his head in apology to Tullia.

Tullia stepped forward, speaking reassuringly in Valdari. She dropped into a crouch, beckoning the child to her.

The child's father let her go and the girl rushed up to Tullia, staring in awe at Tullia's silver temple rings.

Tullia spoke to the little girl with one hand resting on the child's back.

The girl reached for Tullia's temple rings, her chubby hands grasping the shiny rings with their ornate beadwork headband.

The girl's father and Tullia's guards all gasped in unison, but Tullia only laughed. She unhooked her temple rings from her headband and handed them to the child, presenting them like a sweet treat.

The girl snatched them up, squealing. She threw herself at Tullia, embracing the noblewoman with glee. Tullia returned the embrace, clutching the girl's small frame.

When the child finally rushed back to her father, he bowed,

murmuring his thanks to Tullia. He humbly backed away, no doubt trying to disappear before his child asked for more of Tullia's jewelry.

"I love children." Tullia sighed as she watched the child toddle off with her prizes.

"You are quite generous, lady." Brynn suspected both Tullia and Ovrek liked to be complimented.

"I had a little girl." Tullia's smile faded as the child disappeared into the crowd. "Such a pretty thing. She had a laugh bright as dawn and hair dark as my husband's."

"What was her name?" Brynn asked.

Tullia turned to Brynn. Her brow creased ever so slightly. "No one has asked me that."

Brynn knew all too well. "My son's name was Osbeorn."

Understanding flickered across Tullia's face. "I see." The Valdari woman seemed to consider something for a long moment. "Idenna," she said at length. "Her name was Idenna."

"She sounds lovely."

"She was." Tullia finally stood once again. "But that's the way of things, isn't it? Little ones die because of fevers—or accidents or no reason at all." Her mouth moved, but this time it was more of a grimace. "To be a woman is to bear children and to bear children is to lose them."

Brynn wanted to argue with that but couldn't. Most women would conceive at least once over their lifetime and most would bury at least one child. Brynn's own mother had lost a daughter between her and her elder sister. It was so common that some parents would give a new child the same name as their dead older sibling.

Tullia seemed to shake herself, like she was shaking off the sadness of her daughter's memory. "It's best not to place too much hope in little ones and that's what Gistrid has yet to learn."

"How do you mean?" Brynn thought she had an idea, but she wanted to see how much Tullia would confirm.

"Even if she were to bear a son, it's no guarantee. What's more, it's doubtful any son born now would be a man by the time my father dies." Tullia canted her head. "But you know this, don't you?"

"It sounds to me as if Gistrid is not a threat, then."

"Well, not to me." Tullia exhaled. "Though I would not mourn if she were to meet terrible misfortune."

Brynn shifted awkwardly. She knew so little of this woman and the world she came from. It made her feel as if she was walking blind through a field, never knowing when she might fall into a ditch. "You are very honest, lady."

"I am," Tullia agreed. "At least with people who are my friends."

Taking a chance, Brynn asked, "And Gistrid is not your friend?"

"She is not," Tullia answered as the joy from her interaction with the child disappeared. "But she is of no concern to me."

"I would prefer to be your friend, lady," Brynn said honestly.

Tullia's face broke into another grin—the one Ovrek seemed to have given both his children. "Good! I'm happy we understand each other."

Brynn did not think she understood Tullia at all but chose not to say that.

8

Cenric

"We've been making spearheads with ash mixed into the iron," Ovrek explained. He stood over rows and rows of the weapons, proudly displaying the wares to Cenric.

Cenric took in the sheer scale of their work. There had to be hundreds if not thousands of spearheads packed in wood shavings, stacked in pine crates inside the storehouse. Cenric had never seen so many in one place.

Ovrek handed one of the spearheads to Cenric. "See?"

Cenric took the weapon, testing its weight. It was nothing particularly remarkable, but it was sturdy enough to kill. The metal was smooth and sharp.

As if reading his thoughts, Ovrek gestured back toward the forges. "I have a craftsman from the southern continent who has been teaching our smiths to work metal in the way of the great smiths in the south."

Cenric wondered where all this ore had come from. Had they traded for all the iron ingots or had they found a mine somewhere on the islands? "These would be used to arm your men?"

"Those of my household and those of some of the jarls, yes."

Cenric made no comment. A part of him, the boy who had carried a shield for Ovrek, was excited.

The thought of welcoming his old friends, his old liege lord, into his homeland was in some ways thrilling. These were as much his people as the folk of Ombra.

When Ovrek spoke, it was easy to imagine a future with him claiming kingship over Hylden. When Cenric might once again be surrounded by people he understood and who understood him. He loved his homeland, but he had felt more welcomed with the dyrehunds than the people of Ombra for the past years. Not until Brynn had he felt so at ease, perhaps because she was an outsider, too.

But in the back of his mind, he pictured Brynn's reaction if she saw all this.

If they pledged fealty to Ovrek, that would mean a war. Aelgar would not let the northlands go without a fight. Last year, that would not have bothered Cenric nearly as much as it did now.

He had given oaths of allegiance to Aelgar, but he'd sworn loyalty to Ovrek's warband long before. Some would hate him for it, but mostly people in Hylden and mostly those who already hated him for being part Valdari.

Ovrek must have noticed his hesitation. "Have you lost your taste for blood, my boy?"

Cenric didn't rise to the bait. "I am just wondering if I am being threatened."

"Threatened? No. I don't threaten my friends." Ovrek clapped Cenric on the shoulder easily. "I would much rather us stay friends."

So, this was a threat. Ovrek was showing Cenric that he would be taking Hylden one way or another. Cenric liked to think it would pain Ovrek to fight him, but Ovrek didn't seem hesitant.

"If I'd known you were looking for a wife, I could have given you Tullia."

Ovrek couldn't be serious.

"Your daughter is married." Cenric clearly recalled her wedding.

"Newly widowed, as it happens." Ovrek let off a sigh that might have been regretful. "My son-in-law was dear to me, but Sweyn was not appreciative of what he had been given."

That surprised Cenric. Sweyn had been one of Ovrek's fellow veterans who had accompanied him from Kelethi. He'd never been particularly cunning, but he had been fierce. "Sweyn turned against you?"

"Foolish, I know." Ovrek looked toward the entrance of the storehouse, out toward the sea. The king did that often, as if the unconquered lands of Hylden called him. "He joined several others in speaking against me. I had to deal with them." Ovrek sighed. "My daughter hasn't spoken to me since, but she will come around."

Perhaps Brynn was wearing off on him, but Cenric again felt he was being threatened. Ovrek had disposed of one unruly son-in-law. What was to say he wouldn't do away with another?

"You're an alderman," Ovrek added, sounding contemplative. "You can afford two wives, yes?"

Hadn't they agreed last night about only having one wife? Everything about this felt wrong. Cenric glanced over his shoulder. He had the sudden urge to check on Brynn. "One wife is plenty, lord."

Ovrek laughed at that, breaking the tension.

Cenric smiled tightly. This conversation was a jest. It had to be. Valdari men of means did sometimes take multiple wives, and it wasn't unheard of in Hylden, but Cenric had no illusions about ever doing better than Brynn.

They fit together. They worked well together. She was competent as keeper of the household and likeable, even to people who didn't like Cenric. Her lineage would bring prestige to his bloodline for generations to come. She was even wealthy. Cenric knew full well how lucky he was.

Even if Cenric had been of equal status with Tullia, even if he could become rich enough to support two kings' daughters, and even if his patron goddess hadn't made it clear she disapproved of multiple wives, Cenric knew better than to get greedy.

But Ovrek must have been joking, because he dropped the matter. "Will your sorceress kill you in your sleep when she realizes you're siding with Valdar?"

Cenric didn't appreciate that Ovrek assumed he would have Cenric's loyalty, but he tried to hide it. "Brynn could kill me just as easily while I'm awake."

Ovrek laughed at that. Did he think it was a joke? The king gestured for Cenric to follow him back out of the storehouse and into the bustling activity of the shipyards. "The rest of my jarls should arrive by tonight, which means nothing but meetings tomorrow."

Cenric offered a half-smile. "That's the business of being king."

"Bah!" Ovrek spat. "I am not suited to managing the land like a farmwife counting bowls of butter. I have Sifma for that. I am meant for conquest, Cenric. Warring and looting."

That was Ovrek's way of saying he needed more treasure. The coffers he'd taken from his enemies in his rise to power must be running low. This meant he needed to seek wealth across the sea once again.

Come to think of it, Cenric had not seen any gold since arriving in Istra. Had Ovrek run out of it? Perhaps traded it away for the vast amount of iron even now being hammered into spearheads?

This did answer Cenric's question of how long Ovrek could keep giving out as much wealth as he had. Valdari wanted their leaders to be generous, but Ovrek's level of generosity had become unsustainable. To keep giving out lands and wealth, he'd need to keep taking lands and wealth.

Would Ombra be one of those lands taken? Cenric thought of his foretelling last night—an arrow through his own neck as Snapper died and Ovrek's banner waved over their corpses.

And what would become of Brynn if he died fighting his former friends? Would she flee back to Ungamot? Would she be taken by Ovrek as a prize and given to some Valdari jarl? She would be a great prize—a woman with king's blood who had proven she could bear sons. Or, more likely, would she die in battle with Cenric?

It would be far safer to pledge allegiance to Ovrek. At least if they did that, Cenric and his people might be able to keep the fighting out of their lands. They might do the raiding instead of being raided.

Cenric didn't for a moment think that Aelgar would send men to help protect Ombra in a war. The kings of Hylden had always treated Ombra as a shield against the Valdari. A warrior didn't waste time protecting his shield, he cowered behind it, letting it take the brunt of his enemy's assault until he was ready to attack.

Even if Cenric hadn't liked Ovrek as a person, even if he didn't want to swear to this man, did he have a choice? Ombra could put up a strong fight. Brynn could put up a strong fight, but they would eventually be overrun.

Ombra's thanes were used to repelling raids of fewer than twenty men at a time. They would be no match for a fleet of hundreds or perhaps even thousands.

If he swore to Ovrek once again, that would make him Ovrek's man. That would make him the recipient of the king's generosity, one of those gifted treasure and land instead of the opposite.

But Brynn. Would she see it the same way?

"Come." Ovrek beckoned to him. "I want to show you the workhouses. Sifma has over a hundred women weaving the sails for these ships."

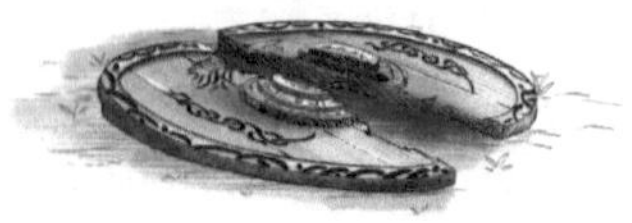

Ovrek was intending to impress Cenric, and he succeeded. The king had shown him the shipyards, the storehouses, and the outside of the massive weaving houses where at least a hundred women worked to weave the sails for the many ships.

No men were permitted inside the weaving houses, but Ovrek showed him the sails ready for fitting outside. They were heavy and sturdy, dyed in bright yellows and pale blues. A single sail might take a woman a year or more to weave, but with dozens working together, the work went faster.

Snapper trotted around them in lazy circles, smelling everything and trying to meet new friends. Part of Cenric wished his life was as simple as his dog's.

By the time Cenric headed back to the tents where his thanes and Hróarr's people were camped, it was late in the afternoon. The feasting would begin at Ovrek's great hall soon.

Cenric reached his tent, finding Kalen slumped against the entrance with his spear at his side. They'd left Kalen with Hróarr's men to guard their camp while the other men were trading.

"Lord!" Kalen leapt up, scrambling. "Sorry, lord."

"My wife?"

"Inside, lord."

"Cenric?" Brynn called at the sound of his voice.

Cenric entered the tent to Guin's excited yipping. The puppy leapt straight for Snapper, the two dogs greeting each other eagerly.

Puppy! Snapper dropped low, slobbering Guin with kisses.

Esa sat mending something in the corner, but it was Brynn who caught his attention.

"Cenric." Brynn went straight to him. She usually greeted him happily, but there was almost desperation in the way she leapt for him.

He caught her, and she clung to him, squeezing tight. Cenric stroked her back. "What's the matter?"

Brynn scared? Snapper asked, cocking his head. Even the dog felt her anxiety.

"I wasn't gone that long." Cenric tried to jest, but something must be wretchedly wrong.

"Esa, Lena, give us a moment." Brynn nodded to the girls.

Esa scurried out to wait with Kalen. Another shape stirred from beside her, what looked to be a Valdari thrall. The second girl ducked out, shutting the tent flap after her.

"Who's that?" Cenric's gaze followed the thrall.

"Tullia's translator." Brynn turned back to Cenric. "She's a sorceress."

"What?" He'd never heard of sorceresses on Valdar.

"She has the ability, anyway." Distress flickered across Brynn's face. "That's another thing. One of many things." She exhaled a sharp breath. "It has been quite a day."

"What else?" Cenric studied her carefully. He could see the worry lines had deepened on her forehead and her clothes were askew as if she had been plucking at them. "There's something else, isn't there? Tell me, love."

Did she know Ovrek had all but commanded his allegiance? Was she going to ask him not to?

"Ovrek's concubine was poisoned."

Cenric blinked, but recovered enough to ask, "How do you know?"

Brynn's hands knotted and unknotted before her. "The atheling Tolvir asked me to see her, so I did. The damage to her internal organs...I think it was pennyroyal."

"Pennyroyal?" Cenric was hardly an herbalist, but he recognized the name. "The plant you use to keep fleas off the dogs?"

"It's used for many things." Brynn waved her hand in the air. "It can also cause miscarriage."

Cenric considered that. "I see." It wasn't unheard of for a woman a third of her lover's age to not want to bear his child, especially when that would make it harder for her to marry after his death.

"No, I don't think she took it on purpose," Brynn clarified. "She seemed genuinely upset, as did her servants. I think someone else meant to make her miscarry."

Cenric pinched the bridge of his nose. Things kept getting worse.

"The pregnancy is over, but I think she will survive."

Cenric straightened. "She was hurt?"

"Pennyroyal can be highly poisonous."

Cenric exhaled. Ovrek would not be pleased to learn someone was poisoning his women. "Does the girl know?"

"I told her and her servants through the translator. I'm not sure they believed me." Brynn made a short, frustrated sound. "I don't know...where to go or who to tell. I feel like I should tell someone, but I don't want to get her in trouble."

Cenric was not meant for this kind of intrigue. Brynn was far better versed at such delicate matters, but she didn't speak the language or know these people well enough. "We must tell Ovrek. If someone is poisoning his consorts, that could be a plot."

"But what if the girl gets in trouble?" Brynn wrung her hands.

"Her life could be in danger." Another thought occurred to Cenric. "Ovrek could be in danger."

Brynn covered her face with her hands. She'd probably been tormented by this all day. "There's more."

"What?" Cenric braced himself.

Brynn dropped her hands. "Tullia..."

"What about Tullia?" Cenric shifted, suddenly uncomfortable after Ovrek's jest today.

"I think she knows who did it. Assuming she didn't do it

herself."

Cenric paused for a moment. "Why?"

"She said she was no friend of Gistrid. Then that she hadn't expected pennyroyal to be so devastating, but I hadn't mentioned anything to her about Gistrid's illness or pennyroyal." Shaking her head, Brynn gestured helplessly. "Then she offered me friendship, and I accepted, but what else was I supposed to do?"

Cenric cursed. Perhaps Ovrek should sort out his own family before planning an invasion. "I don't want to be enemies with Tullia, not any more than I'd want to be enemies with Ovrek, but if I have to choose one, I'd prefer the one without an army."

Brynn's breath hitched. "An army?"

A stab of guilt pierced Cenric at that. "We will be at war with them. Soon. If nothing changes and I do not swear allegiance to Ovrek."

Brynn's eyes widened, but she didn't look surprised. If anything, there was resignation in her face. Her grip on him tightened. "It is like that?"

"It is."

"Can we...is there anything we can do to stop it?" Brynn made a soft whimpering sound. "Tullia told me she wishes to stop the invasion of Hylden."

"Did she say why?" Cenric would have never suspected Tullia of sedition against Ovrek, but he would never have suspected her husband, Sweyn, either.

"She fears Ovrek has angered the ancestors. That his army will be cursed."

Cenric tried to think how Ovrek could have done that. The Valdari ancestors and Havnar, the deified First of Fathers, were not exactly lax, but they were difficult to offend. Honor the ancestors, respect the ancient landmarks, and do nothing that you would not have known to the world—those were their only true commands. "I am not sure what she means. And while Tullia is a force to be reckoned with, I doubt she could stop the invasion any more than we could. The king is set on it."

Brynn seemed to wilt before him. He wished he had a more hopeful answer for her.

Cenric exhaled. "Ovrek offered me a place in his circle. Valdari settlers for the empty farms. We could keep everything we have and gain much more."

"But?" Brynn asked the word softly, sadness weighing her voice.

"But Ovrek will invade Hylden."

Brynn flinched as if she had been struck.

"I had a foretelling last night," Cenric confessed.

Brynn cast him a sharp look. "You mentioned it this morning."

"Yes." Cenric was used to visions of his death by now, but he didn't want to upset Brynn. All the same, she needed to know the outcome, if not the details. "Valdari taking Ombra under Ovrek's banner. I think it is what will happen if I refuse his offer."

Brynn's shoulders slumped. "Even if my uncle did send us thanes from other shires to help fight, it would take time. We would be on our own for weeks or even months before then."

Cenric braced himself, fear tearing at his chest. Fear of how Brynn would react, fear that she might rage against him. Fear that she might leave him.

"You are the alderman of Ombra." Brynn's voice went small, so small that he almost didn't hear it. "You know Ovrek best." She inhaled a deep breath and lifted her face to him. Tears shone in her eyes, but her voice didn't tremble. "If you believe that giving him our allegiance is what is best for our people, then..." Her voice cracked. Brynn closed her eyes for a moment, and the tears fell, but she seemed to compose herself. "I will abide by your decision."

Cenric had come here anticipating an argument, perhaps denial. A part of him had hoped that his wife might have some clever scheme to get out of this. Her mournful acceptance was not what he had predicted at all. "And if I decide it is best to give him my allegiance?"

Brynn didn't falter. "Then he will have mine also."

"If he calls for me to take my thanes and march south with his army?"

"Then I will go with you." Brynn's brow creased, as if she was fighting more tears.

"You would fight against your own people for him?"

"There are sorceresses in the south." Brynn sounded grieved, as if she could already see her people in opposing battle lines before her. "You will need protection from them."

"Brynn." Cenric cradled her face in his hands. "You don't have to do this."

Brynn sniffled, still fighting tears, but she smiled. "I love you," she whispered softly. "I would do this and worse."

"You would become a traitor to your king?"

"I have been loyal to my king for as long as I could remember," Brynn whispered. "And I lost everyone." She rested her hands over his. "If betraying my uncle, my whole country, is the price of keeping you, then...Eponine forgive me, but I will do it." Brynn would be pragmatic enough to know they couldn't repel an attack from several thousand Valdari. Not even with his thanes and her significant power.

Cenric wrapped his arms around her, pulling her against his chest. Brynn clung to him, nestling close against his heart.

He had been so certain he should swear to Ovrek just a few minutes ago. Ovrek was stronger than Aelgar. Ovrek was closer. Ovrek was familiar, someone he liked, and a man he trusted to be generous and fair.

It had been obvious that he should pledge himself and his people to Ovrek. There had just been the vague fear in the back of his mind that Brynn might not approve.

Now he knew that Brynn would be with him no matter what he did, that changed things. There was a weight to that. He had the fate of his entire country on his shoulders, but now Brynn's trust, too. She was deferring to him, letting him decide.

And if he chose wrong, they would all pay for it.

Cenric held his wife and wished it had not come to this. But it had. There was nothing more to be done than to choose which king they would support, and which would be less likely to abandon them to the wrath of the other.

"I could live a thousand years and never earn you."

Brynn let off a sound that might have been a laugh or a sob.

Cenric tucked her under his chin, breathing in her scent, savoring the feel of her in his arms. Sometimes he was still surprised that she was his. He was never going to have a wife better than her and that was something Ovrek would never understand.

"What are we going to do about the girl who's been poisoned?" Brynn turned the subject back to the most pressing matter at hand.

Cenric shifted, feeling as if these twisted intrigues were ropes, tightening around him like a spring calf.

Brynn moved away from him to tilt her head up.

"We tell Ovrek. Then he won't be able to claim you kept it from him if the secret comes out. I don't know if we can accuse Tullia, though."

Brynn bit her lip. "I just want to make sure he doesn't blame the girl for anything."

Of course, Brynn was worried about the girl. That was who she was. Cenric, for his part, was far more worried about Brynn. He didn't know how Ovrek might react if something befell the concubine and Brynn was somehow implicated.

"We can try our best." Cenric couldn't control what Ovrek did once he had the information, but it would be bad if the king learned they'd kept it from them. "Are you ready?"

Brynn adjusted her shawl. He noticed that the silver cuff from last night was back on her arm. Good.

Cenric rested a hand on the small of her back, guiding her out of the tent. It would have been preferable to have Hróarr and Vana's help with this, but he didn't know where they were.

Brynn stayed close to him, almost clingy. Esa stood to go with them.

"Watch Guin," Brynn told her. "I will be back soon. I hope."

Cenric grasped his wife's hand, knotting their fingers together. She clung to him tight, anxiety radiating through her.

The thrall from Tullia followed behind at a respectful distance. She'd probably been told not to leave Brynn's side.

It was late in the day, the shadows lengthening and the sun sinking toward the western sea. It sent golden streaks across the water like rivers of fire.

As they drew near Ovrek's household complex, servants rushed past them. Girls carried bundles of sticks and boys rolled barrels of ale toward the hall in preparation for tonight's feast.

Ovrek would be in the main hall soon if he wasn't already, so Cenric led Brynn in that direction. She stayed close to him, almost like she was trying to keep contact.

Another servant ran past them, this one a young girl.

Voices chattered ahead, mostly female. Someone screamed.

"Oh, no," Brynn gasped. "Oh, no, no..." Brynn broke away from him, running toward a crowd forming at the front of a large house. The building was separate from the others and appeared to be some manner of residence.

"Brynn?" Cenric jogged after her as she pushed through a crowd of onlookers at the open door of the longhouse.

Servants scattered out of their way, but women in jewels with brightly colored shawls didn't move as quickly. Brynn wove between them and Cenric dodged after her.

Brynn reached the doorway, a hand over her mouth as she stared aghast.

"Brynn?" Cenric pushed his way up to stand behind her.

Inside was a sumptuous room lined with carpets. The hearth burned bright at the center and Queen Sifma knelt on the floor, sobbing over the motionless body of a young woman.

Servants hovered around them, but most simply stared in sick fascination. Wealthy women crowded around them, gasps of horror and whispers fluttering between them along with the soft clinking of beads and silver temple rings.

Realizing what this house was, Cenric took a step back from the threshold out of habit. It would be an offense to Ovrek to enter, even if the house's occupant was dead.

Sifma cradled the young woman's corpse. "No, no, no. My poor girl. No." The queen spotted Brynn in the doorway. "You," she growled.

Brynn took a step back, hitting Cenric's chest. She might not understand the language, but she understood the tone.

Cenric reached for his wife, not sure what was happening.

"What did you do to her?" Sifma laid down the girl's body, smoothing back her hair.

Cenric searched over his shoulder. He didn't recognize anyone here. He would have no allies against the queen's wrath.

"You killed her!" Sifma shrieked.

Cenric had never seen Ovrek's stoic wife so distraught nor so angry.

Sifma marched across the room, headed straight for Brynn. "What did you do?"

Two of the onlooking men advanced on Brynn, the object of their queen's rage.

Cenric grabbed Brynn around the waist, pushing her behind him. The two men kept coming, so he drew his sword. Both men drew up short as the surrounding women backed away. None of them wanted to be caught in the middle of this.

One of the men also drew a sword.

Cenric flashed his teeth, a warning, a dare. He didn't care if these men were Ovrek's servants. He'd kill them right here if they tried to touch Brynn.

Sifma drew up short, seeming to recognize him. "Cenric."

"Queen Sifma." Cenric did his best to sound courteous. "What has happened?"

"What's happening?" Brynn asked, her Hyldish words clashing with Sifma's stream of enraged Valdari.

"Steady," Cenric whispered to Brynn.

She held onto his left arm. She didn't tell him to put away the sword, but she kept her attention on the two men.

"She came here earlier today offering her help. Now Gistrid is dead."

"Brynn tried to help her," Cenric retorted.

"What is she saying?" Brynn trembled. "Tolvir asked me to help."

"Did Tolvir not ask for Brynn's help?" Cenric asked, addressing the queen.

"You would accuse my son?" Sifma demanded, eyes flashing.

Cenric frowned at that. "Brynn, did anyone else see Tolvir ask you?" Realizing the Valdari would be unlikely to believe Esa or one of his servants, he asked, "Anyone Valdari?"

Brynn hesitated. "Only him and his friends. And the translator Tullia sent."

"Where is the thrall?" Cenric doubted anyone would trust the word of a thrall, but it might be useful to have her close.

"She..." Brynn turned, then glanced back and forth. "She's gone."

Not surprising. Most thralls knew to run at the first sign of trouble. No one would believe the word of a thrall against a queen anyway.

"Your *wife*," Sifma hissed, "came earlier today and offered to help. Gistrid was recovering, but now she's dead."

If Tullia had been behind this, then Tullia's thrall had led Brynn into a trap. Worse, now Cenric couldn't demand justice without making it appear he was pulling accusations from the air.

But Ovrek had killed Tullia's husband. Who was to say she hadn't killed his concubine in retaliation?

By the corpse, several handmaidens fussed and whimpered. They seemed oblivious to the standoff mere steps away.

Cenric caught the tramp of bootsteps as word spread of the

concubine's death. He tensed, glancing to Brynn.

"She was poisoned," Cenric said flatly. They might as well start spreading the truth. "Brynn told the servants before this. Why would she have warned the household if she did it?"

Sifma turned away, shaking her head. "You should never have brought her here."

"Mother!" Tolvir took in the scene with a gasp, horror washing over his face, but even he hovered back, not touching the threshold. "What happened?"

"She's dead." Sifma seemed to grow larger with fury. "Did you get the Hyldish woman to interfere?"

Tolvir pointed to Brynn. "She told me Gistrid was healed!"

"Foolish boy." Sifma whirled away from her son and back to the girl's body on the ground.

Tolvir spun around, glaring straight to Brynn. "What did you do?" His question was in Hyldish.

Brynn looked to Cenric in confusion. "I don't understand. I healed her earlier today."

"And now Gistrid is dead." Tolvir stepped closer. "You told me she was better!"

"Watch yourself." Cenric angled his sword to the youth.

Tolvir seemed to notice the blade for the first time. "You would dare draw a weapon in my presence?"

"Come closer and I'll sheath it in your gut."

"You wouldn't dare!" Tolvir's nostrils flared.

"Try me."

"Cenric." Brynn might not understand most of what was happening, but she could guess. Her hand stroked his upper arm, like she was comforting a wild animal. "We've all been taken for fools. Please." Her voice dropped to a whisper. "We can't fight our way out."

Cenric wasn't sure he believed that. Brynn probably could fight her way out, just not without a massive death toll. But Brynn was usually right. Cenric lowered his weapon.

"What is happening?" Ovrek's authoritative bellow boomed over the gathered crowd. It was the same tone he had used to shout orders on the battlefield—a voice that made men want to fall in line.

Cenric almost stood at attention out of habit.

Ovrek marched up to Cenric and his son, taking in the two of them with a glare. "Threatening my son?"

Cenric almost felt embarrassed. Almost. "He threatened my wife."

"This woman killed Gistrid." Tolvir thrust a finger at Brynn.

Cenric really should have stabbed him when he had the chance.

"Gistrid is dead," Sifma told Ovrek, mouth tight and face hard. The queen seemed genuinely distraught over the girl's death.

Ovrek took in the scene. He entered the longhouse and crouched beside the corpse, examining her gently. He pinched the bridge of his nose and let off a hard exhale. "Explain," the king ordered, looking to Sifma, Tolvir, and Cenric. "All of you." He continued speaking in Valdari, not even acknowledging Brynn.

Sifma spoke first, her voice cracking. "She had been ill for a few days."

"Why was I not told?" Ovrek demanded.

"I didn't wish to add to your worries." Sifma refused to meet his face. "She recovered partly today."

"Because of Brynn," Cenric interjected. "Brynn healed her."

"Do not interrupt my wife," Ovrek growled, rising to his full height. "Sifma."

"She began convulsing an hour ago and her handmaids sent for me." Sifma turned her face away, tears shimmering in her eyes.

"The sorceress?" Ovrek looked past Cenric to Brynn.

Brynn shifted at Cenric's back, but didn't speak. She was letting him handle his own friends.

Cenric spoke. "The concubine was poisoned. Brynn tried to warn her through an interpreter. Whoever did it must have struck again." Here wasn't the place to accuse Tullia with so many people watching.

"Where is this interpreter now? Why didn't your wife warn anyone else of this?" Ovrek demanded.

"She told me," Cenric answered, realizing how it sounded. "We were on our way to tell you."

"After my concubine and child were dead?" Ovrek's tone had gone quiet, dangerous.

Cenric wasn't sure what to expect. To this man, Brynn was the enemy.

"Nothing I did would have hurt her, lord." Brynn's voice remained soft. She must have guessed what they were saying. "I swear."

Ovrek took in the scene. "I can't deal with this right now." He stepped away from the body of his concubine and weeping queen. He addressed the two warriors who had followed him, stopping over the threshold. "Confine the Lady Brynn to her tent until I decide what to do with her."

Cenric bristled.

"Careful, son," Ovrek growled.

"Cenric?" Brynn's voice was quiet, meek.

"He wants to confine you to our tent until he figures out what to do with you." Cenric ground out the words, each one painful.

"Alright," Brynn said.

"You didn't do anything wrong," Cenric protested.

"No," Brynn agreed, "but..." She swallowed. "We are in their lands." She squeezed his arm tight. "Remember what we discussed."

That Ovrek was probably going to be their king soon. That they needed to be in his favor for the coming invasion. That Ombra wouldn't survive Ovrek's wrath.

Cenric grimaced at the reminder. "I'll go with you."

"Put the sword away," Ovrek ordered. "And clean this up," he gestured to the corpse. "I want all of you in the hall within the hour, do you understand? My dear queen, my dear son, and my dear friend." Ovrek singled out Sifma, Tolvir, and Cenric in turn. "Am I understood?"

"Your woman is dead! And you're planning to feast?" Tolvir cried, lunging toward his father.

Ovrek grabbed the boy by the back of his tunic, slamming him against the outside of the house. "One day, gods willing, you will be king, and when that day comes, I hope you have learned that kingship comes before everything. *Everything.*" Ovrek shoved his son aside, stepping from Gistrid's longhouse. "Don't make me repeat myself."

Tolvir fumed, fists clenched at his sides, but what could he do? His father was Ovrek Fork-Beard, unquestioned ruler of Valdar.

Sifma turned, hiding behind her veil as she faced the motionless corpse once again.

The king stormed away, two men following in his wake, the other two ready to escort Brynn back to the tent she and Cenric had been sharing.

Brynn held onto Cenric's arm. "Be careful," she pleaded. She was afraid, he could tell, but was she afraid for herself or him? Brynn might not understand the language, but she could probably guess what was happening. "Please."

Cenric put an arm around Brynn. "Ovrek wants me to meet him in the main hall after this."

Brynn touched his chest for just a moment. "Then you will go."

"After I see you back to our tent and make sure you have your own servants." Cenric hated everything about this. Everything.

Ovrek's concubine was dead, Cenric's wife was being implicated, and not even his old friend seemed willing to hear them out. As he walked back to their tents, shadowed by the guards, Cenric wondered why things always had to be so complicated.

Would Ovrek believe Cenric when he said that Tullia had poisoned Gistrid? Even if father and daughter were currently at odds, Ovrek had always been fond of her. Would he believe Cenric or assume they were desperate lies?

9

Brynn

She had been too late.

Brynn had tried to warn Gistrid and her handmaidens. She had tried to do the right thing, but Gistrid must have been poisoned again right after Brynn left. Had Tullia decided she wanted Gistrid dead after all?

Gistrid might have been a self-serving, spoiled brat for all Brynn knew. It might have been true that she had wanted to use Ovrek. Brynn still didn't think she deserved to die.

Cenric left Brynn with the two guards standing outside. She heard him growling to them in Valdari, probably threats. But she could protect herself from them. Neither wore armor and their tunics were made of wool. It would be easy for her to use spells to fell both men.

Brynn could fight her way out of this, but then what? Down the beach, their ship had been blocked off by two others. Daven and the rest of Cenric's thanes had been "invited" to sup at the feast being held for the jarls' men. It seemed they were all being watched.

Even if they could escape, Ovrek was about to invade Hylden. If he thought she had murdered his concubine, he would try to kill her. According to Cenric, they needed to give their allegiance to Ovrek to save Ombra, to save their own lives.

Brynn considered killing Ovrek, but quickly dismissed the idea.

Killing Ovrek would only create a power imbalance in Valdar. It might delay the invasion as men squabbled to carve up his kingdom. She doubted Tolvir had the skill or maturity to keep the kingdom in a unified whole. As for Tullia, she was too unpredictable, too unknown. Brynn had no idea if she had the support to seize control of Valdar and even if she did, she might turn out to be worse than Ovrek.

Even in Hylden, where rules for succession had been in place for generations, the death of a king was a bloody affair. Perhaps that discord would be isolated to Valdar, but it might not. For all Brynn knew, it might result in more raids and invasions into Ombra as men starving in the wake of the unrest tried to feed themselves and their families.

At the same time, another king might take Ovrek's place, one just as set on conquering Hylden but without the fondness for Cenric this one had. Brynn did not know Valdari politics well enough to know if there might be another jarl powerful enough to do that.

At the very least, Tullia had known who poisoned Gistrid the first time, but had she been responsible for Gistrid's ultimate death? Could someone else have done that?

Unsurprisingly, Tullia's thrall had disappeared. That did not mean that Tullia was guilty, though.

Brynn stared into the glow of the hot coals in the small pit that served as a brazier, Guin's head resting in her lap, snoring peacefully.

Assuming someone other than Tullia had poisoned Gistrid, who could have done it?

Gistrid had been poisoned when Istra was filled with people. More people than ever, it seemed. From what Ovrek said, jarls and all their attendants as well as farmers, fishermen, and everyone in between would be here from across the country.

It could be anyone. Anyone.

From what Brynn knew, Ovrek had been king for barely a decade. That was not nearly long enough for past grudges and wounds to be forgotten.

But it also didn't make sense. If someone wanted to hurt Ovrek, why not target his son? He only had one and from what Brynn had seen, the boy pranced about Istra unguarded. He would have been an easy mark.

Ovrek also made himself accessible to his men. He might observe the tradition of making them leave their weapons outside his hall, but he walked freely through Istra where anyone could attack him.

Even if someone had wanted one of Ovrek's lovers dead, why not Sifma? She was the one he had given the title of queen, the one who ran his household, and the mother of his two children. From what Brynn had seen, Sifma would be a far greater loss to Ovrek's rule. At the same time, it seemed unlikely that Gistrid would have been a threat to Sifma.

Ovrek had alluded to other concubines. Could it have been one of them? One of their families?

Brynn blew a long breath out of her nose. She couldn't even begin piecing this together.

She sensed *ka* headed toward her tent from outside, about the size and shape of a person. She shifted, thinking it might be Cenric, but it had only been a couple hours and there was no sign of Snapper. She doubted it was him just yet and Esa shouldn't be alone, Kalen should be with her. The two of them had gone to fetch supper for themselves and Brynn. So who?

Voices drifted through the canvas as the newcomer spoke to the guards outside. Words were exchanged for a few moments and then the tent flap opened.

Vana stepped inside, her shawl in place. "How are you?" she asked gently, sounding friendly.

"As well as I can be." Brynn offered a wan smile.

Guin wagged her tail at Vana's entrance, but she stayed lying in Brynn's lap.

"How is Cenric?"

"Furious." Vana took up a place before the hot coals beside Brynn, partially facing her. "But he's trying to hide it."

Brynn should have known. She loved Cenric's straightforwardness. He saw no point in lying. That made him bad at politics, but good at being trustworthy. "Did Ovrek send you?" Brynn watched the puppy as Guin stretched, adjusting her rump and settling back down.

Vana hesitated.

"It's alright." Brynn pushed aside her feelings of betrayal and frustration. She locked them deep down in her chest, to be taken out when she had the time and the space for them. "Ask your questions."

Vana grimaced. She probably didn't like this situation any more than Brynn did, whether she thought Brynn was guilty or not. "What happened?"

"Shall I start with this morning when I first met Gistrid?" It was the only time Brynn would ever meet Gistrid, she realized. That girl's body was even now growing cold.

"Please do." Vana adjusted her shawl.

Brynn told Vana everything she remembered, from the time they had been summoned, to the time they had found the girl's body. She left out the part where Tullia had confessed knowing, though she mentioned walking with the woman.

"We found that thrall," Vana said. "She denies you ever saying that Gistrid had been poisoned."

Brynn quashed her frustration at that. Had Tullia told Lena to lie?

Vana continued. "Is it possible that your healing somehow made her worse?"

"No," Brynn answered quickly. "No. Gistrid's illness was caused by poison. The only way it would have worsened was if she was poisoned again." It was possible for infections to be made worse by giving a person *ka,* but poisons were different.

Vana deflated. Maybe she had been hoping that this could be explained away as an accident—an honest mistake on Brynn's part.

"Magic does not kill slowly. It..." Brynn took a breath to calm herself. "Spells are not living things. They require active participation of the weaver."

Vana nodded, but that meant nothing. This was Brynn's word against everything else. Against every*one* else.

Brynn blew out a frustrated breath. "What will happen if Ovrek thinks I did it?"

Vana hesitated. "I am not sure. He may demand a blood price, or he may want to avenge her."

Brynn had assumed as much. "I see." Was this a scheme to put the blame on Brynn? But why? "What will happen to Cenric?"

"If he complies, nothing," Vana said.

Brynn petted Guin's head, thinking. It would be best for Cenric to stand by and do nothing, but he wouldn't. From the way he had drawn his sword to defend her, even in front of Ovrek, he would never let them hurt her while he was alive.

That thought filled her with a sick sense of dread, but she couldn't quite wish it was otherwise. No one had been willing to die for her in a long time.

"It looks like you did it, Brynn." Vana's words came out slowly, as if she didn't want to speak them. "Intentionally or not."

Brynn ground her teeth in frustration. She should have known better than to try to help Gistrid. It was all being used against her now, turning her into the proxy for murder.

Brynn had killed dozens, maybe even hundreds of people on the battlefield, but she had never been accused of murder before.

"Gistrid's handmaidens said she had been sick for several days," Brynn protested. "Stomach pains and tiredness."

"She was with child." Vana blinked. "That is hardly suspicious."

Brynn didn't expect Vana to be convinced, not really, but thinking out loud was useful. "She was almost dead."

"We have only your word for that," Vana pointed out. "Sifma and the handmaidens said she was getting better."

They were lying. Either they were also trying to pile the blame on Brynn or they feared Ovrek's wrath if he learned just how much they had hidden from him. Maybe both.

Brynn fought to think past her hurt and sense of injustice. "I healed her, and then it looks like she was given a much larger dose." Brynn considered that. "I don't think killing her was the goal, just the baby."

"Why would anyone kill a baby?" Vana protested.

Brynn grimaced. Her own son had been a baby, murdered a year ago. The pain of that loss lingered, but though the boulder of her grief still took up space in her heart, it no longer crushed her beneath its weight.

"The child might not have survived birth, or its first year." Vana shook her head. "It could have been a girl for all we know."

Brynn studied the sleeping puppy in her lap. Vana was right. It made no sense. Brynn was still missing something.

Tullia might well have wanted to make Gistrid miscarry out of spite, but it wouldn't explain changing her mind to want the girl dead. Tullia did not seem the sort to change her mind easily.

Vana exhaled a long breath.

"Why do you think I did it?"

"I did not say that."

"But you do." Brynn watched the glow of the hot coals falter.

Esa would need to stir them when she returned. "Don't you?" She tried not to sound defensive, tried to quash all sense of betrayal deep, deep down.

"I don't think you meant to hurt her."

"And Ovrek?"

"I don't know." Vana sighed. "Tolvir says that you must be a spy for Aelgar."

Brynn supposed that was to be expected.

"Hróarr said you might be trying to sow discord among the Valdari."

Brynn closed her eyes. If she had wanted to do that, she would have attacked Tolvir, not a random young woman. Tolvir was a man of fighting age, despite being young and impetuous. He was by far the bigger threat.

"I don't think word has spread of it yet. They're trying to say it was an accident for now."

Brynn considered it. A king who could not protect his own pregnant concubine would hardly be seen as worthy by the warlike Valdari. They valued strength and power. Maybe someone was trying to discredit Ovrek before his planned invasion.

"Does Ovrek have any enemies besides my uncle?"

Vana let off a little laugh. "Half the men here either fought against him or had a close kinsman who did."

Wonderful. Half the Althing had a reason to hate Ovrek.

"I didn't do it." Brynn stared into the coals. "But I doubt anything I say will make any of you believe that."

"We are just trying to understand," Vana said. "It doesn't make sense."

Brynn felt suddenly tired. It was late and she had been through a great deal today. "Is there anything else you want to know?"

Vana pursed her lips briefly. "There is no way your spells could have hurt the girl?"

"No." Brynn watched the flames. "What I did was heal her from the poison's effects. She was fine when I left her."

Vana made a frustrated sound. "Ovrek is a just man. If you tell him it was an accident, he may be merciful."

Perhaps, but that would not solve the larger problem. Someone had poisoned that girl and until Brynn knew exactly who, there was danger.

If Cenric was correct, they would be welcoming these people into their lands in the next year. They would bring their intrigues and their tangle of debts, offenses, and slights with them. Brynn needed to deal with this now or later, when it might inevitably become an even worse problem.

"I will not lie," Brynn answered quietly. "I did nothing to hurt Gistrid. What I did would not have hurt her. She had no fever, no signs of anything other than poisoning." Brynn spoke the words firmly, as much to remind herself as Vana. "I did not hurt Gistrid," Brynn repeated. "But I understand if you do not believe me."

Brynn and Vana went in circles for several more minutes. Brynn answered the questions honestly, but didn't change anything. She tried not to feel anything, not betrayal, not expectancy, nothing.

Eventually, Vana left, bidding Brynn goodnight in a polite if strained way.

Brynn waited as she sensed Vana's presence fading away. She stayed as she was, stroking Guin's coat.

Would Cenric be back tonight? He might be late. Ovrek seemed to want him to be a part of tonight's festivities. Brynn suspected that tonight had been the whole point of inviting Cenric here in the first place.

Feasts served to remind everyone why a king was king. It reminded Brynn of the nights of revelry her father had often held before going to war, the ones she and her sister had been strictly forbidden from attending.

Brynn stared into the fire, considering her options. If she took the blame for this, it would damage her position with Ovrek and by extension Cenric and Ombra's position with Ovrek. If Ovrek was to be their king, she couldn't allow this.

But how to proceed?

Besides Cenric and their servants, Brynn had no friends here. Not even Vana and Hróarr were on her side.

Voices came from the direction of the campfire. Someone approached.

Brynn sensed the newcomer near the tent. The guards outside left. The newcomer pushed aside the entrance flap.

Brynn straightened. It wasn't Cenric. In her lap, Guin growled. Instinctively, Brynn pulled at her magic.

A man entered, tall, wreathed in shadows. She couldn't see his face.

Brynn remained seated, but her magic shimmered around her, ready. "What do you want?" Brynn's heart raced, but she held onto Guin as the little dog squirmed, growling.

"You killed her."

Recognition struck Brynn. "Tolvir?" Confusion edged her fear.

"You killed Gistrid."

Brynn held onto Guin, adding power to her spells. "This isn't—"

Tolvir lunged for her. It was a bear rush, angry and enraged.

Brynn shoved Guin across the tent and the pup yelped, but she would be out of the way.

Tolvir ran face-first into the shield Brynn had woven around herself. He cried out in pain and rage as the spell burned his skin, leaving a mesh of stinging red marks across his face.

It slowed him down, but it wasn't enough to stop him completely.

Brynn scrambled to the side, clawing to her feet.

Guin leapt up and barked, ears back and tail straight out.

"We can talk about this." Brynn kept her hands out in front of her.

Tolvir was unarmored. He hadn't thought to protect himself

from a sorceress, it seemed.

With only wool and linen protecting him, Brynn knew exactly the spell to fell him. She could slice through his unprotected neck like butter. Unfortunately, killing his only son would do nothing to prove her innocence to Ovrek.

"You know this is wrong," Brynn said. "Else you wouldn't have sent the guards away." Brynn was fully confident that Ovrek didn't know about this.

"You killed her," Tolvir growled. "You're not going to get away with it." His accent thickened with his anger, making him harder to understand.

"The person who killed her is getting away with it." Brynn silently prayed for him to see reason. "But it wasn't me. Think, Tolvir. Why would I hurt an insignificant concubine? Why not your mother? Why not you?"

"She wasn't insignificant!" Tolvir roared.

"Oh, no..." Realization struck Brynn. Tullia had told the truth about one thing, at least. "You poor boy..."

That had been the wrong thing to say.

Face still red from her burns, Tolvir picked up Brynn's leather bag in the corner and swung it at her like a flail.

She raised her spells defensively, but in the tight space, she couldn't retreat far enough. The satchel smacked through the first line of her spells and without Brynn having the space to retreat far enough, Tolvir closed the distance and slammed her against the tent brace, making the whole structure shake.

"Stop now!" Brynn ordered.

Tolvir wasn't listening. His hand wrapped around her neck, slamming her back harder.

Brynn saw stars and darkness claimed the edges of her vision.

Guin bounded across the tent and attacked Tolvir's ankle, snarling and growling. Her little teeth locked onto the back of his leg wraps as she yanked back. Tolvir kicked the puppy, sending her sprawling across the tent with a yelp.

Brynn grabbed his wrist, clawing back his sleeve. She touched bare skin and then it was over.

She sent a jolt of power through his veins. Tolvir screamed, his arm locking up as heat tore up his tendons and muscles. Dark marks singed his wool sleeve and he stumbled back, gasping and crying out in pain.

Brynn inhaled sweet air, staggering to find her balance. She pulled *ka* into herself, healing her neck and vocal chords. "I can do worse to you," Brynn wheezed as her body pulled itself back together. "Leave now and we can forget this."

With his right arm cradled against his chest, Tolvir straightened. He drew his eating knife from his belt, looking back up to her with murder in his eyes.

"Don't," Brynn warned. "Don't try it." Brynn had killed greater warriors than this atheling, faced far worse odds.

Tolvir either didn't know or didn't care. He dove for her.

Stupid, stupid boy.

Brynn wrapped a spell around his neck and cinched it tight.

Tolvir fell to the ground gasping. He clawed at invisible air, helpless and powerless to do anything to defend himself.

Brynn stepped over him, reaching Guin. "Come here, little girl."

The puppy yelped as Brynn scooped her up.

"I'm sorry." Brynn stroked Guin's fur, feeling out the bruises. She didn't appear to have any broken bones, so Brynn eased more power into her, healing her injuries. She left Tolvir writhing on the floor.

Voices came from outside. Brynn went to the tent entrance. Outside, two Valdari came marching toward the noise. She thought they were Hróarr's men who had stayed to guard the ships, but couldn't be sure. They caught sight of the atheling writhing on the ground and from their astonished faces, they recognized the king's son.

Brynn tried to explain. "The atheling is—"

A spear flew and Brynn ducked. The weapon brushed past her head. They thought she'd attacked their king's son. This had gotten out of hand.

"Please." Brynn tried to reason with them, but these men might not have listened even if they spoke her language.

The two men broke into a run, one with his spear lowered and the other drawing a long seaxe knife.

Brynn undid the spell on Tolvir and she heard him draw in a great gulp of air, coughing and croaking in pain. He called out from back inside the tent, groaning. He would be in excruciating pain and Brynn did not feel as bad about it as she should have.

The two warriors weren't slowing. They would not be reasoned with and Brynn had no one here on her side. With the puppy in her arms, Brynn backed away from the tent, trying to reason with them, but they either spoke no Hyldish or didn't care.

One of the men veered into the tent to see to Tolvir. The other set after her.

Brynn brought him down with the same spell she had used on Tolvir, sending him gasping to his knees. More voices shouted, more men drawn by the noise. Ten or fifteen, she couldn't quite tell. Their *ka* was too close together. Brynn couldn't immobilize all of them, she didn't have the time for the concentration necessary.

Several of Hróarr's men had stayed nearby to watch the ships, but though they were supposed to be allies, she knew full well they would side with the other Valdari against her. She could kill Hróarr's men, or she could run. She ran.

Brynn ducked into the darkness beyond the campfire.

Men clamored and she had no doubt the alarm would be raised across the city in a matter of moments. Tolvir had just been attacked, or at least that was how the Valdari would see it.

Brynn needed to get away and let things calm down. She had no plan, other than finding a way to let things calm down. With Guin under one arm, she fled into the darkness.

She raised her shawl, covering her head. In the dark, she would look like any of the other women of Istra. So long as no one noticed Guin.

Shouts continued to ring out.

Brynn slowed her steps, taking a moment to reorient herself. She had come out on the western side of the great hall and its many outbuildings, near the ovens.

She thought about going to Cenric, but he would be surrounded by Valdari jarls and their warriors. She wouldn't get near him before she was stopped and even if she did, he would probably start a fight to defend her.

What she needed to do was find somewhere to lay low and wait out the initial outrage.

Tolvir had been in love with Gistrid. Brynn highly doubted that he'd had anything to do with the girl's death. That was one less potential murderer out of thousands. It did little to help Brynn parse things out.

But if Ovrek had known...no, Ovrek could have just killed the girl outright. No need for the subtlety of poison.

Brynn neared the ovens to find low fires burning. The kitchen was a dome, open to the elements on one side. Women with sooty faces worked to knead bread, turn meats, and tend the fires.

Heat billowed out, driving away the cool breeze. Despite that, Brynn had to wonder. Did these women work like this even during the icy winter months? Surely not.

Slipping into the shadows, Brynn edged out of the main path. She leaned against the warm earth banked over the ovens, heart pounding.

The thralls chattered in low Valdari. She caught Gistrid's name twice, but didn't recognize anything else. Brynn desperately wanted to know what they were saying. They might be able to help her piece together who actually killed the concubine and why.

Guin whimpered and Brynn shushed her, tickling under her ears. The little dyrehund stood on her hind legs, licking Brynn's mouth.

Brynn couldn't talk to her, lest her Hyldish give her away, so she made wordless shushing sounds and patted Guin into silence.

Male voices and the tramp of boots came from below. Brynn shifted onto her knees to see at least a dozen of Ovrek's warriors tramping up the hill. They were expanding their search for her.

Rising, Brynn tried to move silently as the men came closer. She carried herself hunched over, cradling Guin like a baby.

None of the thralls tried to stop her. They were all focused on the armed men coming toward them. Fearful whispers and anxious murmurs went through the thralls as they bowed and sank to their knees. These were people who had been beaten into submission. They had no fight left in them.

Brynn could feel her way by the shapes of *ka* from trees and plants. Unfortunately, rocks did not have *ka*. Brynn stubbed her toe on a stone and bit her tongue to keep from crying out.

As the men barked orders to the thralls, calling out and trying to find her, Brynn wandered into the trees. At any moment, she might hear their shouts and their charging footsteps racing after her.

But it seemed no one had thought she would flee so silently. Or perhaps they hadn't expected her to go into the trees.

Once their voices faded and she could no longer see the light from their torches, Brynn set down Guin. The dyrehund padded alongside her, occasionally stopping to sniff at ferns or nose at the damp earth.

Swallowing, Brynn pulled her shawl tighter around her shoulders. The cold was enough to make her shiver, but the trees mostly protected her from the misting rain and as long as she kept moving, she was fine.

It occurred to Brynn that she knew nothing about the wilderness of Valdar. She had survived in the wilds of Hylden during the war, but she knew precious little about this foreign land. The *ka* was the same and the trees were pines, but beyond that, Brynn had no idea where the rivers, bogs, and mountains might be. She might get herself lost and freeze to death out here, but right now she had no better options.

It wasn't as if she could go explain herself to anyone. No one would listen even if they spoke her language.

Brynn needed time to think. To plan. She kept walking, letting the wilderness of Valdar swallow her up.

10

Cenric

Tolvir had a crisscross pattern of blisters on his face and a huge burn on his arm, so bad that even his sleeve had been scorched by the heat. His neck had a bruised band around it and his voice came out as a rasping croak. He must be in exquisite pain and Cenric took comfort in that.

"The sorceress attacked me," Tolvir wheezed. "I confronted her, and she attacked me."

"Why did you confront her at all?" Ovrek demanded, arms crossed as he stared down his son.

"You had no business with my wife," Cenric growled.

They stood outside the ruined tent where Cenric and Brynn had stayed. The two warriors who had guarded it reported Tolvir had said they were wanted by Ovrek. This appeared to be news to Ovrek, who had immediately turned a hard glare on his son.

Tolvir had attacked Brynn, she had defended herself, and when the men had attacked her, too, she had run rather than kill them. At least, that was what Cenric knew had happened. He wasn't sure if anyone else believed that was what had happened.

Even Hróarr's men who had been drawn by the youth's screams seemed to think Brynn had somehow tricked the boy.

Tolvir glared at Cenric. "If you'd kept your whore in line, we wouldn't be here."

Cenric lunged for Tolvir, but Hróarr caught him, grappling Cenric back.

Ovrek shot a warning look to Cenric. "It is not your place to accuse my son." He turned back to the boy. "Are you alright, son?"

Tolvir coughed, rubbing at his throat with his good hand. "Fine."

"Good." Ovrek smiled in that fatherly way he sometimes did, right before smashing his fist into Tolvir's gut.

The boy doubled over wheezing, but Ovrek grabbed his injured arm and squeezed. Tolvir made a wounded animal noise and Ovrek slammed him back against the side of Cenric's beached ship.

"What have I told you about undermining me?"

"I wasn't undermining!" Tolvir sounded frightened, but at least he didn't beg.

"You went behind my back. You nearly got yourself killed."

"I had her."

"She could have killed you," Ovrek spat. "You think you survived out of skill? The sorceress spared you." Ovrek dropped Tolvir and the boy slumped down.

"She killed your concubine. She shamed you."

"You shame me!" Ovrek roared, kicking Tolvir in the shin and making the youth's legs buckle. "My own son refuses to obey me."

Tolvir whimpered on the ground, choking and coughing. That made Cenric feel a little better, but only a little.

Ovrek whirled on Cenric. "Your wife has attacked my men."

Cenric yanked his arm free of Hróarr's grip. "They attacked her first." He indicated Tolvir's burns. "She could have killed them and the boy. She fled instead."

Ovrek cursed heartily. He turned away, rubbing his beard. Ovrek was a clever man. He had to see that if Brynn had been a spy, she could have killed Ovrek, Tolvir, and all the powerful men here last night.

"Brynn didn't kill the girl."

Ovrek raised a hand, telling Cenric to drop it. "We will find this wife of yours and I will hear her explanation for myself."

"I will find her."

"No," Ovrek barked. "You will remain here." He jerked his chin toward Hróarr. "You will go."

Cenric glared at his cousin. Hróarr had never liked Brynn. To him she was a sorceress and a Hyldish pureblood who would be their enemy soon, if she wasn't already.

"Bring the sorceress back," Ovrek ordered. "Alive."

"And unharmed," Cenric spat, glaring up at Hróarr.

Ovrek heaved a sigh. "Always something." He turned away. "Cenric, with me."

Cenric had to obey. He had come with just a handful of his thanes and Kalen, and the Valdari had successfully separated him from his men for the moment. Hróarr was on Ovrek's side.

Brynn was somewhere out there in the dark, and Cenric had no idea where she was. She didn't speak the language, and she didn't know the land. A part of him was impressed that she had managed to slip away as she had. A larger part of him was worried.

Brynn? Snapper asked. He sent the impression of her scent. Guin was with her and Snapper could track them.

No, Cenric replied mentally. *Not yet.* He hesitated, considering his question carefully. *Is Brynn hurt? Ask Guin.*

Snapper cocked his head for a moment as if listening, then snorted. *Brynn not hurt.*

His wife's puppy would not condescend to speaking with Cenric, but she did sometimes answer questions from him through Snapper. They must not be far if Guin and Snapper could still communicate.

"You and that sorceress will have a great deal of explaining to do," Ovrek growled.

"We have explained everything," Cenric argued. "We have told you the truth."

"You believe that woman?" Ovrek said *woman* like it was an obscenity.

"Yes." Cenric didn't see why that needed explaining.

Ovrek stopped, confronting Cenric face to face. He was taller, but not by as much as when Cenric had been a youth. "Listen to me," he seethed, the words grinding out through his teeth, "you're going to have to choose between being a jarl and being a lovestruck fool. You make yourself my enemy by siding with her."

"Brynn is not your enemy." Cenric tried to keep his temper in check, tried to bottle his frustration, rage, and sense of injustice.

A few hours ago, Cenric had been ready to give Ovrek his allegiance with Brynn's full support. Why couldn't the wool-headed old man see that? Cenric almost told him as much but kept those words to himself. They would only be taken as desperate promises now.

But if Ovrek wanted to be enemies, that could be arranged. Cenric wasn't going to grovel and beg for this man's approval.

So what if Morgi had sent him a warning? He would make sure not to face Ovrek on that particular beach.

"A Hyldish sorceress arrives in my city. The next day, she pays a visit to my concubine, then both she and my child die." Ovrek loomed over Cenric. The torchlight cast his face in an amber glow, but Cenric was sure it must be reddening. "Who should I blame? Queen Sifma reports that no one else but herself and the usual servants saw the girl. How would you explain it?"

It seemed obvious to Cenric. Either Sifma and the servants or all of them were lying, but he doubted Ovrek would want to hear that.

Cenric bit back his outrage, jaw tight. "I see."

Ovrek inhaled and exhaled slowly, probably composing himself with effort. "Hróarr will bring your wife back and then…" He trailed off, then seemed to change his mind about what to say. "Then we will get to the bottom of this."

Cenric wondered if they actually would. Brynn's story wouldn't change, he was sure of that. He believed her even if the rest of them didn't.

He didn't know who had killed the girl, but it had not been Brynn. He didn't understand why Ovrek kept thinking she had when she'd turned down the opportunity to kill so many times already. It made no sense.

But there was nothing he could do to make Ovrek see reason.

Cenric hated that. Brynn had been willing to humble herself. She had been willing to bow before this foreign ruler for Cenric's sake, for his people's sake. And how did this king reward her? By accusing her of sedition and placing her under guard. Not to mention Ovrek's own son had attacked her. That boy was a menace, unworthy of his father and unfit for his position.

Cenric followed Ovrek back into the main hall, to the feasting lords and their warriors. The king returned, immediately transforming into the gregarious, magnanimous man they all knew best.

"My friends!" Ovrek went to a circle of men with flashing rings on their arms and carefully braided beards. Some of them he recognized as having fought for Ovrek in the war, though their names escaped Cenric at the moment.

Cenric glanced toward the door. If he could slip out, he might be able to get lost in the confusion of the festivities and sink into the shadows. If he could find his men, they might be able to ready the *Wolf Star*. If he could find Brynn while they still had cover of night…

Ovrek seemed to read his mind. He placed a hand on Cenric's shoulder, steering him around. "You remember Cenric?"

"Young wolf!" cried a round of voices, men covered in arm

rings and massive braided beards, shield brothers from another lifetime.

Ovrek thrust Cenric into the middle of the celebrations, introducing him to everyone, treating him as an honored guest, but Cenric knew better. He was a prisoner, just as Brynn had been. Their chances of an amicable alliance with Ovrek were looking worse by the moment.

11

Brynn

Brynn found a shelter in a leaning tree and hunkered down for the night. She shivered, not daring to make a fire. Even in summer, the nights were cold.

Guin curled against her, making a comfortable nest under Brynn's arms. At least Brynn had been wearing her shawl when Tolvir had attacked. Perhaps she should have grabbed her cloak, but she'd had other things on her mind.

The forest chirped and popped around her. Brynn stared into the darkness, her heart racing.

She reached out with *ka,* trying to sense every living thing within any reasonable distance. There were shapes she took for squirrels and perhaps a few deer.

There could be wolves in this forest for all she knew. Though she doubted they would be this close to Istra.

Brynn sensed nothing that might be a farm or settlement, so

that was a good sign. She would rather not deal with the Valdari locals just now.

Guin slept soundly in her lap. The puppy probably thought they were out for an adventure.

Brynn drew in *ka,* but while that worked to stave off frostbite, it could do nothing for this seeping, clawing cold. She had nothing to hand that could safely hold heat without burning her. Brynn wrapped her shawl tighter around herself as she shivered. She needed to rest to have the strength come daylight, but she was too cold and uneasy to fall asleep.

During the war, she had sometimes slept on tree roots and in the shelter of wagon wheels, but Aelfwynn had always been there to watch over her. Brynn had been able to sleep knowing her elder sister was protecting her.

Now Brynn was alone. Cenric was back in Istra, though he had probably learned of what happened by now. Overhead, the gibbous moon shone through the branches of the trees, Eponine's face watching from afar.

Brynn exhaled prayers through her chattering teeth with nothing better to do. "Mother Eponine, watch over Cenric. Keep him from being a fool." Brynn squeezed her eyes shut, not sure how else to say it. "I love him and if he loves me like he says he does..." Brynn hesitated. Cenric might truly love her, but he was an alderman, and aldermen had to do what they had to do for the sake of their shires.

Loving a powerful man was to accept that his power would always come first—that was what Brynn's mother had said about her father.

Brynn sat leaning against the damp earth, shivering, and she wondered if Cenric might realize he was better off without her.

They had been married less than a year. She had brought no lands that he would lose by putting her aside. She hadn't given him children yet. It would be easy to put her aside. So easy.

Guin stirred in Brynn's lap, shifting as she settled down again. *If anyone hurts you, I kill them.*

The words of an infatuated boy or a man in love?

Speaking of infatuated boys...Tolvir.

He'd been in love with Gistrid. Even though she had been with his father, Tolvir still cared about her.

Had Gistrid's child been Tolvir's?

Somehow, Brynn didn't think so. Nothing was ever private, not really. Brynn had learned that the hard way when tales had started flying that she was still untouched four years into her first marriage. Rumors that he was impotent had been what finally pushed Paega into bedding Brynn, but as soon as she was pregnant and his virility was proven, he never touched her again.

If Tolvir had been bedding his father's concubine, all of Gistrid's servants would have needed to keep the secret. Not only that, but Brynn could not see Tolvir outright defying his father like that. If he had all the thrall girls as Tullia had implied, why risk death?

Back in Hylden, if a king was cuckholded, he could be declared unfit to rule. After all, if he could not defend his own women, what kind of king could he be?

Raping the wives and concubines of defeated foes was still practiced in parts of Hylden. Brynn assumed the Valdari had something similar. The tradition went back to the days of the wild chieftains when androcide against enemy tribes had been the norm.

But what if someone *thought* Tolvir's affection for his father's concubine had gone beyond unrequited love? It didn't necessarily have to be true, but what if someone assumed?

Someone close enough to Tolvir and Gistrid to want to protect them and prevent Ovrek from finding out.

Sifma seemed the most likely person if Tullia told the truth, but if Brynn was right and pennyroyal had been used, the poisoner had likely intended to induce a miscarriage, not Gistrid's death. That Gistrid had been overdosed and nearly killed the first time implied some inexperienced with use of herbs and their remedies.

My mother could have used the help, I think.

Brynn's stomach clenched to recall Tullia's words about buying a thrall with better skills in herbalism. She must have known from the start. Sifma must confide in her daughter or Tullia had excellent spies. Both were equally possible.

Guin snuffled in her arms, but it was a long time before Brynn fell asleep.

12

Cenric

Every time Cenric tried to leave the great hall, either Ovrek or one of Ovrek's men found a reason to go with him. They wouldn't even let him piss alone. They were treating him like an enemy hostage—an uncooperative one.

Ovrek suggested Cenric spend the night in the hall instead of going back to the tent he had shared with Brynn. Cenric knew that was only so that they could guard him without it being obvious. He hated it. Hated everything about this.

It was an insult.

But he spent the night on the floor, sleeping in the safe warmth of the hall. He imagined Brynn freezing in the forest, falling into a river, or tumbling off a cliff. It was dark and the land was treacherous even in the daylight.

Snapper curled up beside him, quieter than usual. The dyrehund whimpered, whining for Brynn, asking where she and Guin were.

Cenric did his best to reassure the dog as the two of them settled in for a night in Ovrek's hall.

Flames roared against the night sky, consuming storehouses, ships, and anything else in sight. Istra was in ruin.

Bodies lay scattered on the sand, missing legs, arms, heads, and pieces of torsos, as if a great maw had taken bites out of them and then grown bored.

Panting, Cenric was armed with nothing but a shield and a spear he'd taken from one of the dead men. He was soaked in seawater and his boots squished, wet and chafing.

A hiss over Cenric's shoulder made him jump. He turned.

A scaly head rose over him, at least ten times the height of a man. Teeth flashed. He'd never known serpents had teeth.

Red, glowing eyes with black slits focused on him. Claws flashed as the creature lumbered toward him.

Brynn's scream came from his left. "Cenric!"

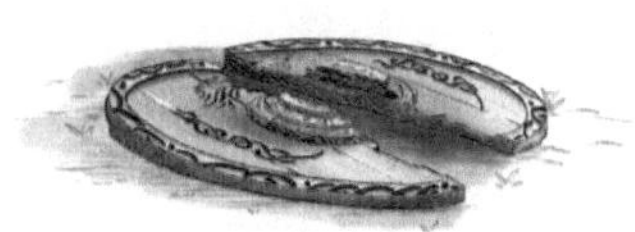

Cenric jolted awake on the hard floor, aching and confused. Had that been a foretelling? It seemed more like one of his nightmares, but as he lay awake with eyes wide open, it did not fade. The memory of it stayed. The feel of the spear in his hand and the sand shifting beneath his feet had been so real. He'd felt his wet clothes sticking to him and his soggy boots squishing underfoot. Why had he been soaked in seawater?

As he thought back, it felt almost like a memory. The fear he'd felt for Brynn the moment she screamed for him still sent icy chills along his back.

But that creature? How could that not be a product of his nightmares?

Cenric had never confused a simple nightmare and a warning from Morgi before, but now he was not so sure. If it was a foretelling, at least it implied that Brynn was alive.

Hróarr had still not returned from last night, presumably still searching the forest for Brynn. Cenric sent out a curse, hoping that his cousin had wet boots.

Cenric would trust Hróarr with his own life, but not Brynn's. Not after all this.

If Hróarr tried to hurt Brynn, Cenric feared she would hold back. She held back most of the time, but she knew Hróarr was important to Cenric. Hróarr didn't care that Brynn was important to Cenric.

Slow movement stirred the hall, voices chattering and low words passing from man to man.

A boy came to fetch him, eyes downcast. "King Ovrek invites you to join him this morning, lord."

Cenric stifled his reaction to that. Ovrek wanted to keep an eye on him, did he? But Cenric could hardly refuse a king in his own house.

"Do you know if there has been any word of Lady Brynn or Hróarr?" Cenric pinned his own mantle in place. He reached for his sword, then remembered Ovrek's men had taken his weapons when he'd entered the hall last night.

"No, lord. Forgive me."

Cenric hadn't had much hope for either. Vana might know more, but he wasn't sure where she was now.

"My thanes? My servants?"

"In your camp, lord."

Hopefully, Kalen was looking after Esa. The last thing Cenric wanted to explain to his wife was why something had happened to her ward.

The thrall led Cenric outside. The early morning light was faint, just the barest blush of the sun against the horizon, but the first king of Valdar was awake, bright-eyed, and laughing with his whole belly.

Ovrek spoke with several men, strangers to Cenric. The men laughed. Ovrek had a way of doing that, of putting people at ease.

The strangers crouched around a fire along the beach, having slept there from the look of it. Their longship crouched nearby, dragged partially onto the shore and tied to the nearby trees. These must be attendants for another of the gathered jarls. Two of the men stood a little apart from the rest with much finer clothes, so they must be the leaders. All the same, Ovrek conversed with all the men around the fire in turn, speaking to each one like an old friend.

Not for the first time, Cenric thought that this was what kings should be. A giver of rings and a leader of men—Ovrek was everything Cenric had ever wanted in a lord. He was the kind of leader who made it easy to follow.

If given the choice, Cenric would never have chosen anyone else—until Ovrek had accused his wife of murder.

Brynn might be Hyldish, but she was an alderman's wife and a lady of kingly blood. If she was not deserving of justice, who was?

"Cenric!" Ovrek caught sight of him behind the thrall boy. "Such a fine morning, isn't it?" Ovrek clapped an arm around Cenric, greeting him like long-lost kin.

Cenric had always appreciated how Ovrek greeted everyone this way, but just now it felt like a lie. A deception, at the very least.

"This is Cenric, son of Wulfram. He's the alderman of Ombra now, but I still remember teaching him to hold his shield." Ovrek presented Cenric like a proud father. Gesturing to the men gathered around, Ovrek introduced their leaders with the same eagerness. "This is Jarl Egill and his son Dagrún."

Friends? Snapper asked, trotting to the two strangers. When they didn't acknowledge him, he trotted off to investigate a patch of grass.

Egill was weathered, a lean man who moved hunched over, like a wild animal guarding a kill. Scars carved a path through his beard in a way that reminded Cenric of rivers carving through mountains.

Dagrún was at least a head taller than his father. Pale with a stringy beard, he was probably still in his teens despite his height.

Though Cenric had met Egill up close only a handful of times, his eagle standard had been well known in the war. Egill was a fierce fighter, or had been. From his hunched posture, Cenric had to wonder if he might be battling some injury or sickness.

"Cenric will be guarding me today. I don't think it's necessary, but he insists!" Ovrek chuckled at that as if it was a great joke. "These Hyldishmen always think a king must be guarded. Even among his own people."

Egill and Dagrún joined Ovrek in laughing at that.

Cenric forced a smile, not quite able to laugh. Even if Cenric had suggested a guard for Ovrek, how exactly was he supposed to guard anyone while unarmed?

Anger simmered deep in Cenric's chest, stoking his fury over the injustice to Brynn. Ovrek was playing games, the exact sort of games Cenric hated. This was a way for Ovrek to keep Cenric close, while flaunting that he had the loyalty of a Hyldish alderman.

But Cenric had never agreed to pledge his loyalty to Ovrek. Even if it seemed obvious yesterday that he would, even if he had as good as told Brynn he would, Cenric had given no oaths and made no pledges. Ovrek took Cenric's allegiance for granted.

Once, that would have made Cenric proud. A younger version of himself would have been glad Ovrek didn't question his allegiance.

After the imprisonment and allegations against Cenric's wife, it was an insult. Did Ovrek really think he could mistreat Brynn and still get Cenric's oath?

That was exactly what the king thought, Cenric realized.

Cenric fought to stay calm as he followed Ovrek. The king spoke to Egill and Dagrún, giving them much the same presentation Cenric had received the day before. Ovrek even used some of the same jokes.

There were unique references to a past life spent sailing with Egill, adventures in the south. All the same, Cenric couldn't help but feel that this whole thing was a performance.

The genuine, authentic image that Cenric had of Ovrek seemed to crumble before him with every step down that beach. This man was a king just like Aelgar, a better warrior, perhaps, but not a better man.

Had kingship changed Ovrek, or had Cenric simply been too naïve all those years ago to recognize the farce?

Ovrek took the jarl and his son down the beach, pointing out the ships his people had constructed. He spoke with animation and excitement, telling of how many men had been gathered, how many spears were ready to sail in a matter of weeks.

Cenric watched the beach. If nothing else, the lie that he was here as a guard gave him an excuse to search in all directions.

As the time of the Althing drew nearer, Istra swarmed with people left and right. Cenric could scarcely see a patch of beach that did not have a ship dragged ashore or a camp set up on the dark sand.

Cenric espied Brynn's servant serving Vana beside a cookfire. It seemed they were keeping the girl watched as well. Kalen crouched not far away sharpening his sword.

It seemed the Valdari had forgotten that Esa was a sorceress, too. Good.

Snapper stopped, ears cocked. *Brynn?*

Not now, Cenric sent back.

Snapper snorted and whined. *Where? Guin?*

I don't know, Cenric sent back. *Hróarr is looking.*

Hróarr! Snapper trusted Cenric's cousin and thought that was a good thing.

Cenric certainly hoped so.

They continued up the beach. Egill spoke very little, but Dagrún asked questions, often glancing to his father. There seemed to be some unspoken agreement between father and son, a kind of easy communication that reminded Cenric of hunters.

"Are all the other jarls aligned with you?" Dagrún asked.

"None have refused yet," Ovrek rumbled in response, as if it was obvious.

"Even Ingmar?"

Ovrek waited just a moment to respond. It was barely noticeable, hardly even a breath. "He's here, isn't he?" The king gestured down the beach to a large ship with at least thirty oars and a boar on its sail.

Cenric vaguely recalled Ingmar. He had been seen by many as a rival to Ovrek when he had first made the claim to kingship. His twin brother had been the jarl before him, and they had fought bitterly against the new king.

But Ovrek had taken his twin's head and Ingmar had taken oaths of allegiance.

"I see Halvdan's ship," Dagrún remarked.

Ovrek didn't hesitate this time. "Halvdan has always been loyal."

Dagrún grimaced at that.

Cenric wondered why. The Halvdan he had known was beyond question in his loyalty to Ovrek. Then again, Cenric himself had once been beyond question. There was a time when he would have sooner carved out his own eye than betray the Valdari king.

With Brynn missing in the forest and being hunted like an animal, the thought of stabbing Ovrek was more reasonable by the moment. Cenric wouldn't stab him in the chest or gut or anywhere fatal. He'd stab Ovrek through the foot where it would take forever to heal and be a wretched inconvenience to a man about to lead an army.

As the king, the jarl, and the jarl's son walked down the beach, through the forges and storehouses, they talked. Some of the questions were the same as those Cenric had asked. He heard names he remembered and some he didn't.

Begrudgingly, Cenric had to admit to himself that Ovrek had put as much effort into awing him as he now put into awing this jarl and his son. Maybe Ovrek really did value Cenric as an ally. Or maybe a part of Cenric was just desperate to believe that was the case.

They made their way from the forges to the weaving house. They were still not permitted inside but stood back to watch as women carried out rolled sails for the dozens of newborn ships waiting along the beach.

"Impressive," Dagrún said.

Cenric was beginning to wonder if Egill spoke at all. He'd seen the man's lips move, but hadn't yet heard his voice.

"My queen is excellent in all things." Ovrek's chest puffed out just a little at that. "Impeccable and above reproach."

Cenric bit his tongue at that. Sifma was the one who had first accused Brynn. Like Ovrek, he'd wanted to believe the best of her. Vana thought the world of her, but Cenric's own opinion was suffering at the moment.

The four men made their way from the women's weaving house toward the animal pens.

Cenric appraised the sky. The morning was mostly gone. Why was there still no word of his cousin or his wife? Surely Hróarr should have at least returned to report a fruitless search?

Something was wrong.

"We will not take all the animals with us, of course," Ovrek said to Egill. "The farms and shires of Hylden are rich with livestock and game."

Cenric thought of his own shire with its farms and forests. He expected that the Valdari would be helping themselves to his herds and flocks if he didn't pledge allegiance to Ovrek soon. It was a matter of time. He could feel Ovrek's ambitions closing in on him like the wooden chutes they forced animals through during Blydmoth.

Ovrek led the jarl and his son to the edge of a wooden fence. Cenric could hear pigs on the other side, rooting through the leftover scraps that would be fed to them by the kitchen thralls.

Cenric had not seen this part of Istra yesterday. Perhaps they had run out of time. Rows of pens separated cattle, pigs, sheep, and a large pen with stocky horses. The fences were new, not yet weather-worn, and the animals probably only gathered here at night or when they were awaiting slaughter.

The king went on, his voice as animated and engaged as ever. For all his dourness, even Egill seemed enraptured. Ovrek had a way of doing that—captivating your attention, making you see his dreams as he did. Ovrek was saying something about cattle and horses now.

Cenric stared toward the forest and the distant mountains. Where was Brynn? Why hadn't Morgi warned him about what a wretched business this trip would be?

The king led them away from the animal pens and back toward the shipyards. "I must show you my banner ship. I shall call it *Sifma,* after my queen. It is the largest ship we have ever built."

The sight of the *Sifma* was not as shocking as it had been the first time, but it was still impressive. Cenric allowed himself just a moment of appreciation—perhaps even envy—at the sight of her more than forty oars. It was a magnificent ship that would loom like a beast over most vessels.

Egill and Dagrún appeared rightly impressed, staring in silence as they wandered quietly in the shadow of its mast.

Around them, workers continued at their labor. The ship was by no means finished and it would need to be if it was to sail to Hylden in a matter of weeks.

"My father has heard tales of this ship," Dagrún broached the topic in a lilting, oddly cautious tone. "

"And what might those be?" Ovrek smiled, but there was a hardness to the set of his jaw that seemed out of place.

"Did you use yew for the ribs and mast?" Dagrún gestured to the great vessel.

Cenric studied the ship more closely. He couldn't see the ribs from the outside, but now that Dagrún mentioned it, the mast was of darker wood than the oaken strakes.

Ovrek's smile wavered for just a moment. "It's good wood." He tensed, as if bracing himself.

Dagrún took several heartbeats to respond, almost as if he had been waiting for Ovrek to deny it. "I see."

Ovrek bristled. "I honor the First of Fathers as much as any Valdari." That seemed a strange response.

"And you honor our holy sites?"

"Of course." Ovrek's tone brooked no argument. "Like all Valdari."

Dagrún went silent at that. The young man was hard to read, but his father's stony glower never moved from Ovrek.

There had to be something Cenric wasn't understanding.

Ovrek's motley assemblage of shipwrights and builders toiled with their backs bent, their focus on their work. Cenric trailed behind Ovrek and his guests, wondering how far he could fall behind before the king prompted him to join them. Could he simply slip away?

His gaze was drawn back to the lurking forest, the mountains. Brynn survived the night. He had to believe she had.

From here, he could see Hróarr's ship again. Vana came into view, speaking with one of his cousin's men. There was still no sign of Hróarr.

Cenric didn't like it. Worry for Hróarr began to wheedle its way in alongside worry for Brynn.

A flicker of motion caught his eye to the left, a figure ducking out of sight. Cenric glanced that way, then away. Another flicker caught his eye to the right. It shouldn't have alarmed him. There were people crawling all over Istra. He was sure it was nothing, but the back of his neck tingled.

Ovrek finished showing his ship to Egill and Dagrún, then headed off back toward his hall and its outbuildings. He took the men along a different route than the one he had taken Cenric. This one was winding through the edges of the town.

Women, girls, and young boys moved past and around them, heads down.

For just an instant, Cenric thought one of the girls was Esa, then remembered she was back on the beach with Vana and Kalen. These people were thralls, most taken from Hylden if he had to guess. They were everywhere in Valdar, especially on large farms and in the households of great jarls, though some smaller farms had them, too.

Thralls had never bothered Cenric before, but that had been before he had retaken Ombra. Cenric was as Hyldish as he was Valdari. If he was a kinsman to Ovrek, then he was kin to these thralls, too.

What exactly would make him better than them when the Valdari took Hylden?

"We have over two hundred thralls in my household." Ovrek's voice was thick with pride. "These Hyldish make good workers, and they learn quickly." He gestured toward the smoking ovens where the evening's meal was already being prepared. "Just think with free access to the Hyldish, what we could do?"

Cenric remembered Brynn, hands tied and neck locked in that

wicked collar, so much like a thrall's, that her mother had used to bind her magic. Thralls had always been an unremarkable fact of life in Valdar, much like the buckets of water they carried and the dung they spread over the gardens. Now he kept envisioning his wife in their place and anger smoldered deep in his gut like molten lead. As the four men made their way between two large huts, Cenric glared at the back of Ovrek's head.

They rounded the huts, heading back toward the complex that Ovrek had built around his hall. He did not have the ancient glory of Ungamot, but he had built something impressive enough here.

"Good timber, better fields." Ovrek shook his head. "Think of the treasure we could bring home."

Cenric caught a flicker of motion to his left again. A prickle along his scalp told him they were being followed.

Speeding up, Cenric came to walk close behind Ovrek. The man insisted he could walk about unguarded, but perhaps he did not think enough like a king just yet.

Cenric glanced to the side, pretending to inspect one of the nearby thrall huts, but he kept the two guests in his line of sight. Egill walked closest to Ovrek on the king's right with Dagrún on the far side.

"Is that going to be a granary?" Dagrún asked, pointing to some partially built structure near the treeline to their left.

"That?" Ovrek shifted, squinting as he partially turned his back. "No, that's—"

Egill reached for his belt and Cenric caught the glint of steel.

Cenric shoved Ovrek full force in the back, sending him straight into a line of firewood. Ovrek smashed into it, knocking over the stack and sprawling on the ground as the logs tumbled under his weight. Ovrek overbalanced and rolled, skidding on the logs like a pig on ice.

It was immensely satisfying, but Cenric had no time to bask in it. He faced Egill, snatching up one of the shorter logs as the jarl came at him with a dagger.

Cenric planted his palm at one end and shoved the short log straight forward like a battering ram. It caught Egill square in the face and his head wrenched back. He went down with a rasping cry, even as his son leapt forward with a second weapon.

Cenric! Snapper barked, dashing back and forth. He was a tracker, not a fighter. *Cenric!*

Help, Cenric ordered. *Get help!*

Snapper raced back down to the beach, barking. His cries drew the attention of other dogs that joined in with a panic.

That would draw the attention of Ovrek's men.

Cenric snatched up another log. This would have been easier if he'd had his sword. This log was about the length of his forearm, but wide enough around that he had to wield it with both hands.

Blocking Dagrún's path to Ovrek, Cenric faced down the other man. "Best get to your feet, lord," Cenric shouted, not looking away from the would-be assassins.

"Pig-humping cocksucker!" Ovrek yelled.

Cenric wasn't sure if the king intended that for him or the traitor Egill. Possibly both. At his back, Cenric could hear Ovrek grunting and cursing as he found his footing. Maybe Cenric had shoved the king a little too hard.

Dagrún came at Cenric with a dagger that had been concealed in his cloak. He slashed sideways.

Cenric blocked the blade, catching it on the log. He swung for Dagrún's head and the younger man skittered back.

Cenric shoved straight out with the log like a spear, putting his weight into the blow.

He missed Dagrún's dagger hand, but he caught the man's elbow. Dagrún yelped, dropping his weapon as he retreated out of reach.

A moment later, Dagrún had a second dagger in his left hand, right arm held protectively against his side.

Cenric picked up another log, but motion from behind Dagrún warned Cenric before two more men came rushing from behind the thrall sheds. Instead of daggers, these men carried swords.

It seemed Egill and Dagrún had come prepared in case they weren't able to finish off Ovrek themselves.

"You dare attack me?" Ovrek roared. "You *dare!?*"

Cenric leapt over one of the rows of chopped wood, still wielding a log as a makeshift weapon.

Ovrek was on his feet, hefting a woodcutter's axe in both hands. It was worn and in need of sharpening, but iron was better than fists, as the old saying went. Cenric took up a fighting stance beside Ovrek, back-to-back.

The two swordsmen came at them, lunging for Ovrek.

Cenric piked another log for the legs of the first man. He missed, but the log skittered past him, tripping up the second.

Dagrún cursed from the other side of the wood pile, right arm still held protectively against his ribs. "Finish him off. Just get him!"

Egill had scrambled back to his feet and clawed toward them, blood streaming down his face, flowing in gory tracts along the scars on his cheek.

"I will feed your guts to the seagulls," Ovrek roared, shaking his axe as he faced down the two swordsmen. "I will use your fingers to bait fishing hooks!"

The first swordsman reached Ovrek, chopping for the king's head. Ovrek ducked, knocking the weapon aside with his axe.

Cenric stepped in front of Egill as the jarl came barreling over the stack of wood, his son at his side. Cenric kicked the stack from this side, wood pieces tumbled and rolled underfoot, tripping up the father and son.

Egill went down, still dazed from the blow to his head. Dagrún kept coming, his knife hand up.

Out of the corner of his eye, Cenric saw the second swordsman recover, reaching Ovrek.

Cenric threw a piece of kindling for the man's head. It missed, but the man ducked, taking his eyes off Ovrek for just a second.

King he might be, but Ovrek had been a warrior first. The old king smashed his axe into the man's collarbone, striking with a ferocity to make any skald proud.

In the moment Cenric had been distracted, Dagrún swept in close, a dagger stabbing for Cenric's ribs. Cenric deflected the knife from his side with another log. He lunged forward, fist smashing into Dagrún's jaw.

His knuckles stung with the impact, but Dagrún stumbled back. Cenric swung his improvised log weapon around again, smashing it into the other man's chest. Dagrún went sprawling, tripping over Egill and stumbling on the shifting pieces of firewood. The younger man collapsed, gasping with the wind knocked out of him.

"Come at me!" Ovrek bellowed. "Come at me, you fatherless shit stain!" The king faced down the last swordsman, a grizzled veteran who scowled from behind a thick beard. Ovrek stood over the dead man, shaking his weapon in challenge.

Cenric snatched up the sword from the corpse. He shoved his last piece of firewood at Dagrún, smacking the younger man in the ribs where he still lay gasping.

Dagrún wheezed while Egill lay dazed. The jarl's arms buckled as he struggled to push himself up. Those two could wait for a moment.

Cenric circled around the last remaining swordsman, his weapon drawn. Cenric attacked, lunging straight for the other man's side. The swordsman backed away, raising his weapon in defense.

Ovrek let off a great bellow and gave chase, like a wolf scenting blood.

The swordsman made to thrust back at Cenric. Cenric deflected, but before he could counter, Ovrek was there.

The king came swinging his woodcutter's axe with a roar, hacking in a wild frenzy. Land Waster—that was what they had called him in his younger days.

Perhaps these men should have remembered just who they were trying to kill.

The swordsman retreated, trying to find his footing. Pieces of stray firewood rolled under them, littering the ground in a treacherous maze.

Ovrek roared, but stumbled, tripping over a log. The king went down with a bellow of rage.

The swordsman saw his opening and dove for Ovrek, sword raised to strike the king's head.

Cenric slammed into the swordsman, his stolen blade punching through the man's ribs and out his other side. He shoved the man over, kicking the man's sword away as the enemy warrior collapsed, blood gushing out his mouth.

Whirling back to where they had left Dagrún and Egill, Cenric stood over Ovrek with his bloody sword. The jarl and his son still appeared worse for the wear.

Egill vomited as he tried to stand, the force of the heaves sending him back down.

The king scrambled back to his feet, cursing the whole way. He righted himself, barreling straight to Cenric. "I had that one!" he roared.

Cenric shifted his gaze to the jarl and his son, currently gasping in a pool of their own vomit and blood. "You can have those two."

Ovrek spun around, face crimson. Red trickled down his temple, probably where he'd hit firewood when Cenric had shoved him out of the way. "You!" he roared, picking up the woodcutter's axe again, advancing on the two gasping men. "You swore oaths to me. I fed you from my table. I made you rich! Before me, you were nothing but a polecat stealing scraps!"

Cenric watched for signs of other attackers as Ovrek marched over to Egill. Voices clamored and it seemed that some of the thralls had taken note of the fighting.

Ovrek began kicking Egill, raving with all the fury of a madman. "You want to be an eagle? I will cut out your lungs and give you wings!"

Snapper charged back up the hill with several warriors racing after him. The men spilled into the space between the thrall huts. The thralls themselves fled, disappearing because they knew what was best for them.

Cenric! Snapper cried. *Cenric?*

I'm fine. Good dog.

Snapper yipped at that, tail wagging.

The warriors took in the sight of two dead men, Cenric with a bloody sword, and their king kicking a vomiting jarl next to his gasping son.

"Lord?" one of the men called, eyeing Cenric suspiciously, gripping his own spear a little tighter.

"Take these whoresons!" Ovrek roared, thrusting a finger at the bloodied jarl underfoot. "Put them somewhere miserable until I think of how to punish them."

Warriors moved to collect Egill and Dagrún, grabbing the men by the arms and hauling them roughly to their feet. Two men moved toward Cenric, weapons drawn.

"Not him, you stupid swineherds," Ovrek snarled. "Cenric was more useful than the whole lot of you." The king finally seemed to be calming down, recovering from the sheer outrage of the whole ordeal. He rubbed at his forehead, wincing.

Cenric studied the sword in his hand, examining the balance of the blade and the wrappings on the hilt. Kelethi, if he had to guess. It was a good weapon, but he would be glad when he got his own back.

Ovrek's men hauled off the offending jarl and his son. Ovrek spat on the corpses and yelled for the thralls to throw the dead men in the sea. They would be denied burial, their spirits left to wander the endless depths of the sea god's realm for eternity.

"Why did Egill want you dead?" Cenric asked, watching as the jarl was dragged off, hardly able to stand on his own.

"Half the islands are in outrage," Ovrek growled. "Men are

saying I don't revere the First of Fathers. But I do! As much as any anyone on these rocks." Ovrek blotted the blood from his temple.

Cenric had to wonder just what Ovrek had done. Dagrún had mentioned something about yew in Ovrek's flagship. Did that have anything to do with it?

"Did you enjoy that?" Ovrek snapped, glaring bitterly.

Cenric wasn't sure if the king was referring to the fight or getting to shove Ovrek face first into a wood pile. Either way, the answer was the same. "Yes, lord."

Ovrek grunted as if he understood exactly what Cenric meant. "You always were an insolent boy." Even as he said it, he swung an arm around Cenric's shoulders once again, like a dear friend. Like a proud father. "You feast beside me tonight, young wolf."

That would have meant far more to Cenric if Brynn hadn't still been lost in the woods, accused of murder.

13

Brynn

Brynn woke shivering, a squirming Guin in her lap. Everything was cold and while she was not quite wet, there was a kind of perpetual dampness that came with being in the forest.

She set the puppy down, letting Guin bounce and pace in all directions. Guin sniffed in an easy circle, marking her territory and chewing on the ferns curiously.

Brynn relieved herself and tried to ignore the gnawing in her stomach. Drawing her shawl tighter around her shoulders, Brynn considered her options. She had few. As it was, she didn't speak the language, and she was obviously Hyldish.

Perhaps she should yield to the Valdari. They would have had time to think over this whole situation and perhaps things had calmed down. But a part of her knew that whoever she might be able to find in order to surrender, they would not be understanding.

Cenric had to be under guard, else he would have found his way to her by now. With Snapper's help, she should have been easy to find.

Breathing deep, Brynn closed her eyes and reached out for *ka*. This forest was ancient, a place where life and death had intersected, overlapped, and comingled for eons. Brynn would be surprised if this place hadn't already been old by the time the First of Fathers had arrived on these shores. Brynn could feel life seeped into the very earth, throbbing beneath her feet even as it blossomed all around her.

Past the trees, she sensed the small woodland animals and insects that made up every forest. Life was a golden haze in this place.

The presence of large shapes flickered into Brynn's awareness. Was that elk?

Brynn wasn't sure that there were elk in Valdar, but if she focused, she could sense the shapes of men on their backs. Horses carrying mounted men, if she had to guess.

Brynn's heart leapt into her throat and she snatched up Guin. They were hunting her.

Adjusting Guin in her arms, Brynn tried to think. This was all a huge misunderstanding, perhaps, but she doubted that a confrontation with warriors would go well. If they attacked her, she would defend herself, and that would escalate a situation that was already beyond rationality.

Guin gnawed playfully at Brynn's hand. She strained, reaching up to lick Brynn's face as she whined. She must be hungry.

Shushing the puppy, Brynn headed away from the riders. She was wandering farther into the forest, away from Istra.

It would be too easy for her to get lost in this unknown island, especially with the sun mostly hidden by the tall trees.

Brynn caught voices at her back. The men must have found her trail. Brynn had no idea how they might be managing to track her in this soggy tangle of a forest, but it seemed the Valdari knew their own land.

Brynn desperately didn't want to fight them. It wasn't that she couldn't win, it was that she probably could. These Valdari were unfamiliar with sorceresses.

"Brynn!" a familiar voice roared. So, they had sent Hróarr after her.

For a moment, she considered surrendering. Hróarr was probably as close to a friendly Valdari as she was bound to face.

Then Hróarr's voice rang out in a loud shout, his words sharp and demanding, more of a snarl. That was not the voice of a man interested in hearing explanations.

She didn't want to risk hurting her husband's cousin. He was the closest thing Cenric had to a brother.

The horses made good time, chasing after her through the brush. Brynn raced, but in her damp dress with Guin in her arms, it was all she could manage.

She could move faster if she dropped Guin, but couldn't bring herself to do it. The puppy bounced awkwardly at her side, woofing and whimpering.

Up ahead, Brynn felt the *ka* shift. Something was off. The feeling of wrongness hit her like a blow.

Brynn broke out of the tree line to find utter carnage. She had never thought of felled timber as carnage before, but that seemed the only fitting word.

Brynn had seen trees cut down for lumber and hauled off, but that had not happened here. These trees had been hacked down and left like so many corpses. Their leaves had withered, indicating they must have been felled some time ago.

The Valdari were pragmatic people and while they might be many things, they were not wasteful. Whoever had done this had acted out of spite.

Boundary stones marked the edge of the tree line, placed every ten paces or so. From their weathered etchings, Brynn guessed those boundary stones had been there long before these trees had been planted.

Between them, *ka* formed a boundary of some sort strung between the stones. The boundary was weakening, but still present. Loose tendrils connected the barrier to the ring that ran between the stones.

Were the dead trees what felt wrong?

The *ka* of this place felt...sick. Brynn had never felt anything like it. Though she could feel the plants, the moss, and some sense of healthy life nearby, she could sense no animals. There were no moles or rabbits or foxes to be felt, not anywhere in this clearing.

Guin growled low in Brynn's arms, her little puppy voice struggling to sound ferocious. Her whole body stiffened, and her ears flicked up, looking ahead.

If Brynn focused, she could sense a band of *ka* running through the boundary stones, connecting them. It was faint, but it seemed to be connected to the dead trees somehow. This was some spell that had been kept in place by the life force of the grove.

Brynn glanced right and left. She couldn't see anything, but her sorceress senses told her something was very, very wrong.

Was the air poison? No, that couldn't be it. How would the trees have been cut down, then? Men would have had to work here.

Horses whinnied at her back. Hróarr was not waiting. From the sound, they had her retreat into the forest blocked.

Brynn took off at a run across the open clearing, clambering over fallen branches and jutting roots. Up ahead, she could see a small ravine, a riverbed, and another line of trees on the far side. If she could just reach the far tree line, the river could help her lose the men.

These dead trees were yew, not the spruce, ash, and pine Brynn had seen in the rest of the forest. The farther into the clearing Brynn went, the more she noticed connecting roots and entwined branches webbed over the ground like veins in a body. There had not been dozens of yew trees, but a single tree with dozens of offshoots.

Brynn had never seen anything like this before. This tree must have been ancient. Yew trees could live for millennia. This one must have been putting down roots before or shortly after mortal feet had trod these islands.

Yet someone had desecrated it—or some*thing*.

As she scrambled up a fallen trunk, Brynn's hands slid over gashes in the wood, four parallel lines. She paused, fear seizing in her chest. Had those been claws? Not even the claws on the giant bear pelt had been large enough for that.

Guin snarled and growled at Brynn's side, making angry puppy noises.

The horses squealed at her back.

Brynn dared to look over her should and spied Hróarr with four other men aboard horses. Their animals reared and stomped, refusing to cross into the clearing.

Strange.

Hróarr and several of the men shouted. They gestured wildly at the clearing and one of them let off something akin to a shriek, clapping a hand over his mouth in horror. Even from a distance, Brynn caught their shock at the sight of the desecrated yew tree.

The men dismounted. Two of them held the reins of their horses while the others took off after her on foot.

"Brynn!" Hróarr bellowed. "You know you can't escape us!"

No, she couldn't. She glanced over her shoulder, counting—Hróarr and two other men. Only three armed men, but unarmored. She could deal with three unarmored men. But she didn't want to.

A stench seeped into Brynn's nostrils. Something cracked underfoot and Brynn realized that bones littered the ground. There were the remains of sheep, pigs, a few dogs, and at least one horse in varying stages of decay.

The choking stench threatened to make Brynn gag. Nothing about this place made sense. What was it?

Hróarr and his men were catching up, but the sickening sensation of wrongness coupled with the stench was enough to bring

Brynn to a stop. In her arms, Guin snarled and howled, her whole body stiff with fury.

Brynn shouldn't have come here. From this spot, she could sense that the yew tree had been connected to that barrier of *ka*, used to strengthen that spell, whatever it was. Now that the tree was dying, and the spell was no longer being fed, it was weakening.

Brynn squeezed the puppy tighter. At least Guin could sense the wrongness, too, and she wasn't insane.

"Brynn!" Hróarr gestured for his men to slow, fanning around her in a semicircle. He had seen Brynn rip a man's head off with her bare hands and was apparently trying to be cautious.

"What is this?" Brynn demanded, gesturing wildly around them. "Where are we?"

"The Grandfather Yew." Hróarr glanced around at the hacked and mutilated limbs of the tree. "This is...was sacred."

"Ovrek?" Brynn wasn't sure why she thought of the king first, but she knew that was wrong the moment her guess left her mouth.

"No," Hróarr said hastily. "What Ovrek did wouldn't have..."

Brynn waited for him to finish that sentence. "Ovrek did something?"

"No!" Hróarr seemed deeply upset by this, but he had a mission for his king. "It's a holy place."

"It's an evil place," Brynn shot back. Her heart raced as she searched their surroundings, trying to understand the source of this feeling. "There's something wicked. Something old."

Brynn knew none of these men had magic, but how could they not feel it? The sense of malice was a palpable thing, a weight that pressed around her.

"You're a foreigner. You shouldn't be here," Hróarr growled.

"None of us should be here," Brynn whispered.

Hróarr extended a hand, though his other rested on the hilt of his sword. "Let us take you back to Istra."

Brynn searched around them frantically. It was irrational, but some deep-seated instinct told her they were being watched.

"We only come here to leave sacrifices, as the First of Fathers commanded."

If that was true, then the First of Fathers must have been a sorcerer. An incredibly powerful one, at that. He'd created a prison held in place by the life force of the yew tree, but just what had he meant to imprison?

"Something is wrong," Brynn whispered.

"This place is sacred and even the wild animals will not come here." Hróarr pointed to Guin, even now writhing in Brynn's grip. "Even your pup wants to leave."

"If no animals come here," Brynn choked down a lump in her throat, "what has been chewing on those bones?" With a shaking hand, she pointed to a large cow's femur, cracked open with the marrow gnawed out.

Hróarr followed her gaze. His expression shifted, a flicker of what might have been fear before he turned back to her. "It's time to go."

"What lies here?" Brynn demanded. "Do you know?"

"The Grandfather Yew." Hróarr sounded annoyed.

"Not the tree," Brynn shot back. "What's *under* the tree?"

Hróarr held out one hand, marching toward her as if he intended to seize and drag her back to the horses.

"It's moving," Brynn gasped.

Before Brynn could decide what to do, a shriek rang out from the direction of the horses. Brynn and the men looked up to see the horses gone as well as the men who had been left behind to watch them. Brynn's heart beat faster and fear prickled the back of her neck.

One of Hróarr's men said something in Valdari. Hróarr answered and then another man pointed back toward the trees.

Hróarr returned his attention to Brynn.

"What happened?" Brynn asked, though she doubted she'd get a straight answer.

"The horses must have fled, taking my men with them."

Brynn looked down to Guin. The puppy's full attention was on the stump of a tree across the clearing. She had gone quiet, her ears pricked and whole body rigid. Afraid of what she would see, Brynn followed the puppy's line of sight.

She saw nothing at first, but then one of the shadows moved. The shape seemed to unfurl like a sail, limbs unfolding from around its body as it shambled out of the cover of the fallen trees.

The creature had brown fur, triangular ears, and a long snout. It seemed not so much a wolf, but the nightmare of a wolf. The creature was too big, rising to perhaps ten feet or more. Its front legs were much longer than its back legs, making the creature shamble awkwardly. Shaggy brown fur hung off the creature's body, draping so that its forelegs almost seemed to have wings.

Crimson eyes took them in as the creature lowered its head, sniffing at the air.

"Wulfwir," one of Hróarr's men gasped, adding something in Valdari. "Wulfwir!"

"What is it?" Brynn asked, her voice coming out as little more than a gasp.

"It can't..." Hróarr trailed off. "It can't." He slipped back into Valdari, speaking to his men.

Brynn's throat went tight. She could swear those eyes were focused on her. Whatever this creature was, it was staring at her.

The creature lumbered toward them.

Guin growled, shifting in Brynn's arms. Her fierce snarls turned into frightened whimpers as she snuggled closer against Brynn's ribs.

Hróarr drew his sword as did his men. "Use your sorcery on it," he ordered Brynn.

Brynn was already drawing on her power, but in truth she wasn't sure if she would be able to stop this thing. Its *ka* was wrong. Whatever it was, this creature was not meant to exist. "There's another one," Brynn gasped, glancing over her shoulder. "Somewhere close."

There were two others, one much larger under their feet and another smaller, but seemed to be moving quickly. Brynn could not see either of the other two, only this frightening lupine aberration.

The large wolf monster broke into a gallop, springing across the ground far faster than its awkward body should have been able to. It did not seem to run so much as to pounce. It bounded across the open space, springing around the tree stumps with an unnatural speed.

Brynn lashed a spell at the creature, creating a whip of power. Her blow hit the creature in the face, making its head snap to the side. Blood splattered, but then the creature spun back around.

Before their eyes, the creature's skin bubbled and popped as it mended, seeming to boil back into wholeness. Brynn had never seen anything like it. It was much like seeing a wound healed with *ka,* but also *wrong* in some way.

Regardless, the creature was upon them within a few thundering beats of Brynn's heart. The creature lunged for Brynn first.

Brynn slashed at it with another spell, stabbing for its soft underbelly this time. She struck, though the hair hid the sight of her strike.

The creature coiled, howling as it shrank back. Because of the creature's unwieldy proportions, it had to crouch down to use its jaws. The motion was awkward, strained, and the creature stumbled as it tried to bite her.

Hróarr and his men set on the creature with their swords, stabbing for its flanks and legs. They were brave, if nothing else.

The creature batted at Brynn with its forepaws, trying to knock her over. It smacked her in the back and Brynn went down, gasping as the air was knocked out of her.

She just managed to keep from crushing Guin as she went down. Brynn struck a stump, but rolled onto her back, facing the creature once again.

The jaws came down, diving straight for her.

Brynn blasted straight up with her power, straight into the creature's face. Her power hit the monster in the side of its jowl, and it shrieked, squalling with a sound like a thousand dying pigs.

Blood splattered as the creature backed up, away from Brynn. It must have decided she wasn't worth it.

Hróarr stabbed at the creature's flanks. The monster spun around, diving for him. It caught his arm near the shoulder and lifted him off the ground. Hróarr yelled, but it was like seeing a crab in the beak of a seagull.

Hróarr spouted a slew of Valdari words Cenric used only when he was particularly angry. Hróarr stabbed furiously at the creature, flailing in its grip ineffectively.

The monster turned and bounded away.

Brynn sent lashes of power after the monster. A spell caught the creature in the back, ripping through its fur and leaving a bloody gash along its spine.

The creature stumbled but kept its hold on Hróarr.

The two remaining men raced after the monster, but it was too fast. How did it move so fast with that crooked gait?

The monster raced away, eating up the ground with its misshapen limbs. The monster slowed and disappeared, diving downward into the earth. Hróarr's bellows of fury echoed across the empty clearing.

Brynn's heart raced. Should they go for help or chase after Hróarr? They didn't have the numbers to fight that thing, but Hróarr would probably be dead in moments.

Guin yelped at her feet, whining and crying. The puppy caught the edge of Brynn's dress in her teeth and tugged, as if begging Brynn to flee. Gone was her earlier bravado.

Brynn scooped the puppy up in her arms, staring to where the monster had taken Hróarr.

His two men chattered in Valdari, pointing to where the monster had disappeared with their lord.

Brynn reached the nearest man and shoved Guin into his arms. "Go back to Istra," she ordered, pointing back in what she hoped was the direction of the town. "And take my dog with you."

The man stared at Brynn without comprehension. He'd glared at her with suspicion earlier, but it seemed he now appreciated her ability to repel monsters. She didn't know his name, but he was one of the men who had visited Ombra with Hróarr in the past.

"Cenric. Tell Cenric." Brynn stepped away from the men toward the direction the monster had disappeared with Hróarr. "You go!" She pointed again. "Take my dog back to Cenric and tell him what happened. Tell Ovrek what happened." Even if Brynn was hardly sure what had happened herself.

"Wulfwir." The man shook his head.

"Is that the name of that thing?" Brynn pointed in the direction it had gone. "Wulfwir?"

The man nodded, eyes wide.

Brynn took a deep breath. Her husband had never mentioned that Valdar was haunted by beasts with tainted *ka* and red eyes. It seemed like the sort of thing he should have mentioned. "Go," she repeated, pointing in the direction of Istra even as she headed after the monster.

"Hróarr," the warrior protested, taking a step after her.

"I'll get him," Brynn promised, even as her whole mind screamed that she was insane. "I will get him, just go!"

Hróarr might already be dead, but she had to try. She had to at least try. For Cenric.

Brynn hated leaving Guin with a stranger, but the puppy had a better chance of surviving this way. Hopefully, the men would do as she told them.

Lifting her muddy skirts, Brynn ran across the field with its maze of stumps and exposed roots. It had taken the monster mere heartbeats to cross this way, but she had to run for what seemed to be forever. They needed more help. She might not be able to do anything.

But Hróarr didn't have time to wait for help. He probably didn't even have the time to wait for her.

Brynn finally reached the spot where the monster—Wulfwir—had disappeared. A burrow sank down into the earth, like what a fox or a rabbit might have, but at least a hundred times bigger.

Hróarr's sword lay beside the opening, where it had been dropped on the way down. Dark patches of blood stained the earth and Brynn could only hope that was from the wounds she had inflicted on the Wulfwir, not from Hróarr.

A man let off a yelp at Brynn's back. Hróarr's man had dropped Guin, shaking his hand.

Guin hit the ground and barreled after Brynn, whining and crying. It seemed she was determined to stay.

Brynn waved to the men to go. They were warriors and proud ones at that, but the Wulfwir seemed too much for even them.

Guin came skidding to Brynn's side, whimpering. Her body shuddered, but she stayed close to Brynn's ankles.

"It will be dangerous," Brynn whispered, stroking Guin's coat even as her own hands tremored. "Can you be brave for me, little girl?"

Guin clung close to Brynn in response. The dog was terrified, but she seemed as committed as Brynn was.

Brynn picked up Hróarr's sword. She cast a final look to the sky, sending a plea toward Eponine for protection, and stepped down into the burrow. The ground was slippery, mud plastered over a maze of roots.

The tunnel sloped down gently, reaching deeper into the earth. Brynn could hear Hróarr shouting from ahead. She thanked Eponine he was still alive and sent a silent prayer for continued good luck. They would all need it.

Guin padded along at Brynn's side. The puppy trembled, but she remained silent.

Roots jutted out of the ceiling, the walls, and made twisted patterns on the ground. The earth here seemed to be made of roots as much as soil. That ancient yew with its many offshoots had created a mesh underground, entwining together in a woven gauntlet.

Up ahead, Brynn could sense the burning presence of evil. That was the only way she could think to describe it.

Brynn had never liked spiders, but their *ka* felt much the same as all other creatures. Foxes and weasels sometimes stole geese, but they did not have this kind of malice to their presence.

Worse, Brynn could sense the presence of at least three of the unnatural beings. One of them was much smaller than the Wulfwir, but one was far larger. Brynn shuddered to think how large.

While she hated the idea of being in an enclosed space with the monsters, if she couldn't escape quickly, that meant that they couldn't, either.

Brynn dared to venture still deeper into the burrow, her eyes adjusting to the near darkness. She imagined this place would be pitch black at night. The burrow was uneven and jagged, not yet worn smooth by use. Some places it was high enough she imagined the Wulfwir would be able to stand, but other places even she had to duck. The roots were gashed in places, like the creature had been forced to claw its way out of the earth by chewing through the roots of the tree.

A dripping sound came from ahead, the telltale signs of water. That river she had seen must run through here. Her heart pounded so loudly, she was sure the monsters would hear that before her footsteps.

Hróarr yelled from up ahead, a roar of pain.

Brynn held back a shudder, quickening her pace. She felt her way along the walls, using the *ka* of the earth around them and her awareness of the monsters. The three fiends were together.

Light came from up ahead and Brynn moved faster.

Hróarr cursed in Valdari.

Brynn came to a branch in the tunnels, but she could sense Hróarr toward the direction of the light, so she went that way.

She stumbled out into what appeared to be some manner of cave. The stone had been carved away by the river that rushed through the middle of the chamber, but roots still dominated most of the walls and ceiling.

Massive roots tangled on the ground, creating a knobbed and crooked surface. Bones scattered in every direction and Brynn had her answer as to what had been eating the sacrifices.

Brynn glimpsed the Wulfwir up ahead, its back to her. She was sure she could sense Hróarr, too. Climbing over the massive roots in her path, she tried to get closer. Maybe she could strike the Wulfwir from behind.

Guin snarled just as Brynn sensed something move at her back. She turned, drawing *ka* into herself in a rush.

Brynn turned, coming face to face with another creature, barely managing to hold in a scream.

It was a little girl—or was supposed to be. She could be no more than ten with black hair and a shift that had long since rotted into tattered rags.

Half her face, left arm, and upper chest had been seared away, leaving nothing but blackened flesh shriveled around the bone. No human child could have survived such a thing, much less been able to stand there, staring at Brynn with a single, red eye.

Half skeleton. The creature was not quite half, but Brynn had no other explanation. *The she-troll.* It couldn't be, but then again, what else could it be?

The child monster opened its mouth to speak and the voice that came out was a rasp, a whisper, and a wheedle all at once. The words sounded Valdari, but they were off. Something about the inflection.

Guin was not having it. The little dog planted herself in front of Brynn, letting off a low growl.

Brynn leveled Hróarr's sword at the child troll, keeping the

Wulfwir in her line of sight. She backed away from the child, careful not to turn her back to either monster.

Guin had the good sense to retreat with her.

"Hróarr?" Brynn called.

The monsters already knew she was here. She might as well let Hróarr know, too.

Bemused cursing in Valdari came from the mercenary, then, "What are you doing here, you stupid bitch?"

"Hyldish," the burned girl hissed, her voice coming out in a lisping rasp because of the flesh missing off half her jaw. "You are a Hyldish sorceress. Have you come to bargain with us?"

It was difficult to understand what the creature was saying with her strange voice, but somehow hearing the thing speak in words Brynn could understand only made this whole thing worse.

"There was one who bargained with us." The burned girl hissed, clawing fingers at empty air. "Before he betrayed us and trapped us down here."

"What are you?" Brynn felt her words belonged to a stranger, far steadier than she felt.

"A child of the moons." The creature's charred mouth curled in the ghastly approximation of a smile. "Like you."

"Eponine?" Brynn didn't know what this fiend was, but it wasn't Istovari.

Amusement twisted the child's lips. "No."

Brynn didn't want to converse with the creature. She wanted to get Hróarr and get out.

"We are grateful to whoever weakened our prison," the child mused, tilting its head back to peruse the roots overhead. "I was able to claw out of the roots, then release my brother. He did the rest. We will *all* be free soon." The child's half-skull gaze fell on the Wulfwir. "Only a matter of time now."

The Wulfwir growled, shifting over the spot where Brynn sensed Hróarr. She wanted to attack both the monsters, but not while the Wulfwir had Hróarr. If she could just get the monster away from him, maybe she could land a killing blow this time.

"Hundreds of years trapped down here while food was piled on the branches of the trees, just out of our reach," the she-troll giggled. "Now food walks in by itself." The girl monster licked her ruined jaw, even half her tongue had been scorched and blackened. "Good. Because we are very hungry. We are always hungry."

Brynn wracked her brain, trying to think. She dragged power to herself, even though that made her even more aware of the sick, tainted presence of these creatures around her. The large one was still nearby, not moving, but still very much alive.

The burned girl crouched down on all fours and cocked her head in the direction of Hróarr. "Is he the father?"

Brynn choked, stunned. She shouldn't have let herself get distracted, but the words hit her like a blow.

The creature made a keening, chortling sound. "Killing families together is always entertaining."

"This is your fault," Hróarr yelled. He must not be able to hear what the rasping monster child was saying and that was likely for the best. "All your fault. If you hadn't come here, if you hadn't come to Valdar in the first place—no—if you hadn't decided to swyve Cenric, none of this would have happened!"

The burned girl glanced in the direction of Hróarr, her one remaining eye sparking in amusement. "So, he's not the father? Interesting."

Brynn chose not to respond to either the monster or the angry mercenary. Heart racing, she forced herself to address Hróarr calmly. "I have your sword." She held it steady, leveled at the burned girl. "Do you want it back?"

Hróarr remained silent for just a moment. "Yes," he answered, drawling the word with an edge of suspicion.

"Alright." Brynn thought quickly, mentally mapping out her next actions.

These monsters healed almost instantly, but she'd still been able to chase off the Wulfwir, which must mean they could be killed somehow. All she had to do was get a killing blow the first time.

Brynn lashed out with her power, slashing into the child's neck. The creature screamed, then its head toppled off.

The child *split*. A being made of knobbed limbs and patches of scaled flesh broke from the corpse. For just a moment, it locked eyes with Brynn, teeth snapping and snarling.

It tried to rush her, but something seemed to be drawing it away, dragging it off like smoke on the breeze. In an instant, it was gone, leaving behind the crumpled body in two pieces.

Beheading could kill them. Good to know.

The Wulfwir creature let off a howl of fury that seemed to shake the earth around them. Brynn sent another spell for its neck, but this one dodged. Her strike slashed across its shoulder instead.

"Hurry up, woman!" Hróarr choked. The Wulfwir held him down with a paw.

Brynn scrambled up the side of another root, coming closer. She lashed a spell in the direction of the Wulfwir, catching the beast in the face. It careened to the side, blood spraying the roots at its back.

Then it spun its head around to her once again and Brynn watched as its face mended before her eyes. Brynn doubted even Cenric had witnessed nightmares like this.

Teeth gritting with determination, Brynn scrambled up the last root between her and Hróarr. She touched it and the root shifted, fleshy and warm under her hands.

Brynn stumbled back, gasping. What she had thought was another of the massive roots was the tail of a great serpent, covered in dirt. It was just the end, tapering off in front of her. She'd been so overwhelmed with the oily, putrid presence of the monsters, she hadn't been able to realize one was right under her.

After everything, she had thought she'd experienced as much horror as she possibly could, but it seemed there was a new depth of horror she had not yet reached.

Guin barked, her little puppy cries seeming so futile in the face of the great beast.

With the Wulfwir looming over them, Brynn panicked. Or perhaps she was just desperate.

She stabbed Hróarr's sword into the scaly hide in front of her. The sword was sharp, but the hide was tough. Brynn was only able to jab it in a hand's breadth or so.

All the same, the entire tail whipped up, striking the ceiling of this strange cave. Brynn kept a tight grip on the hilt and the sword yanked out as dirt and rock rained down around them.

Guin howled in terror, bumping against Brynn's legs in the confusion.

Brynn was blinded, but she could still feel the sources of *ka* to tell her where Hróarr and the monsters were.

Rushing forward, Brynn grabbed Guin's scruff and tucked her under the arm holding the sword, groping blindly through the smog of dirt. Choking and coughing, she found Hróarr.

The Wulfwir let off a howl. The strange serpent, whatever it was, made no sound as it dropped its tail back down.

Grabbing Hróarr's arm, Brynn gripped as tight as she could and dragged him along. Hróarr crawled off the ground with her support.

The way they had come from was blocked by the two monsters, but Brynn followed her awareness of the river. All rivers had a little *ka* in them and the telltale movement gave it away. The river would lead them out, she knew that from her brief glimpse of it from beside the Grandfather Yew.

Brynn handed Hróarr's sword to him in the dusty haze. They reached the edge of the river, scrambling along the narrow ledge beside it. Guin wiggled free to race ahead, yipping to make sure Brynn followed. Brynn pressed one hand to the wall as they plunged deeper into the dark.

Hróarr regained his footing. "Lead me," he ordered, passing his left hand back so she could guide him along the passage.

Brynn took his hand. "It's chasing us." She sensed the tainted power of the Wulfwir loping after them.

Hróarr responded with something in Valdari.

The monster squalled at their backs. Hróarr slashed and hacked as the creature came within range, his battle cries loud enough to be heard even over its shrieking.

Brynn cast spells over her shoulder, lashing for the beast. Some of her attacks landed, but most did not. Everything was chaos and those searing red eyes burned at her back. She couldn't get another clean strike for the creature's neck and none of her other attacks seemed to permanently injure it. She had to kill or nothing.

A plan began to form as they fled, and Brynn dragged power back to herself. She spooled *ka* like thread, weaving her intent into it with feverish determination.

Feeling her way along the wall, Brynn spotted light ahead. Hope surged in her chest. They burst out into day, but with the monster close at their backs.

"Run!" Hróarr ordered, shoving her ahead of him.

Brynn stopped and spun around. "Move!" She raised her hands, releasing the spell she had been preparing.

Hróarr was wise enough to obey, ducking to the side as Brynn let go.

Her power sliced into the roots of the tree over the entrance, shearing through the supportive web that held the stones and earth in place. Red eyes flashed just as the ceiling of the tunnel buckled and folded, crushing the Wulfwir beneath a cascade of stones and earth. The creature lay half buried, still snarling and yowling its fury, too-long arms grasping for them.

"I don't think they can cross the stones," Brynn panted. "Spell...containing them."

Guin whined and barked, pacing around Brynn, not knowing what to do.

Hróarr muttered another string of Valdari curses as he grabbed Brynn's arm above the elbow, shoving her back toward the boundary stones. "Then run, stupid woman."

This time, Brynn retreated uphill toward the stone markers, heart racing.

Hróarr bounded close at her heels, limping just a little. She might have to heal him later.

Brynn could hear the Wulfwir howling as it clawed itself out of the earth like a giant, demented beetle. She hadn't run like this since the war.

The boundary stones loomed before them, their gaps wide and welcoming. A part of Brynn wondered if the Wulfwir would be stopped by the markers. The creature was enraged into a frenzy. Could these old spells really hold them? Brynn supposed they would find out.

Hróarr cursed again. "It's loose. Move!"

Arms pumping at her sides, Brynn forced her body to find another burst of speed. The cold air stabbed into her lungs with each breath and her side ached, but she had to run. She had no choice.

Guin bounded along beside her, struggling to move as fast as she could. The dyrehund bolted, heading straight for the trees as fast as her little legs could carry her.

The scrambling thud of the monster came thundering after them. A scream tried to wrench itself out of her throat, but Brynn didn't have the breath for it.

Hróarr barreled ahead of her, no longer trying to protect her back. He tore headlong across the field, leaving her behind.

Brynn didn't have time to feel betrayal as the Wulfwir's yowling came so close she swore she could feel its hot breath on her neck.

Hróarr crossed the boundary marker and spun around, sword held loose at his side. "Faster!" he yelled back to her.

Brynn was trying. With a last burst of speed, she dove for the line that marked the boundary.

Guin careened past the stones and spun back around, whining

at Hróarr's side.

A claw hooked Brynn's shawl, jerking her back.

Brynn screamed as she fell backward, toward the beast. She didn't even have time to cast a spell before an iron grip caught her arm, yanking her across the barrier marked by the boundary stones.

Her shawl ripped off and pain shot through her shoulder as she crashed to the ground on the safe side of the boundary.

Brynn smacked onto the mud, dead leaves, and twigs breaking her fall. Panting, she spun around to see the Wulfwir looming over both her and Hróarr.

Guin let off a little howl, crawling into Brynn's lap and licking her face. The puppy growled in the direction of the monster.

The misshapen wolf shrieked and howled, pacing back and forth between the boundary stones, but not going past them. The monster prodded and clawed at the earth, but the spells held. Even if the spells felt weak, they held for now.

Brynn crawled onto her hands and knees. She was lucky to be alive. All three of them were.

A great serpent, a she-troll, and a giant wolf, Cenric had said. It seemed that Valdar's legends were not ready to fade into myth just yet.

Hróarr did not offer to help her up as he sheathed his sword, glaring at the Wulfwir. If Brynn had arrived a few moments later, they would have eaten him, he must know that.

Brynn stood, her shoulder sore from where Hróarr had yanked her across the last few steps. "You knew it wouldn't cross the boundary?" Had he at least believed her in that?

"No."

Brynn shook her head. "Then why did you stop running?"

Hróarr tilted his head toward the forest. "Let's go."

"What is it?" Brynn demanded, looking back to the squalling beast on the other side of the boundary.

"I don't know." Hróarr grated the admission like a curse.

"Your men called it Wulfwir."

"I..." Hróarr blinked at the aberration on the other side of the stones as if he still didn't believe that it was there.

"Is it them?" Brynn dared voice her suspicion out loud. "The monsters fought by the First of Fathers?"

Hróarr watched the creature before them. "I don't know."

"The child said that the tree had been weakened and that's how she and the Wulfwir were able to break free and kill it."

Hróarr went very still at that. He pointedly did not look at her.

"You mentioned Ovrek did something. Could he have caused this?" Brynn would not want to accuse Ovrek of anything to his face, but it seemed possible.

"He couldn't have." Hróarr's voice lacked conviction.

"What else, then?"

Hróarr made a snapping motion with his wrist. "It's time to go."

Brynn didn't move. "Do you believe me about anything?"

It went without saying what she meant. Brynn wanted to know if Hróarr thought she had killed the concubine.

Hróar's jaw locked tight. "That's for my king to decide."

Brynn already knew the direction that had been going. She was not optimistic about what Ovrek might decide.

A tense moment stretched between them.

Brynn could escape Hróarr, and they both knew it. She could incapacitate or even kill him. The problem was that she couldn't live forever in this wild land of monsters.

A part of her had hoped that saving his life would at least earn her some credibility, but it seemed that not even that would make him vouch for her.

Had he heard what the child fiend had said about "the father"? If so, Hróarr didn't acknowledge it.

It was possible Brynn could be pregnant. Cenric had been making frequent and passionate love to her for more than half a year. Brynn had started to fear something was wrong, though Cenric had not yet expressed impatience.

The monster might know in some way, though how it would have known when Brynn couldn't yet tell was unclear. Brynn hadn't seen any signs, but it was still possible. She would probably need at least a week before she would be sure and then...

But until she was sure, she wanted to be careful with herself.

Swallowing, Brynn considered her options. "I will...come with you." She glanced back to where the Wulfwir was now gnawing and tearing her shawl to shreds.

"Let's go." Hróarr headed into the trees, seeming to know which way he was going.

Brynn scrambled after him. Cold, wet, tired, and hungry, she wasn't sure what would come next, but hopefully, they could make King Ovrek see reason.

The walk back to Istra was far shorter than it had been in the dark. Brynn followed Hróarr quietly. Neither of them spoke. Guin padded along at Brynn's heels, every so often glaring back in the direction of the monsters.

Brynn wondered if she was being led to her death. Would Ovrek kill her?

Back in Hylden, murder called for payment to the victim's family. The blood price or blodgild was determined by the victim's age and standing within the family.

Valdari repaid blood with blood.

A rock settled deep in Brynn's stomach. She wasn't ready to die. For the first time in a long time, she had been happy. She wanted to live with Cenric for many years yet.

They shambled into Istra as the sun was past its zenith. Voices were raised and people ran to and fro. Something had happened.

"What's going on?" Brynn demanded, looking to Hróarr. "What are they saying?"

The mercenary didn't bother to curse or glare at her, which told her how serious it was. "Someone has tried to murder Ovrek."

Brynn gulped. "Tolvir?" It seemed logical. The atheling had been upset enough to kill her. Perhaps he was grieved enough to attack his own father.

"What?" Hróarr cast her a sharp look.

"Nothing." Brynn took in the people rushing back and forth. No one seemed to have noticed that they had returned. "Where is Cenric?"

"I'll find him," Hróarr assured her. "And my men, too, but first..." He motioned her after him.

Brynn went meekly. She buzzed with worry for Cenric and Esa. Brynn's chest seemed to be filled with a swarm of bees.

People ran in all directions. It was either fear or excitement, it was hard for her to tell. Perhaps a bit of both.

Hróarr took her along a shortcut to the king's complex behind the thrall huts. They reached a large pit, deeper than the height of a man and sheer along the sides. The stench of human excrement came from below.

Brynn dared to look down, noticing what appeared to be the remains of scraps and other trash, though not very much of it. Was this a midden heap?

A hard shove sent Brynn toppling over the edge, into the pit. She landed on the dirt below, gasping as the air rushed out of her lungs.

Rolling onto her back, she saw Hróarr at the edge, glaring down. He had pushed her in.

"Hróarr?" Brynn croaked, gasping as betrayal lanced through her. Brynn cast about, searching for a way out, but there was none.

It seemed that the only way out was to have a rope lowered down and Hróarr had just shoved her in.

Guin let off a howl of protest. She barked at Hróarr, lunging for his boots. The puppy attacked him with a vengeance, snarling and biting.

The mercenary backed away from the edge, out of sight. He cursed at the puppy, trying to get her off him from the sound of it.

Brynn wanted to yell after him, but she didn't have the breath. She had risked her life to save him from the monsters, and this was how he repaid her?

"Hróarr!" a familiar voice cried. He spoke in hurried Valdari. Was that...?

Other voices came from overhead. From the *ka*, there seemed to be a crowd of people headed this way, but they were outside Brynn's line of sight.

Brynn pushed herself onto her elbows. "Cenric?" Her cry was lost in the cacophony chattering above. "Cenric..." Brynn was tired and aching and felt like a fool. Everything had gone wrong and even the things that had gone right had bitten her in the back after all.

Several warriors appeared, dragging two bloodied and battered men between them. From their clothes, the two captives must be important. Their silver arm rings, embroidered clothing, and fur-trimmed mantles hinted at wealth. One was older with scars slashing through his beard and one was younger and taller. The two men were hurled headlong into the pit.

The unfortunate prisoners had even harder landings than Brynn. The older man seemed to splatter into the ground and laid still. Was he dead? The younger rolled onto his side in the mud, groaning and speaking in stilted Valdari.

Brynn was now trapped with the two criminals. Fear spiked through her. She could probably defend herself from these strangers but to be trapped down here with them? For Eponine knew how long? "Cenric!" Brynn wasn't even sure what she hoped he would do. All she knew was that she needed him.

Faces appeared over the edge of the pit. Young men with arm rings and braided beards. Warriors from Ovrek's household. They spat down, but not at her, at the two captives.

Brynn wondered if she had imagined Cenric's voice. Or, worse, if he had ignored her.

Then his outline came into view overheard. Even with the sun at his back, she recognized his silhouette. "Brynn!" He scrambled to the edge of the pit, crouching down.

Brynn took in the sight of him, relief flooding her chest. At least he was safe.

The next instant, Cenric whirled away from her. "Hróarr!" he roared, followed by a string of furious Valdari.

14

Cenric

"You put her in the thrall pit?" Cenric demanded as he barreled toward his cousin.

"I'm keeping her from running away again," Hróarr answered with a shrug. "That's what the pit is for."

Cenric closed on his cousin, fists clenched.

Ovrek stepped between them like a master breaking apart two hounds. "Hróarr. It is good to see you found the sorceress."

Cenric rounded on Ovrek. He had just saved the king's life. Surely his old mentor wouldn't keep his wife imprisoned with the same traitors Cenric had just thwarted? It was hardly just. Ovrek had lost a concubine, but Cenric had saved a king. It seemed the debt, if there had been any, was paid.

At their feet, Brynn's puppy snarled at Hróarr. For once, she'd found someone she hated more than Cenric.

Hróarr bowed to the king. The man's tunic was torn, blood

caked his temple, and he was covered in mud from head to foot.

"Did she put up a fight?" Ovrek asked, gesturing to the blood on Hróarr's face.

Hróarr shook his head. "The bitch—"

Cenric's fist flew, smacking square into Hróarr's jaw, knocking his cousin back. "You are inferior to her in every way!"

If Hróarr couldn't remember that, Cenric would pound it into his skull.

Cenric hurt Hróarr! Snapper made a whining sound. *Bad Cenric.*

Hróarr hurt Brynn, Cenric shot back.

Brynn! Snapper growled, hackles rising. *Bad Hróarr! Bad!*

Now both dyrehunds turned on Hróarr, barking their displeasure.

Hróarr stumbled, but the bigger man didn't go down. His whole body braced, fists drawing up for a fight.

Cenric had already killed a man today. What was one more?

Ovrek's warriors moved aside, giving them space to fight. They had missed the attack on their king, but a scuffle behind the thrall huts might satisfy their bloodlust.

Hróarr moved for Cenric, but Ovrek smacked a hand into his chest, pushing him back.

"Your cousin saved my life today."

Hróarr shot a quick look to his king.

That statement was laden with implication. It meant Cenric was in the favor of Ovrek—at least for now—and it was a reminder to the onlookers that Cenric had been there when they had not. Never mind that Ovrek had been the one to dismiss them.

"Get the sorceress out," Ovrek ordered. He glared down to where Dagrún and Egill still lay where they had fallen. "At least one of my men knows the honor due kings."

Cenric stepped up to the edge of the pit. "Brynn?"

"Cenric." His wife was on her feet, arms drawn close around her. She was filthy, covered in scratches, bruises, and the signs of having been in the forest all night long.

One of the warriors brought a rope and Cenric snatched it from him, lowering it down to Brynn. "Ovrek says you can come out."

Brynn's expression remained tight. Her face was red, though that might be from the cold as easily from crying. His wife grasped the end of the rope, and it took several tries, but she made it halfway up the steep side of the pit and then Cenric was able to catch her arm.

He worried that Dagrún and Egill might trouble her, but he needn't have. The disgraced men had barely pushed themselves off the ground by the time Brynn scrambled free.

She crashed into his arms, clinging to his chest. She lowered her head, curling against him.

Cenric wrapped his arms around her, stroking her back. "I've got you. I've got you, love."

Snapper woofed happily, tail wagging. He licked Brynn's arm, then went back to prancing around them. He dropped to his haunches, ears up as he watched them.

Guin whined, fussing over Brynn. She cast one last snarl in Hróarr's direction before settling against Brynn's side.

"There are monsters in the forest." Brynn's voice was barely audible.

"What?"

"They have a burrow under the roots of the dead yew tree," Brynn whispered, shaking in his arms.

"Did you fight something in the woods?" Cenric demanded, speaking in Valdari to Hróarr.

His cousin deigned a look at him, though his fists remained clenched.

"What was it?" Cenric pressed.

Hróarr shot a glance back to the forest. "I don't know."

"Brynn says there are monsters under a dead yew tree."

At that, Ovrek's attention turned to Hróarr. "Yew tree?"

Hróarr almost looked ashamed as he dipped his head. Conspicuously, he switched into Hyldish. "The Grandfather Yew, lord."

Cenric squeezed Brynn tighter. The Grandfather Yew was the most sacred place in Valdar, miles from Istra. It was forbidden to go near it except to leave offerings and sacrifices and then only with the proper rites. The Grandfather Yew was to remain untouched, by word of Havnar, the First of Fathers.

It was said that disturbing the tree would unleash terror and evil across the islands.

"What happened?" Ovrek stepped toward Hróarr, also speaking in Hyldish for some reason. "What did she do?"

Cenric bristled. He stood, pulling Brynn up to stand beside him. She squeezed his hand, clinging to his arm.

"Nothing, lord," Hróarr admitted. "The yew tree was already..."

Ovrek's eyes widened. "Already what? Speak!"

Hróarr cleared his throat. "It's dead, lord. It's been dead for some time, if I had to guess, lord."

Ovrek faltered. It was just for a moment, but Cenric knew the man well enough to see. "That's impossible," Ovrek shot back. "We barely took—" The king cut himself off.

Cenric glanced between his cousin and the king. Hróarr had turned ashen, jaw tight as if preparing to be struck again.

"It has collapsed, and its leaves are gone." Hróarr continued speaking Hyldish, voice dropping low. "We took too much."

Cenric shifted his attention to Ovrek.

Something flashed in Ovrek's eyes, something terribly like fear. The emotion was there barely a moment before the king spun on Brynn. "You trespassed on sacred ground!"

Brynn flinched against Cenric. "Believe me, I never meant to be in that place."

"What did you do?" Ovrek bore down on Brynn.

Cenric shoved her behind him, ready to fight Ovrek if he had to. If the Valdari king came after Brynn, Cenric would take up where Egill and Dagrún left off.

Surprisingly, Hróarr intervened. "No, lord. She did nothing to the tree, she..." Hróarr hesitated. "There were things inside the standing stones."

"Things?" Ovrek spun back on Hróarr.

Hróarr broke eye contact, almost as if he was embarrassed. "I barely believe it myself."

"It's not like you to waver, son," Ovrek ordered, the endearment barked like a command.

"The Father's Foes." Hróarr's tall frame crouched as he whispered, "I saw them." He glanced to Brynn. "The sorceress and my men saw them."

Ovrek cocked his head, blinking at Hróarr.

The men around them cast each other looks of confusion, but none dared question their king in his current mood.

Hróarr continued. "They had teeth and claws and their wounds healed too quickly. I don't know."

Ovrek seemed to consider that for a long moment. He was not a gullible man, but nor had he ever been one to ignore omens, either. "How did you survive?"

"They wouldn't cross the boundary stones, lord." Hróarr seemed to brace himself as soon as the words were out.

Ovrek's eyes widened. "You crossed the boundary stones? Without the rites?"

Hróarr flinched. "Forgive me, lord." Despite having shoved Brynn in the thrall pit, at least Hróarr was taking the blame for what had happened.

"Your men saw this as well?" Ovrek demanded.

"They saw Wulfwir. They did not see Jormanthar and Hesrid."

"I would speak with them," Ovrek commanded. "Send them to me at once." With the decisiveness that had won him a hundred battles and more, he turned, finally reverting to his native tongue.

"You two." Ovrek singled out two of the younger men nearby. "Go to the Grandfather Yew. Do *not* cross the stones. Return immediately and tell me what you find."

"What's happening?" Brynn's gaze fluttered between them all as they switched back to Valdari.

"Ovrek is sending two men to see if the Grandfather Yew is harmed as you say," Cenric explained.

"It was," Brynn answered flatly. "Someone was quite thorough."

That made the back of Cenric's neck prickle. He gave his personal allegiance to Morgi, but it was never wise to meddle with any god or to disobey the ancestors.

The First of Fathers himself had ordered the construction of the boundary stones and the protection of the yew tree. Generations had offered their sacrifices and prayers twice a year. Most people only made the journey a handful of times in their lives, but villages and settlements from across Valdar sent offerings of animals to the tree.

As long as the Grandfather Yew stood, Valdar would have good fortune. Every child grew up on the tales of how it had been planted to protect the islands and how evil would be unleashed if it should come to harm.

Cenric shot a glance to Ovrek, but the king's attention was elsewhere. He said something to Hróarr, something about the bathhouse.

The pieces clattered into place in Cenric's mind—Tullia calling her father cursed, the questions about yew wood followed by the betrayal from Dagrún and Egill.

Ovrek must have taken pieces of the Grandfather Yew for his flagship as if it was a common oak. The most holy place in Valdar, planted by the First of Fathers himself, and Ovrek had carved it up for timber.

It was unthinkable, an act of hubris that flew in the face of everything every Valdari child was taught from infancy. Nothing worthy of doing should be done in secret and if Ovrek felt the need to keep it secret, he should have known better.

Ovrek must have sensed Cenric's attention. His gaze shifted back to them. "I trust you will escort your wife back to your camp." Continuing to speak in Valdari, he cast Cenric a grin. "I still expect you to feast beside me tonight. Bring her with you, if you like."

It was a command as much as a promise of reward.

Ovrek might have done the worst thing that any Valdari could do, but he was still Ovrek. He still commanded thousands of men and had the power to hurt Brynn.

Cenric bowed as he knew that was what his old mentor wanted. The king might be indebted to him now, but a king was still a king. None of his rewards, not even those that were earned, came without a debt attached.

Brynn had been a *gift* from another king who had also expected Cenric's loyalty. Now it seemed that keeping her was indebting him to Ovrek.

The king turned his attention to his warriors. "Bring me Egill's men. I want them all in this pit before the sun sets."

Cenric returned his attention to Brynn. "Can you walk?"

"Yes." She clung to his chest as if she was hiding from the Valdari men. Perhaps she was.

Cenric guided her back toward their tents. Brynn scooped Guin up in her arms, clutching the little dog to her breast.

Ovrek bellowed an order, and two more warriors broke off, falling in behind them. Brynn was still under guard, it seemed.

"What happened here?" Brynn asked, still gripping his arm. She watched as the king headed away from the thrall huts toward the beach, followed by most of his men.

"Egill and his son tried to kill Ovrek."

"Those two men thrown in the pit?"

"Yes," Cenric confirmed. "At least two of their men were a part of the plot, but I killed one and Ovrek finished off the other, so we won't be hearing their version of the story."

"You fought?" Brynn's grip on his arm tightened.

"It wasn't much of a fight," Cenric said. "I wasn't armed, but I managed."

Brynn took in a shuddering breath.

"I saved the king's life." He felt a little pride at that, but not as much as he should have. The words felt tainted, somehow. Boasting was as much a part of being a warrior as hunting or feasting, but for some reason, Cenric was not entirely sure he had done the right thing this time.

Brynn stroked his arm as if reassuring herself he was real. "Good."

An odd sensation of relief filled Cenric's chest at that. Surely if Brynn approved, he had done the right thing. He wondered if the plot against Ovrek had anything to do with the murder of his concubine. It did seem convenient.

Profaning of the Grandfather Yew seemed to be why Ovrek now faced betrayal. But it might be a mere foretaste of chaos and discord that would follow the tree's destruction.

Cenric glanced at the two Valdari warriors trailing them. He didn't know these two or if they spoke Hyldish. He didn't want to risk it until he had the opportunity to speak with Brynn in private.

"Lady! Lady Brynn!" Esa came running, breathless, with Kalen jogging after her.

"Esa!" Brynn reached for her handmaiden, grabbing the girl in a tight embrace, though she kept her hold on Cenric.

"Lady, I was so worried. We both were." She looked to Kalen. "Two of Lord Hróarr's thanes just returned, and we feared the worst, but before Lady Vana could send out a search for Lord Hróarr, we heard he'd come back."

Esa was confused and using Hyldish terms, but Cenric didn't bother to correct her.

"Where are Hróarr's men now?" Cenric asked.

"They were trying to find help, but with the attack on the king, they were having trouble," Esa panted. "I think Lady Vana went to the queen."

"Lord, the men told stories." Kalen's face was pale as he glanced at Brynn. "Stories of monsters and dead trees."

A cloying feeling of dread bubbled up in Cenric's gut. "Let's keep moving." He kept his arm around Brynn's waist. He could feel the impatience from the men following them.

"Yes." Brynn shivered.

Their odd little band continued toward the camp between *Wolf Star* and Hróarr's ship by the water.

Shouts rose from farther down the beach and Cenric was torn. A part of him ached to join in the hunt. There was violence to be done and something deep in his bones wanted to be a part of it. This was the way of things—insults must be avenged and blood repaid.

The men of Egill's household were all culpable. Their lord had turned traitor, so they would all pay the price. Their women that were here would be divided amongst Ovrek's men and those that had stayed at home had best flee before Ovrek's warriors reached them.

It was just the way of the world. The way of Valdar.

They reached the tent pitched against the side of Cenric's ship that Brynn and Cenric had shared before that disaster last night. Kalen and Esa had set it aright.

Ugba and Anders were the only men of Cenric's thanes present at their camp. They said the others had gone to join the hunt for Egill's men. That was just as well.

Ovrek's warriors waited at the edge of the camp, posted as guards, but giving them the illusion of privacy. Hopefully, this time these two knew better than to leave their posts because some boy told them to.

Brynn sat outside their tent, leaning against one of the front braces as Kalen stoked the fire.

"Lady." Esa knelt at Brynn's feet. "I found this in the queen's garden."

Cenric glanced over.

Brynn accepted a sprig of some plant with purple flower bulbs from the girl. "I thought so. Thank you, Esa."

The girl bowed and set to finding dry clothes for her mistress.

"What is that?" Cenric nodded to the plant.

Brynn surveyed the sprig with a kind of fatalistic acceptance. "Pennyroyal."

"What you think poisoned Gistrid?"

"Yes." Brynn let off a sigh that seemed to come from her very bones. "It seems we have much to discuss, my love. Where should we start?" Guin lay in her lap and Snapper curled against her side.

Cenric exhaled, lowering himself to the ground where she sat near the fire. He kept his voice low, careful so as not to let the warriors hear them. "The monsters you saw. What of them?"

Brynn shuddered. "A creature that was wolf, but not a wolf." She watched the flames as she spoke. "Too big and...wrong. Another creature in the form of a burned girl." Brynn squeezed Guin tighter against her.

A sinking feeling pooled in the pit of Cenric's stomach. "A girl, you said?"

"I was able to take her head off." Brynn's gaze grew vacant. "I'm not sure what happened. Another being seemed to crawl out of her corpse—a creature with scales and misshapen limbs. But she's dead. At least, she didn't chase us. The scaled creature vanished. Like smoke."

Cenric wasn't sure what to make of that.

"That one spoke to me."

"It did?" Cenric shifted at that. His talking dogs were one thing, but talking fiends were another. "What did it say?"

"It knew I was a sorceress. She said that the tree had been weakened, which had allowed her and the Wulfwir out."

"I think Ovrek cut down pieces of the Grandfather Yew to build part of his ship." Cenric felt sacrilegious just saying the words.

"I see." Brynn did not seem surprised. "Your cousin hinted at that, I think."

Cenric briefly wished that his uncle was still alive. Hróarr's father would have thrashed him within an inch of his life. Who else knew Ovrek had done this? It wasn't as if the king could have done it alone. A good number of men must have helped him.

Dagrún had also confirmed the tales right before the assassination attempt. It made sense why Egill and his son would become oath breakers. Even if they had not known the Father's Foes still lay beneath the roots of the great yew, they had known of Ovrek's desecration.

"The burned girl said other things, but most of it didn't make sense." Brynn's gaze turned vacant. "She said they were children of the moon, but I don't think she meant Eponine."

"What other moon is there?" Cenric was no Istovari, but he had seen the night sky often enough to know.

"Moreyne."

"The Dread Mother?" Cenric wanted to argue with that possibility, but under the circumstances, couldn't.

"She was Eponine's sister," Brynn explained. "There were once two moons."

Cenric knew Moreyne only as the cursed goddess, the one that fell from grace. She had been trapped in the Dread Marches by the other gods at the beginning of time. Her children were evil spirits, warped, bodiless creatures forged from shadows and spite. "Does that tell us how to kill them?"

Brynn considered it a moment. "No. I know as much as you."

"We don't need to know everything to kill them." Cenric tried to sound encouraging. "You killed one, which leaves only one, yes?"

"There was also a giant scaled creature, I think some manner of serpent." Brynn's voice shook, as if she hardly believed the words herself. "It was still trapped within the roots of the dead tree, but I don't know for how much longer."

"A serpent?" Cenric's dream from last night burned hot in his memory. "Did it have red eyes?"

Brynn cast him a curious look. "I didn't get a look at the serpent's eyes, but the other two did. Why?"

"I had a foretelling," Cenric admitted. "I thought it might be an ordinary nightmare, but..." He shook his head. "I saw a giant serpent making its way through Istra while the town burned."

"Oh." Brynn seemed to wither with dread.

"You were there."

Her gaze sharpened.

"I heard you call my name and then I woke up."

A serpent, a she-troll, and a wolf. What if the First of Fathers had not been as thorough in his defeat as the legend claimed?

"They had all been trapped under the tree, according to the girl." Brynn ran a hand over her face. "Are we supposed to deal with this on top of everything else?"

"You and Hróarr said they wouldn't cross the boundary stones," Cenric pointed out.

Brynn seemed to deflate, slumping beside the fire. "There were powerful spells cast over that circle. The Grandfather Yew's *ka* was feeding them."

"Spells?" Cenric had attended the sacrifices to the Grandfather Yew a few times in his life. It was a holy place, but of course, he hadn't been able to sense anything magical about it.

"Is it possible that the First of Fathers was a sorcerer?" Brynn asked.

"I suppose." Cenric saw no reason why not. Eponine's power passed along the mother's line, so even if Havnar had been an Istovari, it wouldn't have mattered to future generations unless his wives had been Istovari as well. Cenric had never heard anything about the First of Fathers being a sorcerer, but there weren't many stories about Havnar before he had settled Valdar.

"A master cast those spells, whoever they were. Or perhaps several masters working together." Brynn sighed. "But with the death of the tree, I suspect their spells won't last much longer."

Cenric cursed under his breath. This was getting better and better. "Could you recast the spells?"

Brynn considered it for a moment, then seemed to dismiss it. "Anything I did would be temporary. Without the yew tree to provide a continuous source of *ka,* the monsters would still break free."

"Do you think Ovrek killed the Grandfather Yew?" Cenric wasn't sure why, but he needed to hear her answer.

"Not intentionally," Brynn answered without much thought. "The burned child said she'd had to free herself and the Wulfwir. I think Ovrek just weakened it to the point the monsters were able to kill it."

That made things a little better, Cenric supposed, but only a little. "The monsters...you were able to kill one?"

Brynn closed her eyes for a moment. "I had to strike a killing blow. They heal from everything else."

Cenric ran a hand through his hair. Having an enemy that wouldn't bleed out sounded like a nearly impossible task. It was hard enough to behead fowl with only a single blow of a hatchet. Striking off a head with one attempt took skill, the right angle, and the right blade. Brynn's power was one of the few ways Cenric had seen it done to anything bigger than a goose.

"Does Ovrek still think I did it?" Brynn didn't have to elaborate on what she meant.

Cenric watched the fire. "Ovrek will likely offer me a boon for saving his life, but I don't know if it will be enough."

"To save me, you mean?" Brynn stroked one hand along Guin's fur.

Cenric kicked at the dirt.

"I know who did it," Brynn admitted. "I just can't prove it."

Cenric shot her a glance. "Who?"

Brynn's shoulders slumped as if in defeat. "Sifma. I don't think she meant to do it. I think she panicked after I healed Gistrid.

Maybe Gistrid lied and said I'd been able to save the baby. I don't know. But my guess is that Sifma poisoned her again immediately after."

"She was trying to cause a miscarriage in the concubine?" Cenric considered it barely a heartbeat. "That makes no sense. Even if it had been a son, Tolvir is older and Sifma's position is secure."

Brynn's brow pinched. "I don't think it was jealousy." She stroked Guin's fur.

"Then why?"

Brynn met his eyes then and bit her lip. "Tolvir…" she glanced to where the warriors waited, making sure they were out of hearing distance. "Tolvir cannot keep a secret. His mother must know it."

"What are you saying?"

Brynn leaned over and whispered in Cenric's ear, her voice soft, barely audible. And it was a good thing, too. "Gistrid slept with Tolvir."

Cenric straightened, shaking his head. "Why would you say such a thing?"

"He cannot keep a secret." Brynn's eyes turned sad. "He gave too much away when he attacked me."

Cenric struggled to believe it. Ovrek had been cuckholded by his own son?

"It was probably when the two of them were betrothed, before she entered an arrangement with his father."

That excused Tolvir somewhat, but it was still going to be an outrage if it came out. Cenric swore, hands clenching into fists. As much as he didn't want to believe it, this made perfect sense.

Brynn was a convenient outlet for Sifma's blame. She was a foreigner, from a country that the Valdari would be invading soon. Who better to take the fall to cover up the secret? Sifma must be desperate to keep this hidden, not only for the sake of her son, but her husband as well. This would destroy them both. It would be the death of Tolvir and the destruction of everything Ovrek had ever hoped to achieve in life.

Sifma's guilt was less important than what Ovrek would believe. He hated to be wrong and for him to be wrong not only about Brynn, but also about his own queen might be more than his pride could bear. Cenric had recently saved Ovrek's life, so that might earn him credibility, but perhaps not enough for that.

Gistrid's murder was an embarrassment to Ovrek. For people to learn the murderer was Ovrek's wife who had gone behind his back would be outright humiliation.

There was only one person who could convince Ovrek that Sifma had poisoned Gistrid, and she would not do it unless forced, which meant Cenric had to force her. The realization made him feel cruel and used at the same time.

He had always tried to be honorable, especially with people he respected, but the only option left was far from honorable. Ovrek and Sifma had forced him to this.

Cenric kicked dirt into the fire. He picked up a piece of kindling and snapped it in half before tossing it into the flames.

Brynn seemed to wilt before his frustration. "I'm sorry. I don't...I don't know how I survive this one."

Cenric faced her, resting his hands on her shoulders as he pulled her around to him. "I will deal with it."

Brynn's face was red and blotched. "I know you might not have a choice in what happens. I know you tried."

Cenric silenced her with a kiss. Her lips were cold, but she returned it, her mouth tentative against his, shy as she had been in the beginning. He rubbed her arms, wanting to stir life back into them. "I will be back soon. I'm leaving Kalen, Esa, and the other thanes with you this time."

Brynn bit her lower lip.

Cenric took the sprig of pennyroyal and stood, mind rattling in a hundred different directions. He singled out Kalen. "Stay with them."

The boy's brows pinched in determination as he straightened. He might not be able to prevent another attack from Tolvir, but he would at least be another witness.

He passed the same order to Ugba and Anders, commanding them to watch Brynn as well as the ship. The men both frowned, doubtless bursting with questions about the events since last night, but didn't argue.

Cenric glanced down at the pennyroyal in his fist. It was all they had.

He had faith in Brynn. If she believed Sifma had done it, that was good enough for him. There was a time when Sifma had been above reproach in his mind, but that could be said about a lot of people these days.

Cenric realized he was heading toward the great hall before his plan had fully formed. The beach was abuzz with bloodlust as men scoured the ships for signs of Egill's crew. From the sound of it, most the jarl's men had disappeared.

It wasn't surprising. They must have known that they would be marked for death in the event their jarl failed to kill Ovrek. How many of them had known of the plan?

Cenric found Vana on the way back from the great hall herself, probably having just seen to Hróarr. Her silver torque marked her out as a woman of means and she might be mistaken for a queen herself from the confident way she moved.

"Vana," Cenric called to her as soon as she was in earshot.

"Cenric." Vana's smile was guarded. "Hróarr tells me that he returned your wife."

Cenric wondered how much Hróarr had told her about that. Perhaps it was best not to continue this line of conversation. "I need your help."

Vana raised her chin. "Oh?"

Cenric focused on the great hall over her shoulder, not quite able to meet her eye. "Queen Sifma is in the weaving house. I need you to deliver a message for me."

Sifma, according to Ovrek, spent her days in the weaving house. Men were forbidden from entering, so Cenric would need a woman to at least deliver his message for him. It would have to be a woman who spoke Valdari, could be trusted, and had a rapport with Sifma. Cenric knew of only one.

Vana folded her arms beneath her shawl. "Hróarr says you punched him in the face."

"He deserved it." Cenric glanced to where the warriors were dividing up to search the different storehouses and workshops.

"We're worried about you, Cenric." Vana studied him carefully. "This situation is—"

Cenric bristled. "Will you help me or not?"

Vana exhaled. "Is this about the sorceress?"

"No." It was a half-truth, but if Vana wanted full truths, she should have left Brynn out of this. "This is about the plot against Ovrek."

"Why can't you tell Ovrek about it?"

Cenric fixed Vana in a hard stare. They had been close once. Close enough that Cenric had fancied himself in love with her. But Vana had chosen Hróarr over him, and that had stung at the time, but it was long past. All the same, Cenric hoped now that there were enough tender feelings left that she would be merciful. If nothing else, he hoped there was still some guilt. "If I ever meant anything to you at all, do this one thing for me."

He couldn't tell Vana the whole truth of what he and Brynn had learned. That would put her in danger and the more people who knew, the greater the likelihood it would come out. Even if the secret did come out, Cenric wanted that to happen when he, and more importantly Brynn, were far, far away.

Vana exhaled a long breath. "Fine."

Cenric canted his head in thanks. "This way."

Voices shouted and men ran all around them. It seemed that Ovrek was turning Istra inside out.

Cenric didn't notice any of the ships missing, at least not from what he could tell. The beach was packed. That must mean the men had gone inland, but that seemed odd. The only thing there were trees and rocks and difficult mountain passes. There was a reason Valdari did nearly all their traveling by sea.

Vana walked with Cenric up to the weaving house. The doors were open to let in light and inside, Cenric could see perhaps a hundred women hard at work carding wool, spinning thread, and weaving what would become the great sails.

Cenric stopped well outside the boundary line. He couldn't see Sifma, but she should be there.

"What is the message you have for the queen?"

Cenric handed Vana the sprig of pennyroyal. "Give her this and tell her I am waiting outside."

Vana shot Cenric a sharp look. "What does it mean?"

"The less you know, the better." Cenric was only involving her in this because he had no other way to get the message to Sifma. "But be discreet. I doubt she will want people to know."

Vana opened her mouth, and he feared she would argue or demand more answers, but then she simply frowned. "Very well." She marched up the steps, into the weaving house.

Cenric turned away and rounded the corner of the building, out of sight of the main street. This didn't seem like the sort of thing to be done in daylight. Cenric might be going about this all wrong.

Ovrek would never believe him, but he would believe his dear queen if she confessed—at least, Cenric hoped he would. He didn't have any better ideas, nor did he imagine there was much time to think of a better idea.

Cenric paced, waiting for the queen. He didn't have to wait long.

It was barely a few moments before he spotted Sifma's red dress and glinting temple rings. She appeared with several maids in tow. Vana trailed after her, looking bewildered. Apparently, Sifma's reaction had been exceptional.

Sifma shooed her servants and Vana back before storming the last few steps to Cenric. "What is the meaning of this?" Sifma demanded, coming to a stop in front of him. She was a small woman in stature, but she glared fearlessly.

Cenric might be a warrior and foreign alderman, but Sifma had known him when he was a stripling youth scarfing down bread at her table. More than that, she was the wife of the most feared man on these islands. Cenric bowed to her. "Queen Sifma. You honor me."

"What do you want, boy?" The queen glanced over her shoulder to where Vana and her maids waited, but out of earshot. Normally, she would have kept them close, but it seemed she didn't want additional listeners for this audience. She held up the sprig of pennyroyal in front of her so that only Cenric could see. "What is the meaning of this?"

Cenric remained silent for a long moment, not sure what to say. He was new to blackmail and found he did not enjoy it. "Tell Ovrek the truth—that you killed Gistrid."

Sifma's spine stiffened. "You dare to accuse me?"

"If you will not tell Ovrek," Cenric added, "I will."

"He would never believe you." Despite her words, Sifma's eyes went wide.

This was not going well. Cenric wasn't happy about the concubine's death, but he had never even met the girl. Now these people were determined to blame his wife, and he was not going to allow it.

"Tell Ovrek that you did it or I will tell him why." Cenric spoke the words flatly, before he had even fully considered their implications.

Sifma's nostrils flared, her spine stiffening even more. "Ovrek would never believe you," she repeated. "Such an accusation—"

"No," Cenric agreed. "No, Ovrek wouldn't believe me." He folded his arms across his chest, thinking through his next words. This was a risk, but he was backed in a corner. Brynn was backed in a corner. "If I tell Ovrek the truth, he might well kill me and my wife, too."

Those words didn't seem to soothe Sifma. She cocked her head, eyes narrowed.

"But he will remember what I said." Cenric leaned down, fixing the queen in a hard look. "Perhaps nothing will come of it, but you know your son. Tolvir is reckless and lacks all discretion."

At the mention of the boy, Sifma's face showed fear for the first time. Perhaps she had hoped that Cenric didn't know the whole truth, but he'd just let her know he did.

"Ovrek will remember it and Tolvir will reveal himself at some point. Perhaps not this summer, this winter, or next spring, but eventually, Tolvir will open his mouth and confirm what I say to Ovrek and then..." Cenric let that sentence hang.

Sifma seemed to swell with indignation. "Ovrek found you when you were nothing," she spat. "Just a starveling without an eating knife to your name."

Cenric remained steady. If Sifma called his bluff, he wasn't sure if he would follow through with it or not, but if this was going to work, she needed to believe he would.

"This would destroy Ovrek." Sifma leaned in, her voice turning sharp. "His life, his legacy."

"Yes." Cenric felt no joy at the word.

"You don't want that," Sifma whispered. "I can see you don't want that."

Cenric looked away.

"Ovrek will not hold this against you. I heard of your bravery today." Sifma rested a hand on his forearm. "My daughter is newly widowed."

Cenric did not like where this was going.

Sifma squeezed his arm. "Let this play out."

Let Brynn take the blame, that was what Sifma was asking him to do.

"Please," Sifma whispered as her voice turned pleading. "You will be Ovrek's son, just as you always wanted." The queen bowed her head with something like shame. "He once told me he wished you were his son instead of Tolvir."

Cenric felt a stab of guilt tempered with resentment at that. He had adored Ovrek, idolized the man, but after how Ovrek had treated Brynn, it was too little too late.

If he had truly been so dear to Ovrek, why had his old mentor ignored him for years until the day he wanted something?

"She is one Hyldish woman," Sifma pressed. "What is she next to your family? Your friends?"

"That Hyldish woman is my wife," Cenric growled back. "And I would sacrifice many things for Ovrek, but she is not one."

Sifma's mouth pressed into a hard line at that. "Lovesick children will be the death of me." She snatched her hand away from him.

"Tell Ovrek," Cenric repeated. "I doubt your punishment will be too severe."

Sifma made a vague punching motion with one hand. "Ovrek must be able to trust me."

"You should have thought of that before you killed his concubine."

As if hearing the words spelled out had unleashed something, Sifma's eyes flashed. "I am trying to help him!" She shot a glance to her maids, still watching from paces away "If word of this spreads, no one will ever respect Ovrek again."

"You're right," Cenric agreed. "So, I suggest you tell him half the truth before I tell him the whole truth."

Sifma exploded. "None of this would have happened if not for your meddling Hyldish bitch!"

Cenric had no response for that. Unlike with Hróarr, he couldn't punch a queen in the face.

"Without her, the dose would have worked the first time, and I wouldn't have..." Sifma swayed from side to side, like a trapped animal without the room to pace. "The sorceress deserves to die."

Cenric forced himself to remain calm, to remain unmoving.

Sifma studied him, searching for a sign her words had any

effect.

"Sunrise, Queen Sifma. Tell Ovrek before tomorrow's sunrise, or I will."

"You wouldn't. You don't want to hurt Ovrek. I know you, boy." Sifma's eyes narrowed as if searching for proof her words were true.

Cenric glanced up to the sky, judging the horizon. "I recommend you act quickly."

"Cenric!" Sifma shouted after him, but he was already walking away.

Frustration grated inside him as he walked back toward the camp where Brynn waited. Her life was at stake. She would be far better suited to this than he was, but she didn't speak the language and all they had was him.

Cenric kept his outward reactions restrained. Sifma might call his bluff, she might not. Either way, he was playing a dangerous game. Would threatening the Valdari queen work? Only time would tell.

At his side, Snapper woofed happily, tail wagging.

15

Brynn

In the lair of the monsters, Brynn had been terrified. Somehow, sitting outside the tent she shared with Cenric, she did not feel much better. The two guards Ovrek had assigned to her loomed not far away.

Esa had found her dry clothes and a bread cake with sheep's cheese. Guin hopped around the ground, flipping a scrap of rag into the air and pouncing on it as it came down.

Kalen tended to the fire, quiet and solemn as he did. The boy kept glancing up the beach, probably watching for Cenric.

Ugba and Anders checked the same parts of the ship again. They paced back and forth, trying not to be obvious about staring at Ovrek's two Valdari. The other thanes were still helping hunt down Egill's men.

Cenric was going to have to make hard choices. He wouldn't want to make them, but he would have to. Brynn had been accused of murder by the most powerful woman in these islands. It was the word of a foreigner against the word of a beloved queen.

It was rational, and some would say wise, for Cenric to let Brynn take the blame. They'd probably kill her, but Cenric might be able to spare his own standing with the Valdari. It was the best option to save him and his people.

Brynn tried not to cry. Hróarr had turned on her, despite her saving his life. Vana thought she was guilty and so did all the other people who might have been her friends.

Brynn was sinking into this web of mistrust, suspicion, and blame. What a fool she had been. What a wretched fool.

It was late and even the summer sun began to dip toward the horizon. So much and so little had changed in the past day. Brynn wrapped her shawl tighter around her. Why did everything always have to go wrong?

Then there were the monsters in the forest. They would be free soon, but she didn't know how soon.

More than an hour after Cenric left, Brynn sensed a man approaching their fire with a dog-sized shape at his side.

Snapper leapt into the middle of their campsite first, pouncing on Guin. He grabbed one end of the rag she'd been playing with and the two of them wrestled for it. Guin growled, digging in her little paws and fighting to take it back.

Cenric stepped into view a few moments later, striding past the Valdari guards without a word. He settled down beside her, facing the fire. One hand rested on her lower back, but he still didn't speak.

Brynn watched him, clenching her hands into her shawl. It was going to be bad news, she was sure of it.

"Ovrek wants you to join us in the hall tonight."

That was not the news Brynn had been expecting. "The men Ovrek sent to the Grandfather Yew?"

Cenric shook his head. "I asked around on my way back. They have not returned, but everyone is more concerned with Egill.

Ovrek wants to search for them in the morning."

Brynn bit her lip, feeling sick. She suspected what had happened and from the look on his face, Cenric did, too. "Ovrek is doing nothing?"

"I don't know what he can do," Cenric admitted. "The Grandfather Yew was planted to protect Valdar from evil. It's older than living memory. We can't simply replace it."

Brynn forced herself to remain calm. "He needs to do something. The monsters are breaking free."

"He's distracted by the murder attempt. Egill and his son were caught, but at least thirty of their men are missing." Cenric exhaled a long breath, looking to Kalen.

"All is quiet, lord," the boy said.

Cenric smeared a hand over his face, shoulders slumping on a slow exhale. "I have done what I could for the other situation. At least what I could think of."

Brynn reached for his hand. He lifted her hand to his mouth, kissing the backs of her knuckles. Warmth radiated up her arm from everywhere his mouth touched.

He folded her hand in both of his and laid it in his lap. They sat like that, silent with Kalen tending the fire and Esa quietly moving about the tent and the campsite. There was so much to say and yet nothing seemed quite adequate.

After a time, Cenric stroked his thumb across the backs of her knuckles. "You're worth it, Brynn."

"What do you mean?"

"Whatever happens next. Whatever this costs..." Cenric turned her hand over, fingers tracing the lines of her palm. "I won't trade you." He met her eyes. "Not for all the silver rings in Kelethi."

A lump formed in Brynn's throat. He was saying he'd fight a losing battle with his old mentor rather than turn her over. "Your people."

"You are first among my people," Cenric grated. "Don't try to talk me out of this, Brynn."

Brynn inhaled a shuddering breath.

Cenric leaned over, brushing his lips against hers. It was a soft kiss, gentle. A promise.

Brynn closed her eyes as he rested his forehead against hers. She tried to soak in the comfort of his presence.

She had this moment. She had these past few months. No matter what came next, what monsters broke free of the forest, or what Ovrek and his people tried to do, at least she had been with a man she loved. No one could take that away from her.

Cenric wrapped an arm around her and pulled her against his chest. Brynn curled against his side, her heart aching.

Why did war always have to come? Why couldn't she just be happy for once?

Snapper flopped onto his side, wrestling with Guin over the rag. Growling with her tail stiff, Guin jumped on him, giving her best fight.

Brynn wondered if she would ever see Ombra again. Would she ever return to that wild land with its mountains, ancient trees, and surging rivers? Or would she die here on this strange island? Would Ovrek at least let Cenric bury her in Ombra? She would want that, she thought. She'd want to be buried near Cenric.

Cenric brushed back her hair, tucking the loose strands behind her ear. Her husband might be a fierce warrior, but he was a tender lover. His gentleness made her heart melt every time he touched her. She'd never known a man could be this loving.

They stayed like that, Kalen and Esa remaining silent and out of the way. The poor youngsters probably didn't know what to do any more than she and Cenric did.

Brynn desperately tried to *feel* as much of Cenric as she could. There was nothing she wanted more than to bathe in the warmth of his arms forever.

Someone approached. Valdari voices chattered near the edge of camp.

"Is that Hróarr?" Brynn asked, lifting her head.

"No." Cenric rose as a figure clad in red swaggered into the fire's glow.

Tullia looked magnificent, as she always did. She had a new set of temple rings, and the pelt of a red fox draped over her shoulders as a stole. Her eunuchs flanked her, as did several maids, including Lena.

Lena trembled in the back, head down and shaking.

"Lady Tullia." Cenric inclined his head. "I was not expecting you."

"We have some things to discuss." Tullia glanced around the campsite. "Lady Brynn! So glad you have returned to us. Did you find your exploration of our island to be pleasant?"

Brynn was not sure if that was meant as a joke.

"Come. Walk with me, both of you."

Cenric cast a look to Brynn, almost as if he was asking permission.

Brynn didn't know any more than he did. Rising, Brynn took his hand. They weren't about to defy Ovrek's daughter. "Wait here," she instructed Esa and Kalen.

Cenric repeated the order to his thanes, not taking his eyes off Tullia. However Cenric felt about the Valdari king's daughter, he did not trust her right now.

The two Valdari guards assigned to Brynn trailed after them, but Tullia continued speaking in Hyldish. It seemed Tullia was not concerned about Lena overhearing, but then she didn't seem to be threatened by thralls in general.

Tullia strode a short distance down the beach, Brynn and Cenric following. It was just close enough to the water that the murmur of the waves would muffle their voices.

Snapper and Guin trotted along after them, sniffing at the ground, running ahead and racing back. The dogs seemed perfectly happy.

Turning on her heel, Tullia faced them both. "Quite a mess, isn't it?"

Brynn thought that was a masterpiece of understatement.

"My father realized he is not as popular as he thinks, and my mother is being blackmailed. My brother caused trouble then made it worse, as usual." Tullia laughed, shaking her head. "What a day it has been."

Cenric shifted closer to Brynn.

"You upset my mother, Cenric," Tullia tsked. "She's most distraught at the moment."

Brynn stole a glance to her husband. Was that where he had gone? To see the queen?

Cenric's entire bearing had gone hard. His jaw locked as he squared his stance, ready for a fight.

"Nothing quite upsets her like threats to her darling boy." Tullia exhaled a long breath. "I should have known better than to tell her about his latest folly."

Brynn held onto Cenric. There had to be a point to this.

"I'm curious." Tullia cocked her head to the side. "Why didn't you accuse me of poisoning the bitch?"

Brynn felt as if the wrong answer might be fatal, but she dared speak. "Whoever poisoned Gistrid seemed to be guessing. They underestimated the plant both times."

"And?"

"You would have gotten it right the first time." It had been a gamble, but it seemed Brynn had been right.

Tullia took in those words for a moment and then she smiled. "I like you, sorceress."

"What is the point of this?" Cenric demanded.

"I'm here to offer you both a bargain." Tullia adjusted her sleeves as if bored. "One that gives all three of us what we want."

Brynn did not like the sound of that. From the way Cenric's arm pulled her closer against him, neither did he.

"Kill my father." Tullia's smile never wavered. "I don't care how. I don't care which of you does it but stop the old man's heart before he brings out the wine at the feast tonight."

Brynn didn't believe what she had heard for a moment. "What?"

"You don't mean that." Cenric shook his head. "You love your father."

"I do." Tullia sounded wholeheartedly sincere. "There is no one in the world I esteem as highly as him." For barely a moment, a shadow passed over her face, then it was gone. "But I am not as forgiving as my mother is."

"I saved your father's life today," Cenric said, voice rising. "He trusts me."

"Which gives you an advantage. He'll never see it coming," Tullia purred. "Or you." She pointed at Brynn. "You can kill without lifting a finger, I've heard."

This could be a test of loyalty sent by Ovrek to see if they would betray him. Or this might be a genuine offer and their only chance at escape. Brynn could almost feel the same thoughts radiating from her husband.

"Think on it." Tullia cocked her head to one side. "I am a good friend to have. When I rule Valdar, you will be glad we are friends."

Tullia wanted to rule? So, it wasn't just piety that had turned her against her father. Brynn had suspected as much. Tullia was more experienced and far more competent than her brother. Assuming the Valdari decided to continue having monarchs after Ovrek, Tullia would be a strong contender. Tullia must know this and clearly possessed the ambition to pursue it.

"Ovrek has been good to me," Cenric countered. "I would have nothing without him."

Tullia seemed to find that funny. "Neither would I," she snorted. "But everything has its time. Even the Grandfather Yew."

"You knew?" Brynn blinked in realization. "You knew it had died?"

"Yes," Tullia shot back, bitterness stinging in the words. "He cut down three of the Grandfather Yew's offshoots late last summer. All for that ghastly ship he named after my mother."

"Do you know about the monsters?" Brynn asked, a thought occurring to her.

Tullia locked her gaze on Brynn. "What monsters?"

How to tell this woman that her father's actions were about to unleash the creatures of nightmares on Istra? On the whole island? The men sent to confirm Brynn and Hróarr's report had still not returned.

"Ovrek is my friend." As soon as the words were out, Cenric turned to Brynn.

Squeezing his hand, Brynn offered reassurance.

Brynn did not see Ovrek as a good man. He was an inseparable mix of generosity and greed, kindness and cruelty, vices and virtues balanced on a knife's edge. From what Brynn had seen, Tullia was almost a mirrored reflection of him—neither good nor bad, complicated and simple all at once.

Tullia had claimed that she didn't want Ovrek to invade Hylden, but what if she chose to lead an invasion herself? For that matter, what was to say that she would be the one to take control of Valdar, not one of the many jarls who had been Ovrek's rivals?

"Ovrek has always dealt fairly with me," Cenric continued. "I will not betray him."

"Always?" Tullia's brows rose at that. "My father has been desperately trying to find a woman with king's blood for my little brother. Did you know that the night after you arrived, he discussed taking your wife for Tolvir?"

Brynn's skin crawled at that, like pond scum had been poured down her back.

"Ovrek wouldn't," Cenric growled. "I'd kill him."

"Now you're getting it." Tullia winked at him.

Cenric blanched.

"My father didn't intend to rob you outright, just a forced trade. He meant to compensate you with me, I believe." Tullia's tone turned hard, bitterness creeping in at the edges of her words.

Cenric went very still. Something in Tullia's allegations must have rung true.

Tullia made a dismissive gesture. "My mother was able to talk him out of it, but if he gets the idea into his head again, who knows?"

Brynn gripped Cenric's arm to stop him from doing anything rash. They had only Tullia's word for this. While they might not be able to trust Ovrek fully, this woman was trying to get them to murder her father.

"Before the wine," Tullia repeated, stepping back.

"And if we don't?" Cenric pressed.

Tullia shrugged. "Then take your chances with my father."

"You're not going to threaten us with retribution?" Cenric pressed.

"Why ever would I do that?" Tullia gazed across the water. "My father will never believe it if you tell him of this conversation. And I already have plans to deal with him if you do not." Tullia turned once again to the pair of them. "But I like you, both of you. It's maudlin, I know, but you seem to be in love." Her gaze drifted down to their clasped hands before returning to their faces. "I'm risking much by offering this, but my offer stands."

Brynn didn't know what to say. Cenric remained silent at her side.

"Very well. Think on it. If you plan to throw yourselves on my father's mercy, keep in mind he has very little." Tullia smiled warmly, gesturing for her servants to follow her. She swaggered away, not looking back.

That left Brynn and Cenric alone on the beach with their dogs and the Valdari guards a few steps off, ignorant of what had just transpired.

Cenric stared ahead for a long moment. "Ovrek wouldn't betray me like that," he insisted, voice hard. "She has to be lying."

Brynn squeezed his hand back, neither arguing nor agreeing. "She must have been the one who put Egill and his son up to their attempt."

Cenric's jaw worked as he stared across the water. He cursed, letting off several oaths in both Valdari and Hyldish. "I'm not a traitor." Cenric faced Brynn. "I won't do it. Not...not like this."

"I know." Brynn grasped his other hand. "I don't think we should."

Cenric's relief was almost palpable. "You don't?"

Betrayal was a dangerous line to cross. Even Brynn's mother had wielded that weapon sparingly. "I don't know what Tullia plans, but I don't think we can trust her any more than Ovrek."

Cenric cursed again. "Things were never this complicated during the war."

Brynn offered a wan smile. "Were they less complicated or were you too far beneath politics at the time?"

Cenric cast Brynn a dour look. "You make too much sense sometimes."

Brynn bowed her head, looking to their joined hands. "We can't run. It would only speed your foretelling of Ovrek taking Ombra."

Cenric grumbled incoherently. "He'd never believe me if I said Tullia wanted him dead, but I might be able to warn him there's another attempt coming."

"You might." Brynn didn't really believe it.

"This whole thing is wretched."

"We need to get ready for the feast," Brynn said quietly.

"I suppose." Cenric made no move to leave their spot on the beach. "I don't know what to do. It seems like every choice is the wrong one."

"I feel the same," Brynn admitted.

Cenric pulled her into his arms, tucking her under his chin for just a moment. He squeezed her tight and Brynn pressed her ear to his chest, listening to the comforting thrum of his pulse. They stayed like that for a long space of heartbeats, not moving.

Finally, they broke apart, heading back to their ship and tents. Esa helped Brynn change into a new shift and dress. She pinned

Brynn's hair back under the blue silk veil Sifma had given her and helped Brynn adjust her necklace of carnelian beads. Cenric wanted her to wear the silver cuff he'd received from Ovrek, so she did.

Kalen helped Cenric into his feasting attire with the embroidered tunic Brynn had sewn for him and his rabbit-lined mantle secured with his wolf's head brooch.

Brynn decided to leave Guin with Esa in their tent. Kalen was to stay and guard Esa, as always. Their thanes who had returned from hunting down traitors with Ovrek's men also remained behind.

Brynn stepped outside with Cenric, and her two Valdari guards followed. They said something to Cenric and he answered in clipped Valdari.

Cenric took her hand, tugging her against his side protectively. Her husband was tense, uneasy. She supposed she was, too. She felt that way she had every morning for years after her father had died—taut as a bowstring and expecting danger at every sound.

They reached Ovrek's hall, the towering structure looming over them like a hungry beast. By the fading light of the evening, the doors seemed to be its maw, eager to swallow them all up.

They entered inside with the crowd and their two guards drifted off, disappearing into the throng. It seemed the men did not have orders to continue watching Brynn.

The scene was much as it had been a few nights ago. Brynn recognized several faces, and most people occupied the same benches.

Yet a pall seemed to hang over the room. The death of Gistrid and the attempt on Ovrek's life had left a shadow over them. It was a bad sign. Brynn wasn't sure if news of the Grandfather Yew's destruction had spread yet, but it would soon if it hadn't already.

Ovrek shouted at the sight of Cenric, calling out in Valdari. The king greeted her husband with his usual effusiveness, clapping Cenric on the back and presenting him to several jarls he had just been speaking with.

Cenric let go of her hand to give his full attention to the king, playing the part they both knew he had to. He pulled Ovrek in, speaking quickly and softly.

Ovrek yanked away, shaking his head.

Cenric tried again, but Ovrek waved a hand, dismissing him.

The king greeted Brynn next, though it was in Valdari this time.

Brynn's chest twisted a little at that. It meant Ovrek was more interested in putting on a show for the onlookers. It was a bad sign.

"I tried," Cenric grated. "I tried to warn him there will be another attempt tonight."

Brynn searched her husband's face, though she could already see the answer there.

Cenric's jaw flickered with frustration. "He wants his enemies to try."

Pride. Such pride. It seemed that was the one constant that could be depended upon when it came to kings.

The wine would likely not be served until after a few rounds of ale. What *other means* did Tullia have prepared if Brynn and Cenric declined her offer, as they intended to?

Heart in her throat, Brynn tried to remain composed. She was sure people stared, but the chatter of Valdari continued around her unabated. Brynn's ears itched. She ached to understand, ached to know what gossip flitted on the air around her. She should have asked Cenric to teach her the language sooner.

Cenric was seated at Ovrek's right hand in the place of honor, Brynn on her husband's other side. Ovrek presented Cenric to those gathered around, speaking in long, rhythmic phrases. It sounded like verse. If she had to guess, he was praising Cenric's bravery today.

Cenric seemed to accept the praise admirably, responding with thanks. His eyes were on the crowd, yet one hand gripped Brynn's under the table. He was not letting her go, not even when she was mere inches away.

Brynn understood nothing, though she caught a few names—Egill, Hróarr, and a few other jarls, though she had forgotten the faces that went with some of the names.

Sifma occupied her usual place at the high table. The queen stared straight ahead, barely acknowledging when the rest of the room erupted in cheers or raised their cups in salute.

The cups were still filled with ale—not wine. This far north, it was a delicacy to be consumed only with the greatest fanfare.

Brynn's chest tightened with sick anticipation. Tullia was clever and cunning. She left nothing to chance and if she wanted her father dead, she would find a way to do it.

Snapper flopped against her legs under the table, then rose and circled her, sniffing for crumbs and scraps. He seemed to be enjoying himself, for whatever it was worth.

Hróarr had been seated on Brynn's other side, and it seemed almost spiteful to both of them. He did not acknowledge her, but he had a bruise on his jaw that she suspected had come from her husband. Vana occupied his far side, also not acknowledging Brynn.

Brynn wasn't sure why that hurt. It wasn't as if she had ever been particularly friendly with either of them, or as if rejection was anything new for her. She'd declined two invitations from Vana over the past days, and the beautiful woman probably felt slighted—rightfully so.

After a few moments, Vana rose and slipped behind the tables. She leaned over, speaking to the queen. Sifma clasped Vana's hands, greeting her as one would a daughter. It seemed the queen and Hróarr's concubine were as close as Brynn had heard.

Speaking of Sifma's daughter, Brynn spotted a figure in red across the crowd. Even if she didn't have her spotless clothes and eunuchs at her back, Tullia was the kind of woman who would stand out anywhere. Brynn watched as people nearby bent toward her, bowing and eager to pay her their respects.

Brynn had to search for several moments, but she spotted

Tolvir as well, standing to one side with several other young men. He kept mostly to his peers and out of the way, not mingling with the crowd as Tullia did. He seemed in many ways to still think like a child. Brynn could see he still had blisters and bruises from their encounter. He pointedly did not look in her direction.

The evening droned on.

Meat was brought in earthenware bowls and shared throughout the hall. Bread cakes soaked with butter and herbs, cheese, and every kind of meat one could ask for. Pigs, calf, rabbit, venison, fowl, and several kinds of fish. Ovrek fed his people well, that was true.

Brynn was unable to eat, anxiety twisting her stomach into a hard knot.

When several barrels were rolled in to cheers, Tullia's gaze singled out Brynn. As the barrels were set on the tables and a rich burgundy poured out, that was it.

Tullia cast a conspiratorial glance at Brynn, turning back to her conversation with what appeared to be a rich man and his companion. She laughed and conversed as easily with her father's warriors as she had with that child in the bazaar.

Wine was sloshed into cups and passed around the hall. Thralls and young children darted this way and that trying to keep every cup full and every hand filled with food.

How much longer did this night have to go on? Brynn hated the suspense. She had a feeling she was being toyed with, though she doubted she was so important.

Ovrek raised his voice, calling for silence. The crowd of the hall quieted down, turning to listen as the king's booming voice echoed over their heads. Brynn didn't understand the words, but she had heard enough of these kinds of speeches to guess what was being said. No doubt thanks for loyalty, promises of continued rewards, and boasts of Ovrek's own exploits.

"Are you alright?" Cenric touched her knee under the table.

"Just tired," Brynn answered, casting him a faint smile.

Cenric kissed her temple, rubbing her back.

"Where is Tullia?" Brynn straightened. The woman had disappeared along with her two eunuchs. One moment she had been there and now she was gone.

Cenric went rigid at her side. Immediately, he took stock of Ovrek, but the king stood beside him, continuing his speech.

The doors of the hall had been open earlier, but were now shut. Reaching out with her power, Brynn felt figures at the far end, dozens and dozens of bodies swarming the other side of the entrance. "No."

"Brynn?" Cenric straightened, picking up on her distress.

"We have to get out!" Brynn sprang to her feet, drawing power to herself in a rush.

The moment she did, every eye in the hall went to her.

Ovrek fell silent, glaring at Brynn.

With an icy wash of realization, Brynn saw that she was the center of the entire hall's attention.

"In my country," Ovrek growled, slipping into Hyldish, "one does not speak when a king—"

Cenric rose between her and his old mentor. He faced Ovrek and said something loud in Valdari.

Ovrek was taller and loomed over Cenric. The king rumbled something low, fists clenching as he visibly fought to rein in his temper.

Cenric was unfazed, shouting something back.

At the far end of the hall, two men who appeared to be warriors reached the doors. They pushed, jostled, then one of them slammed into the wood.

There was a moment of stunned silence where the only noise in the room was the sound of the two men trying in vain to open the doors. Brynn saw her own dawning horror wash over every other face in the room.

The doors did not budge. One of the warriors shouted over his shoulder and Brynn didn't need a translator to understand. They were locked inside.

Cenric's hand went to his hip, only to grasp air as he remembered there were no weapons inside the hall. Around the room, other men did much the same.

"There are people outside the hall." Brynn spoke to Cenric, but loud enough that Ovrek and Hróarr could listen if they wanted to. "I think Tullia sent them."

Cenric caught her hand, his face grim.

"Tullia?" That was Hróarr. "It can't be."

"She asked Cenric and I to kill Ovrek before the wine was served," Brynn said.

"You dare accuse my daughter?" Ovrek demanded. "She would never do this."

Brynn felt oddly detached in that moment, like she was seeing this whole thing unfold from outside her body. She looked square into the king's face. "Then who did?"

Ovrek roared a sound like a bear roused from a good winter's rest. He shouted something to his men around the room. Men leapt up to test the two sets of smaller doors only to find them locked, too. Several men tried to smash through the doors and the wood did splinter, giving way to reveal something solid on the other side.

Not just locked but barricaded. Tullia had been thorough. Just as Brynn had predicted, when she wanted someone dead, she got it right the first time.

It started with the stench of burning pitch.

Brynn met Cenric's eyes. She had never seen this happen before, but she knew exactly what this was and from the curses of rage and cries of fear around the room, so did everyone else.

The heat in the room intensified. Kindling had been set outside the doors and a dark haze already filtered through the rafters.

In moments, this place would be filled with smoke and flames would be licking inside. They would all be choking to death long before the fire reached them.

Hall burning was a horrifically effective means of murder.

Ovrek sprang over the table, shouting orders. He seemed to be in denial of the situation. When he realized the doors were secured and his magnificent hall was filling with smoke, he let off a great bellow of rage, hands out like claws. It was as if he refused to believe that this was how it ended, that this was how he would die.

Cenric dragged Brynn down, tugging her low to avoid the smoke for as long as they could. "I love you," he said the words fiercely, like they were an act of defiance. "I am sorry I brought you here to die with me."

"Better to die with you than live without you." Brynn pulled his hands from her face. "But don't count us as dead yet, my love."

Brynn had been fearing the worst, but now the worst had happened. That realization brought with it a strange sense of relief. Now she didn't have to wait any longer, she could act.

Around them, voices chattered with outrage and frustration. Some people howled with despair. Snapper whined and barked, pacing around Brynn and Cenric in a tight circle.

Cenric's whole world seemed to have narrowed to her. "They have blocked the doors. They will be guarding the outside. Even if we can break through, we are unarmed."

"A sorceress is never unarmed." Her eyes stung from the smoke. "But if we die, we die fighting."

Cenric actually smiled at that, excitement replacing the despair of mere moments ago. "What's your plan?"

Brynn didn't have time to explain to him, much less everyone else. "This way." Leading him, she half-crawled toward the back corner behind Ovrek's seat. It was solid wood layered and sealed with mud between the beams. To bare hands, it was impenetrable, but Brynn sensed that their attackers were all gathered at the doors, stoking the fires as they watched the exits.

That made sense, but Ovrek's hall was new. The logs had been cured, but they had been alive not so long ago. Wood was not as workable as leather or sinew, but it kept its memory of life long after leather had rotted away.

"Hróarr!" Cenric yelled, waving his cousin over.

The large Valdari warrior spotted them through the smoke and came to crouch beside them, dragging Vana after him. "Cenric," his expression was grim, "I'm sorry I called your wife a bitch." Hróarr did not apologize directly to Brynn, nor did he apologize for pushing her into the thrall pit, but he had spoken in Hyldish, which was close enough.

"Don't let it happen again," Cenric clipped back.

Kneeling before the wall, Brynn pulled power into herself and inhaled as deep a breath as she could without choking. She released and her spells sliced through the wood. Her power did not so much cut as melt, pushing the log into separate pieces. She sliced down one side, cutting the logs into sections.

Sparks had begun to shower over the doors and screams filled the room until it seemed it would burst. Everything at Brynn's back was darkness, hopelessness, and confusion. They had very little time.

Brynn finished cutting a line down the wall, slicing from about shoulder to knee height. Sweat beaded her forehead, and she coughed.

Snapper whined at Cenric's feet. The smoke was getting to him, too.

Brynn took two steps further down the wall and used her spells to part the logs there, too. The wood was more stubborn on this side, better cured for some reason.

Cenric hovered at her back, sticking close.

"What are you doing?" Hróarr choked. As the tallest of their group, even crouching down, he was the worst off.

Brynn finally finished. Her work was sloppy and haphazard, but this wasn't about looks. Coughing, she shoved at the logs. She had cut the wood, but the planks were still held in place by the daub packed between them.

"Cenric," Brynn wheezed.

Smoke had filled the hall. Brynn could barely see anything, but she could sense the bodies around them, sinking toward the ground either to escape the smoke or because they had succumbed to it.

Brynn felt Cenric's body shift beside her and he slammed his shoulder into the wood. It budged, just a bit.

"Hróarr!" Cenric reached back, grabbing his cousin.

Hróarr must have realized what they were doing. The large Valdari man added his force beside Cenric. They slammed into the weakened wall once, twice.

A crack rang out and both men spilled out, tripping as they tumbled into the clean air of the night.

Snapper leapt out past them, coughing and sneezing.

Brynn couldn't see, but she caught Vana's arm and dragged her toward the opening.

Hróarr and Cenric scrambled free, reaching back for them. Brynn wasn't sure who grabbed her and who grabbed Vana as the four of them tumbled out into the night.

Brynn inhaled the fresh air, the cold breeze rushing into her lungs like the sweetest relief. Coughing, Brynn shoved herself up onto her hands and knees. "Get the others out," she choked. "I'll see what I can do about Tullia."

"You're unarmed," Hróarr growled, sounding annoyed.

Brynn didn't have time to argue with him as she stumbled to her feet. They needed to get the other people inside the hall out of the hall, but the moment they started shouting, they would give themselves away.

It was pointless to break out of the hall only to be slaughtered the moment they did. The people inside were weakened and weaponless.

Someone would have to draw their enemies off or at least hold them off until the survivors were away.

"Brynn!" Cenric scrambled after her.

"Get the others out," Brynn wheezed, fighting to keep her

choking down. "I'll deal with Tullia's men." Or at least she would try.

Cenric turned back to Hróarr, but the other man was already dragging a soot-stained woman and choking man out of the hole Brynn had made. The large Valdari dragged them to the side as he reached back for another person. It seemed at least some people had seen the hole Brynn had made and followed.

"With you." Cenric spoke the words like an oath.

The dear fool was weaponless, but Brynn knew there would be no arguing. She turned and stumbled in the direction of their enemies.

Cenric followed close on her heels, his breathing ragged. Snapper followed, though the dog hung back at Cenric's command. Cenric at least let Brynn go first.

They slid around the outside of the hall. Cries rang out and screams echoed through the night air. There was fighting down in Istra, but it was impossible to see who fought whom.

Brynn thought of Esa, Kalen, little Guin, Daven, and the rest of their thanes, but she could do nothing for them right now. She needed to survive this first and then perhaps she would be able to save them.

The darkness shrouded them, but Brynn was sure Tullia's warriors would hear her rasping breathing. Smoke in the lungs was always difficult to heal.

They sidled around to one of several entrances to Ovrek's hall. Brynn peered ahead, heart thundering.

Warriors with weapons stoked kindling and paced back and forth. They were armed and ready, but Brynn could see necks and faces beneath helmets. They were armed for fighting other warriors, not sorceresses. She didn't see Tullia, but it seemed obvious who was behind this.

Brynn paused, turning back to Cenric. "About forty of them."

"It must be Egill's missing crew," Cenric muttered. "Or some of them."

"I will do my best, but I will likely only be able to fell two or three before they notice me." Without the time to prepare offensive spells or lay traps, Brynn was limited. "Do you prefer a spear or an axe?"

Cenric sounded confused, but answered, "A spear. If it's a good one."

Brynn thought one of the men had a spear that should suffice. "I'll try to get it for you." She pointed to Snapper. "Keep him back."

"What...?"

Brynn lashed a spell at the farthest man in her line of sight, and his head yanked back, his throat sheared open. Several men turned to check on their companion, looking away from her.

Brynn concentrated, focusing on weaving a spell she had not used in a long time. She sent a burst of power straight into the flaming kindling blocking the doors.

Pieces of burning wood, splinters, and smoldering logs swept out as if from a great wind. Brynn didn't remove all the kindling or even most of it from the door, but she blasted away enough of it that men jumped back, swatting at their clothes and screaming as embers burned them.

Curses in Valdari rose from around them and a man who appeared to be their leader stepped forward, yelling at the others. At least three men had been burned badly enough that they slumped on the ground. No one had been killed by that last spell, though.

It seemed that the men around her first victim realized what had happened—but even if they could see his throat had been cut, none of them had fought sorceresses before.

Brynn cast another spell, sending a line of power straight through another man's eye. He collapsed without a sound, his eyeball erupting in a spray of blood. That had been a lucky shot.

She lashed out again for the man who appeared to be the leader. He turned around just as she cast and her spell caught the edge of his helmet instead of his neck.

That man let off a cry, the cut grazed him, but mostly deflected by the metal of his helm. The leader shouted in Valdari, pointing toward her. Two of his warriors separated from the group, weapons raised as they charged for her. Sure enough, the man with the spear was one of them.

"Wait here," Brynn said.

"Brynn!" Cenric reached out as if to grab her, then snatched his arm back, letting her go. Snapper whined but remained at Cenric's side.

Brynn slipped out from behind the protection of the wall, so the enemy could see her. Hopefully, they hadn't noticed Cenric and Snapper in the shadow of the wall.

The two enemy warriors charged for her, one with an axe and the other with the spear.

Brynn retreated with her hands raised, making it look as if she was fleeing. Her heart raced and *ka* swirled around her in golden whorls that would be invisible to anyone without magic. She wanted to get them away from the others, even if only a few paces.

The man with the axe came first. He didn't have a helmet, his hair and beard outlined in the light of the fire.

Brynn sent a spell straight for his face. His head whipped back and he went down.

The man with the spear had a shield and seemed at least smart enough to realize she was doing something even if he might not realize she was a sorceress. He raised his shield as he advanced, charging.

Brynn grimaced. She needed to get around his shield for a clean shot at bare skin. It was possible for her spells to slice through clothing, but it would take more effort, and she needed to save her power for...

A dark shape flew out from the wall. Snapper came bounding across the distance, barking at the spearman.

The warrior spun, probably thinking he was being attacked

from the other side. He slashed for Snapper, but the dog skirted back, still barking.

The spearman turned his head to the side for just a moment and Brynn took the opening. Her spell slashed toward his neck.

The spearman hissed in pain, but from the *ka* that flowed from him, she hadn't struck a lethal blow. He charged her again, ignoring Snapper's barking this time.

Brynn raised both hands and stood her ground. It went against every instinct, but she forced herself not to move as the man came at her, just his eyes showing above his shield. She focused, aimed her power and sent out a whip of *ka*.

This time, her spell caught him full in the face, piercing through his left eye. The man stumbled forward, toppling like a pile of stones.

His spear wavered as he went down, and Brynn caught it by the shaft. She pulled it free and grabbed his shield while she was at it. She ran back to the corner of the burning hall where she had left her husband.

Cenric rushed to meet her halfway. He slung the shield onto his left arm and snatched the spear from her. "Magnificent woman!" Cenric crowed, voice flushed with pride even as he dropped into a defensive stance, pushing her behind him and the protection of the shield. "That's my girl."

The time for praise was short-lived as the other warriors realized they were under attack.

"Draw them away from the others?" Brynn panted, grateful for the first time that most of these men didn't speak Hyldish.

"Can you do anything about the fire?" Cenric asked, not taking his attention off their enemies.

Brynn grimaced. "No."

"You can start fires with your power," Cenric protested.

"Yes, I can *start* fires." Using *ka* to create a flame was possible, but turning the flame into *ka* was another matter. If there was a way to do it, Brynn wasn't aware.

"Can you make this fire bigger?" Cenric asked.

"Bigger?"

"Yes, bigger."

"I could," Brynn answered, not sure where this was going. "But that would endanger the people still inside the hall."

"Anyone still alive is in more danger from these whoresons," Cenric shot back.

Brynn realized what he was saying. It had already been too long, and the hall would already be filled with smoke. If anyone had not gotten out through the hole she had made, they were likely dead. She had no friends or loved ones among the Valdari in Ovrek's hall, but she still felt a pang of anguish. All those people choking to death...what a horrific end.

"Brynn!" Cenric faced down three more men that broke off from the main group.

Inhaling a deep breath, Brynn coughed. Her lungs were still not quite clear of the smoke. She drew *ka* into herself, calling on the power that lay dormant in the air and the earth around them.

Brynn wrapped it into her own chest until it became its own inferno. She coiled it tight around her heart, focusing, focusing.

The enemy warriors drew closer. Cenric could hold off two or three, but not for long.

Brynn punched out with a fist, focusing her intentions down her arm, through her knuckles. Power surged out of her, a golden explosion only visible to her. Magic flared into the fire, too fast and too much for the kindling and the young wood of the great hall to feed.

Heat blasted outward. The men who had advanced on Brynn and Cenric stumbled as fire singed their backs. Even behind the shield, Brynn and Cenric felt the blistering, scorching flames.

Brynn forced the fire to burn bigger, hotter, and faster. The flames needed somewhere to go, and they rushed toward the path of least resistance. The fire washed from yellow to orange, to red, to blue, then white in an instant.

White sparks shot straight up into the night sky. The men who had been standing nearby were engulfed in light so white-hot that it seemed to be starlight.

The whole thing lasted barely an instant. Brynn forced the fire to direct itself outward, spending all its greatest heat.

Darkness descended.

Brynn blinked as her eyes adjusted. The hall still burned, but the kindling had been blasted away. The smoke and fire filtering into the hall would at least be slowing.

The enemy men cried out in confusion and panic. Shadows withdrew around them as their foes fled, probably to regroup. None of them would know what just happened.

Cenric charged for the men now lying on the ground closest to them. He was merciless, furious.

Brynn followed close, staying to his left side, the one most vulnerable to attack when his shield was forward. Heart racing, she gathered more power to herself.

Cenric stabbed for the nearest man, impaling him where his shoulder joined his neck. Another of the flattened warriors tried to rise, hefting his weapon.

Cenric smashed the edge of his shield into the man's face, thrust with his spear the next moment.

Brynn drew *ka* to herself. As soon as she recovered enough from that first blast, she sent a whip of power toward the fleeing men. She could sense the outline of their bodies, but she had no way of knowing who might be wearing chainmail or any other kind of armor. She sent her power for the center mass of their bodies. None of them went down, but from the cries that rang out in the dark, she hit at least a few of them.

Cenric kept stabbing, finishing off the men lying around them. Her husband might not be able to see *ka*, but the hall continued to burn, providing enough light to find his marks.

One of the men leapt up from the ground, running after the others.

Cenric made to give chase, but Brynn caught his arm.

"No!" She dug in her heels, stopping him. "Trap."

Brynn could sense several other figures waiting in the shadows outside the fire, men waiting to attack Cenric if he pursued.

Cenric made a sound of frustration, but didn't argue.

"They're fleeing toward the beach," Brynn said.

Cenric glared after them. For half a heartbeat, Brynn feared he would charge after them anyway.

"Cenric!" Hróarr came rushing after them, a wooden plank hefted like a weapon. He slowed when he saw the bodies of the dead men sprawled in the grass—at least ten, but perhaps more. Brynn hadn't gotten a good count. Hróarr let off several words in Valdari, including what sounded like the name of a god. "You killed all these?" Hróarr crouched to retrieve a weapon from one of the dead men—another spear.

"*We* killed all these." Cenric still watched the darkness where the others had fled.

Several other Valdari men from the hall came rushing after Hróarr in the darkness, snatching up weapons from the dead men. Their voices washed over Brynn in a deluge of foreign words.

Brynn hovered close to her husband. These men ignored her for the moment, but she still wasn't sure they were friends.

The Valdari jarls and other men, those who had followed Hróarr, coughed and choked between their words. They had escaped the smoke and flames, but smoke was a cruel and exacting enemy. It could take hours or sometimes even days to kill and even sorceresses struggled to heal its effects at times.

Beside them, the hall still burned. It crackled and popped as the flames swept higher along with the stench of pitch.

"Where is Ovrek?" Cenric asked, looking to Hróarr.

Hróarr glanced over his shoulder as if expecting the king to be there. "We pulled him out."

"Was he hurt?" Cenric demanded, sounding genuinely concerned.

"No more than the rest of us." Hróarr turned his head, coughing briefly.

"So where is he?" Cenric shot back.

Hróarr grated his response. "I don't know."

Even Brynn knew that Ovrek would want to confront his enemies.

Cenric glanced to Brynn and even in the poor light, she could see her thoughts reflected. They needed Ovrek alive. At the moment, their only alternative was Tullia, and she had just tried to smoke them like fish for winter.

Cenric turned, jogging back to where Brynn had made the hole for their escape. Brynn trotted after him, the crisp evening air stinging her scorched lungs. It was a drastic contrast to the oppressive heat and smoke of the fire.

They reached the back of the hall to find Vana standing over a bedraggled and soot-stained gaggle of survivors. At least a hundred people had been inside the hall when it had been barricaded closed, but Brynn saw fewer than fifty now, counting Hróarr and the men who had come to join them.

"Where is the king?" Cenric demanded, looking to Vana. He shouted something in Valdari, raising his voice, presumably repeating the question.

"He went back in," Vana rasped.

"Back in?" Horror and fear infused Cenric's words. If not for the amber light of the flames, she was sure he would have gone pale.

Beside them, the fire was still consuming the hall. Despite what Brynn had done, smoke was still filling it, just more slowly.

Vana stared toward the burning hall. "He went back for his wife and son."

Brynn thought she must have heard wrong.

"That's madness." Cenric shook his head.

From outside looking in, the hall had become a pit of black smoke broken by flashes of firelight. It was a deathtrap and if anyone inside wasn't already dead, they would be soon.

Brynn pulled her mantle tighter around her shoulders. She focused on the burning hall, trying to sense inside with her power. "Someone is coming out." Brynn straightened. "Someone—"

With a roar, Ovrek burst from the jagged hole carrying a limp form over his shoulder. Warriors rushed forward to pull him free, dragging him and his motionless cargo several steps from the blaze.

Ovrek collapsed on all fours, bellowing angrily between coughs. He surveyed the limp form beside him.

Tolvir lay unmoving.

"Sifma?" Ovrek searched the faces around him. His eyes landed on Vana. "Sifma?"

Vana shook her head, eyes shining with tears by the firelight.

Ovrek staggered to his feet, still wheezing. He stumbled back toward the burning hall.

Cenric and the other men stepped forward to block him.

Ovrek swung his fists. There was a thud and one of the men stumbled back, but the others rushed the king, tackling him to the ground. Ovrek collapsed under their weight, pinned even as he cursed and fought to crawl back into the burning death trap.

Something snapped and a burning beam collapsed over the entrance, blocking the way back inside.

Brynn's chest clenched at the finality. She could still feel *ka* inside, bodies still alive or perhaps newly dead lying strewn around the burning structure. They were so close and yet there was nothing she or anyone else could do to help them.

Ovrek seemed to realize that, too. After several moments, the men let Ovrek up and he stumbled back to the limp figure of Tolvir.

The boy's chest still rose and fell, but it was weak.

"Tolvir," Ovrek rasped and rested a hand on his son's shoulder, shaking as if to wake him. "Tolvir!"

Brynn made to step forward, but Cenric grabbed her arm. "Tolvir is still alive. I can help him."

"You already tried helping that concubine. Besides…" Cenric grimaced and by the burning light of the hall, Brynn thought she saw his thoughts. Not only might Ovrek still blame her if Tolvir died, but it might be best if Tolvir died.

This way, Ovrek would never have to learn of his son's betrayal. In some ways, it was best for everyone.

Ovrek must not have seen Brynn. He knelt over his son, shaking the young man. He muttered in Valdari, low phrases Brynn didn't need to recognize in order to understand. "Tolvir," he whimpered, the rest of his words too quiet to be heard over the crackle of the fire and the murmuring voices around them. The king's shoulders moved. At first Brynn thought he was coughing, but no…Ovrek was weeping.

Male voices demanded blood. Women echoed their outrage, crouched over loved ones and gathered around limp forms on the ground.

All around him, the first king of Valdar's people were in chaos, but he knelt over his son, weeping.

Ovrek was a hard ruler, selfish, often cruel, and he would happily burn Hylden to the ground if he had his way. But Brynn had cried those tears, too. Like Ovrek, she had knelt over a motionless body, calling a boy's name between her sobs.

Cenric still held Brynn back, but she tugged against him, urging him to let her go.

"Tolvir is his son," Brynn whispered, rasping as her voice cracked. It must have been the smoke. "His only son."

Cenric's expression softened a little at that. "Brynn."

"Please." Brynn's attention was on the weeping warrior king. "Please?" Cenric was right that she was risking herself by doing this. Everything she had done for these people had backfired so far, but…she wanted to try.

Cenric muttered something but let her go.

Brynn knelt across from Ovrek on Tolvir's other side.

The king stiffened, looking ready to push her away before he recognized her. "Sorceress."

"Roll him on his side," Brynn ordered. She pushed Tolvir so that he was facing away from her, lying toward his father. She slid one hand under the boy's collar, her fingers splayed over his bare skin. His chest hair was sparse and thin, a reminder of how young he still was.

Cenric stood at Brynn's back, spear planted by his feet—a guard over her as she worked.

Brynn reached into the boy with her power, feeling out the damage done by the smoke. It was not unlike the damage done by poison. Smoke was a poison in its own way.

"Can you save him?" Ovrek asked the question more like an accusation than a plea for help.

"I'm trying." Brynn closed her eyes.

"Save him," Ovrek ordered, as if he could intimidate her power into working.

Cenric said something to Ovrek in Valdari.

The king shot his gaze up to Cenric, lips curling in anger.

Brynn would sort them out later. She focused on the motionless atheling before her.

The inside of his lungs had been badly damaged. If she'd had to guess, he had joined the group of young men who had tried breaking through the main doors and so gotten the worst of the smoke.

She suspected there was still plenty of smoke and soot in his lungs, but for now she just needed to repair him enough so that he could keep breathing. Brynn seeped her power into the young atheling, focusing carefully.

Cenric and Ovrek shot words back and forth. Cenric was still holding a spear, but Ovrek did not seem to care. He growled back, despite being the one kneeling on the ground.

Yes, Ovrek was definitely a king whether Brynn liked him or not.

Her husband and Ovrek argued in Valdari. Cenric was probably still angry about her being accused of murder and telling the king exactly who he had to thank for being alive right now.

Ovrek gave a sharp retort, shifting as if he would stand.

Tolvir gagged, curling in on himself as he drew in great wheezing breaths.

"Tolvir?" Ovrek paused, snapping his gaze down to his son. He grabbed the atheling's shoulder. "Tolvir?"

Tolvir coughed, eyes flying open. His eyes were bloodshot and teary, and he might need healing there, too, but he was alive. He grabbed his father's arm. "Father," he choked. He spoke Valdari, but the meaning was clear. "Father?"

Ovrek dragged his son up, pulling the boy into a rough hug. He squeezed so tight, Brynn was sure she heard Tolvir's ribs crack.

The boy wheezed, choking out a string of words in Valdari.

"Careful!" Brynn reached up, fingers finding the back of Tolvir's neck so she could keep feeding power into him.

Ovrek ignored her. He released Tolvir, squaring the boy at arms' length. He asked Tolvir something, sounding concerned.

Tolvir nodded, though he still coughed.

Ovrek smiled, his forked beard swaying as he did. Then he shook Tolvir with a force to rattle stone. "Stupid boy!" Ovrek roared. "Determined to get yourself killed."

"I'm still healing him," Brynn protested.

"Well, be quick about it," Ovrek ordered.

"Cenric!" Hróarr ran toward them, his huge frame barreling out of the dark. He spoke a hurried string of Valdari, then looked to Vana. "There's fighting in the town. Some of our men and some of theirs. Another band of them is headed this way, most likely to finish us off."

A rumbling sound at Brynn's back startled her. Snapper stood with his tail stiff and hackles raised, glaring down the dark expanse of trees that stretched beyond Istra.

A great flapping, cawing, shrieking sound rose from the trees as thousands of black shapes momentarily blocked the stars. The birds were fleeing the forest, flying up from the trees and frantically seeking safety.

"What's that?" Cenric shifted beside her, coming closer.

Several voices chattered in Valdari at the strange sight.

Chills shot down Brynn's spine as she reached out with her power, straining to feel what living things moved through the dark. There was the usual golden haze of life, but within it, tainted, poisoned *ka* flared into her awareness. Two sources, one large and one massive, larger than any animal she had ever encountered before, but both moving toward them.

"The monsters from under the tree," Brynn whispered, icy fear washing through her veins. "They've escaped."

16

Cenric

Bad thing, Snapper sent to Cenric. *Bad thing coming.*

Cenric had no doubt. He glanced over to Brynn, kneeling beside Tolvir. "Can you sense them? How close?"

Brynn didn't look up from her work. "Close." Her voice shook. "I expect just a few hundred paces from the edge of the town."

Cenric adjusted the spear in his grip, watching the dark line of trees.

Hróarr let off a hearty string of curses. "Egill's men are heading this way, too."

They were grievously outnumbered, and it was about to be worse.

"I need an axe!" Ovrek bellowed. He would not let his enemies take his blood without a fight.

Tolvir scrambled up beside his father, wheezing even as he

tugged away from Brynn. She let him go.

Cenric spotted Hróarr speaking with Vana before pushing her away. At Cenric's feet, Snapper whined, attention still on the darkness of the trees.

"One crisis at a time," Cenric sighed. If Egill's men had returned to finish them off, they might not live long enough to worry about the monsters.

"Draw up!" Ovrek bellowed, taking control. "There are weapons on the dead men at the front of the hall. On your feet!"

The surviving men gathered around Ovrek, following him in the direction of the corpses Brynn and Cenric had killed. By unspoken agreement, Brynn and Cenric trailed after them.

They gathered before the burning hall that had been intended as their pyre. Cenric and Hróarr drew up beside the other men, carrying shields and whatever other weapons they were able to salvage. Brynn hovered at their backs.

Some twenty or thirty of them faced the much better armed and better prepared hundred or so marching up the hill. This group seemed to be in no hurry. They marched in as much of a formation as the uneven slope of the hill allowed, coming to finish off the work of their fellows.

"Egill!" Ovrek bellowed, stepping forward. "Where is that coward?" The king wielded an axe with a long handle, resting it at the ground by his side. "Egill!"

"He's dealing with your men in the town," shouted a familiar voice. A figure stepped forward, a shining helm glinting by the light of the burning hall.

Cenric was sure he had seen this war gear before. The twisting shapes of entwined beasts decorated the helm and cheek pieces. Small overlapping metal plates, each no bigger than two fingers, covered the wearer's torso and formed a skirt around the upper thighs. It was lamellar armor, like the style Ovrek and some of his veterans had brought back from across the sea.

"Tullia?" Ovrek stood face to face with the truth Brynn and

Cenric had tried to tell him. "Tullia?" He blinked as if this might be a mirage or some sort of trick.

"These are my men." Tullia gestured to the warriors around her. "As are Egill and Dagrún."

"You?" Ovrek still didn't seem to believe it.

"Sweyn was my man as well," Tullia said. "And the others you killed for siding with him."

Sweyn—Cenric had seen that armor on Sweyn. Tullia had come to kill her father wearing her dead husband's war gear.

"You tried to kill me!" Ovrek bellowed. "You killed your own mother!"

"She sided with you," Tullia shot back without a hint of remorse. "We have tolerated your insults, your demands, your cruelty, and your greed for long enough," she cried. "Not even the Grandfather Yew was safe from your avarice."

At that accusation, Tullia's men let off a clamor of agreement. Jeers rose, cast toward Ovrek.

"And so you chose kin-slaying?" Ovrek roared. "What manner of vile creature are you?"

Father and daughter continued casting accusations back and forth.

Brynn edged closer behind Cenric. She rested her hands on his arms. He didn't feel anything happening, but her touch was featherlight, delicate. She was weaving magic, he was sure of it, trying to protect him.

"I can't create mail," Brynn whispered. "And I can't stop the force of blows, but that should keep most things from cutting through your clothes."

Cenric cast a glance over his shoulder to Brynn in the dark. "You can do that?"

Brynn squeezed him gently. "It's not very strong, especially against direct hits, so try not to get hit."

Cenric would take what he could get in this situation. "Can you do the same for everyone else?"

"If we have time. I'm not sure we do."

Cenric had to agree. Ovrek and Tullia talked in circles, speaking of broken oaths, honor impugned, and past crimes.

Hróarr lumbered close to Cenric's side. He spoke to Brynn. "When the killing starts, go to the boats with Vana. You might be able to get out of here."

Brynn ignored him, giving no sign that she had heard.

Cenric nudged her. "Go, love. Find Esa, Kalen, and the rest of our men." He gestured to the dog at his feet. "Take Snapper with you."

The dyrehund whined, hearing his name. His attention remained on the dark forest. *Bad things, Cenric.*

Brynn answered softly, yet firmly. "I stay with you."

"Brynn." Cenric wanted to touch her, but one hand held his spear and the other the shield. "Go. It's alright. I'll join you when this is over."

Hurt flashed across Brynn's face. "I thought we agreed not to lie to each other."

Cenric shot a glance to the line of Tullia's men. "If they take you..." He couldn't say it.

Hróarr had no such reservations. "If they take you, they'll take turns raping you before ransoming you back to your uncle."

That was the way things had been done in war for centuries. Brynn might be spared the worst of the abuse if they realized her value as a hostage, but Cenric did not dare think she would be spared entirely.

Brynn didn't even flinch. "It won't come to that." She was just a little too calm. "They'll have to kill me."

They wouldn't take her alive, that was what she was saying. When he'd realized they were trapped inside the great hall as it was being burned down, Cenric's only thought had been fear for Brynn—the horror that she was going to die with him. Now he wasn't just facing the thought of her suffocating in front of him, but a gruesome death at the end of a Valdari spear.

They stood no chance. Even with Brynn, they stood no chance. Cenric didn't want to die, but that was the way of a warrior's life. Someone else would become alderman of Ombra and the world would move on, but Brynn...she deserved better.

"I won't ask you to flee," Brynn said. "You're a warrior and you need to fight, I understand that. But I need to stay."

"Brynn—"

"You die when you run," she interjected, quoting the old warrior's saying.

The bloodiest part of a battle was always after the shieldwall broke and the losing side ran. It was said that to run was to die, either by loss of honor or loss of life. One could still die facing the enemy, but at least it would be a courageous death.

Cenric hated the thought of Brynn in danger, but she was right. She was no stranger to war, and she knew exactly what she was choosing. Brynn was choosing him even unto death. "Stay between Hróarr and I," he ordered.

Hróarr made a sound of protest, but it died in his throat.

"I will try." From her wry tone, Brynn knew that might become difficult once the fighting started.

Go, Snapper. Cenric couldn't make his wife leave, but he could save his dog. *Find Vana.*

Vana? Snapper cocked his head to one side.

Protect Vana, Cenric ordered.

Vana! Snapper whined, looking back in the direction they had last seen her. *Cenric? Brynn?*

We'll follow you, Cenric promised. *Stay with Vana.*

Barking, Snapper rushed into the darkness, seeking Vana and the other Valdari women. Hopefully, the dog would be safe.

Cenric wondered how much of war Brynn had seen. He knew she had fought for her uncle alongside her sister. Unlike a thane, Brynn didn't boast of her time bloodletting. She seemed oddly ashamed of it.

Ovrek's men were outnumbered. Tullia still had at least one

hundred to their paltry band of survivors.

"Enough of this." Tullia drew a sword, leveling it toward the bedraggled group of survivors before her.

There would be no shield wall on their side. This would be plain and simple butchery.

Cenric and Hróarr had weapons, but only a few of the other men did. Most of them had been forced to leave their weapons in the antechamber at the front of the hall and the weapons were now out of reach and far too hot to be wielded.

Below in Istra, fires had caught. Whether by accident or malice, storehouses, barns, forges, and homes blazed like torches in the night. It appeared that even some of the ships were on fire. Tullia hated Ovrek enough to waste good timber?

"Ovrek!" chorused the men around them. "Ovrek!"

Cenric and Hróarr fell in beside the king, joining the ranks that gathered around him. Brynn crouched at their backs, her presence warm and steady. Cenric hated that he couldn't protect her, but he had to trust her to protect herself. Somehow, trusting her with her own life was harder than trusting her with his.

Few of them had shields and that meant Cenric and Hróarr ended up out front.

Other men who had shields fell in around them, but only two or three as best Cenric could tell. Some fifty had escaped the burning hall, many lay dead,

"Ovrek!" their line roared. "Ovrek!"

With the burning hall at their backs, their enemies were illuminated in stark relief before them.

"Tullia!" the traitors cried. "Tullia!"

Cenric caught himself gritting his teeth, as they braced for impact, a bad habit Berdun had always tried to break.

The enemy formed lines in front of them, drawing up in a wall of weapons, shields, and armor here and there. Somewhere in that line might be Tullia herself. Further down the hill, Cenric could see the warriors from the beach fighting the second force of Tullia's men down the slope.

If those men could get through, Ovrek's men would have the advantage of numbers, but for now, they had to fight from weakness. The battle could still go either way. So often, that was all war was—a toss of the sticks and a prayer of favor to the gods.

"Ovrek!" boomed the king's voice. His great bellow seemed to shake the air itself.

The lines surged forward, Cenric and Hróarr at the front.

"Ovrek!" Hróarr bellowed, shaking his axe in challenge. "Ovrek!"

"Ovrek!" Cenric joined in the chanting. "Ovrek!"

"Tullia!" the enemy shouted back defiantly. "Tullia!'

"You will have no graves!" Ovrek swore. "I will feed your eyes to the ravens and your guts to my pigs!"

Not to be outdone, Tullia shouted back. "I will make your son a eunuch and your concubines whores!"

More taunts and boasts flew between the warriors. Most of them lost in the noise.

Cenric's heart raced, more excitement than fear coursing through him. He had never been as skilled with taunts as some, but he knew what to do once the lines met. "Ovrek!" he shouted. "Ovrek!"

The two lines barreled closer. The expectation, dread, and eagerness were so thick Cenric was sure he could smell it.

Despite all the yelling and taunting, Brynn was the first to strike, silent and likely unseen at Cenric's back.

A man at the front of the enemy line tripped and recovered, but then another tripped and another. One man finally stumbled, then went down, pushed forward by the force of his fellows behind him.

As another man reached to help the fallen warrior, his head bent to the side, almost as if an invisible rope had caught him around the neck.

The man who had tried to help buckled, thudding to the

ground. His corpse tripped up the men behind him.

The enemy line jostled, already fragmenting.

"That's my girl." Cenric never took his eyes off the advancing line.

Tullia's men had come prepared with shields and armor, but even when outmatched, no man wanted to die like a coward. Ovrek's line had not been prepared, but they had Brynn.

Brynn tripped up the advancing line, making them stumble in the grass. She took down another man just as the lines closed.

Cenric lunged, stabbing the man to the left of the gap. His spearhead caught flesh and he shoved harder before yanking it out, falling back into formation.

Around him, shouts and screams and grunts and bellows rang out, but Cenric could only see what was in front of him. He was aware of Hróarr to his right, the man at his left, and Brynn at his back. That was it.

The battle turned into a blur, stabbing and blocking. Another spear caught him in the shoulder, narrowly avoiding his neck.

Brynn's hand touched his back, and the pain in his wound was gone a moment later.

The man at Cenric's left stumbled, letting off a cry. Cenric didn't see what had happened to him, but a moment later, Brynn steadied that man, too.

No wonder Aelgar had been able to win after he swayed the sorceresses to his side. If this was what they could do with just one, what was possible with two? A hundred?

Roars rang out as more voices shouting for Ovrek drowned out those shouting for Tullia.

A roar went up from down on the beach. Cenric realized that the other warriors who had not been present at the feast had seized their weapons and now attacked Tullia and her men from their flank. Tullia must not be as unanimously supported as Cenric had feared.

Tullia's own warriors were flanked even as they attempted to encircle Ovrek and his band of survivors. Everything broke down into chaos.

These were Valdari fighting Valdari. Everyone looked the same and that left nothing to do but attack the men who attacked you and hope they weren't friends.

The lines broke and chaos took over.

"Ovrek!" shouted a man to Cenric's left. "Ovrek!"

"Tullia!" bellowed an answering call. "Tullia!"

In the dark, with no banners and nothing else to identify them, the men were calling out their leaders' names. It was as much to keep from killing friends as it was an oath of allegiance.

"Ovrek!" Cenric answered. "Ovrek!"

"Ovrek!" Hróarr howled, swinging his axe as another man came at them.

From around them came answering cries of "Tullia!"

"Ovrek!" cried men farther down the beach. "Ovrek!"

A man came at Cenric with another spear, stabbing for his legs. Cenric caught the attack on his shield, shoving the man's strike wide.

The man screamed, then went down. It took a moment for Cenric to realize Brynn had used a spell, but another man was coming at them before Cenric had the time to praise her.

Cenric couldn't see the man's features, he was a dark, yelling outline tinged in red from the light of the burning hall. This one wore armor, so he must be someone moderately important.

Cenric tried to stab the attacker, but his spearhead scraped along steel lamellar. The man came in roaring, a monster behind his helm's design of a snarling bear.

Sword swinging, the attacker got past Cenric's spear, smashing into his shield and knocking him back. Cenric rooted his back heel as he knocked into Brynn who jostled into Hróarr.

Brynn muttered something that sounded like a curse and Cenric muttered his own as the armored man's sword swung for his head. Cenric ducked low behind his shield, acutely aware that he had no armor himself. He shoved with his shield. The impact rattled up his arm and the boss clanged into the stranger's armor, but the attacker was undeterred. With that lamellar, the other warrior probably hadn't even felt it.

Sparks showered around the man's head and Cenric realized Brynn must be trying to find purchase with her spells.

The warrior flinched back, but recovered, coming in for another swipe with his sword.

On Brynn's other side, Hróarr seemed engaged with his own enemies.

Cenric lost his grip on his spear. Instead of reaching for it, he pushed it to the side so it wouldn't trip him up. Grabbing his shield with both hands, he stepped back just once, then smashed the shield edge first toward the other man's head.

The stranger's sword stung Cenric's upper arm and pain shot up Cenric's shoulder an instant before the shield struck.

The other warrior's head bent back with the popping of bone and he toppled over like a felled tree. The man hit with a hard thud, the fire shining off the lamellar plates. Cenric would have liked to take that helm and armor, but there was no time for looting.

Numbness spread through Cenric's left shoulder, but he was still able to use it. Glancing down, the sword had not cut through his sleeve, but blood seeped through. How had that happened?

"You're hurt." Brynn's hands were on him the next moment, her power sliding into him.

Cenric never could tell when she was working magic, but this time he felt her power like a wash of heat. The pain dulled into an ache and then vanished.

There was no time to thank her as Hróarr let off a great bellow, facing down four men who appeared to be together. These men weren't armored, but they carried shields and spears.

Cenric couldn't see their faces, not in the shifting shadows of the hall fire, but they seemed enemies, so he snatched up his spear again and made ready to face them.

Brynn stepped a little further back, letting Hróarr and Cenric draw their shields closer together.

Two of the men came at the front, closing in. The other two swept out like wings, coming to flank them from both sides.

Cenric glanced left and right.

Then the man circling to his left collapsed. Brynn shifted her attention to the man circling right.

Unfortunately, the man circling right was clever enough to realize what had happened. He skirted back, joining the small formation with his other two fellows.

The men came on with their spears, prodding and poking at Hróarr and Cenric who stabbed back. Several times, the enemy warriors tried to circle, but were quick to remember why that was a bad idea.

"I am going to bind their feet to the grass." Brynn kept her voice low, though the odds were that these men didn't speak Hyldish. "It will only last a moment or so, but it should be enough to trip them."

Hróarr grunted his acknowledgement.

They could use that, especially if they knew the timing. "Signal when you do." Cenric blocked another spear thrust from their enemies.

Brynn rested a hand on Cenric and her other on Hróarr. Her voice was but a whisper as she counted down. "In three, two, one..." She squeezed Cenric's shoulder.

Cenric let off a roar, yelling at the top of his lungs the same instant Hróarr did. Together, they took one lunging step forward. It was an old tactic they'd used before and by no means original, but it worked.

The three enemy warriors faltered, just a little. It was barely even noticeable, but with their feet bound to the grass, it took down the man on the far left, who stumbled back into his fellows on the right.

Hróarr was on the man an instant later, his axe swinging in as his shield blocked the spear. The axe struck and crunched into ribs.

Cenric slammed into the man nearest to him, spearing the warrior's chest just below the collarbone. He'd barely gotten his spear free before Hróarr pounced on the second man, axe slamming into an unprotected forehead.

Pockets of fighting scattered all around them. Groups of four or five breaking out into their own private battles.

Ovrek's voice rang out over the melee. "Ovrek!"

Good, the king was still alive. At least this wasn't for nothing. "Ovrek!" roared the king. "Ovrek!"

Cenric spotted the king himself, armed with a bearded axe, silhouetted by the burning fire of his hall. He had faced two betrayals in a single day, and his fury burst out of him in a storm of rage.

Cenric realized that the line keeping the rest of Ovrek's men from making it up the hill had broken. Tullia's men were routed, crushed between the burning hall and the rest of Ovrek's rallied forces.

What remained of Tullia's line buckled as it was attacked from two sides. A roar went up from Ovrek's men as Ovrek's name was bellowed into the night air.

Ovrek himself shouted above it all, crying his name as if to be heard by the stars themselves.

Cenric stabbed, lunged, and blocked. He raised his shield, lowered his spear, feinted, and charged more times than he could count. He kept close to Hróarr and Brynn.

Every time he reached back, she was there, and every time someone tried to flank them, the man went down before he made it more than a few steps.

Cenric fought and killed until the voices shouting for Ovrek were all he could hear and every man around him seemed to be a friend.

Blood splattered his face, head, and arms. Sweat soaked his tunic and trickled down his back despite the cold night air.

Cenric panted, turning in a slow circle, then looking back to

Hróarr. Had they won?

"Ovrek!" the men of the hillside shouted. "Ovrek!"

The king himself strode forward, the rings in his beard glinting, arms spread wide as he let off a savage howl, shaking his bloodied axe defiantly.

A cheer went up as the survivors descended on the dead, picking over armor, weapons, and jewelry from the corpses. If Cenric wanted that lamellar kit from the dead man, he should probably go get it now.

Brynn swayed, grabbing him for support.

"Brynn!" Cenric caught her, holding her up. "What happened? Are you hurt?"

"No," Brynn panted. "Just...dizzy. I think I'm still recovering from the smoke."

Cenric supported her as best he could, holding onto her. "Fearsome creature." He kissed her forehead. "Magnificent, magnificent woman."

Brynn rested her head against his shoulder. "They're coming," she whimpered. "They're still coming."

No sooner had she spoken than a howl went up over Istra. Cenric wasn't sure how he'd heard it over the noise around him.

But for a moment, the whole world seemed to stop and look toward the darkness of the forest.

Brynn's fingers dug into Cenric's arm. "I don't know how to defeat them."

"We'll figure it out." Cenric chose to believe they were meant to win.

By all accounts, they should have all died inside the hall. They should have died in that battle. Surely the gods hadn't spared them through all that just to have them die a few hundred paces closer to the beach?

Then the screams began again.

17

Brynn

Shrieks filled the air like a great cacophony. A dark shape rushed past, then another and another. Black specks flitted overhead, fluttering as fast as their tiny wings could carry them.

A larger shape barreled past—a horse dragging the fence post it had been tied to. Several pigs followed, along with flapping chickens, and a host of screaming sheep.

The hundreds of animals of Istra were fleeing. From the sparrows to the cattle.

Cenric grabbed Brynn. Hróarr followed and they raced along with the victors back to the burning hall to avoid being trampled. Most of the animals avoided the flaming structure.

"What is happening?" demanded Ovrek. "What madness is this?"

"Have you ever wondered why the animals never ventured near the Grandfather Yew?" Brynn asked, out of breath after their run.

The king's bright eyes fell on her. Splattered in blood with several cuts to his cheek and upper arms, he was a terrifying sight, but Ovrek was no longer the most frightening thing on this island. "Speak, sorceress."

Cenric shifted at Brynn's side, his attention also on the king. Brynn didn't doubt that if it came to it, he would attack Ovrek to protect her.

"The Grandfather Yew was planted to protect Valdar from evil." Brynn glanced to Cenric as she spoke. "When the tree died, it let the evil out."

Whether the monsters had been drawn here by the noise of battle, or the glut of fresh blood didn't matter. They were here now.

Hróarr turned to Ovrek. "My king—"

"This is some trick. I don't believe you," Ovrek said, closing on Brynn.

Cenric inhaled at her side, but Brynn spoke first.

"You may believe what you wish, lord." Even without the pounding of hooves and the flutter of wings, Brynn could feel the rush of animals fleeing from this place. Would Snapper and Guin flee with them?

Beyond the animals, she could sense the burning infernos that were the Wulfwir and something larger. Something bigger than any animal she had ever imagined.

Brynn had heard stories of whales, great beasts larger than ships that sprayed water from their heads with fins larger than a man. Even that did not quite do this thing justice.

How could a beast even grow so large? How was it not crushed by the weight of its own bones?

"They can be killed." Hróarr shoved into Ovrek's line of sight. "Blades didn't seem to hurt them, but they can be killed."

"You killed one?" Ovrek's attention shifted from Brynn.

"The she-troll," Hróarr confirmed. "We killed her."

"How did you kill her?"

"Had to take her head off," Hróarr explained. "No other wounds would affect her. My sword was practically useless."

Cenric cast a knowing look to Brynn, though his question was for Hróarr. "How did you take the creature's head off without a sword?" Her husband had seen her rip men's heads off and even decapitate her mother using spells.

Brynn held his gaze, confirming with her silence.

Cenric's jaw clenched in the light of the burning hall. It seemed he had figured out she'd saved his cousin's life right before he'd pushed her into the thrall pit. No doubt the two men would have a loud and physical confrontation if they all survived this.

"You just have to behead them quickly." Hróarr notably did not meet Brynn's gaze.

"But we can kill these?" Cenric straightened.

"They heal from anything that doesn't kill them," Hróarr said. "Any blow that doesn't kill only slows them for a moment."

Brynn considered their options. Running away was always feasible, but even if she could convince her husband to flee, they had no clear path to the ships. The monsters were closer to the ships than they were, and she had no idea where Esa, Kalen, Guin, and the rest of their people might be. She didn't want to leave them behind. "The Wulfwir is too large and too tall for most men to reach its neck."

"A spear through the heart might work," Hróarr suggested.

Brynn wasn't sure, but it might.

"We attack it the way we do bears," Ovrek offered. "Trap it and strike it from two sides."

Brynn briefly hoped Ovrek *had* killed that bear he'd sent as a gift to her and Cenric. "It would be dangerous. Even more dangerous than a bear, but it might be possible."

"And the other one?" Cenric jerked his head toward the beach.

"I didn't get a good look at it," Hróarr admitted. "But we might be able to kill it the same way."

"You won't." Brynn watched the direction she could feel the

beast coming. The being she felt approaching was too large, too tall. Its neck would be thicker than three men could reach around.

From this distance, it was hard to tell, but she could swear she saw red eyes like pits of fire flickering amongst the trees. Or perhaps it was just the burning town below. Regardless, the Wulfwir was nightmare enough. The serpent was beyond anything Brynn had ever imagined.

That one would almost certainly need to be killed with *ka*. Brynn would need help. If she had five or so mature sorceresses, she might be able to do it. Even if she was able to find Esa, Lena, and perhaps another sorceress thrall or two, Brynn doubted that would be enough.

Brynn had once channeled enough power to flatten grown trees and deepen a riverbed. That was the kind of power she would need to fight the serpent, but that had been after drawing *ka* to herself for several hours. She would need another source.

There was the field of dead bodies, their *ka* seeping out into the earth. But Brynn would need to be touching their blood in a great pool if she was going to draw power fast enough.

The screams down below grew louder. The warriors around her stomped, restless. They would move soon, and she needed some way to fight the serpent, some plan, even an inkling of one.

Brynn beseeched the waxing moon overhead. *Eponine, help me,* she prayed silently. *Eponine, help me.*

The moon's beams shone down, glinting off the waves lapping along the beach. The sky and the sea remained unaffected by the chaos and butchery on shore. Several ships bobbed in the waves as people either sought safety or perhaps some of Tullia's men retreated.

The sea.

Ka infused the waves as surely as it infused the trees and the forests. It was a vast, seemingly endless expanse of rippling power.

Brynn had never tried drawing from the sea before, but she had never needed to. Llyr, god of the sea, and Eponine, goddess of the moon and sorceresses, were said to have a strong friendship. Brynn could only hope Llyr would permit it under the circumstances.

A roar split the night air. After the noise of battle and fleeing animals, Brynn wouldn't have thought that anything could be heard, but the beast proved her wrong.

The clatter of hooves and the rush of animals died down. All the animals that could had fled.

A scream of fury that seemed to come from the very bones of the earth broke the sky over Istra.

Brynn was first to step from behind the shelter of the burning hall, Cenric right beside her. She peered into the darkness and saw it.

The creature rose over the huts, storehouses, and ships, the light from the burning houses casting an eerie glow on its underbelly. She could make out few details, but she saw the glint of fire off scales and the outline of a long, knobbed body. The creature had to be at least five ships in length.

Screams of terror and panic rose from every corner of Istra.

Brynn took in the sight, feeling detached, the way she had inside that burning hall. She was so far beyond fear, so far beyond terror.

At her side, Cenric stared in horror. He held onto his pilfered shield and spear, watching as a creature from his nightmares burst into Istra. "It is real," he murmured. "Morgi tried to warn me."

Brynn wasn't sure what good that warning could have done.

Around them, Ovrek's men stepped out from where they had sheltered from the fleeing animals. Gasps of shock and wonder rippled over the men. Brynn heard appeals to Havnar and prayers to at least four different gods.

Brynn didn't want to fight the serpent. She wanted to flee from this creature with its burning malice and tainted *ka*. She hadn't wanted to come to Valdar in the first place.

But if Esa was still alive down there, she was depending on Brynn. Even Kalen, Vana, Guin, Snapper, that little girl who had admired Tullia's temple rings, and hundreds of others. Ovrek and his men could probably handle the Wulfwir. It would cost them dearly, but they could do it. The serpent was another matter.

Hróarr, Ovrek, and the king's warriors began speaking quickly, conferring amongst themselves. Even if she could get them to listen, that would take time. Every moment was precious if she was going to save the people in the town.

Brynn marched in the direction of the burning city before she could change her mind.

Cenric followed at her side, still carrying his shield and spear. Those might be useful if they faced any more of Tullia's men, but Brynn doubted his weapons would be of much use against the great serpent.

"Where are you going?" Hróarr shouted, his massive hulk trotting after them.

"See to the Wulfwir," Brynn shouted back.

"It's just Wulfwir," Hróarr corrected. "That's its name."

"See to it." Brynn turned back toward the town, moving quickly as she dared.

Ovrek was distracted speaking with his men, and she wanted to be gone before he noticed her leaving.

"What are you doing?" Hróarr repeated. "Cenric!"

Cenric shouted something back in Valdari. Whatever it meant, Hróarr didn't press the issue.

"Does the serpent have a name, too?" Brynn asked.

"Jormanthar," Cenric said. "The Great Serpent."

"I see." Brynn kept walking toward the burning chaos of Istra. "You're not going to try and stop me?" Her voice trembled, but she hoped her husband wouldn't notice.

"I've seen you work wonders before," Cenric reminded her. "Besides, my foretelling showed us together."

Brynn wasn't sure if that was a good thing or not. "I'm not sure I can do this."

"You can." Cenric didn't hesitate.

"And if I can't?" Tears stung Brynn's eyes even as she kept marching.

"Then it's not as if we'll be around for the embarrassment of being wrong, is it?" Cenric sounded entirely too cheerful about the fact.

Brynn continued down the hill, past the corpses of Tullia's men and Ovrek's men alike. In the death, all the bodies seemed to be the same. She did her best to draw power to herself, pulling it in great golden whorls.

Power shimmered off the corpses, off the grass, infusing the summer air. Brynn didn't know how much might possibly be enough, but she would take all that she could get.

Cenric was close, at her side, marching without hesitation. Was he truly so confident or was he just better at hiding it?

Brynn was terrified. She was walking straight toward a monster, but she didn't know what else to do.

"Do you have a plan?" Cenric asked.

"I think so," Brynn said. "I am going to try and draw it into the water."

"The sea?"

"I'm not sure it will work," she confessed. "But I have an idea."

Brynn's uncertainty didn't seem to trouble her husband. "Alright."

18

Cenric

Everything was in chaos.

Thralls worked to carry buckets of seawater to put out fires. Animals that had not been able to flee cried out in panic.

Around them, everything Ovrek had worked for was going up in flames. The carefully constructed storehouses, the barns, and even the remaining animals from the sound of it.

As he coughed on smoke, Cenric suspected Ovrek's dream of conquest would not be realized this summer—if ever.

The darkness of night and the vast expanse of the sea stretched to their left and burning embers floated in the air from the buildings to their right.

Brynn moved beside him, hands at her sides and face set ahead, toward the hulking shape of the serpent as it smashed into storehouses and snapped at shapes on the ground.

Cenric tripped over a body, fearing it might be a friend, but couldn't tell in the anonymity of the dark.

"Cenric!" Brynn's warning came as a man in armor barreled toward Cenric, bearded axe raised over his head.

Cenric skirted back, adjusting the grip on his spear. "Ovrek!" he shouted, just in case these might be allies. "We fight for Ovrek!"

"Tullia!" came the defiant retort.

Three more men in full armor charged after the first. These must be stragglers. The battle seemed petty in comparison to what now stalked the streets of Istra, but these men must not think so.

Nothing for it, then.

Three of the men charged Cenric, probably counting on the advantage of being armored while he was still dressed for feasting. The last man barreled for Brynn.

Cenric dodged the first swipe of the axe, then the second. He caught a spear thrust on his shield.

A body hit the sand—the man who had charged Brynn lay with his head half-severed.

Cenric's three attackers turned, startled. They must not have known Brynn was a sorceress. Two of them spun, diverting to her.

That was enough. Cenric jabbed the nearest man with his spear, catching him in the space between his helm and the collar of his chainmail.

The stabbed man stumbled, collapsing as he gasped and choked. It would take him some time to die, but he wouldn't be getting up.

Scrambling, Cenric turned to help Brynn face the remaining two men.

Cenric fell on the nearest enemy, his spear slamming into the man's side, just above the hip. His spearhead didn't go through the armor, but it did knock the man off balance.

Brynn took the opportunity to strike at their fourth enemy. She feinted to the left, seeming to stumble.

Cenric's heart dropped as her foe stabbed for her side. The next moment, Brynn dodged, a spell ripping through the man's cheek in an explosion of teeth and blood.

Cenric barely had time to notice as his own opponent recovered, trying to back up and regroup.

The remaining enemy warrior let off a yell, his own spear lowered as he charged for Cenric. Cenric had heard that cry before. It was the cry of a man who knew he was going to die and had nothing left to lose. There were few things more dangerous.

Cenric swiped with his spear, but the enemy warrior got past it, blocking Cenric's spear with a shield.

Cenric sidestepped, getting inside the enemy's spear so he was face to face with the armored man, both inside the other's defense.

The warrior took but a moment to react. He drew a long knife, aiming for Cenric's chest.

The surf roiled at Cenric's back, lapping against the sand. The warrior was counting on Cenric not wanting to get into the water.

"Cenric!" Brynn called. She wouldn't have a clear strike for their enemy without risking a hit to him.

Cenric swung at the man's head with his shield, dropping his spear. He grabbed the knife between himself and the other warrior, his grip wrapping over his opponent's hands. Whether he had control of the knife or not, the other man was still armored and he wasn't.

Instead of trying to force the knife around to stab the enemy in the neck or head, he yanked backwards, toward the lapping surf.

"Tullia!" barked the warrior straining in Cenric's grip. "Tullia!"

"Tullia is dead," Cenric spat back, willing the words to be true. He yanked the other man backward just as a wave broke on the sand, washing over their feet before sliding back out. "And so are you."

"Cenric!" Brynn cried from the shore as he dragged the remaining Valdari warrior into the knee-high water. The man struggled, pulling back.

Cenric fought to hold on, but the man twisted out of Cenric's grip. The Valdari warrior crashed backward, splashing.

The knife disappeared into the water.

The armored warrior fought to reach it, but Cenric dropped his shield and tackled him into the waves. Pinning the enemy down, he grabbed the back of the man's helmet and shoved it under the water.

That armor had been an advantage on land, but in water it was a death trap.

Cenric dug his knee into the middle of the man's back as cold salt water lapped around him. The man bucked and struggled under Cenric—no warrior wanted to drown like an unwanted pup—but Cenric braced his foot against the sand and held the man under until he stopped kicking.

Cenric staggered to his feet as the waves sloshed around him.

Brynn met him in the surf, crashing into him. She gripped his arms, pulling him back toward the shore. "Are you alright? Are you hurt?"

"Fine," Cenric muttered, smearing salt water off his face. "Wet, is all." He waved toward the burning buildings, his sleeve dripping with seawater. "At least I'll be able to warm up by a fire."

Brynn clung to him, not seeming to care if she got soaked, too. She didn't chide him for his actions, though.

Over his shoulder, Cenric could see Ovrek's hall crumbling as it burned. "Most people will see that and assume Ovrek is dead."

If Ovrek was assumed dead, along with so many of his jarls, there would be widespread panic. People would flee the Althing while other men, who may not have had anything to do with Tullia's attempt at taking power, might try to seize power for themselves. The rich and powerful might try carving up Valdar for themselves, as it had always been feared that they would. If word didn't spread of Ovrek's survival soon, it could be a disaster.

But they could only deal with one disaster at a time.

"We can worry about that later." Brynn felt him over as if checking for damage before releasing him.

"Yes." Cenric gathered up his spear and shield and they continued deeper into the ravaged Istra. To draw the serpent toward the sea, they first needed to find it.

Cenric led the way, following the sound of the serpent's roars. He'd never known a snake could do aught but hiss, but this was not a natural creature.

The howls and bellows of Wulfwir could be heard from the northern part of Istra. Hopefully, his cousin and Ovrek were dealing with that one.

Cenric and Brynn rounded a storehouse with a burning roof and came upon utter carnage. Brynn gasped, a hand going to her mouth.

Bodies lay strewn in every direction—men, women, children, and dogs. Why dogs had stayed, but no other animals, Cenric couldn't begin to guess. Thankfully, none of the dogs were Snapper or Guin.

The corpses lay missing limbs, heads, and in some cases chunks of rib cage. Most of them appeared to be dead, but a few were still moving, groaning on the sand. But he doubted even Brynn's power would be enough to save them.

He had a strong stomach, but the sheer malice of the act made his stomach turn. This had not been the work of a hungry beast or an animal trying to feed itself. This had been an act of pure evil. Cenric had a stunning moment of clarity as he recognized the scene from last night's foretelling.

A hiss over Cenric's shoulder made him jump.

19

Brynn

Cenric slammed Brynn into the shelter of the burning storehouse before the serpent struck. He covered her body with his, the shield raised over them.

It missed, its teeth smashing into the ground instead. The creature let off a bellow of anger, clawed foot smashing into the burning roof as if to bat it away.

"The beach," Brynn panted. "We need to get to the beach."

Cenric had lost his spear but held onto his shield. He grabbed her arm with his free hand, pulling her after him.

The serpent turned at a sound, red eyes fixed on something on the other side of the buildings.

Brynn gathered power and lashed a strike for its face. Her spell cut into the creature's snout, sending black blood spurting free.

The creature roared and spun. Red eyes fixed on her. It didn't speak and she was grateful. She wasn't sure she could take the creature taunting her on top of everything else.

Shouts and cries rose from the other side of the building. It sounded like a group of Valdari were trying to attack the beast.

Fools. Brave and utter fools.

The serpent turned with a hiss, lunging for the unseen people on the far side of the building. The creature lunged and there came wet crunching sounds as screams erupted once again.

Gritting her teeth in frustration, Brynn pulled Cenric to a stop. "Jormanthar!" she shouted. "Serpent!"

The scaly body lashed back and forth on the opposite side of the storehouse, busy attacking the men who had dared attack it.

Brynn had hoped for a head start, but she would need the creature to be close for her plan to work. For a neck as thick as that, she would need power and focus and as little distance as possible.

If it had been any other enemy, she could have whipped it with hundreds of tiny cuts and weakened it either for her own attack or for spearmen. Because the serpent and its skin healed instantly, she had to give more effort.

Brynn gathered as much power as she dared and sent a lash for the creature's exposed back. Her spell ripped into its hide, leaving a great gash in the dark brown scales.

Squealing, the creature's head swept up, fixing on Brynn once more.

Brynn and Cenric started running again, heading toward the beach.

The serpent didn't follow. It blinked at them with those glowing red eyes.

How hard could this be?

Brynn sent another lash of power for the serpent's jaw. Jormanthar jolted, hissing as its mandible split, then repaired itself.

"Come on!" Brynn shouted. "Chase me, you wretch!"

Cenric snatched up a rock and hurled it at the creature's head. He missed, but the stone bounced off the serpent's large back.

The serpent let off a low growl, shifting toward them. The

thing seemed more annoyed than anything else. It lumbered in their direction.

The creature had been feeding and its belly distended. Even though it had only been taking a bite or two out of its prey, those bites had added up.

Getting chased by the monsters had been terrifyingly easy back under the Grandfather Yew. Brynn hadn't thought getting the serpent to follow her would be this difficult.

Jormanthar let off a low rumble. It lunged, tromping through the burning remains of the storehouse that had blocked the way between them.

Brynn and Cenric backed away, watching to make sure the creature followed.

Brynn cast another spell at the beast, shearing cuts along its nose. The beast sneezed, shaking its head and snapping at the air.

It cleared the broken remains of the storehouse, illuminated by the light of the burning buildings. The creature wasn't formed quite like any Brynn had seen before. It had a long neck and a head that swiveled in all directions like an eel. But it had scales and tiny legs, almost like it had been a common lizard that had far outgrown its intended size. The creature's proportions were off, much like Wulfwir. Jormanthar was not so much a serpent as a frightened child's idea of one.

Brynn and Cenric reached the sand beyond the wooden buildings, the beach lined with burning ships and scattered corpses. The sea was in sight, less than a hundred paces off.

Jormanthar growled and stopped, nostrils flaring at the sight of the black waves at their backs.

It's afraid of the sea, Brynn realized with a surge of hope. Perhaps her plan was onto something, not just desperation.

"Be moving!" Cenric bellowed back at the thing. "Let's go!"

Jormanthar hissed in response, head swaying.

Movement up the beach caught Brynn's attention. A gaggle of men carrying spears and axes charged down the sand, thumping their weapons against their shields.

"Not now!" Brynn cursed. "Idiots!"

Jormanthar swung its head in the direction of the men.

"That will be Ovrek," Cenric muttered.

"How can you tell?" Brynn cast him a sideways glance.

"He'll want to fight the greatest beast. I'd hoped we'd be able to deal with the serpent before he realized where we'd gone."

"He's going to get himself killed." Brynn's fists clenched, her frustration mounting. "He'd have a better chance of defeating the Wulfwir."

"A glorious death is better than an ignominious life," Cenric said.

"I almost had it!" Brynn watched as the serpent cocked its head, swaying in the direction of Ovrek's line of warriors. "What are their spears and axes going to do to this thing?"

Cenric observed as the beast withdrew, moving toward the line of warriors. "You want it near the water?"

"I'm going to try and use the *ka* in the water to work a spell," Brynn explained.

Cenric considered the advancing Valdari. "They might be able to flush it this way."

"You know they won't." Brynn sent another lash toward the beast. Her spell ripped along its back and even in the dark she saw blood splatter the sand. The creature growled, continuing toward the line of men.

Ovrek drew his warriors into formation, creating a shieldwall. It was a good formation. Most of the men had managed to acquire weapons. They must anticipate being able to attack it the way they would an enemy army, but it seemed none of them accounted for just how quickly it would heal.

Had Hróarr not told them? Or perhaps Ovrek had simply not wanted to listen.

"You seem to be striking it from this distance," Cenric pointed out.

"I need it to come closer," Brynn said. "The strength of the spell I'll need to cut all the way through that neck in one blow..." She groaned with frustration. "I'm not sure I'll be able to do it at all, but definitely not from a hundred paces or more."

Cenric was silent for a moment, watching as the serpent drew closer to Ovrek's line. The warriors formed a solid formation, spears bristling from between their shields. Jormanthar would batter through them like sticks.

A volley of javelins broke from the shieldwall. Most of them went wide, missing the beast entirely. A few struck the creature, but it shook itself and the javelins fell loose as if they were nothing but thistles.

"I'll bring it to you."

"Cenric?" Brynn's chest tightened.

Cenric pecked her cheek. "Get ready. I'll get the serpent." He pulled away from her, running up the beach.

Brynn's hands grasped after him instinctively, but she forced herself not to protest. Cenric trusted her, she needed to trust him. Even though her heart seemed to be clawing its way up her throat, Brynn turned. She ripped off her boots, letting them flop away onto the sand. She tore off her wool stockings and shed her leg wraps. Fortunately, they came off much faster than they went on.

Pebbles jabbed at her soles and cold water stung her shins as she rushed into the surf.

"Please, please, please," Brynn prayed, glancing toward the moon. "Eponine, please. Llyr, please." It was not her most eloquent or thought-out petition, but hopefully the gods wouldn't mind under the circumstances.

As the water touched her skin, Brynn pulled at the *ka* she had always sensed in the waves. Power rushed into her in a great torrent, mending the cuts and bruises from the past hour and surging strength through every sinew.

As she watched her husband rushing back up the beach, Brynn kept whispering "Please, please, please."

Her plan seemed to be working so far, but she could only hope it would be enough and that she wouldn't miss. That was assuming Cenric was successful.

20

Cenric

Getting in front of an ally shieldwall was something Cenric had been told never to ever do. Especially when projectile weapons were involved, it was one of the stupider ways to get oneself killed. Berdun had pounded that lesson into him, but if there was ever a special circumstance, this was it.

Cenric could see several of the javelins that had missed the serpent lying half-buried in the sand. He snatched up one to find it had bent. He tossed that one aside to grab another.

Jormanthar loomed over the shieldwall, swaying back and forth as if to find the easiest place to attack. The beast dove down, teeth crunching into the tight press of bodies.

Men yelled as spears jabbed at the snake's jaws as soon as it came in reach. The serpent tossed a single man into the air and let him crash down on top of his fellows. The line swayed and buckled for a moment, but it didn't appear anyone had been killed yet.

Cenric finally found two intact javelins. They were small and barbed at the ends, intended for hunting, not warring. Good enough.

Jormanthar reared over the shieldwall, making a thrumming, purring sound. It swayed, cocking its head. Despite being almost indestructible, the creature seemed to prefer the path of least resistance.

"Serpent!" Cenric shouted, trying to capture the beast's attention. "Jormanthar!" He had no idea if the beast would answer to that name, but his shouting at least drew its notice.

Its massive head with those red eyes turned and fixed on him. It blinked once, as if not sure what to make of this.

Ovrek's line took advantage of the beast's distraction. They surged forward, stabbing and hacking at the beast's sides.

Jormanthar reared back and struck down, biting at whatever it could reach and forcing the men back.

Cenric cursed at that. He'd almost had it. Then again, perhaps he could use this. The serpent seemed to prefer the easiest targets it could find.

Cenric rolled his right shoulder and then his whole arm, warming up the muscles. His tunic was still wet and restricted his movement somewhat, but he thought he'd still be able to make the throw.

Over his shoulder, Cenric spotted Brynn amid the waves. She stood in the water up to her knees. Her hands were at her sides, rigid and outstretched. He couldn't see her expression from this distance, but he knew her eyes were on him.

Was she ready? He hoped so.

First of Fathers, let us kill this beast and finish what you started.

Cenric cocked back his arm and hurled the first javelin.

The blade embedded itself in the serpent's right eye.

Jormanthar shrank back, shaking its head as a keening, shrieking sound broke from its maw. The eyes were the most sensitive part of the body, even for monstruous beasts of legend.

The creature tried to paw the spear free, but the moment its claws touched the javelin, it cried out in pain. It could probably heal from that wound, but in order to heal, it would need to pluck out the shaft.

Screaming in rage, the serpent spun on Cenric. Fury burned in its one uninjured eye as it let off a wail that was equal parts pain and wrath.

Ovrek's line advanced on the beast once again, but this time Jormanthar did not care.

Cenric hefted his second javelin, and the beast lunged.

Jormanthar's too-small legs scrambled after Cenric, its massive hulk and open jaws snapping after him.

Cenric ran straight back toward Brynn. His wet clothes stuck to him too tightly and the soft sand drew him down. It would have been a minor inconvenience any other time, but now it seemed far worse.

Jormanthar keened.

Cenric glanced over his shoulder to see the beast slow and then stop. It hesitated at the edge of the damp sand, glaring at the waves.

Brynn stood almost thirty paces off, shaking her head. She needed it closer.

Cenric faced the serpent and drew back his arm once again. He rocked forward, putting his body weight into the throw. The javelin hurled forward, striking the serpent in the second eye.

The First of Fathers had guided his arm. There was no other explanation for two perfect strikes.

Jormanthar shrieked loud enough that Cenric thought his ears would burst. The creature screamed, pawing blindly after Cenric. It stumbled forward, its jaws snapping after him with abject rage.

21

Brynn

It had worked. Cenric had thrown two javelins with perfect precision, and the creature was barreling after him, blind but enraged.

Power crawled up Brynn's legs, her hands, and everywhere that her skin touched water. It was different from drawing *ka* from the air. Strength came in pulses, much like the rhythm of the waves, but strong and abundant. As her heart raced, each moment passed at once too fast and not fast enough.

"Please, please, please," Brynn chanted, pulling magic to herself in great surges. "Please, please, please."

It seemed the only word that could capture her gnawing desperation. Whether she was begging Eponine to help, Llyr to show kindness, or Cenric to run faster, she couldn't have said. Maybe all three.

Cenric raced toward her, the serpent in pursuit. Now that the creature was blinded, it seemed less afraid of the water.

Brynn drew more power, growing lightheaded with the sheer magnitude of *ka* rippling through her. She wrapped her spell into a lash, the largest she had ever made before.

Cenric came closer, the serpent gaining on him. Cenric reached a few paces in front of her and skidded to a stop. He met her gaze in the moonlight and grinned.

Smiling at a time like this? What was in Valdar's air that made men such fools?

The serpent roared toward them. Close. Closer.

Jormanthar opened its mouth, swooping for Cenric.

Brynn released her power straight into its maw. Her spell burst out in a great rush, slicing up into the top of the serpent's skull.

Its pierced eyes guttered from red to black.

Brynn and Cenric scrambled out of the way as the top half of the beast's head splashed into the waves. Cenric grabbed her, pulling her to the side as the creature's neck smashed down the next moment.

Brynn had decapitated it from the jaw up.

The creature's massive hulk collapsed. It crashed into an incoming wave and splashed Brynn and Cenric backwards, making them lean on each other for balance.

Just like the burned girl, the serpent split.

A mangled phantom with beetle's wings and a vaguely human shape burst out of the corpse. The creature tried to scramble toward Brynn and Cenric, clawing at them like it might have dealt its revenge, but it flickered out of sight, dragged backwards as if by an invisible breeze.

Brynn leaned against her husband, staring at the dead beast beside them. She hadn't realized how truly massive it was until she was standing this close.

The thing must be as long as three ships, perhaps larger. Its legs were like tree trunks yet still seemed too tiny to have supported its size.

Cenric trembled beside Brynn. He made a low snorting sound.

"Are you laughing?" Brynn demanded, turning an accusatory glare at her husband.

"You are amazing!" he crowed, grabbing her waist. "Wonderful, wonderful woman."

Brynn could hardly believe it. "You've gone mad."

Cenric laughed harder at that, pulling her against him. They were drenched in sea water and the blood of the serpent swirled in the waves, staining them both. He squeezed her in his arms.

"How can you be celebrating?"

"My wife just killed a beast that not even the First of Fathers could vanquish," Cenric said, exultant. "If that's not worth celebrating, what is?"

"You stood there! Smiling when that thing was chasing you!" Brynn pushed him away, jabbing a finger into his chest.

Cenric shrugged. "I knew you would kill it."

"And if I hadn't?" Brynn wasn't sure why she was angry, but her temper flared.

"Better to die with you than live without you," Cenric said, echoing her words back to her.

A lump formed in her throat. "Cenric."

He rested a hand on her back. "Come on, love. Let's get out of the water."

Brynn glanced over to the limp corpse of the serpent. She could feel that the poisonous life force that had inhabited the thing was gone. Now it was just an ordinary corpse of an animal, its *ka* leaching out by the moment.

All the same, she moved past it uneasily. From beside the beast's haunches, it seemed possible that it was just resting, waiting for the moment to roar back to life.

Brynn and Cenric made their way back onto the shore, soaked in saltwater, serpent's blood, and caked in black sand. Cenric had not removed his boots or leg wraps and his steps made wet sucking sounds. Brynn walked barefoot, her own stockings, leg wraps, and boots soaked through as well.

These clothes were ruined, Brynn decided. Needing to have new feasting clothes made for herself and her husband was a small problem in the grand scheme of things. All the same, Brynn's mind wandered to where she would find the time to embroider a new tunic for him before Blydmoth. He would need it for the autumn feasts.

She would need Esa's help…

"Esa." Brynn pressed her hand against Cenric's shoulder. "And Kalen. What about the Wulfwir?"

22

Cenric

"We'll see to all that." Now that the exhilaration of victory was wearing off, Cenric started to feel the strain of the past hour or so. Weariness was taking over. *Snapper?* he sent out.

Cenric? the dog's answer came faint, but eager. *Brynn?*

Brynn, Cenric answered, assuring the dog she was safe. *Vana?*

Vana, Snapper answered. *Snapper protect Vana,* he confirmed proudly.

Good dog.

Snapper's pleasure echoed across the distance.

Cenric and Brynn trudged onto the beach to find the king's band of warriors staring at them. Ovrek stepped forward.

"You greedy bitch!" Ovrek shouted. It was hard to know if he was serious or not, but he spoke Hyldish, intended for Brynn. "Had to take the beast for yourself?"

Cenric bristled. Why did people keep calling his wife a bitch?

Was he going to have to kill Ovrek after all?

"Wulfwir is headed this way." Brynn cast her gaze to the burning expanse of wooden structures around them. She shifted closer to Cenric. She was unsteady on her feet, they both were, but she watched straight ahead. "Cenric."

Ovrek's gaze sparked as he hefted his axe once again. He called to his men back up the beach and they fell into formation.

Wulfwir burst from the darkness, red eyes flashing in the dark. The creature lunged for the men.

Hróarr's voice rang out over the beach. "Wall!" he roared. "Shieldwall!"

Cenric almost dove forward at the familiar call, the order driving home years of practice when obeying that command had been a matter of life and death. Only Brynn's weight against his side reminded him that he was now unarmed, and some things were best left to his cousin.

Ovrek made to charge forward, and join the fray, but he had left the line to come toward the beach. Now the line closed without him, meeting Wulfwir head on.

Wulfwir seemed to realize the serpent was dead and attempted to flee. Javelins pelted it and this time, they were not so easily plucked out.

Cenric saw Wulfwir go down as the men fell on the beast. It fought back, struggling and kicking. One man went flying, hitting the sand some twenty paces off.

Wulfwir disappeared under a wave of bodies as Hróarr led the attack. Cenric shifted, looking to Brynn. Would she need to deal with this one, too?

Brynn touched his arm. "Hróarr will be fine," she assured him, as if hearing his thoughts. "I think this one is personal."

A roar went up, but not from the beast. A shape burst out of the melee—Hróarr carrying the severed head.

His cousin was splattered in blood and gore with cuts and gashes on his chest, torso, and arms, but he was standing while the

Wulfwir lay hacked to pieces.

As the tight press of warriors withdrew, Cenric could see that they had hacked its legs off to keep it from running. It seemed the beast hadn't been able to heal severed limbs.

As Hróarr and the men celebrated, Brynn and Cenric were left with the king, standing a short distance away.

Brynn pulled her wet stockings and boots back on, steadying herself against Cenric. "I think some of Tullia's men are still about."

"Word will spread of her death soon enough," Cenric answered.

"Is she dead?" Brynn sent a probing gaze toward Ovrek.

"Probably." The king showed no feeling at the words. "Her ship is one of the ones burning on the beach and no one saw her retreat."

"I don't think she would have retreated," Brynn said.

Cenric had to agree with that. Tullia had been committed to her course. She had too much of her father in her.

"She should have been born a son." Ovrek looked back in the direction of his burning hall. "Why did the gods not make her a son?"

Cenric didn't know what to say to that. From the burning town and the hard-fought battle, being a woman had never stopped Tullia. Ovrek was the only one who had been limited by her being a daughter, not Tullia and certainly not the hundreds of men scattered across the city who still battled in her name.

Cenric! A grey shape leapt from the darkness. *Cenric! Brynn!*

"Snapper!" Cenric stepped forward to meet the dog.

"Snapper," Brynn sighed, sounded relieved.

The dog whined, slobbering his tongue over Cenric's cheek before bounding to Brynn and leaping up to try licking her face. *Cenric! Brynn!*

"Can Snapper find Esa and Kalen?" Brynn asked. "Can he find Guin?"

"He should."

Brynn gripped his arm. "We must find them. Vana, too."

Brynn was right. Tullia's forces were defeated, and both monsters were dead, but the danger was not past.

"Hróarr!" Cenric shouted. "We're going to find Vana and the others!"

Hróarr dropped the head of his defeated foe. Jogging toward them, he held onto his bloody axe. "Vana?"

"We're going to look," Brynn said.

"I'll come with you." Hróarr's jubilation was gone. He looked to Ovrek.

"Go." The king turned back to the light of his burning hall. "I should make sure my daughter is among the dead."

Cenric wondered if Ovrek would kill Tullia if he found her alive. Would the king slay his own flesh and blood? His firstborn? There was a time when Cenric would have never even asked the question, but he was not so sure now.

He turned back to Snapper. *Find Kalen.*

Kalen. Snapper sent back an image of the boy. He let off a bark, bounding ahead.

Cenric needed to find Vana, Esa, and Guin, too, but it was easier to give the dog one set of instructions at a time. Not to mention that Snapper was already getting caught up in the screaming and the riot of noise and smells.

Snapper led the way, tail wagging. He leapt over the debris and flotsam of the beach, only growing solemn when they came across bodies.

Some people were still alive, and Brynn stopped, trying to help those she could. Others were past her skill and Cenric had to pull her away. He was sure that only the thought of Esa and Kalen allowed her to abandon her efforts.

"Kalen!" Cenric shouted, searching the darkness. "Kalen!"

Hróarr jogged beside Cenric, bloodied axe in one hand. "Vana!" he roared into the smoke.

Shouting as they ran down the beach, Cenric finally spotted a familiar ship with its deer heads in place on the prow. It seemed that Hróarr's ship was intact, if nothing else.

The *Wolf Star* had been unanchored and a deep groove in the sand stretched back several paces, as if someone had tried to push it out to sea, then been stopped.

"Kalen!" he shouted. "Where are you, boy?"

A body lay on the sand in front of Cenric and he feared the worst for a moment, but as they drew closer, he realized it was a Valdari man. The stranger's neck had been sliced open in a clean wound, almost like...

Kalen! Snapper sent the name with an image of the boy crouched beside the ship. *Kalen!*

Cenric followed the sound of whining as Snapper licked the boy's face, hopping and dancing in the sand with glee. "Kalen?"

"Lord?" Kalen sputtered. His voice came from the shadow of the ship, hesitant.

"Are Vana and Esa with you?" Cenric called.

"Vana!" Hróarr barreled toward the sound of the boy's voice. "Where is Vana?" he demanded.

"Hróarr!" The pale woman flew from the darkness, meeting him in a tight embrace.

Hróarr pulled her against him, cradling her in the shelter of his body.

"Esa?" Brynn stepped forward, voice shaking.

"She's here, lady." Kalen reached back to pull Esa out of the shadows.

Esa emerged, looking shaken by the light of the fires, Guin clutched in her arms. The puppy squirmed, squeaking for Brynn.

Brynn caught her ward in her arms, Guin clutched between them. Brynn stroked the girl's hair, pressing her cheek to the top of Esa's head. "I'm so glad you're safe. Both of you."

"You too, lady," Esa whimpered. "We were so frightened when we saw the fires of the hall."

"Daven and the other thanes went to find you, lord," Kalen said. "We thought for sure you were dead, but then Vana found us, and we dared hope."

Cenric saw no sign of his men. "Where are Daven and the others now?"

"Still searching for you, lord."

Istra was burning. Confusion and chaos reigned. It was unlikely that Cenric would be able to find his men in this mess, and he'd probably have to wait for them to return to the ship.

Cenric assessed the dead man on the sand, then Kalen. "Good work, son." He pulled the silver ring from his right arm and passed it to the boy. He'd given one to Kalen before, but he deserved another for saving Vana and Esa.

"Thank you, lord." Kalen inclined his head, not taking the ring. "But that was Esa. She used her magic."

Brynn shifted away from Esa, one hand on the girl's arm. "Esa?"

The girl nodded. "I did it, lady."

Cenric passed the arm ring to her, and she took it in a shaking hand, not seeming to understand what was happening. "For your courage." Cenric tugged an iron ring from his left arm and passed that to Kalen. "For your honesty." Cenric took in the damage done to the city of Ovrek's dreams.

"There will be no invasion of Hylden," Brynn said, stating the obvious. "Not this year."

"No." Hróarr kept one arm around Vana.

Too much damage had been done. It would take years to recover from this, at least three, if Cenric had to guess.

Ovrek would build back, that was his way, but it would take time.

Anything could happen in three years. Anything at all.

23

Brynn

Brynn did not know Ovrek personally. She knew only passing details of his history, but she had no doubt that last night had been the worst night of his life.

His queen, his daughter, and his concubine were all dead. He'd lost hundreds of men and years of work. His hall, the symbol of a lord's power, had been burned. Not only that, but terrors from legend had ravaged his people.

Worst of all, Ovrek had not killed any of those terrors himself. He had faced the serpent and Wulfwir and even Tullia, but he could not claim the glory for besting any of them.

In a way, Brynn sympathized. He had done what he was supposed to do—lead fearlessly in the face of danger. But the glory would go to others.

Brynn and Cenric had killed Jormanthar. Hróarr had killed Wulfwir. There had been dozens of witnesses to both. No one knew who had killed Tullia or if someone did, they were wisely not taking credit. Though Tullia had been a traitor, it was unlikely Ovrek would reward the man who had slain his daughter.

Daybreak saw Ovrek alone on the hill beneath the smoking remains of his hall. He'd chased off everyone who had tried to speak to him—Cenric, Hróarr, Berdun, and even Tolvir—shouting incoherent threats and curses.

Vana had wanted to try speaking to him, but Hróarr had wanted her nowhere near Ovrek while the king had an axe. Brynn had volunteered because she had the means to protect herself and Ovrek might not see her as a threat. He tended to underestimate women.

Cenric, Hróarr, Vana, Berdun, and a jarl by the name of Ingmar waited a short distance down the hill. Snapper and Guin waited with them, watching to see if Brynn might have better luck. It had been six hours since the battle, and the sun had climbed its way out of the eastern sea. Perhaps Ovrek had the chance to calm down, or perhaps he was simply tired by now.

"King Ovrek," Brynn called, not sure if he would try chasing her off, too.

The king did not respond. He remained with his head bowed, staring at the corpse laid out before him.

Brynn ventured closer.

Ovrek's axe lay at his feet. He'd have to reach for it and that should give her ample warning if he did try to strike.

"Lord?" Brynn dared to venture even closer.

"What do you want?" Ovrek growled, not looking up.

"Your people need you."

"They did just fine without me last night," Ovrek spat back. The bitterness in his voice unmistakable.

"Vana would ask your permission to search for Sifma's body," Brynn said. "She wishes to prepare your queen for burial."

Sifma's remains were somewhere in the smoking ruin of the hall. Vana hoped she would be recognizable by her jewelry, but after flying into a rage, Ovrek had not permitted anyone close enough to look.

"Vana?" Ovrek seemed to think hard to recall the name, but after a moment he relented. "Yes. Vana can look."

"Thank you, lord. That will mean a great deal to her." Brynn could see that Sifma had been dear to Vana, like a mother. As soon as she realized Hróarr was alive and they had won, she'd broken down in tears.

Ovrek hesitated. "She'll have women help her?"

"She'll need some of the men to help move the bodies, but yes."

Ovrek's shoulders rose, squaring.

"Cenric and Hróarr," Brynn added quickly. "And perhaps your son? No one else."

Ovrek was quiet for a moment. "That's fine. But no one else."

Brynn dared to venture closer.

Ovrek didn't respond, allowing her to sit beside him on the edge of the small berm where the corpse had been dragged last night.

Tullia's helm was missing, as was one of her bracers. The looters probably hadn't realized it was her or even that it was a woman in the dark, but Ovrek had been incensed when he'd caught them.

He'd killed two of his own men without question. He had raved and roared like a madman, swinging his axe at anyone who came near his daughter's body.

Brynn understood all too well. She'd found her sister's corpse naked on the battlefield and knew what that meant. There was a reason she had never told anyone where her sister was buried. Better for Aelfwynn to lie in anonymity than to be violated further.

"I shouldn't have named her Tullia." Ovrek's voice cracked. "Her namesake died young, too. It was unlucky." The king didn't say more, and Brynn didn't press him.

She stared down at what remained of Tullia.

Bodies had a way of paling and shrinking in death. It was eerie. The form at their feet was Tullia and yet it wasn't.

It appeared that a blade had gotten under Tullia's armor and stabbed her inner thigh, probably a spear. She'd bled out but had kept fighting if the corpses around her were any indication.

Her two eunuchs lay not far off, covered in wounds. They too had sold their lives dearly.

"She fought well," Brynn said softly. "She died well."

Ovrek tilted his head back, looking to the sky. "She did."

Brynn had felt an odd sense of kinship to the other woman. Even after Tullia had tried to kill her and Cenric, along with everyone in that hall, Brynn couldn't rejoice over the woman's death. Tullia was so familiar. She had been so much like Aelfwynn.

But Brynn couldn't picture Aelfwynn locking her inside a burning hall as Tullia had done to her younger brother.

"She will be buried in the armor." Ovrek spoke the words like a decree. "No one takes it off."

"We can arrange that, lord." The war gear was exquisite, even in its battle worn state. Brynn couldn't even begin to imagine how much it would have cost, but that wasn't important to Ovrek now.

"We'll bury her eunuchs with her." Ovrek gestured toward their corpses. "They should attend her in the next life, I think."

"I'm sure she'd like that." As to what the men would have wanted for themselves, Brynn would never know. They would be buried as grave goods for their mistress by people who likely didn't even know their names.

"I will bury Gistrid with Sifma," Ovrek continued. "It seems fitting."

Brynn had no comment. She inhaled and exhaled carefully. The morning breeze had carried away most of the smoke, but her lungs were still sore. She might find it difficult to breathe for some time.

"My queen told me an interesting story before the feast."

Brynn dared not speak.

"She said she had poisoned my concubine." Ovrek made a growling sound of frustration. "She refused to tell me why."

Brynn followed his gaze, staring out at the water. "I am sure she had her reasons."

Ovrek finally deigned to look at her. "That is exactly what she said."

Brynn had the impulse to turn from his probing gaze, but she didn't.

"I suppose this means Cenric can keep you." Ovrek glared down the hill to where her husband waited with his cousin.

A flutter of relief stirred in Brynn's chest. At least that was confirmation Ovrek wouldn't be trouble for them—for now.

"I owe you a favor, Lady Brynn." Ovrek rested his hands on his knees.

"A favor, lord?"

"You killed the serpent," Ovrek reminded her. "Every man on that beach saw it. An arm ring hardly seems sufficient."

"Ah, yes." Brynn glanced down the hill at Cenric. "I'm not sure that is needed."

"Why not?"

"I killed Jormanthar for Cenric."

Ovrek didn't seem to quite understand. "What does that mean?"

"I fought the serpent for him. Just as I was ready to swear allegiance to one," Brynn replied softly, "if he'd asked it of me." She gazed down to the beach, where Ovrek's black serpent banner had been staked to let everyone know that the king still lived. Whether that was an extra banner or if Ovrek's banner had been somehow spared when his hall burned, Brynn didn't know.

"But he did not ask it of you?" Ovrek seemed to catch on.

"It looks as if it won't come to that." Brynn stared out over Istra.

By daylight, the damage was not as bad as it had seemed when fires were all one could see. Many of the storehouses had been partially damaged, but only a few had been destroyed entirely.

Most of Tullia's men had behaved in a typical Valdari fashion, seeking to steal instead of destroy. Apart from the obvious exception of the hall, Brynn wasn't sure that any of the other fires had been started intentionally. They might very well have been accidents as fires were left untended in the chaos of the battle. Many of Ovrek's unfinished ships had been burned, but most of the completed ones had only been taken farther down the beach.

Hundreds of people had died, and the Althing had all but dispersed before it had begun. Rumors of Ovrek's death still fluttered about the town, but Ovrek's men were working to tamp them down.

It could have been so much worse.

Stories of Hróarr slaying Wulfwir and Cenric's two perfect javelin throws into the serpent's eyes were already spreading like ringworm through a pigpen.

Down on the beach, people stared at the massive corpse of Jormanthar, milling about, seeing the decapitated body for themselves. Everyone could see no blade had done that. Brynn had heard her own name whispered by Valdari tongues on the walk here.

"I will rebuild," Ovrek growled, the words like a vow.

"You will," Brynn conceded.

Even once word of what he had done to the Grandfather Yew spread, Brynn had no doubt Ovrek would keep control of Valdar. He was not a man to let something as trifling as facts hinder his aspirations.

All the same, Ovrek would not be able to invade Hylden this year or next. He would need time. That would give Brynn and Cenric time, too.

With time, they could build palisades, strengthen defenses. They could train more warriors and establish more forts.

One day, Ovrek might very well have to court Cenric's favor instead of demanding his allegiance.

Ovrek folded his arms across his chest, leaning back. He might have floundered in his grief moments ago, but it seemed thoughts of conquest pulled him back.

"If you still wished to grant me a favor…" Brynn weighed her next words carefully. "There is one thing I think would benefit us all."

"And that is?" Ovrek seemed interested now.

"Recognize Cenric as jarl of Ombra," she said.

"That will do nothing," Ovrek shot back. "He's already an alderman."

"He is," Brynn conceded. "But if you invade Hylden, my husband will need the respect of your men."

"If?" Ovrek growled.

Brynn continued as if she hadn't heard him. "You punish jarls who steal from other jarls, don't you?"

Ovrek muttered his confirmation.

"Raids from a few farm boys here and there are inevitable." Raids were a problem, but Ombra had always dealt with those. "But by giving Cenric the same honor as the other men of your circle, you will make it clear who you want to hold Ombra."

Cenric had lived most his life among the Valdari, but since his own uncle's death had never had a place among them. He'd fought and bled for Ovrek, but his home had always been across the sea.

Brynn could see many of them liked him and respected him, but he needed more than that. He needed Ovrek's blessing. Not just a few former thralls turned warriors to retake his home, he needed Ovrek to outright recognize him as rightful lord of Ombra.

If Ovrek publicly acknowledged that Ombra belonged to Cenric, then there was no way Ovrek could carve up pieces of the shire for his other jarls. At least if he did, Ovrek would have to publicly turn on Cenric first.

After the events of the past two days, that would be difficult to justify. Cenric had saved his life at least twice and everyone within fifty miles knew it already. As soon as the remaining Althing dispersed, every island in Valdar would know it. Brynn had also saved Ovrek's life and word of that was spreading, too.

Ovrek could not repudiate Cenric without exceptional cause,

not without making every other follower question if they might meet the same fate. If Ovrek could not be trusted to reward such a show of loyalty, could he be trusted at all?

"You cannot make demands of me." Ovrek's voice hardened with offense.

"I thought we agreed Cenric already holds Ombra and it would change nothing?"

At the foot of the hill, Cenric watched her, arms folded across his chest. He didn't think Ovrek would recognize him as a jarl, but Brynn thought Ovrek was smart enough to see that he should. Rewarding Cenric would reassure Ovrek's current followers that he was generous. Ovrek's followers needed reassurance about now—the promise of wealth to help soften their king's sacrilege. It might also incentivize Hyldish lords to join Ovrek when the time came.

Brynn already had an explanation if her uncle questioned it. There was no Valdari word for alderman. They would tell Aelgar that it was just a translation. As long as they continued paying proper tributes, her uncle would have no reason to question it.

"Your uncle is the king of Hylden." Ovrek stated the obvious.

"He is." Brynn inclined her head slightly. "And he's a good man. A good king, too."

Ovrek watched Brynn like a warrior watching the approach of a strange ship, not sure if it was an enemy vessel or not.

"But he is sick," Brynn said, her voice soft. "He has been sick since he was born." Not a month had gone by as children when Brynn hadn't heard of some malady that ailed her uncle. He had all the best healers and sorceresses the kingdom had to offer, yet it was a miracle he continued to live. "I expect he will be the last of his line unless the gods are exceptionally good."

Aelgar had a son, but his son was still a toddler. Kings in Hylden did not inherit by virtue of birth. All kings must be the descendants of kings, but they must also be elected by the Witan, the council of aldermen who ruled the shires. It was made up of proud elders and grizzled veterans. It would be over a decade before the boy would even be considered by the Witan as a candidate, even if someone else ruled in his stead until he came of age. Hylden did not have queens, but they did not have boy-kings, either.

If Aelgar died before his son was at least sixteen, Hylden would have another war. A king needed to be armor-strong—grown enough to wear the helm and war gear. Even if Aelgar's son was a man by the time of his father's death, there might still be a war. It was impossible to say. Some other Hyldish warlord might decide he would make a better king than Aeldred.

If another king of a different family replaced Aelgar, Brynn and Cenric's children would forever be a threat to him. If Aelgar's bloodline ended, that would make Brynn the last surviving descendant of her grandfather, King Aelmar, and her children would be the sole heirs to his legacy. Aelmar's legend was powerful. Many regarded his reign and the reign of Brynn's father as a golden age.

The events of last autumn had reminded Brynn that though she might consider herself outside the royal succession, not everyone did. Brynn doubted any upstart king would tolerate the risk she and her children posed, especially if she had another son. Brynn and Cenric needed a bulwark against the death of Aelgar.

"You are sharpening your sword on both sides." Ovrek sounded vaguely amused. "You wish to remain loyal to Aelgar while keeping the option to join me if it suits you."

"Does that not suit you?" Brynn kept her tone mild. "You and my husband remain friends. Valdari ships will be welcome to trade in our harbors, if they please."

"When Aelgar dies?" Ovrek slanted his head to the side. "When I am again ready to invade?"

"Then we will have much more to discuss, won't we?"

If Ovrek wanted to use Brynn and Cenric to gain a foothold in Hylden, they would use him to protect their future. The aldermen and sorceresses of Hylden were dangerous, but so was the Valdari king. Last year, Brynn had wanted to disappear into obscurity for the rest of her life. She still hoped that would happen but doubted more and more that it would.

Ovrek gave a noncommittal grunt. He joined her in staring out across Istra, leaning to rest his elbows on his knees. "You are like Tullia."

Brynn wasn't sure how to take that. She resisted the urge to glance down at the corpse by their feet. "How so?"

"Clever."

Brynn stayed quiet, sensing that they were venturing back to the topic of Ovrek's betrayal and loss of his daughter.

"She was everything I've always wanted my son to be." Something about those words sounded almost like confession, almost. "Yet every day I lose hope the boy ever will be."

"She fought you." Brynn reminded him, trying to be gentle.

Ovrek shook his head. "It's natural for a boy to fight with his father. It's part of becoming a man." Ovrek gestured in the direction of Hróarr and Cenric. "Those two are better sons than my own flesh and blood."

Hróarr and Cenric were here, Tolvir was not. Brynn didn't know where the young atheling might be, though she had seen him alive this morning.

"Everyone seems to be a better son than Tolvir," Ovrek complained. "Not just Cenric and Hróarr. I trained an entire army of sons yet can't seem to train one." The king seemed to be sinking into self-pity once again. "Sifma didn't want to foster him, and so I allowed her to raise him herself. She spoiled the boy."

Brynn wasn't sure that was fair to the dead queen, but didn't argue. She glanced down to the foot of the hill and an idea came to her. Hróarr probably wouldn't like it, but if Brynn could provide wise council to Ovrek, it might help strengthen their new alliance. "Now that Hróarr will not be needed for your invasion for some time, I expect he will return to being a mercenary."

"Likely." Ovrek sounded uninterested.

"He will need men for his ship," Brynn pointed out. "I know

he lost a few last night."

Ovrek cast Brynn a hard look. "What are you saying?"

"Perhaps there are some things we can't learn from our parents," Brynn explained. "Perhaps Hróarr could teach your son what you taught him."

The king stroked his beard, looking down the hill. "It might do the boy good."

Brynn inclined her head. The thought of Hróarr having to deal with the spoiled atheling brought her a smug sense of satisfaction. Maybe she *had* been holding a grudge over the thrall pit.

Ovrek inhaled a deep breath, looking over his burned town. "My people need me, you said?"

"Yes, lord."

Ovrek slapped his thighs. "Let's go, then."

A little surprised, Brynn stood with the king.

The two of them walked down the hill side by side in silence. They were a strange set of companions, the Valdari king and a foreign sorceress. Brynn was grateful that Ovrek left his axe behind.

They reached the foot of the hill, met by Cenric, Hróarr, Vana, Berdun, Ingmar, and a small gathering of other warriors who had waited out of sight.

Cenric caught Brynn's hand. "Impressive," he whispered in her ear. "None of us could even get close enough to talk to him." Cenric kissed her cheek, tugging her closer to his side.

Berdun and Ingmar greeted Ovrek in Valdari, inclining their heads. The other warriors bowed. No matter what happened last night or with the Grandfather Yew, they were still loyal.

Ovrek seemed to transform, back straight and chin up. He was grief-worn and had to be exhausted, but in that moment, it was easy to see why the Valdari had allowed him to become king. It was hard to look at him and see anything else. The king spoke softly, looking to Vana.

The Valdari woman bowed at his words, and rushed up the hill, Hróarr following close behind.

"Your wife is a wise woman, Cenric," Ovrek said.

"She is, lord." Cenric fitted her hand more snugly in his.

Ovrek's gaze fell on Brynn once again. "My son could have used a wife like you."

Brynn might not have thought anything of it but for Tullia's words to Cenric last night—*Did you know he considered taking your wife for Tolvir?*

Brynn couldn't prove it, but in an instant, she was certain that Tullia had told the truth.

From the way Cenric inhaled sharply, he came to the same conclusion.

"Lord?" Brynn squeezed Cenric's arm in warning.

Ovrek cocked one brow.

"There have been bad omens for serpents lately." Brynn looked pointedly to the great corpse that lay on the sand, the creature whose likeness adorned the Valdari king's banners. It was a risk, but she hoped Ovrek would catch her meaning without taking offense. "Do be careful."

Ovrek threw back his head and laughed, one of the great belly laughs that seemed to be a staple of his personality. "You have a way with words, sorceress."

Around them, the air seemed to shift. With the return of Ovrek's laugh, the men seemed to breathe a collective sigh of relief.

Except for Cenric. His jaw clenched, pulling her closer.

"Let it go," Brynn pleaded.

"The insult!" he hissed.

Brynn grabbed the collar of his tunic, pulling his head down so she could whisper in his ear. "If he mentions it again, I'll deal with his men so you can fight him, but just this once, let it go."

Cenric exhaled a long breath. He was still angry but let her have this one.

The king was too busy answering questions from his men to notice their conversation. They surrounded him, visible relief in having Ovrek among them once again.

Berdun led the way with several others, heading back toward Istra at a jog. The people needed to see Ovrek, to reassure themselves that he lived. Their whole group began to move onward toward the town.

Ovrek stopped abruptly, his back to her. "Lady Brynn?"

"Yes, lord?"

"You will look after Tullia?" Ovrek's voice did not falter, but his entire spine remained rigid as he awaited an answer.

"Yes, lord," Brynn promised. "I will look after her."

"Good." Ovrek marched away with his men and this time didn't look back.

Instead of attending the Althing, they attended two funerals. It took the better part of a fortnight to see to the many preparations for the burial of three great ladies.

The head of Wulfwir was left on a rocky expanse of beach to be picked clean by seagulls and crabs. Once the flesh was gone, Hróarr wanted to mount it on the front of his ship to use in place of a wooden wolf's head.

The cleaved head of Jormanthar was massive, even in half, and had been left where it fell. Once the creatures of the shallow water finished their work, Ovrek wanted to move it to the place of the Grandfather Yew.

The body of Jormanthar had been too large to move and had begun to stink. So, men had hacked it to pieces and dragged the pieces down the beach. There it had been rolled into the waves where it would be food for the creatures of the deep.

As much meat as there was, eating the flesh of the ancient monster was too much for even the pragmatic Valdari.

Brynn couldn't have said why Ovrek trusted her, but he charged her with overseeing Tullia's burial. Vana was tasked with tending Sifma and Gistrid.

Cenric and Hróarr had to move both Sifma and Tullia. Ovrek wouldn't let them take the armor off, either, so Tullia was that much heavier.

Cenric showed Snapper Tullia's corpse and the two of them spent an entire day with Kalen, searching the campground of the Althing. They returned with her missing bracer and helm in the late hours of the evening. Cenric told Brynn they'd been taken by a stripling youth who broke down crying and swore he hadn't known whose corpse it was.

That was believable enough. It had been dark, and everything had been in chaos.

Cenric returned the stolen armor. When Ovrek demanded to know who had taken it, Cenric truthfully answered that he didn't have a name.

Tullia was buried in her late husband's lamellar armor, upright in a wooden seat with her eunuchs standing beside her, held up with wooden posts. The sword she had wielded was bent and placed in her right hand. The shield was split with an axe before being leaned by her feet.

A young mare was killed and set before her, along with two hunting dogs from her household, and a cat she had brought from across the sea on one of her journeys. Precious stones, a silk robe, a small box of polished wood containing amethyst, a jar of perfume, combs, eating knives, and a cask of mead were buried with her.

It was the burial of a warrior in every way, worthy of a jarl. Some people questioned Ovrek's decision, but no one dared question it to his face.

When going through Tullia's belongings to find goods for her grave, Brynn came across a child's toy horse carved from soapstone. It was tucked in a chest inside a leather oilcloth along with several dried daisies and a baby-soft lock of black hair.

Brynn made sure the oilcloth pouch was placed in Tullia's lap under her left hand, the one not holding the sword.

Ovrek sacrificed his great, profane ship to be Sifma and Gistrid's grave. The vessel with its mast and ribs made from the Grandfather Yew was dragged to the hillside, into a massive trench. The ship alone was a lavish act of mourning, a sacrifice of wealth greater than most people would hold in their lifetime.

Brynn had to wonder if sacrificing the ship at the heart of the past days' bloodshed was an act of penitence. She doubted Ovrek would ever admit to something so humbling, but the king did seem repentant.

Sifma and Gistrid were buried reclined on the deck with Gistrid by Sifma's feet, denoting their rank. Sifma's body had been badly burned and little besides her skeleton remained.

Vana and the servants still did their best, but Sifma's clothes had mostly melted into her charred flesh. They had to wrap her funeral clothes over her feasting garb.

Sifma was buried with lush furs, arm rings, a magnificent silver torque not unlike the one Vana wore. The deck of the ship was neatly arranged like a small house with chickens, a pair of oxen, three ewes, and jars of salt. Sifma's spinning wheel and distaff were placed beside her, as was her loom, much of her jewelry, and a mirror of polished brass that had been a gift from Tullia.

A magnificent tapestry depicting the tale of the First of Fathers had adorned the inside of Sifma's house. That was pulled down and used to decorate the edges of her grave, the painstaking detail and meticulous designs buried beneath the earth.

Gistrid was buried with just a few of her own goods surrounding her, the cushions and furs that had adorned her house.

The graves were sealed at midday when the sun was at its brightest, ensuring that the spirits of the dead would not be wandering and become lost. Drums beat to draw the attention of the gods, hopefully to earn their protection over the dead.

Brynn stood beside Vana, watching with the other onlookers as Ovrek and Tolvir cracked open casks of ale and poured them out over the freshly turned earth.

Vana wept silently, Hróarr's arm around her. The tall mercenary glared at Brynn every so often, but he had been doing that ever since Ovrek had asked him to take Tolvir onto his ship. Hróarr had agreed—it wasn't the sort of request that could be refused—but he hadn't wanted to. Brynn admitted that some dark, spiteful part of her enjoyed that.

Cenric watched beside Brynn, a jarl now as well as an alderman. Guin leaned against her feet, and Esa and Kalen stood at their backs.

It was difficult to reflect on the past few weeks. Nothing had changed and at the same time, everything had.

Brynn squeezed Cenric's hand as the drums continued to beat.

24

Cenric

Little about these past weeks in Valdar had been enjoyable. Cenric was returning richer than he had left, laden with cloth, ivory, and furs his men had traded for, but also gifts of walrus ivory, silver cups, lapis lazuli beads, and iron ingots from Ovrek.

The king always gave good gifts, but that he was still giving so generously after the grievous blows of the past month was telling. He wanted Cenric's alliance.

He doubted he would be able to forget that Ovrek had considered trying to take Brynn for Tolvir. For now, he took Brynn's advice and pretended not to know. Deep down, he vowed never to trust Ovrek again.

Loading his ship in Istra's harbor, Cenric was glad to be leaving. Valdar was in his blood, but it was not in his bones the way Ombra was. He was eager to return home.

A yelp caught Cenric's attention. He turned to see Tolvir rubbing his head, glaring at Hróarr from the deck of Hróarr's ship. It seemed the man had tossed one of the bags up and Tolvir had not caught it fast enough.

"Watch yourself!" the boy snapped.

"Watch your surroundings," Hróarr answered drily. "I called out, but you didn't respond."

"You have no right—"

Hróarr hurled another of the bags, this one even bigger than the first. It hit Tolvir square in the chest, and the young man stumbled back, fighting to catch it. Hróarr had volunteered to accompany Cenric back to Ombra before he headed south once again. It was only fitting that a jarl had a vanguard, Ovrek had said.

Cenric picked up one of the bundles of tent poles with Daven. They handed it up to where Kalen and several of the younger men worked to arrange their goods on the deck.

Kalen never complained, a fact Cenric was coming to appreciate more by the moment. Maybe he should give the boy another silver ring just for that.

Snapper watched over Guin, who appeared to have found a mussel shell farther down the beach.

Brynn and Esa worked to roll up the tent canvases and pack up what remained of their small camp. Lena, the thrall girl, helped them with her head down, jumping at commands and skirting to obey even soft-spoken Esa.

Brynn had asked Ovrek if she could take all of Tullia's Hyldish thralls back to Hylden. Unfortunately, Ovrek had already given all the surviving thralls along with the other goods in Tullia's household to the jarl Ingmar.

Ingmar had been the one to rally his men and attack when he realized Ovrek's hall was burning. He deserved a reward.

Cenric went to Ingmar with Hróarr and offered to buy the girl. "My wife is fond of her and wants a translator," had been his excuse. He had not mentioned to Ingmar or anyone else that the girl was also Istovari.

Ingmar had relented. Brynn being so obviously in Ovrek's favor likely hadn't hurt, either. Ingmar had given Lena as a gift to Brynn, under the condition she did what she could to heal several of his men who had been injured in the battle.

Around them, Hróarr's men worked to load the ship. They were a few men short after the battle over a fortnight ago. Hróarr's band had taken losses, though it could have been worse.

Several of the storehouses had been burned down or partially burned down. Thralls were still sorting through the rubble of many of them.

Stakes had been driven into the ground in front of Ovrek's burned hall. Atop the tallest one was Egill's head, with the heads of his son and warriors staked on the others. Nails had been driven through their mouths to hold them in place. Seagulls and crows had pecked their skulls nearly clean, leaving patches of scalp and jowl behind.

Tullia might have been buried with honors, but none of the other traitors had been. That was Ovrek's way. That was how the King of Valdar dealt with his enemies and how the warriors of Valdar and Hylden had dealt with enemies for generations.

Ovrek was gathering men to storm Egill's lands in the coming days. Cenric knew he would lay waste to everything and kill or enslave everyone he found.

If the survivors of Egill's family were smart, they would flee somewhere far, far south. Somewhere far enough that Ovrek couldn't be bothered to chase them. But Cenric doubted they would flee. People always tended to deny their doom until it came upon them.

"Faster!" Hróarr bellowed, calling to all of them. "The tide waits for no one!" The large Valdari man paced around his ship, checking the hull and inspecting the vessel from prow to stern. He still seemed unsure that Egill's men hadn't tampered with it, but they'd found nothing wrong.

Cenric's men had found nothing wrong with *Wolf Star* either, aside from a few scratches from the failed theft attempt.

"Ovrek!" Someone shouted the name the way they might call out a sighting of a whale while at sea.

Cenric turned to see the king.

Ovrek no longer walked about Istra alone. Two warriors flanked him, men from his personal household. It was a concession the king had not wanted to make, but his remaining jarls had worn him down.

Vana trailed a short distance behind, a servant at her back. She was different, somehow. Grief had made her paler, leaching color from her cheeks and lips the way Cenric had seen in men who lost too much blood.

"Ovrek." Hróarr stopped hurling bags at Tolvir long enough to bow, not a hint of shame.

Tolvir came to the edge of Hróarr's ship, looking down. "Father?"

Ovrek nodded up to him. "Farewell, son. I hope you will have much to tell when you return."

Tolvir straightened just a little. "Yes, lord."

Ovrek turned his white head toward Hróarr. "Teach him well."

"I will." Hróarr spoke the words solemnly, like a vow.

The king seemed like his usual self, though there was a shadow over his every word, lurking in the corners of his eyes. Who could blame him? He'd lost so much in a single night. When the Valdari king reached Cenric, he extended his hand. They clasped forearms.

Come next summer, Ovrek had promised to send settlers to farm the empty lands and reap new harvests. With Brynn, their flocks and herds would be kept healthy, and Ombra would be strengthened.

Cenric would send an annual tribute of ten adult pigs and three pots of honey back to Ovrek. It was a pittance compared to what Ombra owed to Aelgar every year. Cenric was surprised

Ovrek had agreed to so little, but it was the spirit of the gesture, more than the amount. It was an acknowledgement that Ovrek had the right to tribute at all.

In exchange, Ovrek was to stop raids into Ombra. He was far more confident he could do it than Brynn and Cenric were, but it was a good deal for Cenric thus far. Even if some of the people of Ombra might not like the newcomers, many of them already had Valdari kin. And they had accepted Cenric as alderman, so perhaps there was still hope.

Brynn came to stand beside Cenric.

Ovrek bobbed his chin to her once.

Brynn bowed, not speaking.

Ovrek moved on, conversing with members of Hróarr's crew and even a few of Cenric's men who had once fought for him.

Hróarr approached Vana. He rested a hand on her arm, the big warrior becoming suddenly soft. "Come with us."

Cenric exhaled, a vicarious feeling of resignation in his chest.

Vana caught Hróarr's hand, peering up at him earnestly. "Stay with me."

Hróarr ground his jaw in frustration, looking over his shoulder to Cenric.

Vana looked at him as well, but what was Cenric supposed to do?

They were both dear to him, precious friends from boyhood. There had been something comforting about knowing that his two dearest friends were looking after each other, but it seemed their fates had diverged.

"We're going to Arnza." Hróarr offered a hesitant smile. "I will dress you in the finest silks and feed you on persimmons, your favorite."

Vana smiled back sadly, shaking her head.

"Please, Vana," Hróarr pressed, taking her hands in his. "I want you with me."

"Ovrek needs someone to run his household," Vana said.

"Then he shouldn't have dismissed his other concubines," Hróarr growled.

Ovrek had several other concubines in his household who had been summarily dismissed as soon as they began fighting over who would take Sifma's place. It was one of those things that no one had dared question.

"Why does it have to be you?" Hróarr pressed.

An unmarried, unrelated woman running the household of a man recently widowed? They all knew what would happen next. Either Vana would soon be in Ovrek's bed, or she would make an arrangement with one of his household warriors.

Vana had no family, no close kin, and no inheritance. Women like her had to make do with lovers. She might have stayed as part of the household under Sifma's governance, but without a lady of the household, becoming Ovrek's woman was likely inevitable.

"He's old enough to be your father," Hróarr hissed, dropping his voice.

"He's strong enough to fight and wealthy enough I won't go hungry, even in spring," Vana clipped back. "Not that it would matter if you stayed," she added, tone softening into a plea.

Cenric had heard pieces of this argument from the two of them over the past weeks. If Hróarr stayed, Vana would remain with him. If he left, it would be over.

Vana wanted a household, somewhere to set up her spindle and loom and tend her own fire. Something she had apparently been telling Hróarr for some time now.

"I can't stay in one place, Vana," Hróarr said. "I've tried. The sea is in my blood. It always calls me."

"The land calls me." Vana's face creased with sadness. "I wish it was different." Vana was, in her bones, practical. It was why she had chosen Hróarr over Cenric all those years ago. It was why she was choosing Ovrek over Hróarr now.

Just as Cenric had not blamed her then, he did not blame her now. She knew what she wanted and Hróarr couldn't give it.

"Vana..." Hróarr let off a slow breath. He tilted his face to the sky for a long moment, then he gathered her into his arms.

The big warrior squeezed her tight, tucking her under his chin. Vana wrapped her arms around his thick waist, burying her face against his chest.

They stayed like that for a long moment.

Cenric could feel a heaviness behind his breastbone as realization set in for everyone watching.

It was over.

The two former lovers pulled apart, Vana smearing tears from her cheeks. She fumbled for the silver torque around her neck.

"No," Hróarr murmured softly.

"It was your mother's," Vana protested.

"Keep it." Hróarr brushed the tears from her face, hands lingering as if to memorize the shape of her features. "It always suited you."

Low words passed between them before Vana walked away and Hróarr threw himself back into the work of loading the ship.

All the while, Ovrek ignored the exchange. He wouldn't steal Vana, but he wouldn't object to her choosing him, either.

Cenric rested his hand on Brynn's lower back for just a moment. These past few days had been a whirlwind of madness. He still wasn't sure how they had come through it alive, but he was glad to have Brynn. She was like bedrock surrounded by silt, a guiding constellation in an endless expanse of night-dark sea. Her wise counsel, loyalty, and unwavering faith in him made him...more. He was more a warrior, more an alderman, and more a man than he had ever been before her. Partly because she made him better, but also because she made him believe he could be.

Brynn had known and lived with great men all her life. Surely, if she saw the seeds of greatness in Cenric, they must be there.

He thought of her uncle Aelgar then. The current king of Hylden had gifted him Brynn to start with. Certainly, Aelgar would not be pleased by their dealings with the Valdari.

Brynn shared some of Cenric's concerns, but they had made no oaths that Aelgar could find troubling. If he questioned them sending tributes to Ovrek, they would tell him the truth—that it was to prevent raids.

The whole arrangement was far better than Cenric would have dared hope for, but it was delicate, a precise balancing of the scales.

Ovrek had been weakened. What would happen when he was once again strong?

Brynn peered up at him, offering a slight smile. "We'll deal with it when the time comes." It was as if she had read his mind.

Cenric brushed back a loose tendril of hair from her cheek. "I know."

"Don't fret." Brynn squeezed his arm. "I promise I fret enough for both of us."

Cenric kissed her, her mouth soft and giving in response. There didn't seem to be anything more to say.

25

Brynn

"Have you told Lord Cenric yet?" Esa did her best to keep her voice down.

Brynn offered a wan smile. "Not yet. You're sure?"

"Everything appears as it should to me." Esa shrugged awkwardly. "But you are more experienced than me."

"It can be a challenge to sense *ka* in our own bodies sometimes." Brynn exhaled a long breath. "Thank you for confirming, Esa. That is a relief."

"Lady?" Lena approached them, head angled carefully toward her feet and shoulders bowed.

Esa scrambled away from Brynn as if she'd been caught doing something wrong.

"Lady, the jarl wants to know if you would sleep in his tent tonight." Lena frowned. "He says he's tired of Snapper trying to steal his woman."

Brynn laughed at that.

Lena shifted, seeming deeply troubled.

"Snapper is his dog," Brynn explained. "He likes to climb into bed with me. He's been doing it since our wedding night."

Lena's face remained grave, not understanding the humor of the situation. The girl remained perpetually on edge, like a fox trapped in a longhouse. She constantly seemed to be on guard watching for a threat.

"Tell my husband that yes, I will share his tent."

Lena bowed and scurried away.

"I'm trying to help her," Esa said. "But she's afraid of me."

"Give her time." Brynn watched as the former thrall retreated, head down like a frightened mouse.

"Will you teach her as you do me?" Esa asked.

"I hope so," Brynn replied. "We can use more sorceresses in Ombra."

Lena would have much catching up to do, but she was a sorceress. Brynn was sure of that. She'd not yet learned much of the girl's mother apart from that she was dead and had been taken by the Valdari when she was very young. Lena did not know who her mother had been before.

Brynn had to wonder if there were more thralls in Valdar who had been taken from the Istovari as children, before they had honed their power properly. Perhaps she would be able to persuade Ovrek to free more of them at some point. It wasn't as if he had any way to train them himself.

The *Wolf Star* and Hróarr's ship had sailed through the day, reaching one of the islands halfway to Ombra. They were stopping for the night, having set up camp along the deserted shore.

Across the camp, Cenric worked to secure the ship and the canvas they would be sleeping under. Just one more night and then she would be back with her husband in their own house and bed.

Hróarr sprawled beside the fire, glaring into the flames. He was either drunk or well on his way there. He'd been silent for most the day and as soon as camp had been set up, had demanded a keg of ale. He must be grieving the loss of Vana.

Brynn knew grief well, but she had to wonder what that particular grief was like. What was it to mourn a person you loved and who loved you? What would it feel like to know that love had not been enough?

Guin trotted up and sat by Brynn's feet. Brynn reached down, stroking her fur and ruffling her behind her ears. Guin leaned against Brynn's leg, panting happily. She might never be as friendly or easygoing as Snapper, but she was affectionate with Brynn.

Brynn rose, patting Guin. With a brief nod to Esa, she headed into the trees behind their small camp, seeking privacy.

Guin trotted after her, sniffing at the trees and roots and the remains of an eagle's dinner lying scattered beneath the pines. It was mostly dark, but Brynn could sense *ka* in the life force of the world around her.

Brynn found a tree a few paces off and squatted to relieve herself. She took her time on the way back, letting Guin explore.

Brynn paused beside a smooth boulder, sensing a shape stepping into the trees after her. She might have thought it was one of the other men, but she sensed Snapper bounding beside him.

"Cenric?" Brynn turned around. She saw him approaching, outlined by the firelight of the camp beyond the trees. Her heart flipped in her chest as he came closer.

"Brynn." He reached for her, and she reached back. He caught her hand and pulled her in. His mouth found hers in the dark, his breath hot against her face.

Brynn curled against him, enjoying the solid warmth of his body and how his arms felt curled around her. She closed her eyes, savoring the warmth of his kiss. He was here. They were safe. She clung to him as a little whimper escaped her.

Cenric cradled the back of her neck, tilting her head to the side as he left kisses along her throat.

Brynn gasped, her fingers clenching into his mantle. "Cenric," she whispered, not sure what else to say.

"Yes, wife?" Cenric nuzzled her cheek before kissing her temple, her forehead, her nose, and then back to her mouth.

"We'll be home tomorrow," she rasped, fighting to keep her voice from being too loud.

"I don't want to wait until tomorrow," came Cenric's flat answer. He pushed her against the rock, the one that blocked her from the view of the campfire.

The stone was cold against her back, but Cenric was warm as he pressed against her front. His kisses grew harder, more insistent. His hand caught her skirt and hiked it up, exposing her knee.

His hand found her skin, stroking up her thigh. Brynn reached under his mantle, gripping the sides of his tunic as she felt the hard lines of flesh underneath. Real. This was real. She held on tighter, wanting to cling to this moment as tightly as she clung to him. Anything might happen in the coming days or months, but she could have this moment with his body pressed to hers, his caresses setting fire to her skin.

Just a taste. She'd wanted just a taste and now like a drunkard she couldn't seem to stop.

"The others might hear," Brynn whispered, even as she kissed him, breathing in the smell of him, the solidness of him. He was alive. *Alive.* She'd been so close to losing him, to losing this.

Snapper and Guin wandered around the trees. Dogs were strange that way. There was nothing unusual or noteworthy to them about mating.

"We're married," Cenric growled back. "Everyone knows we swyve." He pressed her against the boulder, nipping her neck where it joined her shoulder.

Brynn bit her lip, fighting to be quiet. She dug her fingers into his sides, wanting everything, but afraid to take it.

Cenric drew up her skirt, exposing her thighs. He did it slowly, watching her face by the dim light of the distant fire. When she didn't stop him, he dropped to his knees.

Brynn bit down on her knuckles as his tongue slid into the space between her legs. Pleasure flared through her, hot and delightfully forbidden.

He pushed her legs wider, his tongue doing those wonderfully wicked things to her most secret places.

Her mind turned heady, and her power rippled around her. Cenric might not be able to see it, and most the camp wouldn't, but Esa would. Lena might. Brynn fought to control herself, but she couldn't control her body and her magic at the same time. *Ka* rippled around her in shimmering lines, magic responding to her pleasure in golden coils.

Pressure built deep in her core as Cenric licked her with delicate strokes. He reached up to knead her breasts through her dress, finding her nipples and pinching just so through the linen and wool. How did he make this feel so good?

With her skirt around her waist, she was exposed and vulnerable, the cool night air reminding her of that. It felt dangerous, wicked, but also thrilling.

Brynn climaxed, doubling over as she fought to contain her moans. She gasped, whimpering and shaking.

Cenric caught her, chuckling as he straightened, his wet mouth leaving kisses on her cheek and temple. "That's my girl."

Shameless. Cenric was absolutely shameless.

Brynn gasped into his chest, leaning heavily against him. "I love you," she squeaked, still fighting to be quiet. "You do such wonderful things to me."

"Sweet wife," Cenric murmured, nuzzling her cheek. "My sweet Brynn." His erection pressed against her thigh, rigid and needy. Pleasuring her always excited him. He was never so hard as when he knew she was enjoying herself.

Heart pounding, Brynn reached under his tunic for the belt that held up his trousers. If she was going to be this exposed, this bare, and this helpless, it was only fair that he should be, too.

Cenric's grin was visible even in the dim light as she freed his manhood, stroking along the warm length of him.

Brynn pulled him toward her, inviting.

Cenric rested his hands on her hips and turned her around so she was facing the boulder.

Flashbacks of another time with another man froze her with fear. This was how Paega had always wanted it—in the dark, her bent over and facing away from him. Her first husband hadn't wanted to look at her and he hadn't cared if she enjoyed it or not. In hindsight, he had probably hoped she wouldn't.

"Brynn?" Cenric's voice came soft, concerned. "What is it, love?"

Brynn tried to collect herself. This was Cenric. She could trust him. All the same, maybe she could ask for another position or offer to kneel for him and use her mouth the way he had for her.

"Brynn?" Cenric leaned over her but didn't move to lift her skirts again. "Are you alright?"

"Yes." Brynn inhaled a deep breath. "I'm just...not used to this."

Cenric leaned over, pressing his cheek to hers. "Not with me, you mean."

Brynn didn't like talking about her first husband, especially not when she and Cenric were like this. She wished she could just forget him, but Paega had been her whole life.

Brynn didn't care so much that he had taken her virginity or even that he had taken six years of her life. She resented him for taking her hope, her naivete, and any innocence she'd had left after the war. He had drained her girlhood down to the last dregs. Though she had a good life now, and a good husband, Paega had taken her youth, and she would never get it back.

Cenric pulled away from her. "I'm sorry."

"No." Brynn grabbed his arm, holding him in place. She didn't want Paega's memory to have power like this. "No, I want to."

Cenric leaned over her so his chest pressed against her back, his hands braced on the rock on either side of her. "Are you sure?"

Brynn's heart raced, the dare in his tone making her body quiver just a little. "Please," she whispered. "Show me how you do it."

Cenric pressed her against the stone, kissing her shoulder, her neck, his hands reaching back under her skirt. "You can always tell me to stop. You know that, don't you?"

"Yes." Brynn's heart raced as his hands pulled her skirt back up around her hips. The cold air nipped at her skin, but then Cenric's hands were stroking her, exploring her.

She was already good and wet from his ministrations, and he pushed inside her easily. His entry came with a flurry of sensations that fluttered along her spine and deep in her core. Her body welcomed him eagerly, like they had been made for each other, like this was how things were always meant to be.

"You're so warm," Cenric murmured, his cheek pressed against hers.

Brynn closed her eyes, stifling a moan. She never understood why his cock felt good, but it did.

He rocked his hips slowly at first, gauging her reaction. "Are you with me, love?"

"Yes," Brynn whispered, her breath coming in a ragged gasp.

"Say my name," he ordered, dropping kisses on the back of her neck.

"Cenric," Brynn replied.

"Who's inside you?" he pressed.

His name broke from her as a whimper this time. "Cenric."

"Good." She could hear the pride in his voice as he said it. "Do you like this?" He rocked his hips faster, just a little harder.

Brynn gasped, bracing her palms against the cold rock. "Yes." She arched her spine, pushing her hips back to meet him.

She was out of control again, helpless. She felt as if she were freefalling, but Cenric would catch her. He never let her hit the ground.

"That's my girl." Cenric's voice brimmed with pride as he

drove in and out of her, harder and faster until he had her splayed against the stone, her back arched against him, fighting to hold in her moans.

"You feel good." Brynn clenched her jaw to hold in a scream. "Gods, you feel so good."

Cenric reached around to the front of her sex and found the bud between her legs again. His fingers stroked and teased as he shoved in and out of her.

Brynn felt her body tightening and coiling again, building toward a wave of heat. "Cenric," she gasped, "you're going to make me..."

Her second climax hit her and her legs buckled. Only Cenric's arms and the boulder kept her from falling.

At her back, Cenric muttered endearments and praises against her ear, the Valdari phrases he always used when he was caught up in his emotions.

Cenric thrust harder into her, faster, almost desperately. He drove in and out of her seeking his own release.

He climaxed with a growl, shoving harder into her and driving himself to the hilt as he did. Bowed over her, his chest pressed to her shoulder blades, he kissed her hair, her neck, her cheek, anything he could reach.

They stayed like that for a long moment, both panting, with him doubled over her.

Slowly, Cenric straightened, pulling out of her and lowering her skirts again. He turned her back around, kissing her, framing her face with his hands.

It was so gentle, so loving, so tender. It was a sharp contrast to the primal need from a few moments ago. He gathered her into his arms, cradling her against his chest.

Brynn pressed her ear to his heart, listening to the pounding of his pulse against her cheek.

"You're such an incredible wife," Cenric praised, tone turning playful. "Such a good lay, too."

Brynn smiled a little at that. "You don't have to flatter me." She knew her skills were still catching up. She had been married before, but she had years of bed tricks to learn.

"I mean it," Cenric insisted. "You're the best I've ever had."

Brynn giggled, heady with the aftershocks of her climaxes. "You're a liar."

"That's a matter of opinion," Cenric shot back, pulling up his trousers and securing his belt again. "And in my opinion, you're the best." He snatched her face, pulling her in for another kiss.

Brynn fought to catch her breath, resting her hands on his chest. "I'm pregnant."

Cenric froze, his face hidden by the shadows.

Brynn cursed inwardly. She hadn't meant to tell him yet, but the words had slipped out.

"What?" Cenric's voice shook as his arms slid around her. "What did you say?"

Brynn swallowed. "I'm pregnant."

"How long have you known?" Cenric sounded suddenly winded, his voice coming out in a rush.

"Not long," Brynn admitted. "I suspected for a while, but I wanted to be sure, and...yes, I'm sure." Her heart fluttered in her chest, nerves wrenching through her at her confession. "I'm a few weeks along."

This could hardly be a surprise to him. They had been making love almost daily for months now. If anything, it had taken longer than expected. Still...the last time she'd spoken those words to a man rattled sore and raw in her memory.

"Weeks?" Cenric's tone turned hard. "That means... Hróarr!" Cenric straightened, glaring toward the campfire.

"What about him?" Brynn blinked in confusion.

"He pushed you in the thrall pit when you were pregnant," Cenric grated. "He could have—" He growled furiously. "I'll kill him."

"I'm fine," Brynn promised, gripping Cenric's arm. "The

baby's fine. I had Esa check to make sure."

Hróarr had already been reminded that he'd pushed Brynn into the thrall pit again and again over the past fortnight. Cenric had stopped mentioning it these past few days, but after this, Hróarr was probably going to hear about it for the rest of his life.

"You're sure?" Cenric's fingers fluttered over her face.

"We're alright." Brynn's throat went suddenly tight. Cenric was already trying to keep her safe through this pregnancy. It was going to be very different from last time.

"Well, then I suppose I don't have to kill him." Cenric's lips met hers, gentle, tender. "My sweet wife."

Brynn dared a smile even though he couldn't see it. "Are you pleased?"

"Pleased?" He let off a choking laugh. "I think my chest could burst." Cenric pulled her into his arms, tucking her under his chin.

"We might be at war soon," Brynn reminded him. "And if Aelgar's son fails to take the kingship after him, this baby might be a threat to his successor. And if it's a girl—"

"Shush." Cenric cradled the back of her head. "We'll think about those things when the time comes." He kissed her forehead, then leaned down to nuzzle her cheek. "The woman I love is giving me a little one to love."

Tears sprang into Brynn's eyes. Everything about this time was different. Everything about this *would* be different.

Thank you for reading!

You can expect more soon from Brynn and Cenric! (And Snapper and Guin, too!)

Visit my website <u>elisabethwheatley.com</u> for latest news, updates, and early bird sign-ups.

About the Author

Elisabeth Wheatley is the author of High Fantasy with Epic Romance. She lives in Austin, TX with her husband Christian and their former trash cat, Yumi.

You can find her at elisabethwheatley.com

www.ingramcontent.com/pod-product-compliance
Lightning Source LLC
Chambersburg PA
CBHW032339310726
48973CB00007B/1771